Praise for Jeffrey Thomas:

"Punktown is sear...
and it is humane, ...
done something w...

"Thomas is ...
detailed ima...

"With brutal elegance and chilling subtlety, Thomas pulls his readers into his dark visions immediately from every opening line..."
—Paul Di...

"Thomas's stories...
stored in fragments...
together they create a...
of their parts—while...
great impact, a collection of which anyone would be proud to have written just one tale."
—Michael Marshall Smith, author of *Only Forward*

"Jeffrey Thomas's imagination is as twisted as it is relentless. If there is such a place as hell, the demons have a suite reserved in Jeffrey Thomas' name."
—*New York Times* bestselling author, F. Paul Wilson

"Jeffrey Thomas's visions of Hell... are as compelling and as beautifully horrific as any ever put down on paper."
—*World Fantasy Award* winner Jeff VanderMeer

"A dazzlingly complex and detailed future vision as poetic as it is horrifying, full of insights and images that cling to the mind."
—Ramsey Campbell, author of *The Overnight*

DEADSTOCK

A PUNKTOWN NOVEL

JEFFREY THOMAS

SOLARIS

First published 2007 by Solaris
an imprint of BL Publishing
Games Workshop Ltd, Willow Road
Nottingham, NG7 2WS
UK

www.solarisbooks.com

ISBN-13: 978 1 84416 447 9
ISBN-10: 1 84416 447 0

10 9 8 7 6 5 4 3 2 1

A CIP catalogue record for this book is available from the
British Library.

Designed & typeset by BL Publishing
Printed in the UK

To Hong—for taking care of me.

Profuse thanks to the crew at Solaris for inviting me aboard their starship and encouraging me to fly it to Punktown (guiding me through an asteroid belt or two along the way): Christian Dunn, Mark Newton, and George Mann. A tip of the fedora to the hard-boiled gumshoe James Ambuehl for inadvertently giving me the initial spark. And a "cam on, Ba Xa" to my wife Hong for her inspiration, empathy, and the entrancing scalp massage that helped me reset my brain and arrive at a certain crucial epiphany. My hands need yours, Em Yeu.

*Why are all these dolls falling out of
the sky? Was there a father?*
    —Anne Sexton

*Tear off your own head
It's a doll revolution*
    —Elvis Costello

PROLOGUE
TRASH

THERE WERE NEIGHBORHOODS in the city of Paxton where the police did not readily go—if at all. Tin Town, for instance, or Warehouse Way; the former given over mostly to mutants and the latter to squatters in its nominal disused warehouses. Sometimes fires in such regions were even left to burn themselves out, despite the fact that the city firefighting units were mostly automated in nature.

Beaumonde Square, however, was not one of these shunned sectors of Punktown, as the megalopolis had come to be known over the years since Earth colonists had built it upon the humble foundation of the native Choom city that preceded it, like a great cathedral atop an ancient pagan altar.

No, Beaumonde Square was one of the more affluent areas of the city. In its environs were Paxton University and the Beaumonde Women's College. There were plazas and narrow streets either retaining the cobblestones of the original Choom lanes, or replicating that quaint effect. Neatly spaced trees fronted rows of upscale shops, as did stone benches upon which to sip one's cappuccino. There was Quidd's Market, with its countless booths offering food from a cross-section of Punktown's many sentient species, human in aspect or otherwise. The mall-like structure's central rotunda was meant to represent this planet Oasis, raised in an invitation to the first colonists, and to lure them to the market to do business. Money had paved the streets of Beaumonde Square as surely as its cobblestones, from the start.

But even the sorriest of Punktown's citizens who had legs to walk with could plant their feet on those cobblestones. Law enforcers—or forcers, as they were simply called—did not shy from this nexus of streets, and rousted as many troublemakers as they could, but the crime in Punktown was of legendary proportions. Its war zones often chased their inhabitants out into the less anarchic sectors, the way over-development had once sent coyotes, deer, and bears into suburban neighborhoods on Earth (back when there had been such animals, outside of zoos). Of course, many times it wasn't that these blighted people were fleeing a portion of the city gone so rotten as to be all but unlivable. Sometimes they were merely curious; daring explorers, like those first Earth colonists. But even they had been likened by some to the initial cells of a cancer.

Brat Gentile had taken the Red Line to Blue Station, and the Blue Line to Oval Square. From there, he had gone up to street level, and soon found himself on Beaumonde Street itself.

Despite having bought his white leather jacket only a month earlier, he gazed longingly into shop windows at automatonic mannequins as they struck a succession of programmed poses in even more updated varieties of this popular style. But admiring these items of clothing, Brat had to snort in disgusted amusement. So the youths of Beaumonde Square were trying to look like gang kids, huh? Wearing cloned leather jackets like these, and trendy rubber swimming caps on their heads like the pink cap Brat wore, and using the gangstyle lingo. To him, they were like a local moth he had seen in a VT program, which had spots and markings on its abdomen to imitate the face of a snake.

Then again, his resentment toward the more advantaged citizens of Punktown, seemingly instilled in his very cells since birth, had been tempered in recent months by his relationship with Smirk. Smirk, as he had nicknamed her, didn't live in Beaumonde Square herself, but her family could have if they'd cared to. That she had come into his life, and fallen in love with him... *him*... still amazed him to the point of confusion.

But that she had now disappeared confused him even more.

He wandered more or less aimlessly, letting the last of his anger drain from him. He had asked his two best friends from the Folger Street Snarlers to accompany him in his exploration this afternoon, but they had made their vague excuses. They didn't care for Smirk: distrustful, because of her money. They'd hinted that she was just playing at being dangerous, wearing him on her arm like these uptown kids wore their gangstyle fashion. Well, Brat suspected his friends were secretly envious of his golden girl, too. Finally he had even asked his ex-girlfriend, Clara, to join him on this excursion, but she claimed to be babysitting her sister's kids today. He had doubts about that excuse, of course. Why should she want to help him find his current girlfriend? But to Brat, she should think of him as a fellow gang member first, and a former boyfriend second. So much for the loyalty of friends. Fuck them. All gang affiliations aside, Brat had no problem going solo when he had to. Sometimes he even preferred it that way. Yeah. Like a shark, on one of the nature programs he and his brother Theo had enjoyed as boys and still liked to watch together in the apartment they shared with Theo's wife. He didn't doubt that Theo would have joined him today, but he and his wife were off in the city of Miniosis for a while, staying with her family. Over the phone, he had told his brother about Smirk and Theo had been concerned, so Brat knew Theo wouldn't have let him down like his friends had.

In all fairness, though, he had to admit that it would have helped if he'd been less vague with them about Smirk's disappearance. But then it was vague enough, still, to him.

Brat went into one end of Quidd's Market and came out the other end with his fingers greasy from a bag of fried dilky roots he'd polished off, an ice cream cone now in his fist. His mission hadn't blotted his sense of curiosity, nor his hunger. He still had the ice cream in hand and was beginning to gnaw the cone itself when his wandering legs finally brought him to Steward Gardens.

That was the name given on the large plaque outside the structure, its letters deeply recessed into a slate-gray background, like an epitaph carved on a tomb: STEWARD GARDENS.

"Huh!" Brat said as if in surprise, though he had come here in search of a place by that name. As if he hadn't truly expected to find it. As if this place—and Smirk's voice on the phone—had only been figments of a dream.

"I'll be at Steward Gardens," she had said to him, her voice all but lost in a storm of static. "He'll bring me... Steward Gardens..."

He had shouted into the phone, pleaded for more, but there was only the static after that. *He?* Who was *he?* Someone who had kidnapped her? When the chill had left Brat's flesh, he'd had the notion to turn on his comp and look up Steward Gardens on the net. He hadn't found much, but he had learned its whereabouts. Beaumonde Street.

Now that he had in fact located the place, he didn't know what to make of it.

Punktown was filled from one border to the other with as many diverse buildings as it was varieties of intelligent beings. There were certainly far more unusual, inventive edifices in this city. For instance, he liked to stare at the exterior walls of the library on the subterranean or B Level of Folger Street, into which were set sizable aquarium tanks swarming with jellyfish from a number of planets (an especially mesmerizing sight when he was high on purple vortex). A skyscraper one could see from the upper level of Folger Street was lit at its summit with a flickering green flame, like a titanic candle, though he didn't know whether the flame was fed by gas or merely holographic.

This building was less showy, more somber. Still, it held his eye and made him run his gaze over its surface, into its more shadowy corners and creases. He found himself drifting nearer as he unconsciously nibbled his cone. How much should he search for her now? How wary should he be of kidnappers? She'd be here, she'd said. But not yet?

He walked up the front path, through what passed for the gardens. These front grounds, which set the building itself back from the street, had once been landscaped with flower beds and shrubbery, and there were even trellises made from black wrought iron that enclosed metal benches, spaced along the sides of the front walk. But the flowers had wilted and decayed, the shrubbery was bristling into chaos with dead leaves snagged in its branches like the husks of flies in a spiderweb, and the vines interwoven through the iron trellises were brittle and leafless. The grass was in need of trimming, but looked matted down and yellow, except where the flotsam and jetsam of colorful trash had blown onto the lawn.

Still, for Brat, whose neighborhood of Folger Street's B Level was lucky to see a weed teased from a crack in the sidewalk by the artificial lighting, this aspect of Steward Gardens alone was enough to capture his attention. It was even a little disorienting, like venturing into a verdant jungle with a mysterious ruined temple secreted in its depths.

The wide front walk branched off into little strolling paths, and in the center of the walk, not far from the front doors, was a circular pool that had once been a fountain. Now the water was oily looking and black in the spaces that showed through its epidermis of fallen leaves. With its vile stink, he figured the water was probably full of algae. He knew about algae from VT, too.

From the edge of this basin, prodding the water with a gnarled stick he'd picked up, Brat again lifted his eyes to the structure itself.

Two wings of three floors each flanked a lower central section, no doubt a lobby, though he couldn't see through the opaque black glass of the front doors (or were they clear, and the lobby unlit?). What it lacked in height it made up for in its sprawl. Along the fronts and sides of the two wings ran three levels of covered balconies that gave access to rows of black metal doors. The surface material of the building proper was the same dark slate-gray color as the plaque that had told him the place's name.

Maybe a hotel, but more likely an apartment complex, he guessed. Its three areas of roof were flat, and likely provided parking spaces for helicars, though from here he couldn't see any. There was a parking lot to the right of the building, which curved around behind it, but this was vacant as far as he could tell.

Intending to break off onto one of the branching lesser paths, Brat first tossed the remnant of his cone into the fountain pool. The disturbance caused the water to bob and he noticed an object floating on the surface. He poked it with the stick he still held. It was a decomposing bird, its remaining metallic blue feathers identifying it as a species nicknamed a pig-hen, which made itself a pest in the city, speckling statues and tripping up pedestrians, snuffling about for morsels of food with little tapir-like snouts. Now he understood the source of the fountain's stench.

Brat skirted close to the edge of the building, but he still couldn't see through its windows. He figured they had all been adjusted to an opaque tint or else they were one-way, protecting the privacy of the apartment-dwellers. He glanced over his shoulder at the hovercars riding low along the road in front of the building, but they were safely distant and traveling quickly, so he squeezed between two hedges to vault over the wall of the ground floor walkway, which corresponded with the two balconies above it. As he passed them, he saw that the black metal doors spaced along the smooth gray wall (was it concrete? ceramic?) were marked with silver numbers.

He moved toward the rear of the building, and as he had suspected he found this arm of the parking lot empty, too. So this building had been abandoned, then. Shut down. After all, it certainly didn't look brand new, yet to be opened, from the condition of the grounds. What had happened? Another bankruptcy? Even with the depression over, businesses and stores folded in great numbers yearly and half the factories of the city had closed shop over the past two decades, so he supposed it must be the same with apartment complexes, too. Wherever there was money to be made, there was money to be lost.

An abandoned building would be a great place for a kidnapper to bring a girl. But it might also be a great place for a girl to send her boyfriend, if she were playing games with him. She was definitely a bit of a devil, this Smirk. Could her disappearance only be that? And she had left her phone behind on purpose, so that she might spook him by calling him on it? Making him think that she was kidnapped or, worse, already dead—it being one of those Ouija phone gadgets? Not that he knew much about them.

If she wasn't dead, and this turned out to be a game, he'd make sure she wished she *was* dead by the time he was done with her.

There was one unique feature about the building, after all, but from a distance its bland general shape and sullen color had detracted from the effect. Now Brat was right on top of this detail, could reach out and touch it. Between each and every black door, on all three stories of both wings, there was a niche recessed in the exterior wall. A niche with a bullet-shaped top. And standing in each niche was a statue of that same slate-gray hue. They were stylized human figures with barely defined features and rudimentary limbs, standing straight like soldiers ranked at attention. They reminded Brat of pictures he had seen of the outdated motion picture award called the Oscar, minus the sword. They might have been considered Art Deco in style, but that term he wasn't familiar with.

He wondered how many there were, but since there was one between every apartment door, he assumed there was one figure to every apartment.

Had the former occupants felt safe at night with these nearly faceless sentinels standing guard outside, like cold suits of armor? Now, they resembled nothing so much as an army of men fossilized right into the structure's hide.

Brat imagined that these statues *were* the former inhabitants. That unwelcome little fancy gave him a shiver.

At the back of the building—the middle section, with its lower roof—he saw a very large trash zapper unit, its sides caked with streaks of corrosion and refuse. Its mechanized arms were retracted and folded in repose, and the red bulb glowing on its side indicated that it was not currently digesting a meal; it might not even be functional anymore. There were a few doors back here at ground level, no doubt for maintenance crews to use. The litter about was dense, as were the piles of leaves. This was where the wind deposited most its treasures.

Brat returned his attention to the wall beside him, at the end of the walkway. The balconies did not extend to the rear of the building; there were no rear windows either, no doors other than those for apparent service access. This last apartment door beside him had some unfamiliar insignia spray-painted on it in glowing green pigment. It resembled the warning sign for radioactivity, with three Ts in its center. A local gang? If so, he wasn't familiar with it. He made that snorting amused sound again. Some Beaumonde Square gang. The kids of wealthy families, emulating the kids of poor and struggling families. Healthy kids emulating junkies and muggers. That old disdain arose in Brat, and he dug inside his white leather jacket.

Not for the gun he always carried, of course, but for his own tube of highly concentrated spray paint. Except that his color was red—an angry, fiery, blood red.

Over that luminous green insignia he sprayed the insignia of the Folger Street Snarlers. Then, for good measure, he sprayed an erect red penis on the gray statue that stood between the last two doors on this side. It made him snicker. Looking up into its eyeless face, for the first time he noticed a number was etched into the forehead. 12-B. It corresponded with the last door's number.

Let Smirk see his handiwork and guess that he'd been here. If she wasn't already watching him from inside. He was more convinced by the second that she was toying with him. He was glad now that his friends hadn't helped him check this place out. And he had to concede that he'd often had the same doubts about Smirk that they held. Sooner or later she had been bound to tire of her feral pet. Had that time come now?

Brat emerged from under the walkway's canopy and floated toward that trash zapper. Its flank was crying out for him to paint some message for Smirk or at least a larger version of his gang insignia there. But that was not bold enough. Why not use all this wasted blank space at the back of the building itself? He smiled and approached the wall, but stepped on something lumpy and soft in the bed of washed-up leaves. Looking down, he brushed them aside with the side of his shoe, then hissed a profanity, backing off immediately. Again, he had been fooled about the stink he smelled, assuming it came from the trash zapper.

The leaves at his feet hid the bodies of dead pig-hens; heaps of them. And all of them looked crushed or mutilated in some way. One might have thought a cat had killed each one, and left them here as a tribute to its owner. But it would have taken an army of cats to deposit this many bird corpses here. Had someone shot them, and meant to zap them in the machine, but upon finding it inoperative simply dumped them on the ground instead?

Brat left the mound of dead birds, moved around to the opposite side of the trash zapper. The leaves on the ground were thinner here and he saw only a half dozen of the dead pig-hens, easier to step around. He kicked one out of his way as he approached a nice expanse of wall begging for his paint as a blackboard begs for chalk.

Allowing his artistic impulses to guide his hand, across the gray surface he sprayed a life-sized figure, like a blueprint for another of those statues, but with one arm raised in an obscene gesture. He chuckled. There were no features yet inside the head's outline. Well, the last door was 12-B, so why not paint a 13 on this figure's forehead? He was about to accomplish this, when a crunching sound distracted him and caused him to turn about quickly.

A crunching sound like feet crushing dead leaves.

The briefest flash of a figure, darting behind the opposite side of the trash zapper.

Brat became mindful of the handgun holstered under his jacket. He eased himself one stealthy step forward, leaning ahead so as to peer around the body of the disposal machine. If it was the member of some Beaumonde Square gang, with his pretty green paint and a white leather jacket his Mom had bought for him, and he was trying to defend his territory from this stray outsider, he was in for a *real* education in gang behavior. Or if this was a kidnapper, or even Smirk, they were in for some harsh brand of punishment, too.

While Brat was straining his hearing forward, another sound came from behind him. A metallic squealing sound. Loud, rasping, screeching. He whirled to confront it, his hand darting for his pistol, in time to see the great mechanical talons a second before they seized him in their grip.

Brat was lifted into the air and squeezed at the same time. The breath was jetted out of his lungs. Though his quick hand had slipped out his pistol, his arm was crushed against his chest and the weapon dropped from his fingers into the leaves below.

Kicking his legs, unable to cry out, Brat looked down and saw three things in the final moments of his young life.

He saw the cover of the trash zapper slide open with a grating noise. He saw the green bulb on its side come on instead of the red.

And in wildly looking around for help, as the mechanical arm lowered him toward that humming maw, he saw that a person was standing near the edge of the building, watching him calmly and making no effort to come forward and shut the zapper down.

A person with a huge red phallus painted on his front.

CHAPTER ONE
MY LITTLE DEITY

"BURIKKO SURU" WAS the Japanese expression for this popular look. It meant, "to fake-child it."

His client's daughter and her three schoolmates were sixteen years old—Jeremy Stake knew that part already—but they all seemed shorter perhaps than they should have been, not even five feet tall, as if they had willed themselves to remain so petite in order to further their cute and child-like appearance. Stake wondered if they had undergone some process that, at least temporarily, would suppress their height to engender this effect.

They all had the same figure, too, as far as he could make out: slender, delicate, with coltish legs. The legs were particularly noticeable, because as part of their uniforms they wore very short, pleated tartan skirts in black and gray with a touch of blue. Their trim blazers were black, with their private school's crest emblazoned in metallic gold and

blue thread. They wore white blouses and blue
ascots.

"Hello, mister—I'm Yuki," said one of the four
girls, smiling shyly, blinking her long lashes under
a mathematically straight fringe of bangs.

He could already tell she was Yuki, because she
was the only one without a kawaii-doll. Despite
the sameness of their uniforms and bodies, there
were small touches of individuality about the four
friends (but if one looked at all the girls from their
school, one would no doubt see these individual
touches widely repeated). One girl wore white
ankle socks. Another wore very baggy knee-high
white socks, bunched up in folds that contrasted in
an interesting way with her smooth brown thighs.
Another wore knee-high white stockings that
instead clung tightly to her calves. Yuki wore socks
like these, but hers were a deep navy blue color.

"You're here to see my father, aren't you?" Yuki
went on, when Stake had smiled and nodded to
acknowledge her greeting.

"Yes," he admitted, trying not to let his eyes flick
down to her legs again. Her thighs were glaringly
empty. The other three girls had dolls resting on
their laps.

Yuki had long blue-black hair and huge eyes that
were both black and luminous at once. There was
another girl of Asian origins whose hair was dyed
a reddish color. A third Asian girl had her inky hair
cut very short, but with bangs like Yuki. The
fourth girl appeared to have a more Hispanic
bloodline, her long hair bunched into two tails on
the sides of her head, floppy like the ears of a cartoon rabbit, but her thin features had a kind of

imperious sharpness that disagreed with the cute effect. Yuki's two Asian friends might have been going for pouty but came off looking bored or sullen. Stake thought that only Yuki really pulled off the soft, sweet, innocent look that they were all shooting for.

"It's about my doll, isn't it?" Yuki said. "My father is asking you to find it for me."

The girls sat on a marble bench within the garden-like courtyard of the company that Yuki's father owned. It was a cylindrical building hollowed by this open core, the bright blue sky of the planet Oasis showing far above them like a telescope's view of heaven, but it was a deceptive view. Beyond the walls of this structure, Punktown was anything but heavenly. At least this courtyard seemed like a microcosmic paradise. A double-helix sculpture twined up from the fountain at the center of the garden, reaching almost to the top of the building like a ladder. Brightly blossoming vines had entangled the bronze chain's loops. Encircling windows looked out upon this rising symbol, so significant to the work being done within the building's offices and labs. Stake had passed through a lobby area, and been directed to wait here for Mr. Fukuda to join him.

"I really shouldn't discuss the business I have with your father," he said to the girl politely.

"Well, I'm sure my father will want you to question me about Dai-oo-ika's disappearance." Yuki smiled again, but her lips quivered and her eyes suddenly took on a moist sheen. The reddish-haired girl reached over to clasp her hand on one of Yuki's legs consolingly. Stake tried not to look at the small hand upon the plastic-smooth thigh.

"I'm sorry about... your doll," he said awkwardly. "So it's name is what?"

"Dai-oo-ika," said the short-haired girl. "It means 'great king of squid.'"

"I see." Stake nodded, and now took in the three kawaii-dolls of Yuki's pals. "Kawaii" was a Japanese word for "cute," and kawaii-dolls of all types had been the rage with children in the Earth colonies for the past few years. Of course, the more expensive and elaborate dolls held more value for collectors, and hence more appeal—more esteem. Stake had done a little reading about these toys on the net this morning and could tell that these three dolls were of the highest order.

The short-haired girl watched Stake staring at the dolls, so took it upon herself to introduce them. She hugged her own and said, "This is Mr. Gau." It seemed like a very realistic bear cub in some ways, but its eyes were too large and it had no nose or mouth and only stubby vestigial limbs. The lack of a mouth and ineffectual arms and legs were a common theme with kawaii-dolls, to make them look helpless, vulnerable, submissive. Stake had read that critics of the dolls viewed this as a conspiracy, sending signals to young girls that these passive qualities were what would appeal to men when they became adult women.

There was a little metal straw extending from between Mr. Gau's legs. Yuki's friend uncapped it, held the teddy bear up and sucked at the straw, keeping her eyes on Stake's. At this, the bear lifted its head higher, blinking, and made a rumbling sound like a purr or muffled growl in spite of its missing mouth. Its tiny half-limbs swam in the air. Finished, the girl recapped the straw and the bear went immobile again. She smiled, licking her lips. "Ruou gau is a rice wine the Vietnamese like, made with bile from a bear's gall bladder. The Chinese used to have bear farms where they put catheters in live bears to drain it. But Mr. Gau is filled with pineapple CandyPop." She giggled.

"Mm," Stake said. He hadn't realized the dolls could be so educational. But however slight his knowledge of animal anatomy, he knew a bear's gall bladder was not between its hind legs.

"There were only a hundred-fifty copies of the Deluxe Mr. Gau made," the girl announced proudly. She gestured to the reddish-haired girl's pet. "Suzu's doll is number four in a series of only a hundred!" She pouted as if in sad envy. Suzu giggled, less sulky all of a sudden, and held her doll higher for him to see. It was a thing like a clockwork robot from some long-antiquated future vision, made from a goldish tarnished metal (or plastic resembling metal), somewhat turtle-like in form. The whole time they had been talking, this thing had been watching Stake avidly, turning its head ever so slightly to track his smallest shift in position. He found it unsettling.

Not to be outdone, the Hispanic girl spoke up loudly with a kind of arrogant pride to say, "Mine is only one of four hundred. That's still pretty rare!"

Yuki was able to speak again. "Maria got hers for her Sweet Sixteen party two weeks ago, like I got Dai-oo-ika for my Sweet Sixteen party last month." At the memory of this event, she looked like a woman who had watched her child murdered before her eyes. Stake saw Suzu's hand give Yuki's thigh a squeeze.

Stake recognized that Maria's kawaii-doll was not an animated toy like the other two, but a bioengineered organism. Its functions were simple; despite its seemingly higher evolution, it was as primitive a thing as a starfish. It was little more than an anthropomorphic starfish in shape, too: four pointed pink limbs and a pointed pink head with eyes like black marbles pressed in dough, and no other features but for its outie navel. The near-mindless organism squirmed with the uncertain slow-motion movements of a newborn infant.

"Yuki's dad's company makes Stellar," Maria said. "And he made Dai-oo-ika, too. But there's only *one* Dai-oo-ika."

Sniffing, Yuki nodded. "Dai-oo-ika is the rarest kawaii-doll in Punktown, Daddy says." Her voice came close to breaking as she squeaked, "And I love him, too!"

During an awkward moment in which he was at a loss as to how he might properly console a person in this situation, Stake heard the ring of a hand phone. "Oh... oh," said the short-haired girl urgently, digging the tiny device out of her blazer's pocket. "The channel is open." Maria leaned in close to gaze at its minuscule screen. The short-haired girl pressed some keys, then brought the phone to her ear. "Hello? Hello? Can anyone hear me?"

In a whisper, Suzu explained to Stake, "It's a Ouija phone."

"Ah." He nodded.

Another craze with the kids. At first, skeptics had accused the phone makers of recording false ghost voices that callers could tune in to, and there were a few disingenuous services where live people posed as dead people (when hassled by consumer groups, such services protested that their operators were sensitives, channeling the voices of the dead), but in fact the majority of these instruments did what they purported to do. The technology for them was based on the findings of government-commissioned Theta research groups, as they were called, which sent probes— and even researchers themselves—to investigate other planes of existence. Whether one chose to consider them souls in the religious sense, or merely sketchy traces of electromagnetic life energy imprinted on the ether, the voices on the Ouija phones didn't so much interact with the callers as moan and lament in more or less inarticulate despair, though some kids claimed to establish bonds with certain spirits. Other kids just liked to talk dirty and taunt them.

"Hello? What?" said the short-haired girl. She visibly shuddered and gave a nervous smile to the others. "Can you say that again?"

"What channel are you on, Kaori?" Maria asked, whipping out her own Ouija phone. It was shocking pink with tiny skull-and-crossbones all over it.

"Have you ever tried one, mister?" Suzu asked, watching Stake's face as he observed Maria's attempts to tune into the same frequency her friend was using.

Stake thought of the men who had died beside him, all around him, in the Blue War. But what would they have to say to him, if any of them should indeed be in that junkyard of spirit scraps? Would they rage at him in envy for returning home alive in their place? And then, what of the people he had killed? What would *they* want to tell him? Stake hoped his own shudder was not visible to the others.

"No," he said. "I haven't."

"Want to try it?"

The short-haired girl, Kaori, was saying into the mouthpiece, "Can you tell me your name?"

Before Stake could say "no" again, a male voice behind him said, "Mr. Stake?"

Stake turned around a little too quickly, to meet the gaze of a tall and handsome Asian man in a five-piece suit, terracotta in color, expensive but cut loose-fitting and comfortable so that he didn't suffer that embalmed bureaucrat look. He grinned and extended a hand tipped in shiny manicured nails. "I'm John Fukuda."

"Mr. Fukuda."

"I trust my daughter and her chums were keeping you entertained?" He looked past Stake at the group of uniformed girls. "And what are you ladies doing here?"

Yuki pouted. "I thought you might need me to join you, Daddy, to talk to your friend about Dai-oo-ika."

"My dear, if I need you to talk to Mr. Stake I will be sure to summon you. But you just trust me to take care of this. For now, I will tell him all that you've told me, and we'll go from there—all right?" He reached out to cup her lovely face. "I know how much this hurts you."

She nodded miserably.

Fukuda faced his guest again. "At the end of the day I customarily use the gym here for an hour. Would you mind accompanying me? And you're welcome to use the equipment, too, while we talk."

"Um... it's fine to talk there. Any place you like."

"Very good. I'm a creature of habit. Habit is the closest I can come to self-discipline," he joked.

"Can you give us a ride to the Canberra Mall on the way home, Daddy?" Yuki spoke up.

"Yes, yes, very well. If you don't mind waiting another hour. Why don't you girls go sit in the cafeteria or something?"

"Okay, Daddy."

"And I wish you'd stop using those morbid phones," he added, but with a weary sigh rather than disgust. "This way, please, Mr. Stake."

"Nice to meet you girls," Stake said, his eyes drawn back to Kaori with her Ouija phone cupped to her ear. She was intent on whatever it was she was hearing, ignoring the conversation of the living people.

THE FITNESS CENTER of Fukuda's company consisted of two floors, and its facilities included a swimming pool, though it was currently hidden by its retractable cover. The windows looked out upon the central garden where the girls had formerly been sitting. Popular music played over a sound system.

Whether it had been arranged this way or not, Fukuda and Stake were the only two people currently in the gym. Fukuda had quickly changed into a T-shirt, shorts and sneakers in the men's locker room, though Stake hadn't even removed the jacket of his rumpled, mustard-colored suit. He sat on the edge of a weightlifting bench, watching his client pump his legs in an elliptical walker. He saw that Fukuda's arms and leg muscles were rock hard. Most of those people who could afford them took nonprescription meds to control their weight, but many others like Fukuda preferred to shape their bodies through a more personal process. They no doubt found the ritual of exercise rewarding in some very primal way; maybe it put them more in touch with themselves. Was it a source of pride, a narcissistic achievement, a self-intimacy like masturbation? Personally, Fukuda's pedaling looked quite boring to Stake, mindless, like a hamster racing in a wheel.

At thirty-three, Stake figured himself to be at least five years younger than his client. Others found his age hard to pin down. He was of average height, and average weight without the intervention of either exercise or meds. Because of the blending of races over many generations, most people of Earth ancestry had dark hair and dusky skin. Stake's short hair was dark, and his skin was somewhat olive. But upon very close examination, despite a normal smoothness of texture, his skin had an oddly grainy look, as if pixilated. There was a blandness to Jeremy Stake's face that made him more than nondescript; he was almost unfinished looking. There was something both eerily infant-like in his face, and mannequin-like. A drunken young woman he had once tried flirting with in a bar had asked him if he were an android. It had killed his own half-drunken lust for her.

Fukuda was looking over at him, and Stake knew his host was speculating on his appearance. Stake straightened his slouched posture, hoping the man didn't think him lazy for not joining in his workout.

"I heard about you from one of my people," Fukuda explained in a voice only slightly strained. "Do you remember a Troy Leman?"

"Yes. He had me follow his wife. I figured there might be a connection between you two, when you told me who you were."

"Her boyfriend attacked you, and you took care of that situation very, uh, adeptly. Clearly a case of justifiable homicide." He smirked. "But an ice swan?"

"It was a Christmas party, in a posh hotel. I didn't have my gun on me at the time."

"I see. I appreciate resourcefulness. Well... I have a security team here, Mr. Stake, but this is out of their range of expertise. It's investigative skills that I mostly require. Still, if you need me to give you a little extra manpower, by all means just ask. But I was impressed that you're able to handle things on your own when they get ugly."

"You don't expect this to get too ugly, do you, sir? I mean, it's got to be another kid at school who stole this thing, from what you told me on the phone."

"That is the obvious answer. But even then things could become unsavory, getting the doll back. You don't shy away from the unsavory, do you, Mr. Stake?"

"Unsavory comes with my job description, Mr. Fukuda."

Fukuda slowed his pedaling to the point that he could step down from the walker. He switched to a crunch machine, set the weight level, gripped its handles, then began sitting back and forward, back and forward, breathing in and out accordingly. In between that, he managed to go on, "Security at Yuki's school is tight, as it well should be, but I'll make some calls so that you'll have access to question teachers and even students, discreetly, should you need to do that. I have influence there."

Stake didn't doubt it, from the looks of this building. This business. But its exact nature was still somewhat unclear to him. The private investigator glanced toward the windows, that massive double-helix sculpture looming up from below. "What do you do here, sir, if I might ask? Do you make... toys?"

Fukuda laughed, and stopped pumping his body like a bellows to look over at his guest. "Yes, we make toys, Mr. Stake, but I'm not a toy maker. This isn't the North Pole." He laughed again. "Fukuda Bioforms designs and manufactures a wide variety of bio-engineered life forms, for any number of purposes, depending on our clients' needs. Everything from microscopic, organic and partly organic nanomites for the repair of people and machines alike, to very large organisms such as deadstock."

"Deadstock?"

"Sorry; it's an unappetizing slang we use for comestible battery animals."

"Ahh. Livestock. Deadstock. I see. A fitting name for a lot of chickens and cows with no heads or limbs."

"Do you know we bought out Alvine Products after that scandalous situation they had a couple of years ago? We rebuilt their facility and grow our own meat products there, now."

"Oh yeah, Alvine. They turned out to be owned by a religious cult. They weren't just growing deadstock, but some kind of army of... monsters, too. They thought Armageddon was coming."

"Something like that. It was run by Kalians. Religious fanatics. There was an attempt to cover it all up, afterwards, and I have to say I've helped to blot out that facility's history myself. It's all in the past now and we don't want to be associated with those former activities. No Armageddon army for us." He chuckled.

"But you do make toys, too. Living toys, like that girl Maria's doll, there. And like your daughter's 'great king of squid.'"

"Dai-oo-ika. He is a one-of-a-kind. I suppose it was naive of me to think that no one would dare steal him. Even at a good school like that, people are people. Of course, Yuki was envied for Dai-oo-ika, and envy in little girls can fester into very ugly shapes."

"What do you estimate his... *its* value to be?"

"There's nothing like him, so even if you look at the collector's guides for kawaii-dolls, it's hard to say. But comparing him to other one-of-a-kind dolls, even a conservative estimate would put him in the tens of thousands of munits. Maybe a hundred thousand munits or more."

Stake whistled. "For a toy."

"Not just any toy. A kawaii-doll. And a custom-made kawaii-doll. But it isn't so much the money, at the end of the day, is it? The thing is, this creature belongs to my daughter." For the first time, Fukuda's face looked hard. He at last betrayed the cold force that a person needed in order to raise up a business of this size. "Whoever did this has made my daughter unhappy. And my child is everything to me, Mr. Stake."

"I'll do all I can, sir."

"Good man. So now, I'll run over everything that happened to Yuki that day, as she related it to me. I'm trying to keep her out of this in case it does get, uh, unsavory. But I'm not afraid of unsavory, either. Not when someone has brought pain to my child. Still, should you need to talk to her in person, just ask me and I'll arrange it promptly." Fukuda rose, picked up a towel to mop his face. "Care to sit with me in the sauna as we go over this?"

"I don't really like heat, sir."

Fukuda smiled. "No? I find the sauna to be a soothing discomfort. Let's go to the upper level and have a juice, then, instead. And I'll tell you the plight of our dear, lost Mr. Dai-oo-ika. He's become a sort of grandchild to me, I suppose."

Stake smiled a little at Fukuda's joke, his eyes wandering restlessly around the room. This was his habit. He had tried not to let his gaze remain on John Fukuda for very long. And yet...

Fukuda startled him by reaching out and taking his chin. It was not a forceful gesture, but Stake complied with it and let his client stare directly into his face. "Amazing," Fukuda said in a tone of fascination.

With every moment since they had been alone together, Jeremy Stake's eyes had subtly grown narrower. They had even, at last, developed a fold of skin over their inner corners in what is called the epicanthus. Thus, his eyes had become slanted, like Fukuda's. Even his muddy irises had grown darker, nearly black. His lips thinner. His skin more taut over his cheekbones.

"You don't do this on purpose, then?" Fukuda marveled almost boyishly.

"No. Some can do it at will. Not me. I have no control over it, except to look at someone. Or not look at someone."

"*Caro mutabilis,* isn't it?"

"It's in that broad spectrum. But my specific disorder is called *Caro turbida,*" Stake explained. Even his voice was oddly undistinguished, unaccented, like a machine's. "It means 'disordered' or 'confused' flesh."

Fukuda lowered his hand, and nodded as if with satisfaction. "Frankly, Mr. Stake, it's another of the attributes that compelled me to hire you."

Stake was uncomfortable talking about it. He was always uncomfortable talking about it. "If you don't mind, sir, how about that juice?" he said.

CHAPTER TWO
BLAH BLAH

THE NINE MEMBERS of the Folger Street Snarlers ascended from the subway station at Oval Square, bumping elbows with other pedestrians and glaring into faces, puffed up and bristling, because they had come in search of their missing brother. Brat Gentile.

They split up into three groups of three, so as to spread out and cover as much ground as they could, not knowing precisely where Brat may have gone yesterday—knowing only that he had been headed for Beaumonde Square because he had asked Clara, his once-girlfriend, and his two best friends, Hollis and Mott, to accompany him there to help look for his current girl, whom he apparently felt was to be found there. These three friends had banded together in their search for him now. They all three experienced an unpleasant mix of guilt and, knowing something bad might have happened to him, shameful relief that they had not joined him yesterday. But whatever the risks, they had to find him now. Still, they felt better knowing that they were here in numbers, and fully armed inside their lumpy white leather jackets.

Hollis was black, with white Maori-style tattoos on his face, and wearing a purple rubber swimming cap. Mott was a Choom, Oasis's dominant native race, human in all regards except for a mouth that sliced back to both ears, his jaw heavy with multiple rows of molars. Instead of a swimming cap, and instead of the crew cut most Choom males favored, he wore his hair plaited into tight braids clinking with red glass beads and little polished ornaments carved from bone. Clara was pretty in a sneering and surly way, her long curly hair dyed a metallic crimson, and as one of the Snarlers she was just as quick with a gun or knife as her two comrades.

They sauntered ferally through the length of Quidd's Market, pausing here and there just long enough to buy some meat on a stick or little white bags of exotic candy. As they continued on, Mott bit into a chocolate, saw that its center consisted of live bluish grubs, and tossed his own little white bag into the next trash zapper he came to. There was barely a hiss as the bag of candy was disintegrated.

Hollis laughed, slapped him on the back, and proffered his own bag of candy.

"Stop playing, you stupid dung-dongs," Clara chided them. She was scanning every face behind every one of the counters, swiveling her head from left to right and back again, as if to intimidate one of these people into giving away a suspicious mannerism. She had disentangled herself from Brat romantically within the past year. He was just too childish, too insecure, monumentally irritated with each slight real or imagined, but she had never wanted anything bad to happen to him. She still had feelings for him, and this situation stirred up an eddy of bittersweet memories.

They were just emerging from the end of Quidd's Market, into the brisk late autumn air, when Hollis's hand phone beeped. He slipped it out of his leather jacket's pocket, and saw the leader of the Folger Street Snarlers, Javier, on its tiny screen.

"We found something," Javier said grimly. "Where are you?"

"We just came out of Quidd's Market."

"Good. We're right down the street from you. Come to an old apartment building called Steward Gardens. You can't miss it."

JAVIER DIAS WAS wiry, tightly wound, with a pompadour of curly black hair he never hid under a swimming cap, and he talked out of one side of his mouth and through gritted teeth in an effect that seemed as much like partial paralysis as it did toughness. At twenty-five, he was overripe for a gang leader, like an alpha lion getting too aged to master its pride, but no younger male would try to supplant him. It didn't usually work that way. Usually, a maturing gang leader might try to get in with one of the big crime syndys. Or he or she might even settle down, get a legit job, like Brat Gentile's own brother Theo had a few years ago.

Theo had been a Snarler himself, up until then. Theo was married now, with a decent occupation, and a year younger than Javier. Well, often a gang leader wouldn't live much longer than twenty-five to have to worry about plotting long-term goals.

When Clara, Hollis, and Mott had joined him, he pointed to the last apartment door on the right-hand side, ground floor, of the building the sign out front had labeled Steward Gardens. There was a silver 12-B against the black metal, but besides that they could see an insignia in glowing green paint on the door, partially covered over with their own gang insignia in red paint: a stylized dog's head baring its fangs.

"What's that sign he covered?" asked Big Meat, another member of their band. All nine of them had converged at this spot. "Another gang?"

"They probably saw him painting over it, and jumped him," said Mott, through clenched rows of molars grating against each other menacingly.

"A gang tough enough to jump one of ours, here in Beaumonde Square?" Big Meat said.

"Hey, there are gangs everywhere. This is Punktown," Javier said.

"Brat did this, too." It was Clara. She was pointing toward the groin of a life-sized but oddly incomplete-looking gray statue standing in an arched nook beside the door. There was one of these statues standing between each of the apartment doors here, but this was the only one with a big red penis painted on its crotch.

"What's that smell?" Mott asked. Then his eyes went wide. "That isn't..."

"Follow me," Javier commanded.

At the back of the building, he led them toward a large rusting trash zapper with a red-glowing function bulb on its side. Clara cupped a hand over her lower face. "Oh God," she moaned, when she saw a mound of leaves beside the zapper. The rotting stench emanated from there.

Javier kicked through the leaves, and a dead pig-hen tumbled toward them, flopping and broken. "It's these. A lot of them. But we thought it was him, too, so we came back here to look. When I poked in the leaves, I found this." From out of his pocket, their leader produced a semiautomatic pistol, small but mean looking. "This is Brat's gun. I know—I gave it to him for his birthday a couple years ago."

"It is," Clara hissed, staring at the weapon. "It is his."

"Someone got him... someone got him." Hollis began pacing back and forth furiously, scuffing up leaves. He inadvertently uncovered a dead pig-hen himself and his boot sent it into mock flight.

A small creature like a monkey had been clinging to Big Meat's shoulder all this while. He was Tiny Meat. They were brothers that complemented each other symbiotically, working in conjunction like this on their own world. They had glossy helmet-like skulls, scarlet in color, but their faces were wrinkly masses of flesh like the caruncle of a turkey, as if badly sculpted out of raw hamburger. Their squinted eyes seemed lost in the heaped red tissue, but a long bone-white tube extended from the chaos by way of a nose. Due to his diminutive size, Tiny Meat's voice was high and squeaky, and as he shifted excitedly from one to the other of his sibling's shoulders, he said, "Look at this place—it's a fucking squatter's wet dream! If a gang jumped our boy, it's for sure they're holed up in here! We need to get inside and blast these fucking punks!" Tiny Meat had a vicious temper and was not to be messed with; even his big brother was cowed by his anger at times.

"T.M.'s right," Javier said, running his eyes over the surface of the building. "This place is derelict; it's gotta be filled with squatters, Beaumonde or not. Maybe that rich bitch Smirk is posing tough with another crew now. Wanted to impress them, and lured Brat here to set him up." He glanced at Clara. In her current regretful state of mind, he saw a flicker of pain cross her face at that particular scenario.

"So we're going in, right?" raged Tiny Meat.

"I don't wanna try the front door just yet," Javier mused. "Too much in view of the street. We'll try other ways first." He nodded. "But yeah. We're going in." He motioned for his people to spread out and approach the three service doors, apparently used by the building's staff back here at the rear of the building. He approached one of them himself, and tapped at the keyboard set into the wall beside it. "I don't wanna set off no alarms," he murmured.

"Look out," Tiny Meat snapped at Hollis, who was examining another door's control strip.

Hollis could tell by the eye-watering, ammonia-like smell wafting out of Tiny Meat's snout that he was getting ready to jet his corrosive bile from that bone nozzle. He backed off fast and started to protest, but in his blubbery wet voice Big Meat expressed Hollis's concerns first. "Don't! You'll just fry the thing and jam it for good!"

"Hold on, don't get excited, scrotum-face... let me try my skeleton card," said another member of the Snarlers, a girl of Vietnamese heritage named Nhu, her long black hair flowing in a ponytail out a hole cut in the back of her lime-green swimming cap. She was reaching into her white leather jacket. It looked child-sized, to go with her miniature frame; only Tiny Meat's jacket was smaller.

"Who are you calling scrotum-face? Me or him?" he huffed.

"*Both* of you."

Javier hissed over at them, "All of you quiet the fuck down. If there is a gang inside, you want them to hear us coming and arm themselves up?" No doubt anticipating the possibility, he still gripped Brat's pistol in his right hand. He nodded at Nhu. "Try that card."

Using her home computer system, acquired under dubious circumstances, Nhu had impregnated a blank data card with hundreds of thousands of randomly generated key codes. There was a card strip in the keyboard unit, and Nhu swiped her card through it several times, flipped the card over, tried it again, tapped a button or two, gave a few final swipes—all to no avail. She shook her head at Javier.

"Let me try something," said Patryk, a very tall and pale youth with a crew cut and bland features. He was the most solemn and silent member of the Snarlers; his family had been forced to relocate to Folger Street when his parents were laid off from their jobs, replaced at the plant where they both worked by automatonic laborers. He always carried a backpack, and he slung this off his shoulder, extracted a pair of black rubber goggles with dark red lenses that his father had once used in his work. He fitted them onto his head. Javier and then the others followed him around the corner of the building, treading more quietly across the crunchy leaves now, back to that door where they had found their familiar insignia superimposed over an unfamiliar one. Patryk pressed his forehead right up against the glass of the last window in the wall.

"If this glass is one-way," whispered Tabeth, the final member of their group, a tall and solidly-built black girl with a pretty face and hair slicked close to her skull, "someone can shoot you right in the face, Pat, and you wouldn't see it coming."

"Nice apartments like these got weapon-proof glass," Javier told her, watching Patryk work. "But Pat, even if you get us into one apartment, that doesn't get us into the rest of the building."

"Maybe," he murmured, as he adjusted a knob on the frame of the goggles cupped over his eyes. So far, his artificial vision couldn't penetrate through the opaque-tinted glass. "But sometimes these upscale apartments have two means of exit for insurance reasons, in case of a fire or something else dangerous—like home invasion. One door leading outside, and one door leading into the rest of the building."

Patryk touched a keypad on the goggles, and suddenly it was as though a light, albeit a dim one, went on in the room beyond the glass. It was a gray, smoky, watery view. A smallish bedroom, maybe, but it was hard to tell from the absence of furnishings. He could see an open doorway on the opposite side of the room, maybe leading into a living room. He was reaching to adjust another small knob when a pale smudge passed across that dark, open threshold. He flinched, almost withdrew his face from the glass. It had only been a blink, but had that been a person?

Javier's sharp eyes had caught the tensing of his body. "What?"

"I don't know. Hold on." Patryk focused his goggles until, at last, the features of the room became sharply delineated. On the same wall as that doorway he saw the only piece of furniture: a built-in vanity unit with a large mirror. Shifting his position slightly, he concentrated on the mirror. He could see himself in the glass; the window he peered through was reflected, and it was indeed a one-way view. But more importantly, at the base of the window's sill he could see a little strip with a series of buttons. Patryk smiled thinly. He touched another keypad, and then a single purple ray pierced through the black window into the room, projected by a tiny lens on the goggles. He moved his head, until the beam struck the mirror. It bent sharply back in his direction, reflected off the silvered glass. By angling his head further, he inched the refracted beam toward the buttons directly below him, beneath the window's sill. Finally, he aligned the beam with one of the rubber buttons, and then he thumbed a little notched wheel set into the goggles, increasing the intensity of the ray until the purple light was almost a nonluminous black; almost a solid black rod.

With a little whisper, as of escaping sealed air, the window slid upwards. They were in.

"I got point," Hollis hissed, pulling a large hand-gun out of its holster beneath his jacket. He started to slip past Javier. Javier almost grabbed his arm to stop him, not liking that Hollis hadn't waited for him to give his orders, but decided to let him go. Brat had been Hollis's close friend. And why take point himself if someone else was chomping at the bit? But Javier held his gun ready to cover the black man as he pulled himself through the open portal.

"Careful," Patryk whispered urgently, "I thought I saw somebody inside."

"I'll take care of that," Hollis said ominously.

"It might be Brat!" Javier reminded him. He climbed through next. Mott was a close third, and the others all followed, Patryk bringing up the rear. As soon as he was through, he unholstered his own gun as the others had—all except Tiny Meat, who didn't use a gun, though they could smell the sharp chemical bite of his rising bile.

Satisfied that the last of his friends was now inside, Hollis moved to the open doorway across the room, pistol held ready.

"Moron," Javier barely uttered under his breath. He motioned for Patryk to hasten and cover Hollis. Patryk nodded, flicking a switch on the goggles he still wore to avail himself of their basic night vision function. Only he would be able to see clearly into the murk beyond this room, but that hadn't stopped Hollis from approaching the threshold and peeking around its edge.

Hollis's black market firearm was a Scimitar .55, an expensive semiautomatic, silvery glitter sparkling across its dark purple enameled body. It had an internal silencing feature. The gun that killed Hollis did not. A crude revolver, its thunder in these dead rooms like a detonation inside the head of every one of the Snarlers. But it was only Hollis who was actually struck by its lead projectile. The bullet smashed a sizable chunk out of the right side of his tattooed face, taking one peeking eye with it. His body slumped back almost gently, folded to the floor, and Patryk jumped over it as he took Hollis's place.

"Blast!" screamed dreadlocked Mott, surging forward with his own gun ready. "Blasting fuckers!"

"Mott, keep back!" Javier roared.

But Mott had learned a little from his friend's death, and plastered himself to the wall behind Patryk, ready to follow him into the next room should Javier give the word.

"Oh God… oh my God," whimpered Clara, backing toward the open window they had clambered through only moments earlier. Despite having a gun of her own in hand, she wanted to flee right now—even if it meant abandoning her friends in the face of great danger—but she was more afraid of incurring Javier's anger than that of whoever was lurking in the gloom beyond that doorway.

"Who is out there?" called a muffled voice from within the next room.

"We're here to kill you, you motherblasting fuck!" Mott bellowed, with eyes bulging.

"Mott, shut it!" Javier snapped. He edged closer to Patryk, and called over his shoulder, "Who are you?"

"Don't shoot, okay?" the voice replied. It sounded strangely distorted. "I'm sorry…"

"You're sorry? You're fucking *sorry*? You killed our friend!" Mott yelled.

"I said shut it," Javier told him. He again addressed the voice in the darkness. "I asked you who you are!"

"We're squatters here. We came in to squat. Please, please don't shoot! I didn't mean to kill your friend… I thought he was one of those things."

"What things?" Javier demanded.

"The Blank People."

"What fucking Blank People?"

They all heard Clara scream. They all turned. They all saw her being pulled backwards out the open window they had climbed through, by two pairs of gray arms.

And then she was gone, and then her screams really began.

CHAPTER THREE
GHOSTS

JEREMY STAKE PREFERRED riding a hoverbike, a leftover trait from his days in the Blue War, but sometimes his job called for him to use a hovercar instead, and he owned one of those, too. Similarly, when he was off the job, or on a job that required him to look casual, his clothing style was quite different from the nondescript black business suit he wore now—a generic look useful for any number of environments. He adapted to the occasion. But the regulars at the Legion of Veterans Post 69 recognized him in either casual or business-like incarnation, and they had tired of teasing him about whether he was off to the stock market or—when he needed to use the toilet—if he were headed for the "boardroom."

The veterans' former taunts aside, his suit wasn't quite that spiffy, and the hovercar he parked in front of LOV 69 was dimpled and dented here and there. He climbed out of it, and entered into the little building's cavernous shadows. Bass-heavy music thudded from a jukebox, a sports program played on one giant VT screen and a muted soap opera (watched avidly by several drunken gray-haired men) on another. Neons glowed fuzzily through cigarette smoke, and a genie-like holographic woman belly-danced inside a large plastic bottle advertising Knickerson beer. He seated himself on one of the stools at the bar.

Without having to be asked, the bartender pulled a tap to fill a glass with Zub beer and placed it in front of him. This man, Watt, was a Choom veteran of the Red War, older than Stake, his crew-cut hair silvered and one arm replaced from the elbow down with a nimble-fingered, plastic prosthesis black as an insect's limb. Despite his grunt of greeting and perpetual glower, he was one of the few men in the Post whom Stake spoke with at any length. Stake returned the greeting by asking, "Any wars broke out since last time I was in?"

"Not this week, unless I'm forgetting something."

Stake picked up and sipped the foam off his beer, swiveling on the stool a little to scan the other occupants of the barroom. Sitting at a table in front of glass cases containing framed portraits of past Post commanders, various plaques and medals of valor, and trophies won by school sports teams the Post had sponsored, were some more Red War veterans and some similarly boozy-looking women. The Red War vets seemed to predominate at this Post. That was okay by Stake. He didn't really want to reminisce all that much with other Blue War vets. But then, he asked himself sometimes, why did he even come to this place when he felt in the need of a brew? Maybe it was a distant camaraderie, safely filtered. Maybe it was something like a programmed behavior. He was used to that, from those bloody years.

Watt had told him what some of the older vets had claimed: that two decades ago, a crew of veterans from the Klu-Koza Conflict had come in here from time to time. Could that be true, when some said there had been no survivors of that conflict, and others held to the belief that the engagement had never happened at all? Well, those mythical men were gone now, if they had ever been here. Ghosts hung in the air like the cigarette smoke. Ghosts of veterans now dead, and the conjoined ghosts of all the people they had killed. The live souls who hunched over the tables and bar, wearing baseball caps and windbreakers thick with military pins and patches, were embalming themselves with alcohol; ghosts in the making.

Is that what I am? Stake wondered. *Is that why I come here?*

"Want a shot with that?" Watt asked, scooping up the one munit tip Stake had dropped beside his coaster.

"No thanks," Stake replied without looking around at him. "I'm on a job this afternoon. Just killing time."

"Time's all we got left to kill these days, huh?" slurred a hulk down at the end of the bar. It was a man named Lark. Stake had been trying to ignore the fellow Blue War vet's presence. In the past they had occasionally compared notes, but Stake had found nothing like comfort or pleasure in the exercise. Lark hadn't seemed to like being dismissed, and so it wasn't unusual for him to take a poke or two at Stake before subsiding into conversation with whatever dumpy barroom floozy he could coax beside him with a bottle of Zub.

"Depends on what you do for a living," Stake mumbled.

"Oh, that's right, you're a private detective. You still get in a little gunplay, do ya, huh? I thought you mostly looked through a camera's sights these days, Jer. Following cheating wives and all that."

"Yeah. And when you want me to follow your wife, you just call me, okay? I'll give you a discount."

The woman beside Lark, not his wife, chortled. Lark growled, "Blast you, Stake! At least I have a wife, you stinking mutant. Who the hell would want you?"

"Ease up, boys," Watt said disinterestedly.

Lark went on, "Course, a guy can always pay for it. I expect you had a few blue-skinned prosties in your time, huh? I know I did." Lark turned his attention to Watt. "Those Jiini women, man. Beautiful. Beautiful like a cobra is beautiful. But you know what gets a Ha Jiin man the hottest? It's *hands*, man. They have a *fetish* for hands. See, in the Ha Jiin culture, aristocratic women always showed off their status by making sure their hands looked dainty and delicate. No calluses, no scars. It got so crazy over the years that these women started dipping their hands into this stuff like liquid nitrogen, to crystallize them. It petrifies them, man, turns them as hard and useless as the hands of a statue. All smooth and white."

"I've seen a show about it on VT," Watt told him.

Lark went on as if he hadn't heard. "See? They're showing they don't need to use their hands. No manual labor for them. So after that practice began, the regular not-so-aristocratic girls started wearing white rubber gloves to at least make their hands look like they're petrified." He chuckled. "I tell ya, nothing pops a Ha Jiin guy's cork like having a lady stroke him off with one of those cool white hands, though most guys have to settle for the fake ones. I had me the real deal once."

"You told me about it," the Choom bartender grumbled. "More than once."

But Stake hadn't heard the story, and he found himself tensing up inside, as if he knew what was coming. As if the woman Lark was referring to was Thi. But it couldn't be Thi. His Thi. She had not possessed crystallized hands, as glossy—and immobile—as alabaster. She hadn't even worn imitative gloves. Her small hands had been only too mobile, and nicked with scars, even with little black hairs on the knuckles; a working woman's hands.

A killer's hands.

Lark continued, despite Watt's words. "We captured this plantation once. These rich bastards, with their own private army of guards. Well, they didn't stand up to us long. Anyway, the family had a few daughters, and the oldest daughter had those frozen white hands, man, just like her mom, only the mom was old. Those Jiini women are the most beautiful women in the universe, but when they hit a certain old age—bam—they shrivel up fast. Anyway, this daughter... *oh*. I took her upstairs, and I had me a look at that blue skin. But she didn't like my pink skin, I guess." He turned to laugh at the woman beside him, but she only gaped at him with a fish-like expression.

Stake was remembering Thi's blue skin. Her eyes, gazing up into his. Her unreadable eyes.

"When I was done with that little blue bitch, I left her alive. But I broke her hands with the butt of my rifle. I broke 'em to pieces, man, you should have seen it. Hell, she didn't need them anyway, did she? Aristocratic little..."

Watt's eyes had followed Stake off his stool, and down the length of the bar. He could have stopped Stake, or tried warning Lark, but he didn't. He didn't like Lark. And he was just a little afraid of Stake. He trusted him not to make too much of a mess.

"...bitch," Lark said, a second before Jeremy Stake grabbed him by the back of his collar and slammed his face onto the bar. Out of respect for Watt, he didn't smash the vet's face into his glass and spill his Knickerson, but there was still a spurt of blood from the man's split right eyebrow. Stake let go of Lark, watched him thump bonelessly to the floor.

"Fucking barbarian," he muttered.

"I'll tell him he got too drunk," Watt sighed. "Slipped off his stool and bashed his face."

"I don't care what you tell him," Stake said. He glanced at a clock advertising Clemens Light beer. "I gotta go."

"Hey," Lark's would-be pick-up griped, "what are you, some kind of blue-lover? They were the enemy, weren't they?"

"Keep out of it, Joy," Watt advised her.

"Yeah? Well this guy cost me my next beer."

"Here." Stake tossed some munits onto the bar. "It's on me." He then went to the door, and after the tomb-like darkness of the Post the brightness of the city made him squint as if in pain.

STAKE HAD ANTICIPATED a weapon scanner at the school, particularly as this was an upscale private school, and so he had made sure not to be packing anything today. It wouldn't have gone over well, regardless of the fact that Yuki Fukuda waited for him, smiling, inside the lobby. Visitors, even parents, had to pass through this separate entrance. After having him stand on the scanning platform for a moment, the guard (himself unquestionably armed) waved Stake through. He signed into a log at the reception desk. The woman behind the counter said pleasantly, "Yuki tells me you're a business associate of her father's, who might have employment for her after graduation."

She had, had she? Stake smiled. He wasn't sure Yuki would find his line of work very rewarding financially, or very palatable for that matter. He often found it unpalatable himself. Did she have the proper qualifications as a masochist? "Well, it's never too soon to contemplate the future," Stake said, setting the pen down on the logbook.

"Thank you. Right through there, Mr. Stake," the woman said.

Stake passed into the high-ceilinged lobby of the Arbury School. The crest he had seen on the blazers of Yuki and her friends was reproduced gigantically on the lobby's polished floor, like some cabalistic symbol awaiting all manner of hedonistic rituals, orgies of students divested of their primly seductive uniforms. Stake banished that image as best he could as he approached his client's lovely daughter with her bright, shy face.

"Nice to see you again, Yuki." He shook her tiny hand.

"Thank you, Mr. Stake. It's lunch time... do you want to join me in the dining hall?"

"You don't mind sitting openly like that? What will your classmates think of me?"

"They'll think you're my boyfriend," she joked, then she hid her giggle behind her hand. "I'm sorry."

Stake felt weirdly shy himself. "Ah, well, if you don't mind people seeing us, then I don't mind. But have you told anybody that your dad hired a man to look for your kawaii-doll?"

"No. If anyone asks, I'll tell them you're a business associate of my father's, who—"

"Who might have employment for you after you graduate. The receptionist told me. Good story."

"Thank you. Okay, then. This way, please."

If Stake had felt shy before, he was ready to pull his head into his collar like a turtle when they entered the cafeteria together. It would have been easier, he thought, had the students not all been female. It just felt *wrong*, as if he had blundered into a convent. Yuki seemed unconcerned about it, and maybe even liked showing off her male guest in some perverse way. He supposed at her age, and in the competitive mind-set of the wealthy, any attention was good attention. He was only somewhat relieved when they found a small table to sit at alone.

"I'll spare you from going through the lunch line; I'll get your lunch for you," she told him, then recited today's menu. He chose the same meal she was having—sushi—but asked for a coffee to go with it. She giggled again. "Coffee with sushi? If you like."

Soon Stake was breaking up an eel roll with a pair of chopsticks and transporting the morsels to his mouth with a modicum of grace. He glanced around the vast room surreptitiously, trying to get a feel for the Arbury School's environment, both physical and psychological. Yes, Fukuda had given him Yuki's story, but now he wanted to hear it from her own lips, and in the place that it had happened, to see what impressions might be gleaned firsthand. And so he had called Fukuda this morning, and Fukuda had given him the go-ahead to visit Yuki at her school, as he had offered the day before. Fukuda had then called the school to clear it with them. Had he been honest about Stake's mission, or had he given a story similar to that which Yuki had told the receptionist?

Over the heavy buzz of youthful female voices, gathering at the ceiling like a solid mass, Yuki asked him, "Did my Daddy show you pictures of Dai-oo-ika?"

"Yes, he did."

"Oh. Well, I have more right here, if you want to see them."

Stake switched to a small cup of miso soup and took a sip while he watched Yuki awaken the computer she wore on her wrist like a bracelet. It was a more feminine version of the one he himself wore. She touched some minuscule keypads, then extended her arm toward him.

The screen was tiny, but when he positioned his eyes directly above it the image was transmitted to his brain in such a way that it filled his vision to the exclusion of all else. In the lower right corner of this enveloping virtual screen there was a sort of window that showed the wrist comp's controls, so that he could still view them in order to operate the device, but it was Yuki's delicate fingers that he saw resting across the keypads now.

She gave him a slide show of Dai-oo-ika in various poses. On her living-room couch, propped up like a sofa cushion. On her bed, slumped against her pillow. In her lap, as she sat grinning in childish pink pajamas with a pattern of cute-eyed jellyfish swarming across them.

"Great king of squid." He had understood the name when Fukuda had shown him his own, more clinical pictures yesterday. Dai-oo-ika looked as plump as a beloved doll should be, but not so inviting to the touch. His Buddha-like body was shiny, glossy, gave the impression of being clammy. His belly was a bloodless white, but his translucent flesh shaded to a grayer color toward his back. There was a scattering of black speckles there, too, and on the back of his hairless head. Two chubby arms like those of a baby, and two even chubbier legs, all ending in webbed paws. From that speckled back sprouted two cute little wings, ribbed rather like the fins of a fish. And the face...

Well, there was no face, really. No eyes, no ears, no nose, no mouth. The lumpen head possessed no features other than an outgrowth of thick tendrils like those of an anemone in the place where a nose and mouth should have been, had Dai-oo-ika been a human infant. These tentacles were ringed in alternating bands of black and an almost metallic silver.

Stake remembered the kawaii-doll of Yuki's friend, Maria. Stellar, it was called. Primitively alive. Eerily squirming. He envisioned Dai-oo-ika, a kindred creature, doing the same. Bio-engineered doll. A golem to take to bed. A homunculus to squeeze and kiss.

"Cute," Stake told her.

She had a proud, tragic sheen in her eyes as she returned her wrist comp to sleep mode. "Thanks. At first when Daddy surprised me with him, I was disappointed that he didn't have eyes, but I think it makes him so helpless and dependent on me. One time when I was hugging him it really seemed like his tentacles were stroking my face!" She made a spidery motion along her cheek with her fingers.

Stake imagined that as a less than endearing sensation. He took another slurp of his soup, then observed, "So it's safe to say that our culprit is right here in this room."

"It has to be one of them," Yuki said in an urgent whisper. "They've all seen me with him. They all envied me for him. It's been a week now, exactly, since he's been gone! And I've only had him for about a month. It's so unfair!" Her voice was near to crumbling. "I always take good care of him; I never ever put him down and turn my back on him. If I can't have him with me, like in phys ed, then I keep him in my locker. And that's what happened! I came back from my shower, and there was my locker—open. And Dai-oo-ika was *gone!*"

"Does anyone else know the code to your locker, or was the lock forced?"

"It wasn't forced, but it could have been hacked."

"What about maintenance people?"

"Um, I don't know, they might have access to the lockers."

"I'll look into that. What about your friends; they wouldn't know the code? The ones I met the other day?"

"Oh… Kaori, Suzu and Maria are my best friends! And they have their own kawaii-dolls."

"But not as good as your doll, no matter how good theirs are."

"No, no, they wouldn't. Besides, what good is a kawaii-doll if you can't show it off to people?" she said with plain honesty. "You wouldn't just hide away with it."

"Unless someone was doing it specifically to hurt you."

"Right. To hurt me." Those oversized eyes under their border of bangs had begun to film over wetly. "That has to be it. Someone so jealous, they wanted to get back at me. I just hope they haven't hurt him. I hope they ask for a ransom or something. I'd get Daddy to pay it, I don't care!"

"So do you know any girls who dislike you? Who are especially jealous of you? How about teachers? Have you had problems with any of them?"

While he conversed with the girl, he let his gaze alight on her face only briefly before it fled to another table, or a supporting column of the room, or the wall of bright windows. If it lingered too long on her face, he would begin to feel the familiar rustle of his cells (even if that sensation were largely imaginary) as his features began to remodel themselves. Again, his eyelids would take on the epicanthic fold, but in imitation of her eyes instead of her father's. The length of time it took for this process was not always the same. Sometimes it was fairly swift, and other times it was more gradual, but unless he was preoccupied he usually had a subconscious awareness of when it was going to transpire, despite the fact that he had no conscious control of his ability. He felt restless with Yuki's own eyes upon him. Had Fukuda told his daughter about his "gift?" Was she even waiting to see it happen for herself?

"A teacher? Oh no, all the teachers like me! I don't have a problem with any of the phys ed teachers who would be in the locker room. But I have had a problem with some of the girls here, in the past few years. It's always like that. Cliques, you know?"

"Sure. Right now—but don't make it obvious— do you see anyone taking extra interest in our conversation? Anyone who's been hostile toward you in the past?"

He saw Yuki involuntarily turn her head just a fraction, but her glistening eyes rolled about in wide, morose arcs. "A lot of people are looking at us."

"Mm," Stake agreed, peering over the rim of his coffee cup as he sipped from it, and taking in the many curious glances.

"Oh," Yuki fretted, "maybe it wasn't a good idea to meet in public, after all! What if we scare the person into destroying Dai-oo-ika, to hide the evidence?"

"I'm sure they wouldn't do that, not with his value. In fact, we might spook them into coming forward and saying it was all just a harmless prank."

Yuki returned her gaze to him. "One of the nastier girls, one of the ones who've been really mean to me, disappeared last week, too. She's in my biology class."

Stake looked directly at her now. "Disappeared how?"

"Well, she had an older boyfriend, and the rumor is she ran away with him because her dad didn't approve. But one of her friends—her name is Krimson—one of Krimson's friends swears she heard Krimson trying to talk to her on her Ouija phone. And that would mean Krimson is dead." Yuki hugged her arms and visibly gave a shudder.

"Huh," said Stake.

Lost in thought for several beats, he frowned toward the floor. He tended to do this a lot. No faces to see down there. It was hard to escape faces in a city. In his apartment he didn't even have pictures of people, whether they be photos or paintings or holoportraits, displayed on the walls. Except for one: a picture of himself. If he came home looking like someone else, staring into this photo as if it were a mirror helped him speed up the process of looking like himself again. In the wrist comp he wore he could store pictures of faces, the countenances of people he might want to metamorphose into for this or that reason, by staring hard at their image. But he had also filed a picture of his own face in his wrist comp. He could gaze at it to hasten the restoration of his neutral appearance (his "factory" or "default settings," as he joked to himself), like a man with amnesia remembering who he truly was again.

Lost in her own thoughts, Yuki said, "My mother died when I was just a baby, you know."

This comment, seemingly out of the blue, caused Stake to meet her eyes again. "I'm sorry. I lost my mother when I was just a child, too." He regretted his own admission as soon as it left his lips. Why tell this young girl such a personal thing, regardless of what she had revealed to him? He didn't elaborate on his mother, and thankfully she didn't ask him to.

Yuki continued, "My mom. I think… I think I've heard her, too."

"Heard her? You mean, on your Ouija phone?"

Yuki nodded, doing her best to keep a cap on her emotions. "I swear it's her voice. She's trying to tell me something. Something important. But I can't hear her well; just little bits and pieces, really far away, and full of static."

"Huh," he said again.

"Please don't tell my father I told you that, okay? He hates those Ouija phones. I don't want to upset him. He loved my mom a lot."

Half a sob gushed out, and Stake found himself reaching across the table to take her hand. He was a bit embarrassed when he realized what he'd done, but here he was, so he gave it a comforting squeeze. Yuki looked down at their joined hands tearfully, then smiled up at his face.

"People will really think we're boyfriend and girlfriend, now," she joked, trying to restore her composure.

"Well, I'm honored if they'd think that." But he felt it was prudent to let go of her hand now.

"You're cute, you know?" she confessed, and giggled behind her palm. "I'm sorry."

He was more embarrassed than ever; her compliment caused him to feel flattered and self-conscious and bewildered all at once. No one had ever said that to him. "Cute, huh?"

"Yes," Yuki told him. "You have a face like a doll."

CHAPTER FOUR
PERMUTATIONS

"CLOSE THE WINDOW, close the window—don't let them in!" cried the distorted voice from the room beyond this one.

"Clara!" Tabeth yelled, pulling a gun out from underneath her white leather jacket.

"Oh God!" Nhu blurted, jumping back from the window through which the four gray arms had dragged their friend and fellow Folger Street Snarler.

"Don't hit Clara!" their leader, Javier, barked as he saw Tabeth aim her pistol outside. He dashed forward to join her.

From the other room, the owner of the frantic voice rushed forward impulsively, a whitish blur in the murk. This was what Mott, still poised around the edge of the doorframe behind Patryk, had been waiting for. He reached around Patryk with his own handgun, and squeezed its trigger at the ghostly shape responsible for the death of his close friend, Hollis, who lay near his feet with blood coming in a tide from a head broken open like that of a doll.

Tabeth had begun firing outside only a microsecond before Mott opened up with his gun. Javier, caught between the two sounds, spun around toward the latter, thinking that the shots might be coming from the same person who had—accidentally, they claimed—killed Hollis. But he saw Mott's extended arm, his handgun bucking.

"Mott, hold your fuckin' fire!"

"I got him," Mott said, his Choom face a caricature of an insane grin. He lowered his gun as ordered, but he gloated, "I got that piece of dung!"

From the room beyond, terrible screams and confused shouts. Screams of pain from the one who'd been hit, or screams of despair from that person's comrades, whoever and however many they were.

From where she stood, though a bit removed from it, Nhu could see out the window. She could see what was happening to Clara. She shrieked. Her shriek dipped and rose again when she saw Clara's body flinch as it was inadvertently struck by one of Tabeth's projectiles. But considering what those two gray figures were doing to her, Clara had to be dead already. If not, then getting struck by Tabeth's bullet was a blessing.

"Oh... oh..." Tabeth said, lowering her gun. Bile rose into her throat.

Big Meat had his gun pointed toward the window now, as he surged toward it with Tiny Meat clinging to him, Tiny Meat letting loose a fusillade of high-pitched obscenities. Big Meat pushed past Tabeth, who had gone into stunned mode at having hit Clara. At having seen those things *tear* Clara.

But Nhu was already darting back toward the window, into Big Meat's range of fire, and he barely checked his trigger finger. Tiny Meat barely checked the spray of acidic bile from the bone nozzle in his face. "Out of the way!" he screeched.

They could see the two gray entities—now gray and red—drop the thing that had been Clara, turn their heads in unison, and break into a sprint toward the open window. The way they were running, it appeared that they would dive straight through it, side by side, like two trained dogs through a hoop.

Nhu was good with anything technological, but her fingers froze a moment above the buttons on the sill, as if she had never encountered so simple a thing as the controls to raise or lower, tint or make opaque a window. A mad thought sprang into her head: what if the beam from Patryk's goggles had damaged the controls? Disabled them? What if the window wouldn't close?

Javier saw the gray things coming. Like Big Meat, he was pointing his gun out there but afraid to hit Nhu, and instead of moving forward to push her out of the way or aim past her, he commanded, "Close the window!"

The faceless beings had almost reached it. Though their smooth, abstracted bodies were devoid of muscular detail, Javier still saw in their body language that they were tensing themselves up to spring at any moment.

Nhu's index finger jabbed a button on the control strip. The window began to lower with the barest whisper.

One of the gray beings sprang. Then the other.

A thud against the safety pane. Palms spread across it with a splat like suction cups, first one pair and then the other. Palms that squealed down the surface, smearing red. The pane was still lowering. There was a gap at the bottom. One of the suction cups came off the window, flashed down and slipped under the lowering edge. A gray hand like a giant spider clawed at the air.

Big Meat lunged forward. Now he pushed Nhu out of the way. But it was Tiny Meat who jetted the groping hand with his bile, even as the edge of the window pinned the wrist against the sill. The gray flesh sizzled, bubbled. Dripped something clear instead of crimson. Fingers were reduced to nubs. There should have been bone inside those fingers, revealed by the acid. There wasn't.

Holding his breath against the strong chemical smell of Tiny Meat's bile, Javier rushed forward also now that Nhu was out of the way. Not waiting for Tiny Meat's bile to finish dissolving the hand, he pointed his gun at it and fired. The foaming blob splattered into chunks. Was gone. And the window completed its serene downward passage, meeting the sill and sealing. Locked. Glancing back to make sure her fellow gang members were done spitting and shooting, Nhu moved in and touched the button that activated an alarm on the window, should the things manage to force the pane open somehow with those three remaining, spread palms. She imagined, though could not hear, the squeaking sounds they made against it. She tried not to see the faceless faces behind those palms. Or the streaks of her friend's life fluid.

"It's still tinted one-way," she said numbly, straightening. "They can't see us."

"How do you know?" raged Tiny Meat. "Blasting things don't have eyes, anyway, but they saw Clara!"

Patryk and Mott hadn't left their post by the threshold to the next room. From the chaos of voices in there came a more articulate exclamation. It sounded female. "You killed our friend!"

"Sounds familiar, huh?" Mott shouted. "So now we're even!"

"Shut it," Javier growled. "Hey," he then called into the other room. "You said you're squatters. What the hell is going on here? Why are you fighting these 'Blank People?' I want answers, unless you wanna keep fighting us, too. And I don't think you want that!"

"You're the ones that wouldn't be wanting that!" an arrogant male voice bellowed in return. But the female voice overruled him.

"We'll come out and talk if you promise not to shoot. It was all an accident. We don't want any trouble with you—we just want to get out of this place!"

"So do we."

"Right. So we need to talk. Promise not to let your friends shoot."

"Then throw out your guns first!" Mott yelled. But it was Javier's gun, suddenly, that pressed hard under the Choom's heavy jaw.

The leader of the Snarlers did just that, through gritted teeth. "Are you trying to steal my job, wanker?"

Mott looked back at his friend from the corner of his eyes. "No, man, I just..."

"What do I got to do to get you to listen to me? Make that hole in your ear bigger? We're going to talk to these people. It sounds like those gray things have got them pinned down in here. And it looks like we're pinned down in here, too. We might just be on the same side."

"They probably killed Brat!"

"Don't be stupid. We found his gun outside— where those things are."

"We didn't kill your friend!" the female voice called. Javier was surprised; he hadn't thought they'd been discussing it loudly enough for her to hear. "He was outside. I didn't sense it until he started screaming. The trash zapper out there picked him up, and fed him inside. I heard him screaming inside my skull."

"What are you talking about?" Javier demanded.

"I have a gift."

"Mutants," Nhu whispered.

Javier lowered the gun from Mott's jaw, where it left a red indentation. "Let's talk. Come out. We'll keep our guns down if you do."

"Don't, Mira," that angry male voice rasped. But she wasn't listening to him. The female came out first, her arms raised above her head.

Arms as short as those of a small child.

"Mutants," Patryk echoed Nhu belatedly.

The first person to emerge from the darkened room, into this room where the surviving

Snarlers were clustered, was an adult woman in her mid-twenties compacted into a condensed form. A dwarf, with a normal-sized head and fairly normal-sized torso, but with chubby stunted limbs, her somewhat bowed legs giving her a waddle. Her hair was long and black, cinched in a messy ponytail, her dark eyes large and striking. Her clothing looked like it had been donated to a homeless shelter by a parent whose daughter had outgrown it: a pink T-shirt with a cute cartoon jellyfish on the front, outlined in flaking glitter, and white shorts. But the clothing was dirty and frayed, speckled with dark stains of old blood.

Had he only seen her face, Javier would have found the young woman very attractive, with those heavy-lidded eyes and her strong nose and full lips. But besides her dwarfism, there were also dark purple veins on both temples, running up into her hair, like tattoos of forked lightning. A gift, she had said she possessed.

"I'm Mira Cello," she told him, stopping in the center of the room. The Snarlers hadn't put their guns away but they didn't point them, either. For a moment, the only movement was the gray palms sliding down the windowpane, then moving back to the top again.

"I'm Javier Dias. This is my gang. What's left of it. The Folger Street Snarlers."

Mira glanced down at the body of Hollis, then away with a wince. Slowly she let her arms drop, having established that she meant no harm. And then the rest of the squatters timidly began filing into the room after her. A couple of them carried guns of their own, but kept them lowered as the Snarlers did.

Javier had the irrational thought that the next person into the room was the man Mott had shot, but that man was dead. The reason for this impression was that the mutant's head was an impossible ruin, looking as though it had been run over with the tread of a construction robot. It was crushed into a half-flattened mass, with only one eye showing through the rubbery folds that twisted the mouth into a drool-slicked hole. More like a crumpled Halloween mask than something with a skull, let alone a brain, inside it.

"This is Nick," Mira said.

The Choom man who followed Nick crawled into the room on all fours, like some giant white spider. He was naked but for a pair of filthy shorts, his bony body making him look as though he were in the terminal stage of starvation. His strangely bent stick limbs each had two extra joints, and it appeared that his too-long fingers were supernormally jointed, as well. A wispy-haired head wove like that of a cobra atop a slender neck twice as long as it should have been. The young man smiled shyly at pretty Nhu. In his hollow, wasted face, his already broad Choom mouth seemed a death's head grin. Nhu had seen a lot of mutants and nonhuman beings in her young years, but something about this man's eerie movements made her shiver. She quickly looked away.

Mira introduced him. "This is Haanz."

Another woman came shambling in, hefty and wheezing, a too-small dirty gray sweat suit straining to contain her bulk. Javier counted five faces of varying sizes crowded onto her single shaggy-haired skull. Oddly, the one normal-sized face appeared insensate, its mouth drooping and eyes rolled up white. Only two of the smaller, rudimentary faces appeared to be cognizant, with sharp, alert eyes. One of the three dead faces was positioned upside-down, with hair trailing from its scalp to partially obscure the half-formed suggestion of a sixth face.

"Barbie," said Mira.

Finally came the owner of the angry voice. He too resembled some giant insect, though black and bipedal, stalking in like a mantis with a soft pneumatic hiss. He was little more than a black man's bald head perched on a stubby, grub-like blob of a body, harnessed into a cybernetic frame. Javier had seen badly wounded war veterans reduced to moving about in this sort of mechanical "pony," though in this man's case his limbless state was obviously congenital. His mother had either not wanted him aborted, when obstetrical scanning disclosed his anomaly, or she had been too poor to have received advanced medical care at all. Orange flames had been stenciled onto the sides of the open thorax that held his nude little body in place, and decals had been pasted on the pony's skeletal limbs, but the machine had seen better days; one arm was silver instead of black, with a different sort of claw hand—a replacement part. The other arm gripped a big Decimator .220 revolver in its fist.

"I'm Satin," he introduced himself, his eyes moving over the Snarlers with a challenging menace.

"And this is Hollis," Mott said, sweeping his arm at the dead man on the floor between them.

"Yeah? Well our friend Chang is in there with his throat shot out." Satin flicked his head back over his little nub of a shoulder.

"Wanker shouldn't have been so trigger happy!" Tiny Meat said.

"Enough," Javier said. "None of us are happy what happened to our friends. But I think we can agree that the real problem is out there." He pointed his pistol toward the window.

"What are you doing here?" Big Meat asked the mutants.

"Like we said, we're squatters," Mira told him.

"We're the Tin Town Terata," Satin elaborated proudly. "The Triple Ts."

"Yeah, nice alliteration," Patryk muttered.

"So you're a gang, too," Javier noted. "That was your insignia outside, in green? Not smart, putting it there. You were begging the forcers to see it and come in here to investigate."

"It was there to warn other gangs that this is *our* place now."

"But now you want to leave," Mott snorted.

"Funny, our two gangs both coming to this same place, here in money land," Javier said.

Mira replied, "Not so unusual, when you're talking about a big abandoned building. We were surprised there weren't any other squatters already in here. Until we found a homeless man in one of the hallways. What was left of him, anyway, after *they* were done with him."

"But how do Tin Town mutants find their way to Beaumonde Street?"

"There was a war," Mira confessed. "The other mutie gang was bigger. The only way out for us was to escape Tin Town. Some of our enemies kept chasing us, so we had to go further and further, until they stopped chasing. We finally got on a train, and got off the train here. Before the war there were thirty-one of us. Sixteen of us made it to the train." She swept her arm at her friends. "Now we're five. The Blank People got the others, before we were able to lock them all outside."

"God," Tabeth moaned.

"What are you doing here?" Nick mumbled, his wet words barely decipherable.

"Our friend you say was put into the trash zapper," Javier answered. "He came out to Beaumonde looking for his girlfriend, and he didn't come back. We tracked him here."

"Why would the trash zapper do that to him?" Nhu asked dubiously.

"The same reason the Blank People killed all the pig-hens they caught on the roof," Mira said. "The same reason they killed that homeless man. And why they're trying to kill us. I think it's because they see us all as pests. Pests to be exterminated."

"And the trash zapper thinks the same way?"

"The zapper and the Blank People must've been programmed to recognize and take action against us *undesirable* types," Satin growled.

"Undesirable is right," Nhu whispered to Tabeth. More loudly she said, "It still doesn't make sense, with a trash zapper."

"So what the blast are these Blank People, anyway?" Javier asked. He wandered closer to the window, now trusting that the Tin Town Terata would not shoot him in the back as he did so. He had to fight his own reluctance to near the window, however, reminding himself again and again that the things could not see them through the one-way tinting. But was that true? Who knew what senses they relied on? A kind of sonar, like the blind Waiai race, that could penetrate the bulletproof pane?

"Androids," Big Meat stated.

"No," said Mira. "They're not mechanical, anyway. They just have a chip in their heads. The rest is all organic. We know—we put the bodies of the ones we killed in apartment 6-B."

"And we've been putting the bodies of our dead friends in apartment 5-B," Satin added. "That's where we'll put Chang. I suggest you start using apartment 4-B." He nodded down at Hollis.

Mott squeezed his gun's handle tighter. "What do you mean, 'start?'"

Mira glanced up at Satin. "We've got to all work together here, Satin. Right?"

"This is easy enough," Tabeth said, pacing nervously, and digging a hand phone out of her jacket's pocket. "We just call the forcers down here to get us out past those gray things."

"Yeah! Of course!" Nhu lifted her arm, on which she wore a new—stolen—wrist comp like a bracelet.

Javier blinked at them a few moments before he said, slowly as if speaking to far younger children, "Think for a minute, if that's possible. We call the forcers to this building in rich old Beaumonde Square, where our two gangs are inside with guns in our hands and a room full of dead mutants? And a couple of people with bullet holes in them?" He motioned toward Hollis. "And I bet more than one of us has go some illegal substances on 'em, am I right? Dung, girls, we'd be going from this prison to another prison."

"Javier's right," Tiny Meat said. "We're the Folger Street Snarlers. Since when do we need to go crying to the forcers for help? We'll fight our way out of this—right, Big?" He slapped the shoulder of his larger twin, who presently carried him in the crook of one arm.

"We can try," Satin said. "But I hope you got enough ammo, little fella. There's twelve apartments to a floor, and three floors, and two wings. And there's one of those Blank People for every single apartment."

"So how many does that make?" Tiny Meat said.

"That makes seventy-two of them," Patryk replied softly.

For a few moments, nobody said anything.

THE BODY OF the mutant named Chang was carried to apartment 5, here on the ground floor of B-Wing, by Patryk and Nick, escorted by Tabeth and Barbie with guns in their hands. Patryk held his breath when the door slid into the wall and the stench of the makeshift morgue rolled over him. Tabeth hung back in the hallway and stifled a retch. Patryk saw indistinct forms crudely wrapped in clear plastic tarps the mutants had scrounged from somewhere in the building. Some of the forms were on the small side—either creatures like Mira, or else the Blank People had *made* them that small.

Next, this same crew carried Hollis into apartment 4-B, as Satin had facetiously suggested. They laid him on the floor, all out of tarps to wrap him in. They'd already taken his pistol and ammo, and a candy bar they'd found in a jacket pocket to add to the food Javier was pooling together, but now Barbie pointed at the corpse, and two of the supernumerary faces on the side of her skull rasped in unison, "We should take his jacket. It's cold in here."

"I wouldn't do that if I was you," Patryk advised her. "That's a Snarler jacket. Mott or Tiny Meat see one of you Teratas in that and Javier might not be able to stop 'em in time."

Barbie nodded, seeing his point. They left Hollis in the room, looking very alone on the barren floor, devoid of all furniture, but the door slid shut to close off the image.

The others had abandoned apartment 12-B where Hollis and Chang had died, as much to escape the blood on the floor as those two Blank People still lingering at the window. Looking back at them as he left the room, Javier said, "I don't think they're trying to get in, now. I think they're just reminding us that they're out there."

They all moved to the room in which the Terata had set up their own little camp: apartment 1-B, just off the front lobby that bridged the two wings of Steward Gardens. In 1-B there were some chairs and couches that the Terata had stolen from that lobby, on which they had since been sleeping. Glancing around at the other items the squatters had salvaged from here and there, Mott whispered to Tiny Meat, "I don't think these last five are the toughest, and that's why they're still alive. Dung! Look at them. The only reason they're still alive is the Blank People probably killed off the best fighters first. The only one of these sad fucks that I'd be worried about is that Satan bastard."

"Satin," Big Meat corrected. "You two remember what Javier said. Our gangs aren't at war; we've got to team up against these Blank People."

"Shut up," Tiny Meat told his brother. "Were we talking to you?"

"Listen," Mott said to Big Meat, "I hate to say this, but Javier's getting soft in his old age. How does he know these freaks didn't kill Brat themselves, like they did Hollis, even if it was just by accident? More believable if they'd said those Blank Fucks got him, instead of that trash zapper story."

Javier swept together the small store of edibles he had gathered from his crew. He saw the mutants all glancing at it as if it were a steaming, aromatic buffet. "What have you folks been eating?"

"We had some food with us when we started out, because we knew we'd be out of Tin Town for a while," said Mira. "But it's almost gone now. We found a pig-hen in one of the rooms; it must've flown in before we sealed everything off. So we ate that, yesterday." In a lower voice, she admitted, "We were talking about, you know, maybe having to eat our friends. I know that sounds crazy, but..."

"I understand."

"Anyway, first I suggested we try eating one of the Blank People. They *are* organic. Though in a way, that sounds even more terrible."

"I don't think we'll have to resort to that," Javier reassured her. "How long have you folks been trapped inside here, anyway?"

"Eleven days."

"Dung," he said, wagging his head.

"So," Nhu pointed at the humble pile of food, some of it purchased at Quidd's Market only hours earlier, "we divide up our food, and the Teratas ration their own stuff, right?"

"No," Javier said. "It all goes in one pot."

"There's too many of us all together!" she protested.

"Well that's the way it's going to be, until we get out of here. Clear? Anybody gets caught sneaking into it, and I don't care if you're a Snarler or a Terata, you'll be eating my bullets instead. Trust me. I'm going to put Patryk in charge of the food."

"Oh, you are, huh?" Satin said. But Mira reached up and put a hand on one of the flippers that would have been a leg, to reassure him. Still, Satin asked, "And why him?"

Javier shrugged. "Because he's got a backpack. And because he does what he's told."

"What about water?" Nhu asked.

"There's running water," Mira said. "And this place is self-sufficient for power. It must have its own generator system in the basement."

Nhu headed into the little kitchen unit of 1-B. "A nice place like this, there has to be a food fabricator."

Mira followed after her, waddling quickly. "I wouldn't do that if I was you."

Nhu flicked on a light, glanced around her, moved to a control strip set into a faux black marble counter top. "Is there anything still in the fabricator stores? Did you try?"

"Of course we tried, but..."

Nhu started tapping the keys without waiting for the tiny woman to finish. A screen lit up, showed a menu of meals the fabricator could create from the generic soup in its banks (a raw material that consisted largely of fermented bacteria). She punched up something simple: imitation chili con carne. After a hesitation, then the sound of rushing air, there was a gurgling and a tray was pushed out of the processing unit onto the counter. In a ceramic bowl fizzed a foamy black sludge that smelled like pond algae.

"Oh, wow," Nhu said, cupping a hand over her nose and mouth.

"It's gone bad," Mira said.

"How long has this place been abandoned, then?"

"Well, I think the soup sat in the banks but never got used," Mira replied. "Because I don't think this building *was* abandoned. It seems to me like it never even opened in the first place."

CHAPTER FIVE
WRAPPED IN SKIN

ON THE WAY from his flat to the Arbury School, Stake became mired in traffic. His battered hovercar was wedged in a stream of vehicles of every sort, some even riding on wheels. He glanced up in envy at the helicars that swarmed more freely above him, though their flight paths were still limited to invisible channels beamed in layers between the ranks of towering buildings. These too were of every stripe. Skyscrapers with sides so smooth and featureless (with vidscreens on the interior, instead of windows) that one might think they were solid granite monuments in a graveyard for dead gods. Other buildings that looked like they'd been pieced together from thousands of odd-matched parts salvaged from stripped factory machines, steam curling out of grids and grates in their complex flanks. Buildings with snake skins of multicolored mosaics. Buildings wearing an armor

of riveted metal plates, like retired warships looming vertically with their sterns jammed into the
street. Flat roofs upon which perched smaller
buildings, symbiotically. Other structures tapering
to needle points that seemed to etch the clouds
upon the blue glass of the sky. Stacked apartments.
Stacked businesses. On street level: shop fronts,
and gang kids squatting on tenement steps, glaring
insolently at the slow sludge of traffic. In many an
earlier traffic jam, he had seen such kids walk
across the roofs of vehicles to attack someone in a
car who they felt had gestured or looked at them
in a challenging way, or simply in order to rob a
certain individual too boxed in to escape. He now
saw a group of small but hard-faced teenage boys
loitering outside a Vietnamese *pho* restaurant,
who wore as their identifying garb clear plastic
jackets that brazenly showed off the guns they
wore in holsters beneath them.

Ah, Punktown.

A movement caught his eye, distracting him
from the banner advertisements he had begun
watching numbly as they scrolled across the top of
his dashboard monitor. A hoverbike, weaving
slowly but deftly through the deadlocked larger
vehicles. The person astride it was slight in frame.
A woman, most likely. And though a helmet
enclosed her head, he saw the blue of her bared
arms.

Stake's heart was jolted. A Ha Jiin, he thought.

Thi, he thought.

But it could not be Thi. What were the odds of
her being in this city? No, Thi was not on this
world of Oasis. Not even in this dimension.

Thi was not the only Ha Jiin woman in existence, was she? Though for him, she might as well have been.

He continued watching the woman on the bike as she worked her way between the idling cars with a stubbornness, a tough determination, that he felt was characteristic of her race. And watching her, Stake felt transported back to the teeming city of Di Noon. The buildings were not nearly as tall as these giants which cast an icy sea of shadow over the street. And it was primarily motorbikes, in staggering numbers, that flooded the streets in place of all these bulkier crafts. Smoothly humming hoverbikes, noisily buzzing older bikes with wheels, and even bicycles—all of them miraculously seeming never to collide with each other, though he had seen, and himself barely evaded, countless near collisions. It was in Di Noon that he had developed his preference for riding outside on a bike rather than packaged up inside a car. Cutting through Di Noon's hot, tropical mugginess and smog of exhaust. Out in the blaze of twin blue-white suns that wrung the sweat from his skin and steamed the blood in his heart. The throng of life, so intense and immediate, and him immersed in its very substance, corpuscle in a vein.

The Blue War had been the only war that Earth had participated in—thus far, anyway—in which the soil of battle was not only that of an alien world, but an alien plane of existence. The blue-skinned people themselves might very well be a parallel incarnation of his own kind, for all the Theta researchers knew. The Colonial Forces had gone there to support the new Jin Haa nation as it fought to maintain its sovereignty from that of the Ha Jiin, and Di Noon where Stake was initially stationed was the capital city of the Jin Haa. This support from the Earth Colonies of course had nothing to do with the rich clouds of gas that seethed and fermented in pockets beneath the surface of the blue-leaved jungles, waiting to be bottled up for transportation back to their own dimension.

Watching the elusive figure of the woman on the hoverbike recede, Stake vividly recalled in every cell of his being the first time that he and a large group of fellow soldiers had seated themselves inside one of the big metal pods, in two long rows facing each other. Also aboard the transdimensional pod was a small team of Theta agents, the research branch that explored and mapped whatever alternate material planes they could pry their way into. This car which now confined him felt like a smaller, more personal version of that pod. And he shivered, as he had then. He shivered, as if again he experienced his body being sifted through the veil, filtered through the very weave of the universe, squeezed out like strings of hamburger to be reconstituted in another realm as far away as infinity and as close as the opposite side of a thin sheet of paper.

Something in the logjam seemed to break, and the river of steel and plastic began to flow forward again. And a moment later, he lost sight of the woman on the hoverbike altogether.

* * *

SITTING ON A bench outside the Arbury School, under the watchful eye of the guard in the visitors' entrance scanning vestibule, Stake tried not to be obvious about eyeing a girl in blazer and plaid skirt and navy socks that clung to round hard calves as she knelt down to gather the books she'd spilled. Her silky, blue-black hair made him think she might be adorable little Yuki, but when she straightened and turned he saw the swimming clear tendrils that sprouted out of her eye sockets, and realized she was of the humanoid Tikkihotto race. Most of the girls at the school were Earth colonists, though he had spotted the occasional Choom, and a minute ago he had seen a female alien more akin to a giant dust mite walking upright on her four hindmost legs. However exclusive this private school was, it couldn't get away with racial exclusivity, though money was often the best way to filter undesirables. Because of her anatomy, the mite being wore only a diagonal band of the same black material as the blazers across her body, the school insignia displayed on this. The alien girl who had been walking beside her, though, with her gaping face like that of a deep sea hatchetfish, had been wearing the typical uniform, her tartan skirt giving Stake a look at knobby legs shimmering with silvery-gray scales.

"Mr. Stake?" He looked up to see a woman approaching him, smiling. She wore something like the same blazer the students wore, but with a skirt of matching solid black. Stake felt embarrassed, as though the woman had caught him luxuriating in this churning sea of teenage femininity. "I'm Janice Poole," she introduced herself, as she briskly clicked closer.

He stood and extended his hand. "Thanks for meeting with me."

She shook his hand. Her grip was strong. "I know John Fukuda; a very pleasant and charming man. He allows me to tour my biology students through his facility every year. I told him I'd be happy to cooperate in any way. Yuki is one of my favorite students—a very dear girl. I hate to see her upset like this. I really don't want her work to suffer as a result."

"Mr. Fukuda recommended you as someone I could talk with discreetly, so I thought I might ask you some questions about a classmate of Yuki's, who she mentioned is also in your biology class. A girl named Krimson?"

Janice Poole gave an odd smile. "Krimson. Yes. Well, we could go back inside to my office, Mr. Stake—the school will be open another hour before it locks up for the day. Or would you rather go to your office, or a café nearby?"

His office. He didn't have one. His flat was all he needed, and he never met with his clients there. "Do you know a good café?"

"Sure. Care to take my car? And I can drop you back here afterwards."

"Certainly; thanks."

As they drove in her sporty new hovercar, Stake stole glances at the woman beside him. He liked Janice Poole's profile of strong pointed nose and pointed chin. He liked that she had not dyed the gray that prematurely and attractively threaded her shortish, shaggy dark hair. He judged her to be older than himself, in her late thirties. Her skin was very white, her figure inside her sharp uniform apparently full and womanly, and she was nearly the same height he was. She seemed confident. Sure of her place in the world. That always intimidated him about people a little. Or maybe it just mystified him. In that regard, a human could sometimes be more alien to him than a nonhuman being.

They seated themselves at a small table in an upscale café; their young waitress sported a pixel tattoo that covered her entire face, making of it a movie screen. She could probably play any number of film loops across its surface, but right now it showed a close-up of the shifting and glistening feathers of a peacock's tail. "Terrible," Stake muttered, watching her move away to submit their order. "She'd be beautiful without that thing, as far as I can tell."

"Beauty is subjective," Janice chuckled. "My nephew has one of those on his face; he plays vids of his favorite music groups. I saw a man on the street who was playing porn vids on his." A smile. It had a kind of open suggestiveness to it. In that moment, Stake thought: she's been to bed with John Fukuda. A "pleasant and charming man."

"I just don't understand people defacing their faces," he said.

"It's a fad. They'll have them removed, and go on to something else." She leaned her elbows forward on the table. "So… Krimson."

"Yes. Yuki told me she disappeared about a week ago—the same time that Yuki's doll vanished from her locker. She tells me the girl is hostile toward her. Since you know both girls, I was wondering what you thought the chances are of this girl taking the doll—maybe for its monetary value—and running away from home. Yuki said she has an older boyfriend."

"I don't know about any boyfriend, but I suspect I know why this girl might be hostile toward Yuki. Her name is Krimson Tableau, and her father owns a company here in Punktown that raises and harvests battery animals. Tableau Meats."

"Ah... yes."

"Fukuda Bioforms recently purchased and assimilated the old Alvine Products company. So now they're direct competitors in the same market, in the same city."

"Well, then my hunch seems valid. But there's a complication. Yuki said one of Krimson's friends has heard Krimson on her Ouija phone. Which, if true, would indicate that Krimson hasn't run away, but is dead. And at her young age, dead could very well mean murdered."

"Hm." Janice nodded absent-mindedly to the waitress as she placed their coffees in front of them. The girl's face was now a soundlessly pounding ocean surf. "Well, there are some bogus Ouija phone services. And the fragments of voices the kids hear on those things are wide open to interpretation. So I don't know how reliable that theory would be."

"I know. I'm not too trusting of that source, myself, though I have to admit I know little about those phones. Please don't repeat this to Mr. Fukuda, but Yuki even swears she's heard her own mother on one of them."

"Really? That's rather spooky. Speaking of murdered: did you know that Yuki's mother was murdered? And please do me a favor, too, and don't tell him I told you that. I don't know that he cares to have people discuss it."

Stake set down his mug and looked at Janice intently. "Murdered? No, I didn't know that. She only told me her mom died when she was a baby."

"When she was a baby? I thought I'd heard it was more recent than that, like four years ago or something. Maybe Yuki told you that to hide the more painful reality. Anyway, yes, her mom was killed. I guess they never found out who did it. My knowledge is pretty limited, so it might be unfair of me to bring it up at all."

"Huh." Stake stared into her face, lost in thought. She was watching him very intently herself, and it was as though he could see himself reflected in her eyes. Before he realized what was happening, so distracted was he by this string of revelations, he saw Janice's expression become one of surprise.

"Oh my God—you're a changeling! A chameleon!"

Instantly, violently, he looked away. But she reached over and took his hand.

"I'm sorry; I don't mean to make you self-conscious. Please look at me again."

"I'd rather let this pass." How much did he look like her already? The long pointed nose? The pointed chin? Maybe even gray threads through his short dark hair? Maybe even his somewhat olive skin gone ivory white?

She squeezed his hand to reassure him. "It's remarkable. Really, I'm not repulsed. I'm fascinated."

"Well, you are a biologist."

"I didn't mean it that way. Maybe a little. So, were you genetically designed for this, or—"

"No," he said, a little too harshly. He looked at her again. "I'm not a belf." It was a derisive slang for bio-engineered life form. "I'm a mutant." But was that much better than being a belf?

"Yes, I see. Ah, *Caro*—"

"...*turbida*," he finished.

"Restless flesh."

"Confused flesh."

She still held his hand. "Please don't be offended. Do I look like it bothers me?"

"No. But it bothers me." That was too frank. Women brought that out in him. Especially those he found attractive. As long as he was spilling his guts, he went on, "I was born in Tin Town. The mutie slums. My father was normal, but my mother was a mutant. She died when I was a kid."

"Very sorry. So your dad raised you."

"Not really. He sort of lost himself in drugs after that. He loved her a lot, see; he didn't care what she was. So I pretty much grew up on the streets. I avoided the gang thing, and I ended up enlisting in the military as soon as I could, to get out of Tin Town the best way I knew how."

"Was your Mom a... could she change like this, too?"

"No. She had physical deformities. But no 'gifts,' if you want to call it that."

"Wow." Janice digested all this. "I appreciate your candor, Mr. Stake. Can I ask your first name?"

"Jeremy."

"Jeremy," she repeated, staring at him so raptly that he couldn't stop himself from flicking looks at her eyes again and again, despite how much he had trained himself.

The waitress returned to ask if they were enjoying their coffee and if they needed anything else. Her eyes, in a field of yellow flowers rippled by a summer breeze, looked confused, as though she thought another customer had come in to replace Stake. The woman's twin brother, perhaps.

Janice dismissed the waitress, and then whispered to Stake, "Hey, do you want to get out of here?"

She still hadn't let go of his hand.

HE HAD BEEN wandering around her living room, admiring her collection of paintings (they apparently paid teachers unusually well at the Arbury School), but he rejoined her at the bar. "What would you like?" she asked. He noticed a bottle of bright yellow Ha Jiin wine; he could tell by the giant centipede coiled inside the bottle, preserved by the alcohol. He tapped the bottle with a finger, and Janice poured some into a small glass. "Be careful, it's very potent. And did you know it's supposed to be an aphrodisiac? I'm sure that long, thick centipede has nothing to do with the belief."

He sipped the barest few molecules of his drink but it still took his breath away. He hadn't had any of this in a few years; not since angry vets had protested it being stocked at the bar in the Legion of Veterans Post 69. Why put money in their former enemies' pockets? This, in spite of the fact that it was probably their allies, the Jin Haa, who had exported it.

He noticed a bottle of sake amongst the diverse collection of bottles. "How well do you know Mr. Fukuda?" he asked in an offhand way.

"How well does anyone know anyone, Jeremy?"

She was being playful, or evasive. He turned around, and she was standing close, too close, a glass of white wine in her own hand. He knew his face held onto the change, a little or a lot. When he concentrated on it, his mind could reach out and tell. He could also activate the mirror feature on his wrist comp's screen to look and be more sure—and he could even call up his natural face on that screen, and pore over it until he slipped this mask—but he did not raise his arm. He was a little embarrassed to do so. To show that it bothered him that much. He had revealed enough vulnerability already.

"I like it," Janice purred. She set her glass down on the mini bar.

"Like what?"

"That you look like me now. I don't know; I find it very intriguing." She took the glass from his hand, rested it beside hers, and then her arms went around him. Their twinned mouths came together...

In her bed, she straddled him with her full breasts swaying down heavily in his face. He sucked at one of them as if to feed, his craving making him an infant. It had been a while since a woman had gone to bed with him. And the last time had been a prostie. Not many women found his turbulent flesh so "intriguing." As she undulated atop him, Janice said huskily, "When I was thirteen, I used to kiss my reflection in the bathroom mirror as I—you know—touched myself. Huh. I guess I sort of lost my virginity to myself." Her eyes didn't leave his face. "Look at me... please," she said.

His closed eyes dutifully opened and stared up at her. She leaned lower and dragged her nipples across his cheeks. She grinned, her shaggy hair falling about her face.

"We're all narcissistic," she said in a lustful voice, more like panting. "We're all just masturbators."

Yes, thought Stake. Because we're all alone. Even when we're together.

And that made him think of Thi. And it was a good thing he did not change his appearance simply by thinking of another person, as some who suffered his disorder did. Or right now, Janice would wonder why he was beginning to resemble a Ha Jiin woman instead of herself.

She dug her fingers into his breasts, which had swelled up in a fair imitation of her own, and her undulations grew more intense. Beneath him, under her driving weight, Stake felt her sheets rub against him. When she had led him by the hand into her bedroom and pulled back the blankets, she had revealed that her bed linens were sheets of pink, living skin. A thin flexible tube ran from both the mattress sheet and the cover sheet to a nutrient tank in the corner that kept the bio-engineered flesh alive. Stake had never been in a bed with sheets of this nature before. It made him feel all the more infantile and helpless. Inside a womb.

Their entanglements grew more varied. Finally becoming more actively involved, less passive, Stake shifted behind Janice. He preferred looking at the back of her head, felt strengthened by the break in their eye contact. He remained there until he climaxed hard against her. They collapsed to the bed together, he on top of her, sucking at air. Janice had squeezed the mattress sheet in her fists, and when she unclenched her hands she saw that her nails had dug into the smooth skin. Beads of blood rose from the little wounds. "Damn," she said.

Stake lifted his head to look. "I'm sorry."

She reached up behind her to stroke his face. "Don't worry, it will heal."

CHAPTER SIX
SHADOW CITY

BENEATH PUNKTOWN THERE WAS, in effect, a shadow version of itself. When they'd run out of room to build sideways or upwards, city planners had looked downwards instead. This underground district had come to be known as Subtown. Its borders were not nearly as extensive as those of the city proper overhead, but it still encompassed a sizable area.

The rays of the sun did not reach down here; its citizens, many of whom might not venture aboveground for months at a time, lived and worked under the artificial glow of lamps set into a concrete sky. As evening fell, some of these lamps dimmed and others were shut off completely, to give something of the effect of night (though Subtown was not made so dark as to give criminals undue cover for their activities). Because of the limits set by the ceiling, buildings were smaller, tending toward flat-roofed tenement structures, often with shops on the ground floor. There were factories and warehouses, too, but these had not been safe in their subterranean shelter when financial plagues had swept through the city, and manufacturers had migrated in flocks to the Outback Colony or even to overcrowded and much-blighted Earth in a reverse colonization. Wherever labor was cheaper, or perhaps restrictions were laxer about how many living workers companies were required to employ to balance out their automatonic laborers, whom they didn't have to pay at all.

Behind the Perez Valve Company there was a pair of loading docks, but these had been claimed by other street people, who had used scrap material from the derelict factory's inoperative trash zapper to build enclosed shelters upon the elevated platforms. So last night, the homeless person had simply lain against the factory's graffiti-splashed flank, using his bent arm for a pillow. He didn't have to worry about being rained upon, after all, and the temperature was regulated down here, always comfortable unless there was the occasional glitch in climate control. Therefore, he didn't really need to build a shelter. He simply slept in this alley or that, at most pulling a plastic tarp over himself. When he had first found the blue plastic tarp, he had dragged it behind him loosely in his wanderings, but later he realized that it was better to roll it in a tube and carry it with him that way during the hours that corresponded with daylight. Finally, he had had the notion to tear a hole in the center of the sheet and wear it over his head like a long poncho, covering his previously naked body.

He had awoken hungry, as he did every day. So hungry. Yesterday he had seen two street people scrounging through a trash zapper behind an Indian restaurant. The spicy smells of cooking from inside had made his innards gurgle, but when he had shambled toward the two men to join them, they had yelled and thrown trash at him to chase him off. Forlornly, he had moved away.

Now, as always, he tried to keep to the alleys as he navigated Subtown. Peering out from one of these, he spotted an outdoors café (if it could be spoken of as such), spilling onto the sidewalk. He lingered in the alley mouth until a nicely dressed couple got up from their table, leaving behind a little coffee in their mugs and half a croissant on one plate. He emerged from the alley and went to the table, snatching up the piece of croissant just before the waiter reappeared and started shouting at him. He hurried away, glancing over his shoulder to see the waiter protectively gather up some slips of colored paper that the nicely dressed couple had also left behind them on the table.

He ducked into another narrow passage between buildings, and there brought the croissant up to his face. Some of it had flaked away in his tight grip, but he studied the smashed bit that lay in his palm. He stared and stared at it, so hungry. But he could not think of how to get the succulent morsel into that empty place that yawned inside his body.

Two youths stepped into the end of the alley, laughing, holding a woman's handbag between them. As they clawed through the pouch, little bits of this and that dropped to the alley floor. Coins. A container of mints. A little glass bottle that smashed with a tinkle and emitted a strong flowery scent.

Giggling, babbling. Their happiness inspired the homeless person. He moved forward out of the shadows, shuffled toward them. Maybe they could help him. Show him what to do.

"Whoa!" said one of the youths, looking up at the homeless person's approach.

"Dung, man," the other laughed, to hide the fact that he'd been startled. "What the hell you want, you mutated freak?"

The homeless person stopped a few paces away, almost the same height as the two boys but bulkier. The rustling plastic cloak he wore made him look bulkier still. He lifted his arm, extended his fist and opened it, revealing the smashed remnant of croissant there. He wanted to make the noises they made, but he could not. All he could do was hope that they understood his mute gesture. Helped him to feed, and appease this perplexing hunger.

"Thanks, freak, but I'm not hungry," the darker-skinned of the two boys said. He stepped up to the homeless person and slapped the piece of croissant out of his hand. It went flying, landed on the ground. The boy then backed off, sputtering laughter. They both laughed.

The homeless person looked down at the morsel on the ground. He then looked up again, and moved closer to the boys imploringly. So confused. So hungry. He continued to hold out the empty hand in which the croissant had rested.

"Get back, wanker," the lighter-faced youth snapped, lunging and shoving at his shoulders. "Go beg someplace else."

But the homeless person was heavy, despite his hollow hunger, and barely moved when pushed. He did not drop his extended arm.

The dark-faced boy tore something out from under his jacket. Was he taking pity? Knowing that he had not been able to find a way to get the croissant inside, did the boy have something more suitable to offer him? But the hard black object he gripped in his fist did not look like food, and it did not look like he was willing to hand it over, either. The gun made a little electronic blip to announce that its safety feature had been thumbed off.

The homeless person reached out his arm a little further. He tried to touch the lighter-skinned boy on the arm.

"Get off me!" he cried, stumbling back against the alley wall.

"Blasting freak," the black boy snarled, lowering his gun and putting one shot into the homeless person's distended belly.

This stolen gun did not fire solid projectiles, but a short beam of light of an intense purple color. Like an arrow, it pierced his belly, its entire length disappearing inside him. The arrow of light left a black, puckered hole. A little dribble of clear fluid, as thick as syrup, wept out of the puncture beneath his poncho.

Had the boy meant to feed him, by injecting some sort of nourishment directly into that hungry place? He didn't think so. It only made him feel more hollowed out in there. And besides, it hurt. It hurt badly.

The homeless person didn't like to hurt. He didn't like these would-be friends.

He swept his other arm, and it struck the black boy on the wrist. There was a snap of bones and the hand flipped over at an extreme angle. The gun he'd been holding went sailing down the alley, skittered across its floor. He began to scream, but the homeless person's other hand clamped across his face, and squeezed, and lifted. Between thick digits, the boy's eyes darted madly. The hand squeezed tighter, causing one of the maddened eyes to be ejected from its socket, bulging out between two of the fingers. When the homeless person slammed the boy's limp, dangling body against the wall again and again, the other eye stopped moving, too.

"Dung, dung, dung!" the lighter-skinned boy cried, bolting out of the alley. He even tried racing through a gap in the street's traffic, but he misjudged his trajectory and the speed of the vehicles he plunged between. A silver hovercar tapped him enough to spin him around, but a red hovercar struck him hard enough to sweep him right out of the homeless person's range of sight.

He released the black boy, watched him flop to the alley floor at his feet. The smell of the red fluid leaking from the splits in the youth's skull made his innards gurgle all the more insistently, but he didn't know how to get that stuff inside him, either.

Tensing up his body against the molten pain inside him, he turned and sought out the dropped morsel of croissant. He went to it and stooped to retrieve it. This action made the pain stab him more deeply, but he dealt with it. Straightening, he studied the morsel again. Then, he lifted the edge of his makeshift cloak, and crammed the food into the little black hole the boy had burned through the blue plastic, burned through his flesh.

Using his finger, he pushed the crushed pastry inside as far as he could. But it did not even begin to alleviate his hunger.

Later in the day, as he resumed his wandering through the labyrinth of alleys, his body finally pushed that crumpled piece of croissant out of him again. There was one good thing, however. The black hole closed, sealed up, and was gone as if it had never existed. And shortly after that, the hot pain inside him subsided as well.

But the hunger remained.

CHAPTER SEVEN
THE DOPPLER EFFECT

As HE FOLLOWED John Fukuda to their table, Stake took in the people who had already sat down to their lunch. Most of them were men in expensive five-piece suits, some of whom had left overcoats and bowler hats—the current fashion for the stylish businessman—with a robot attendant which would not misplace a single item. But one article of clothing that many of the men continued to flaunt proudly caused Stake to give a derisive smirk. Tucked into a pocket of their jackets like a handkerchief, these men wore a soiled pair of teenage girls' panties. Preferably white, though sometimes with a soft flowery pattern or even cute—kawaii—designs such as the adorable jellyfish that proliferated on clothing lately. Other men, though, wore their panties tucked into the collar of their shirts, hanging down their fronts like a tie. One gentleman who was just being seated actually wore his pair across his lower face like a mask to filter his breathing. Presumably he would remove it in order to eat. The two sharply dressed adult women being seated with him appeared utterly indifferent to this accoutrement, apparently not insulted by the fact that their own larger personal garments would not be coveted in this way.

Stake touched Fukuda's elbow, causing him to pause and face him. "What do you think of this fad with the panties, Mr. Fukuda, having a teenage daughter of your own? I've heard girls even younger than Yuki sell their underwear to panty brokers, who put them in those vending machines you see around."

Fukuda's hands were tucked into his jacket pockets. He withdrew his right hand just far enough to reveal a shimmering membrane of white silk that he rubbed between his fingers. "Cotton is most popular, but I find the touch of silk more calming." His eyes twinkled, testing Stake's reaction.

Stake couldn't stop himself from stammering, "Those aren't... Yuki's?"

Fukuda lost his twinkle immediately, exchanging it for a look of dismay. "What? Of course not!" It seemed to take him a moment to compose himself, after the rattling suggestion that he might fetishize an article of his own child's clothing. "Mr. Stake, in the community of Luzon, here in town, a man might savor the taste of dog. But he will not eat his own. And he will protect his dog from ending up on someone else's plate, too. Do you catch my meaning?"

Stake caught it only too well, but he wanted to pursue the matter and ask how his client would feel if he learned that one of these businessmen were right now wearing his daughter's used dainties, sold by Yuki to one of those entrepreneurs who in turn dispensed them through vending machines in subway stations, malls, and even in the washrooms of upscale nightclubs, but he decided not to poke the man about his hypocrisy. It was no different from a man having no qualms about a woman selling her body—so long as he had not sired that body. Anyway, they were now holding up traffic behind them, and needed to seat themselves at their own table instead of standing in the midst of these others.

The executive cafeteria of Fukuda Bioforms was smaller, more intimate than the one in which Stake had lunched with Yuki Fukuda. It was more of a restaurant, really, and once they were settled a wait staff served them their drinks and salads. Though Stake was sure the general cafeteria for the hordes of office drones and lab techs was considerably less swanky.

Hemmed in by tropical potted plants and subdued lighting, Fukuda and his guest hovered over their blood orange martinis until their steaks arrived. Fukuda had insisted on ordering for Stake, after first determining that he was not a vegetarian. He watched avidly as the private investigator cut off a tender chunk of filet mignon, popped it into his mouth and chewed.

"Mm." He nodded. "Mmm. Don't tell me—from your deadstock, right?"

"Oh, Mr. Stake, you ruined my surprise. Yes, it is. Wonderful, eh?"

"It really is. Very delicious. Thank you."

"Janice Poole phoned me to say that you had talked with her about the daughter of Adrian Tableau. And talk of that butcher Tableau put me in mind to treat you to something of a far better quality than the blobs he churns out at Tableau Meats."

"The consumer gets what he pays for, I guess." Mention of Janice Poole made Stake want to casually establish how well acquainted with her Fukuda truly was, but he knew it wasn't relevant to the matter at hand, and he couldn't say he was jealous enough, yet, to obsess over it. So instead, he focused on Fukuda's relationship with this Adrian Tableau. "Then you two are definitely not fond of each other."

"He's the one who seems to have a problem with me, though there's room in the market for us both. This is a hungry town, and we both ship our product as near as the city of Miniosis and as far as the planet Earth. But our client base is a little different. As you say, his products appeal to those with less discriminating tastes."

"And less money."

"Yes. Not that our products are overpriced, just of a higher grade. Well, I suppose that after the Alvine Products scandal and the closing of their plant, Adrian grew used to having the market all to himself for a few years."

"Do you think he hates you enough to have someone steal your daughter's valuable kawaii-doll? If not his daughter Krimson, then another girl?"

"It's a possibility. I was aware that his daughter had gone missing, but I never put that and the disappearance of Dai-oo-ika together until Janice brought it up to me in her call. Still, it's a pretty indirect way for Tableau to attack me, unless his daughter did it on her own purely out of spite."

"Yuki told me that a friend of Krimson's claims to have heard her on a Ouija phone."

"Bah." Fukuda waved his fork dismissively, one cheek bulging with his own bite of steak. "I'm not convinced about those things. And even if they do enable people to speak with the trace energies of the departed in some alternate existence, it isn't healthy. It isn't meant for us to throw stones into the well of souls, so to speak, in some irreverent form of play."

"Maybe we can learn from the dead."

"I'll find out about it firsthand one day. I can wait until then."

"I think the kids are less afraid of this stuff than we are," Stake observed. "More open-minded about the technology."

"Or more naive. Or it could be that being older, we're more uncomfortably aware of our own mortality."

Stake wanted to ask Fukuda about his wife, then, especially now that he knew from Janice Poole that she had been murdered. But that had no bearing on the matter at hand, either. How could it? As Yuki had warned him, her father had loved his wife dearly. Why upset him if there were nothing to gain from it?

"Well," Fukuda went on, "this is food for thought, anyway. Pardon the pun." He poked at his steak with his knife, looking pensive. "I should hope it wasn't Tableau behind it. I wouldn't want to imagine why he'd want that doll."

"I'll look into it. Though honestly, I think it's more likely that the daughter would do it on her own, instead of her father putting her up to it. But I don't want to make limiting assumptions."

"Mm," muttered Fukuda, digesting thoughts that tasted decidedly less appetizing than the meat he savored. He looked up at last and studied Stake's face. And smiled an odd, sad smile. "I don't mean to make you self-conscious about it, so perhaps I shouldn't mention it, but in the past few minutes you've started to take on a resemblance to me again."

Typically, Stake dropped his gaze. "Sorry."

Fukuda laughed. "Why apologize? I don't consider it a personal violation. As I've said, it intrigues me a great deal." His smile faltered, took on that melancholy aspect again. "But seeing you this way does fill me with a strange emotion. You see, I had a twin brother—James. He died some years ago."

Stake was plainly surprised. First Yuki's revelation about her mother, and now this. Was their family under some curse? But then, Punktown was a dangerous place. Even so, shouldn't the Fukudas' wealth have insulated them a bit better from that?

"I didn't realize," he said. "I'm very sorry to hear it." He didn't know what he should say, how much curiosity was prudent. He couldn't help it, though; it was his job, and thus his mind-set, to be curious. He asked, "Was he, uh, a fraternal twin or identical?"

"Identical. Like you're becoming."

"I'm not *that* good at this."

"Good enough. It's uncanny. So, this ability of yours must come in handy in your line of work."

"It's been useful. I can program faces into my wrist comp, like masks I carry with me." He tapped its screen. "It gets me in places. It gets people to talk to me when they might not otherwise. I control it the best I can. If my look starts to slip, I just stare at my comp again. And if I need to be me again, I have my own face in here, too."

"It's all so amazing."

"Sometimes I think what's more amazing is that people's cells are constantly being replenished, replaced, and yet they *maintain* their appearance. It's like they clone themselves over and over and over again. Right down to every last mole and scar."

"Hm. Yes." Fukuda prodded at his meat some more. "We are fascinating organisms, aren't we? The flesh is the ultimate clay; how could we as a species not want to mold it? We have tattooed it, pierced it, exercised to tone and build it, tanned it and tamed it. Modified it and improved upon it with bio-engineering." He wagged his head, then sipped his martini. Observed his guest as if contemplating himself in a mirror. "Is that all you've been, then, a hired detective? Was that your dream from an early age? A romantic, idealized sort of profession? Or did you just fall into it?"

"More fell into it. I don't know that I ever had a dream occupation, just a dream to escape Tin Town. I was born there."

"Ohh, I see."

"I joined the military at eighteen, to get out."

"Really? And did you see action?"

"A full four-year stint in the Blue War."

"You lived through that hell, eh? Thank God for that. And did they take you in spite of your mutation, or because of it?"

"They were enthusiastic about it. They started training me straight off for deep penetration missions, behind enemy lines."

"You did that in the Blue War? Then, can your skin take on a blue color, too?"

"It tries. It gets... bluish. I ended up using a dye for that. But the dye didn't wash off too quickly, and it almost got me shot by my own people a couple of times even after my face had reverted to normal."

"You've had an interesting life."

"Think so?"

"Yes, very much so. Maybe not lucrative, but lucrative and interesting do not necessarily walk hand-in-hand."

"You sound like you have regrets."

Now it was Fukuda's turn to avert his eyes. "We all have regrets, Mr. Stake."

AFTER LUNCH, THE rich food and drink sitting in his guts like its weight in gold, Stake returned to his flat. This was on the top floor of a squat tenement building at the very end of Forma Street, one of the town's longest and most colorful avenues. Unfortunately, one of the presiding colors was red. But perhaps in some masochistic way, the street suited Stake's mood, though he could have afforded to live in a somewhat less raucous neighborhood. He joked to people that the gunfire at night reminded him of his soldier days.

He wasted no time in changing from his generic black business suit into something much more comfortable: a pair of jeans and an old T-shirt. This was in camouflaged shades of blue, from pastel to indigo. Barefoot, coffee in hand, he stood at his windows and watched the daily Mardi Gras for a few minutes before turning away to sit at the banged-up secondhand desk that was all he really had by way of an office, though the computer equipment arranged atop it was fairly state-of-the-art.

He was juggling a few other cases concurrently with John Fukuda's, though it was more conventional stuff. He checked his messages and did a little research into this or that ongoing investigation. One of these involved a runaway daughter, Yuki's age, but her scowling photo on one of Stake's array of screens suggested she was far less innocent. At this point Stake was pretty sure that the girl had run off with a thirty-four year-old boyfriend, down south toward the Outback Colony. This girl put him in mind again of Krimson Tableau, whom Yuki had said might also have run off with an older boyfriend. When Stake did a net search on her name, however, he found little that was useful. A missing persons report had been filed by her father, Adrian Tableau, over a week ago, apparently one day after she had failed to return home from school. But there was no mention of any boyfriend that the police had been asked to seek out and question. Maybe just schoolyard gossip? After all, if Yuki's story about Krimson speaking over a Ouija phone could be believed, the girl was not a runaway, but more likely a murder victim.

Murder victim.

Stake's next net search had him looking into the death of Yuki's mother. John Fukuda's wife. Just out of nagging curiosity.

Again, he found little. Yuriko Fukuda had been murdered four years ago. (Janice had been right; she hadn't died when Yuki was a baby, as the girl had claimed.) Shot to death in her home by an unknown assailant, possibly in a bungled robbery of their high-class apartment. Attached to the news report was a holoportrait which Stake rotated on one of the other screens. A stunning woman. He could see where Yuki had got her looks.

Stake rolled back a bit in his chair, still staring at the revolving disembodied head of the beautiful woman, and yawned. He thought he might steal a nap, then get up and head down to LOV 69 for a dinner of burgers and brews. He wondered if the Legion of Veterans Post bought its cheap hamburger in bulk from Tableau Meats.

BEAUTIFUL HEAD. SPINNING and spinning. Beautiful face. Turning away from him, then turning his way again.

She had been so beautiful. As beautiful as the monastery, with its outer and inner walls tiled in mosaics that told the story of her faith in place of a holy text. (It's a comic book, joked one of his fellow soldiers as he followed the story. Then the soldier had gunned away the brightly glazed little tiles that composed the face of their prophet in one of the "comic book" panels.)

The monastery had been secreted away in the heart of a jungle where every frond and blade and leaf and vine was a vivid shade of blue. Blue lizards basked in the broken rays of twin blue-white suns. Lovely insects fanned their blue wings as they rested on blue flowers. Deceptively like butterflies, they were. But they drank blood, not pollen.

It was ironic that the monks themselves could not see the mosaics, but they spent hours each day reverently running their hands over the raised and contoured shapes as if reading a bible printed in Braille. It was the first time some of his fellow soldiers had seen the Ha Jiin's clerical caste, and they were horrified. Their horror made them angry and rough as they herded the monastery's ten monks together, prodding them where they wanted them to go with the muzzles of their guns.

They wore beautiful flowing robes of azure silk, embroidered with raised religious symbols also seen worked into the mosaics. On their heads, black three-cornered hats. And because the holy caste started smoking their incense as children, each of the ten monks had a whorl-like hole in place of a face. Like a huge knothole in leathery blue tree bark. The incense had cancerous properties that ate their features away over the years, obliterating their identities so that they were all identical servants of their faith. The cancer eventually reduced their fingers to nubs so that the hands they rubbed along the tiles were more like blunt flippers, fleshy mittens. They sacrificed their fingers by pinching the hot glowing incense out of the bowls of the pipes they smoked. Then, they pressed the ash to a point in the center of their chests until over time a smaller vortex wound opened there, like a window straight to their hearts. They humbled themselves this way day after day. Until they were fully transmogrified. Until they needed the incense no more.

"This is how hardcore these people are," marveled one of the soldiers, wagging his head in awe. In fear. "This is why they're so fucking tough to fight!"

Devoted to their faith. Devoted to win their war against the emerging Jin Haa nation. And the Earth Colonies' military forces that supported it.

It was because of this fierce devotion that Corporal Jeremy Stake was a little surprised that the two Ha Jiin fighters who had taken refuge in the monastery surrendered when the Earth soldiers surrounded it. Stake was in command by the time they captured the monastery, because their unit's lieutenant and sergeant had both been killed by sniper fire.

The captured fighters were a woman in her early twenties and a boy of maybe nineteen with a badly infected leg wound that had slowed them down and forced them to hide out in the monastery. Stake ordered their medic to see to the boy. Their guns were collected. From the woman they took a sniper rifle; a sophisticated Earth weapon she had no doubt taken off a corpse at some point.

"Let me shoot that bitch!" Private Cortez raged, aiming his own gun at the now unarmed woman, her fingers linked on top of her head. "She's the one who killed the lieutenant and Sergeant Lindy—has to be!"

"We don't execute prisoners unless they attempt escape," Stake intoned, quoting regulations.

"She looks like she's gonna make a run for it to me" remarked another unit member, leveling his bulky, multi-barreled assault engine.

"She was picking off our officers," Cortez said. "You would've been next, man!"

"I mean it," Stake told them. "Just get some restraints on them."

"Sir," said Private Henderson, calling him over to examine the sniper gun they had confiscated. He pointed to some Ha Jiin characters etched or burned into the weapon's stock. "Can you read this?"

"What's it say?"

Henderson met his eyes gravely. "'The Earth Killer.'"

Overhearing this exchange, Cortez bounced on his feet and jerked his gun at the woman, raging anew. "It's her! She's the Earth Killer! That's what they call her! She's snuffed I don't know how many of us, Stake! We need to riddle this fucking bitch *now!*"

"I told you to back off, didn't I?" Stake snapped. "Don't argue with me or it goes in my report."

"The corporal's gunning for general," wise-cracked another man, but he ignored it.

The Earth Killer. Her own people had dubbed her that. A legend, almost, even to them. And it had worked its way to the ears of the Colonial troopers. A cold-blooded little beauty, carrying a gun almost as big as herself, with a patient trigger finger and an instinctive eye for drilling solid projectiles and various types of ray beams into enemy soldiers at great distances, even through the intervening chaos of jungle vegetation.

But Stake wanted to know her real name, and he stepped closer to her. He asked her, in his crude fumbling attempt at the native language. She said nothing, staring at him unblinkingly. He edged closer, to intimidate her. But not too close, because he was intimidated himself, though she was five feet tall at best, slim as an adolescent boy, and had had her wrists banded together in front of her. Those cat-like eyes. He stared into them. He repeated his question.

"Thi Gonh," she answered this time, in a voice surprisingly dark and strong for her small frame. And then she gasped. And Private Cortez broke into laughter.

"You're starting to mimic her, Stake," he said. "And she looks like she just saw a ghost!"

Stake realized he had been looking at her too intensely, and severed his eye contact. But he hadn't been able to help himself. The young woman was indeed a beauty, as the rumors had indicated. The shape of her face was delicate, with fine cheekbones, the mouth feminine but hard with a kind of composed arrogance. Her nose looked like it might have been broken at some point, but this—like the black mole below one corner of her mouth—rendered her beauty more individual, gave it a flawed humanity to blend with the ethereal loveliness. There was a fold of skin over the inner corners of her eyes in what is called the epicanthus, giving them the slanted look of the Asian peoples for whom Stake felt the Ha Jiin were this dimension's analogue.

The woman's flesh was the robin's egg blue that made these people so eerily lovely, like ghosts. Her waist-length hair, parted in the center and gathered loosely behind her head, stray strands hanging in her face, was midnight black—and yet, it had a metallic red sheen where the light slid across it. Similarly, the pupils of her eyes were black as volcanic glass, but when they caught the light a certain way glowed a bright, unsettling red. Demons, some of the Earth soldiers called the Ha Jiin. It made it easier to kill them.

Stake had the woman patted down for secreted communication devices or weapons, a blade or such. When he saw the soldier give her chest a double squeeze, thinking that the corporal didn't see him grin in the woman's glaring face, Stake growled, "Show some professionalism, you stupid fuck! Put her in one of the rooms we can lock. Stand guard outside it."

"Leave her cuffs on?"

"Yeah, for now."

This private and, at Stake's urging, the more professional Henderson escorted the woman away. Stake thought better of it and had a third man follow them, gun ready. Even without weapons, the Ha Jiin could fight like panthers.

Stake went on to check the medic's progress with the wounded boy, who had been taken to one of the tiny bed chambers—containing little more than a thin mattress on the floor—that each of the monks had been using before the Earth soldiers had corralled them all into one large room where they could be guarded. The boy had spoken English when the two Ha Jiin had been captured, and Stake had hoped to question him, but the medic had put him out in order to safely work on him.

Instead, he made contact with his superiors and gave a report of his unit's status. The loss of the two commanding officers and two infantrymen, the seizure of the monastery, the capture of the Ha Jiin fighters. He mentioned the words etched on the female's Earth-made weapon. And he was commended for his work.

Stake was told to hold the monastery until another ground unit rendezvoused with them in a few days, and then together they would go onward to the next X on the map, the next block on the chessboard. Since none of the Colonial Forces soldiers were so badly wounded as to require that a medevac fly in and transport them out, a flier wouldn't be sent in just yet to collect the prisoners; probably not until the joined units were ready to move onward together to their next destination. Due to the sensitivity of their operations, Stake as yet had no idea where that destination might lie, or what his people were to do when they got there.

He was ordered not to harm the clerics, as it could make for bad press. They would not be taken away when the flier eventually came in. Though small probing bands of the Colonial Forces wormed their way through this part of the jungle, officially they were not even supposed to be here due to the area's great religious significance. (Here, the valuable subterranean gases that certain parties wanted to harvest leaked from occasional fissures, coiling into the air like spirits to be worshiped.) Stake felt that his superiors wanted to digest the situation better before sending in any conspicuous aircraft. It might even be that the joined units would be required to bring the prisoners along with them on foot. When the orders came, whatever they were, he would obey them.

Ultimately, as night began to fall, Stake checked back on the captured woman. The guards were rotated, and Henderson reported that he had managed to exchange a few words with the reticent prisoner in her own tongue, aided by the up-to-date translation chip he wore in his head, programmed with the Ha Jiin language and so many others. Smiling, he told the corporal, "You really spooked her. She called you a Ga Noh. That sort of means a chimera or a shapeshifter. A mystical kind of being; part human, part god. Maybe good, maybe evil."

"Did you tell her that I'm only some Tin Town freak?"

"No sir. It could be useful if she's in awe of you."

"Just like you are, right, Henderson?"

"Exactly like that, sir."

Stake looked at the closed door of the room she was kept in, a thick panel of blue-glazed wood. "I'm going to go in and have a look at her."

The woman was sitting cross-legged on the mattress, her wrists bound in her lap. She and the boy had reverently kicked off their sandals when first brought into the monastery. Stake's eyes took in her bare feet, the spacing and stunting of the big toe (did the thong of the sandals do that, over time?) making them look somewhat prehensile, and there were even little spurts of coarse black hair on their knuckles. Monkey feet, the Colonials joked about the Ha Jiin, to dehumanize them further. The woman's feet were small, like those of a child. Self-consciously, he lifted his eyes from them to meet her gaze. Her own eyes presently flashed that disturbing red color, as if lit from within.

Stake knelt down in front of her, at the edge of the mattress. "I'm Corporal Jeremy Stake," he told her, touching his chest. In halting snatches of the Ha Jiin language, he tried to tell her that he was the commanding officer, though surely she knew that already from the insignias on his blue-camouflaged uniform and from observing him take charge of the others. He had no doubt now that it was she who had picked off the lieutenant and sergeant, and that she was only too familiar with reading insignias of rank in her rifle's magnifying screen.

She said nothing. But she held his gaze. She was waiting for him to start changing again, he realized. Watching to see her own face reproduced on his, like a reflection appearing through subsiding ripples after a pebble has broken through a pond's smooth surface.

Several little flies hovered through the room, and one alighted on her chin, crawled toward her mole as if might be some rare berry. The woman turned her face toward her shoulder and crushed the bug against herself. When she returned her eyes to Stake's, he saw the tiny insect smeared across her lower lip in black flecks.

Without thinking, seemingly without willing it—but aware that the heavy door was closed behind him—Stake reached out with his thumb and wiped the flecks from her lower lip.

She opened her mouth, and closed it around his thumb.

For a moment he expected her to crush her jaws together. Then shake her head from side to side like a dog with a cat in its teeth. Instead, she sucked on his thumb. Keeping her eyes fixed on his. They were black again, at the same time mysterious and full of meaning.

And that was when Corporal Jeremy Stake knew that he and the Earth Killer were going to be lovers.

WITH HER STILL sucking on his thumb, and swirling her tongue around it, he heard a strange sound from beyond the thick door. Unearthly, uncanny. Between the sound and the woman's actions, the hair rose on the back of his neck. He realized it was the sound the monks made through the spiral hole where their faces had once been. All ten monks were making the sound together. It was a time for chanting. They could see no timepieces, but it must have been an hour they felt arrive inside them.

The noise grew louder. Louder. It hurt his ears. Became deafening.

Stake no longer saw the woman. He saw only his pain. He clamped both hands over his ears, and opened his mouth wide in a cry of agony. His mouth widened. Widened. The sound of the monks was now coming from his own mouth, which widened more and more. His mouth was going to open until it swallowed his nose, then his eyes. Until all that was left was a gaping hole screaming in the center of his face.

Oh my God, he thought. I'm changing into one of *them*.

His eyes sprang open, his palms still pressed to his ears. That horrible sound still pouring out of his wide, wide mouth. Jeremy Stake scrambled out of the chair in front of his computer station, awake once again, and staggered into his bathroom. Terrified of what he would see in the mirror there.

But when he dared to activate the mirror-screen (which reversed his reflection for him, so that he might appear to himself as he appeared to others), Stake saw that his mouth was not locked open wide, and spreading wider, after all. It was more of a drooping grimace, really. And he panted through it, gripping the edge of the sink. Gazing at his reflection, he muttered a chant of his own.

"Jeremy Stake. Jeremy Stake. Jeremy Stake." As if he were his own prisoner of war, giving his name, rank and serial number.

CHAPTER EIGHT
THE FLESH MACHINES

"THESE ARE THE ones we've killed inside the building," said Mira, waving a plump little arm. A neat row of five mostly intact bodies lay on their backs in the gloom of apartment 6-B of Steward Gardens. "Five to the ten of us they've killed."

"I didn't notice the missing spaces when we were outside," Javier said, referring to the narrow alcoves the Blank People occupied. He stepped closer to the corpses and prodded one's leg with the toe of his shoe.

"Like I say, this is only five out of seventy-two of them. No wonder you didn't notice."

"So they're not androids, huh?" Javier said dubiously, crouching down beside one of the bodies. Even this close he smelled no decay from the corpses, just a faint fishiness from the raw wounds where the Tin Town Terata's guns had blown chunks out of them. Most of the killing wounds were to the heads. He lifted a slender but heavy arm, completely blown off at the elbow. It was rubbery to the touch and in consistency. He noted the whitish filaments that dangled out of the stump in place of veins, or maybe nerves, or maybe tendons.

"They're belfs," Mira stated. Bio-engineered life forms. "But very simple ones, not like real people. They're like *organic* androids."

Javier laid the limb on the floor again, and bent closer to this creature's decimated head. The interior was as gray as the exterior. A slime of clear fluid coated the insides of the creature's wounds, and a viscous pool had spread under its body, but he saw no shards of skull. He saw no brain. Just solid gray meat throughout, interwoven with a network of those white filaments. However, inside the gaping head he did spot a corner of the shattered programming chip that Mira had alluded to. "So these chips are all turned on."

"All I can think is that the people who would've opened this place, but never did, left the Blank People active to keep out intruders and vandals. And they're probably all tied in to one computer server, along with the generator."

Javier looked up at her. "Okay, but if the power in this place is on, and if these things and the homicidal trash zapper are all running off one server, then why can't the computer just open every window in this place and let all the Blank Fucks inside to finish us off?"

"Well, I can't tell. Maybe the owners programmed the computer to just communicate with these things, to use them as security, and the trash zapper is either an oversight or they left it fully active because the owners still needed to use it. But the weird way it attacked your friend makes me think its program is crossed with the Blank People's program. They're following the same purpose."

"A mixed purpose. To dispose of us trash."

"Yeah, but even the Blank People's behavior can't be normal. The way they're acting, it wouldn't have worked out for this place. Can you imagine these things waking up and killing every visitor, every deliveryman? They're too aggressive. Their program is glitched. Who knows; maybe the owners of this place didn't leave them turned on. Maybe a virus got into the system just recently and woke them up. It could be that homeless guy they killed triggered the initial effect, by messing around in here somehow. Being the first person to trip a security alarm, and bring the things out of a dormant state, but now they're filling their role in a distorted way."

Javier got to his feet and smiled his city tough's sneering smile. "Huh. You're pretty smart, you know that?"

He saw her beautiful face redden. "My body is stunted. Not my brain."

"So are you the leader of your gang?"

"Oh no. No. He was killed by the gang we were fighting, before we even got out of Tin Town."

"But the others seem to do as you say. More or less."

"They respect me, I guess." She shrugged humbly.

"I wish my people would be respecting me a little better. They've always been rough dogs to rein in, but lately I don't know. Maybe because I'm getting old for this dung. I'm twenty-five. I ain't a teenager anymore. Hell, most of the original Snarlers have all gone off and gotten married and whatnot. These kids you see me with all came later."

"Maybe with us mutants that's not an issue so much. We're together more out of survival than to, um…"

"Than to what—be criminals? Sell drugs? Mug people? Torch cars and abandoned warehouses for a cut of the insurance money?" His tone had become defensive. "Yeah, I've done all those things."

Mira stammered, "I just mean, our gangs in Tin Town can have people of all ages."

He drew in a breath to calm himself. "Well, I'm definitely feeling ancient for the Snarlers. Twenty-five is like being a worn-out old grandpa."

Mira smiled. "You don't look worn out to me."

"I should get a job, I suppose." He gazed down at the five dead Blank People again. "But doing what? Being what? I can't work in some office. And labor work… ha. Most of the factories in this city are boarded up, and the jobs they do have are filled with robots and clones. Even these fucks here had a job."

Mira had no answers for him. Being a mutant in one of the most impoverished slums in Punktown, her own dreams had always been so limited that she had no imagination for them.

He looked up at her suddenly. "So, you have this gift. You heard Brat die; you saw it in your mind. Can you control it?"

"A little, but mostly it's random. I catch bits of other people's thoughts. They sort of come through the static, if you know what I mean. And sometimes people even hear my thoughts, so I guess I must be transmitting and not just receiving."

"Can you read my mind right now?"

She grinned shyly. "No."

He smiled back. "Good," he said, with teasing ambiguity. In fact, even he didn't know what he meant by it. Was he flirting with her? A dwarf from Tin Town? He knew some men sought out the city's mutant brothels for the express purpose of experiencing things like that. Maybe small people appealed to their inner pedophile. Personally, Javier had never been into mutants, amputees, and the like. He had slept with women who'd undergone some wild body modification, however, and he also found some of the alien races attractive: he'd dated a Choom, and he'd once had a crush on an exotic Kalian girl, though with her strict culture she hadn't given him the time of day.

Looking shyer than ever, and maybe even a bit wary that he might be mocking her, Mira stumbled back to their earlier subject. "You know how I was saying the Blank People are all linked into one server, most likely? I think I've even picked up on the computer's thoughts a little. Kind of like a gibberish that I can't even put into words. More like listening to bugs making sounds."

"Hold on. You can read machines' minds, too?"

"Well, if that's what I'm hearing, it must be an encephalon mainframe. You know—a computer made out of bio-engineered human brain tissue. So it would be partly organic."

"Ahh. Yeah. Too bad your power isn't stronger, so you could order that thing to shut these Blank People down."

"I wish I was that powerful."

Lost in thought for a moment, Javier placed his foot against one of the Blank People's heads and turned it on its rubbery neck so that he could better make out the number recessed into its forehead. 9-A. He then observed, "I wonder if these things were more than just guards. Maybe they were meant to be servants, too."

"I've thought of that. Especially given the name Steward Gardens."

"Why, what does 'steward' mean?"

"Well, a steward is sort of like a servant. Or a waiter, or a guy on a ship who might take care of the passengers. You know?"

"Nice. Everyone with their own slave slash bodyguard. But the apartments themselves are all pretty small. One bedroom each. Not a good place to raise a family."

"More likely it was geared toward unmarried young professionals. Office drones in cubicles, who wouldn't mind cubicle apartments. But they'd pay big money for them because it's right in the heart of one of the city's best sectors."

"Six apartments to the front of both wings, and six on the sides. What's at the back of the building?"

"Maintenance offices, and the elevators and stairs to the upper floors."

"Ah. But what about the middle in both wings? The apartments line the *outer* walls, so what's behind the opposite side of the hallways?"

"Come on, I'll show you."

They left 6-B, closed its door behind them, and found themselves in a murky carpeted hallway. Javier followed the miniature woman further down the passage until they came to one of the far-spaced doors on the opposite wall from that in which the apartment doors were set. She opened this, and they stepped into a single large chamber.

Mira's voice echoed somewhat as she explained, "On the ground floor of B-Wing, we have this big empty room that I figure must have been a function hall the occupants could have used for parties, business meetings, whatever. On the floor above us is a tennis court. And on the third floor, a swimming pool, but it's empty."

"Now I can really see why they'd pay big munits to live here. What about A-Wing?"

"On the ground floor, a little café, mostly vending machines and a few tables." She saw Javier's mouth open but cut him off. "The vending machines were never stocked. On the second floor is a gym. On the third floor is a little movie theater."

"Nice place. And I can't wait to get the hell out of it." Javier looked about the dark, cavernous function room. "How about the roof? There must be a heliport up there. Have you gone up?"

"Yes. But the Blank People came out of their nooks and started climbing right up the walls. Like I said, they've been killing all the pig-hens they find up there."

"So they stay in their nooks when they're not directly attacking, huh?"

"Yeah. I don't know if they sleep, exactly."

They left the function room and shut its door. Together, they started back toward their camp in 1-B. Walking slowly out of deference to Mira, Javier asked, "You got a gun?"

"No."

"Take this one. I got one of my own." He handed her a pistol, explained, "That was my friend Brat's. I gave it to him for his birthday one time."

Mira examined the mean little pistol as they walked, and smiled as if he had given her a flower plucked from a field they wandered through. "Thanks." She tucked it in the waistband of her white shorts.

With her hands free again, she reached up to rub her temples in circles with her fingertips. Seeing this, Javier frowned. "What? Headache?"

"Yeah. I get bad ones a lot."

"Related to your gift?"

"I guess so."

"My mom used to get bad headaches, so she had me rub her feet."

"Her *feet?*"

"I guess she thought it was like acupuncture, where one part of your body is connected to another."

"I think that's just a story you tell girls so they'll let you rub their feet. It's so innocent. 'I did this for my mom, baby, really.'"

He chuckled. "Yeah, maybe you got me on that."

Mira glanced up at him, embarrassed. "I mean, not to say that anyone would want to rub my feet."

"What? Why wouldn't they?"

"Well, they're so small."

"Come on. So who likes girls with big feet?"

By now they had returned to 1-B—and in the middle of a heated argument. At first Javier expected it to be between the Snarlers and the Terata, until he saw the fury twisting the faces of Nhu and Mott. Nhu was holding her forearm as if she'd been injured. The Choom whirled toward his leader and said, "She was trying to use her wrist comp to call the forcers down here, man!"

Javier glared at the Vietnamese girl. "I thought I told you—"

"How long should we stay in here, Javier? The muties have been here eleven days! Maybe they got no place better to go, but I have a family waiting for me! This is crazy—all we have to do is make a call! We're right in the middle of Beaumonde, here! Cars are driving right past us! We aren't stuck on some other planet."

"We can't get the forcers involved in this. We'll be thrown in prison."

"I'd rather be there than here."

"Oh, really? I don't think so. We can get out of here, and we will. Where's your comp?"

Mott held it up. "I got it."

"You almost broke my arm, you dung-dong!" Nhu screeched at him.

"Blast you."

"All right, everyone give Patryk your hand phones, comps, whatever."

"Why Patryk again?" Nhu sulked.

"Because he's one of the only people I can trust anymore, looks like. Besides, he's got a backpack."

"Nobody better steal that boy's backpack," the mutant named Satin quipped. "They'll have all the food *and* all the phones."

"Nobody should be panicking," Javier snarled at Nhu, but then he ran his hot eyes over all the other faces, whole and mutated, as well. Barbie with her five. "We lose our nerve, and our cooperation, and we die. You wankers think I've lived to be twenty-five by acting all panicky every time I was in danger?"

"Yeah," Tiny Meat told Nhu. "You get out of Folger Street and suddenly you forget what you are?"

"Shut it, scrotum-face."

"Bitch."

"All of you!" Javier roared. Silence prevailed at last.

Tall, quiet Patryk collected a few devices and stowed them in his backpack. Nhu had begun to sob. She backed into one wall, slid down to its bottom, and wrapped her arms around her legs. "I'm sorry, okay?" she whimpered. "I'm sorry."

Near her, the spidery Choom mutant named Haanz cooed, "You'll be all right. It will all be okay." He started to reach out with his extra-long fingers to stroke the silky black hair that hung down to obscure her face, now that she had freed it of her lime-green swimming cap, but Nhu lifted her head abruptly.

"Don't touch me!"

The mutant withdrew his hand and averted his eyes shamefully.

"Patryk," Javier said, taking him aside, "get on Nhu's comp and look up Steward Gardens on the net. Maybe you can find us something useful, blue-prints or whatever. Maybe something we can use to fight or shut down those zombies out there."

Patryk nodded, and moved into the next room.

Javier sighed, then lifted one arm and sniffed at himself. "So the showers work?" he asked Mira.

"Yeah. Come on, I'll show you how to use them." She preceded the leader of the Snarlers to the bathroom.

"I'm sure he isn't quite that dumb that he can't figure out how to use a shower," grumbled Satin, strapped in his cybernetic pony.

Flattened-faced Nick gave a snort of amusement. "Jealous, man?"

Satin turned his bald head and gave his friend a withering look.

In the bathroom, Javier watched Mira lean into the shower stall to point out the various controls to him. When she was done explaining, she turned around to see that he already had his shirt off. She seemed stunned by the bared sight of his lean upper body, with its scattered scars and tattoos. The stylized dog head baring its fangs, the insignia of the Folger Street Snarlers, adorning his left pectoral.

When he saw her embarrassment, or whatever else was there on her face, Javier smiled and said, "Sorry."

Her eyes moved to a long raised scar above his collarbone. She reached up to touch it lightly with one finger. "What was this?"

"We got into it last year with a Tikkihotto gang. They had those axes of theirs—what do you call 'em—e-ikkos. This kid whacked me with his e-ikko.

I could've had this smoothed away, but that's money, and…" He shrugged. Obviously he was fond of his battle scars.

She still rubbed the scar with her finger, her face as absorbed as a doctor's. When she finally started to lower her hand, Javier closed his own over it. He guided it down his chest, her finger like a pencil. Tracing across his nipple, lingeringly. Down the steps of his ribs. Into the hair of his belly.

His eyes held hers. Neither of them smiled now. It would be too vulnerable, just then, to do so. Or it might make things seem joking. This was not a time for joking. Their situation was very serious, here: in matters of war, and in matters of attraction.

CHAPTER NINE
BED GAMES

STAKE DESPISED THE situation comedy called *Buddy Balloon*, starring a mutant discovered by the producers in Tin Town, by the name of Buddy Vrolik. Buddy was a 150-pound sphere, without limbs, without facial features, without anything but artificial ports into which nutrients were fed and from which wastes were pumped, these substances contained in tanks stored under the motorized cart he rested in. He could move this cart about via a chip implanted in his brain, which resided inside that globe like a yolk in an egg. Similarly, he could have his thoughts expressed through a speaker in his cart, in the form of a synthetic voice.

In Tin Town, prior to his discovery, his sister had let Buddy sit all day in a child's plastic swimming pool in her living room, soaking up a nutrient solution usually fed to malnourished infants from a baby bottle.

In the comedy, Buddy—whose mutation, Stake had read, was called *Acardia amorphus*—was the centerpiece of a lovable if trouble-prone family, berating them or giving them smart-alecky wisecracks in a city tough accent. He was famous for his lewd comments and double entendres, when female friends visited the apartment.

Stake couldn't fault Vrolik for humiliating himself this way. It was a better life than he'd ever known. He'd been able to move his family out of Tin Town. But Stake knew that Vrolik's benefactors had not been motivated by concern for his welfare. And if other mutants, each more grotesque than the last, became the subjects of their own sitcoms produced by rival networks, then it would not set into motion a wave of public concern for the horrendous living conditions of Tin Town, the epidemic lack of health care for the poor, the toxins in the air. It would set into motion a wave of laughter, from viewers smugly relieved that they had two arms, two legs, two eyes.

Janice Poole returned to the bedroom, wrapped in a purple silk robe and toweling her gray-threaded dark hair. She saw what he was watching as he still lay nude on her bed, but with the skin sheet pulled up to his chest. "Oh, this guy is so funny," she said, sitting down on the edge of the mattress. "I saw him interviewed on VT a few weeks ago and he really is funny in real life, too."

"The indomitable human spirit," Stake said drily.

Janice looked around at him. "I missed you in the shower, lazybones. We could have had fun in there." She leaned down over him and pressed the side of her face to his crotch, the living flesh of her bed sheet forming a thin barrier between his flesh and hers. She pretended to be listening to a baby inside the womb of its mother. "I hear something kicking in there."

Stake ruffled a hand through her hair in a gesture more obligatory than affectionate. He had not been too lazy to shower with her. He had needed the few minutes alone, after the hours they had spent in bed together tonight. They had been watching movies on the entertainment system opposite the foot of her bed. Some of her favorite movies, starring some of her favorite actors.

She had instructed Stake to keep his eyes on the screen. Occasionally she had even touched her remote in order to freeze a huge close-up, so that he could focus on his subject all the better. Like a sniper, keeping her target in her sights. In this way, Janice Poole had at first made love to the hot new actor, Crow Tidwell. And after she had had her fill of Crow, she had exchanged him for the leading man Harris Docker, but in a movie a few decades old, from when he'd first become popular. Stake had not objected. He had complied, passive beneath her, or even behind her. Once in a while stealing a look at her skin, instead, to keep himself aroused.

She raised her head to smile up at his face. "My toy," she said. She was so honest about it; how could he hate her for it? "Back to your 'default' mode, I see."

"Sorry."

She narrowed her eyes perceptively, but didn't say anything. She followed his gaze back to the screen, watched Buddy Vrolik for a few moments. In a slapstick scene, his rascally sitcom nephews were trying to roll him down a bowling lane in the hopes of winning a competition. It was VT; of course they'd get the trophy. Janice said, "How come your face isn't turning all blank right now? What keeps it from trying to copy him?"

"My subconscious seems to know when it's something beyond my reach. I don't try to turn into a Bedbug," he said, referring to the bipedal insectoid race, from an alternate dimension like the Ha Jiin. "I won't even try to mimic a Tikkihotto." This of course was one of the handful of alien races that were truly humanoid, but whose "eyes" were squirming nests of clear ocular filaments. "I could reproduce their faces in general, but because their eyes are so different my gift shuts down and refuses to try."

"Okay, so if your gift is controlled by your subconscious, can't your subconscious be controlled by drugs? Or a chip? Or even therapy?"

Stake met her eyes. "Why? Are you anxious to lose your toy?"

She arched a brow at him. "I'm only saying, why didn't you ever do that?"

"I guess I feel this is who I am, now. It came in handy during the war. Comes in handy in my job. And, I suppose it makes me feel a bond with my mother. She was a mutant, too."

"You don't think there's something masochistic about not dealing with it?"

"What do you mean?"

She held up her hands to ward off potential anger. "Never mind. I'm being too personal, maybe. Things always deteriorate when men and women stop fucking and start talking instead." She sighed. "I'm not good with long-term relationships."

"Me neither," he muttered. Though he resented the way she had used him tonight, at least she had wanted him in some way. He had found it difficult to meet a woman who wanted anything from him at all. If she wanted his money, that made it easy enough, in a brief and barely satisfying way.

"Has anyone ever played these games with you before?"

"Well, I once had a woman hire me to find her missing husband. It turned out he'd been murdered by a business associate. She was devastated; especially because she'd doubted him by thinking he'd run off with another woman. A few months after I found him, she contacted me again. She, ah, paid me to take on her husband's appearance. We met a few times for sex." He shrugged. "Then, about a month after we stopped that, I heard she committed suicide."

"Wow."

"I wondered, for a while, if I made her problem even worse, by doing what I did."

"Oh no, don't say that. She was badly messed up already. You take on people's faces, Jeremy, but I think you take on their pain a lot, too."

Again, he met her eyes. It was a more insightful and sensitive observation than he would have expected from her.

In a moment, however, she was back to being the playful Janice, smirking and asking, "Did a man ever pay you to impersonate a lost *female* lover?"

Stake confessed, "I guess the last time I met with John Fukuda, when I was leaving him, I was kind of afraid of that. Afraid he might ask me to take on his dead wife's form. He'd been looking at me very strangely through lunch. Especially after he'd had a few drinks. I thought I saw tears in his eyes. Then again, he'd talked a little about his twin brother, earlier."

"Mr. Fukuda did adore his wife, from what I hear. But I don't think he'd accept a man as a substitute. He's very much a fan of the ladies."

"You sound like you speak from experience." Stake had finally come out with it.

Again, the smirk. "Jealous?"

"Curious. It didn't develop into anything major?"

"I guess we're both too restless, he and I. Restless in here," she tapped her chest, "instead of here." She reached over to touch his cheek.

Stake thought of the Ha Jiin clerical caste, with their vortex faces and the smaller vortex in the center of their chests. "I'm restless in both places."

She slipped under the sheet with him, but thankfully kept on her robe, content to lie on her back and stare absently at the VT screen. "How is the Fukuda case coming along?"

"I brought up Tableau Meats to him. The possibility that Adrian Tableau's daughter might have stolen Yuki's doll out of hatred, because their fathers are rivals. I'm going to follow that angle for now. In fact, I think I'm going to try to meet with Tableau in person."

"Who knows, maybe he'll even hire you to look for Krimson. Or would that be a conflict of interest?"

"Technically, maybe not, but I think I'd have to decline at this point if he asked."

"So, how much do you know about John's meat company? The former Alvine Products? It has quite a history behind it."

"I know the basics of the scandal."

"Oh, I was fascinated with the whole thing when it came out."

Like Tableau Meats, Punktown's other large meat supplier, Alvine had been in the business of manufacturing livestock—or deadstock, as Fukuda had told Stake they were nicknamed. Battery animals, as they were more formally referred to by bio-engineers. Chickens without pesky heads or feathers, rapidly grown by the thousands in great tanks of nutrient solution. Headless cattle with rudimentary limbs. Hogs that were little more than pink blobs of meat for the harvesting. Tikkihotto hetreki, which were like giant sloths, and llama-like reptiles called glebbi, from the planet Kali. In fact, the top executives of Alvine Products had been Kalian; apparently the leaders of a bizarre religious cult.

"They were growing an army of monsters, right there along with the meat," Janice related. "Spawn of Ugghiutu, they called them. Ugghiutu is sort of the Kalian God and Satan in one body. Supposedly, Ugghiutu is one of a whole race of god-like beings called the Outsiders, who once ruled the universe but got shut out of our dimension and put into a sort of suspended animation. So there are these really fanatical schism groups of Ugghiutu worshipers who try to call Ugghiutu out of his sleep. They want to bring about an apocalypse to end our reign, and return Ugghiutu and I guess the other Outsiders to power."

"So what kind of monsters were these things, anyway? The place was so badly damaged in the big quake."

"Yeah, that's how it all came to light with Alvine, because of the fire fighters and rescue teams going in there. Anyway, who can tell what would have happened if they'd unleashed all those creatures. No one seems to know just what they would have been like when they were fully grown. The leaders of the cult were either killed in the earthquake themselves, or hunted down by another sort of cult called the Children of the Elders, that seems to be at war with the Outsiders cult."

"Jeesh. So strange," Stake mused. "But why would Fukuda go to the trouble of rebuilding the same structure and assimilating their business, instead of just starting up another similar company elsewhere? I should think that he'd want to distance himself from all that. Controversy can be good publicity, but we're talking about something people put in their bellies, here."

"Well, John's a bit on the mysterious side; do I need to tell you that? Mainly, I think he was just fascinated by the whole thing with Alvine Products himself, given his profession. They were obviously doing some very strange experimental stuff behind the scenes in Alvine." She turned toward Stake meaningfully. "I've been thinking of that a lot since you and I first talked about Tableau Meats."

"What are you thinking?"

"Yuki's doll. It's a belf. A primitive life form John created for her."

"Yes."

"And his name, Dai-oo-ika. In Japanese it means—"

"'Great king of squid,'" Stake cut in.

"Yeah. Well, like I said, they didn't find out much about what the cult was growing at Alvine; what the things would have ultimately developed into. But some rescue workers were killed inside by a couple of these monsters. They were on fire and all crazed."

"One guy was eaten," Stake said. "I read an interview with a rescue worker who saw it happen."

"I read that, too. It sounds like he wasn't eaten so much as absorbed, in something like phagocytosis."

"Which is?"

"The way an amoeba eats. Hell of a way to die, huh?"

"Right. I hate when that happens."

"So anyway, these eyewitnesses said the things were very big, and that they didn't have faces. Just tentacles instead, like those of a mollusk."

"'Great king of squid,'" Stake mumbled again, remembering the pictures of Dai-oo-ika that Yuki had shown him on her wrist comp. "My God, Janice."

"Yeah," she said. "So, what I was thinking is, was John able to salvage some of the research or technology at Alvine? And did he use that when he designed Dai-oo-ika for his daughter?"

"Janice," Stake said, "if I ever need to hire a partner, you're in the front running." He sat up in her bed, the gears in his mind fully lubricated now.

"So what if that were true, and Tableau suspected it, too? Put it together like you did? Would he want to steal Dai-oo-ika from his rival not so much out of spite, but because he wants access to that research himself?"

"Hard to do a job for John when he keeps you in the dark, isn't it?"

"I'd like to know just how much dark there is. The first time he told me he bought up Alvine Products, he admitted that he did a lot to cover up the situation there himself."

"Can you come right out and ask him about this stuff?"

"He'd have told me if he wanted me to know. He might feel it's not relevant to the task he's given me. He might not trust me with knowledge like that. But if I need to confront him, then I will."

"Still, you're not a forcer solving a crime, you're a private dick collecting a paycheck."

"Exactly."

"You're my private dick, too." She squeezed his groin beneath the skin sheet.

"You mean Crow Tidwell's dick," Stake remarked.

"Ohh, jealous of your own face now, huh?" She rolled on top of him. "It's still you, isn't it? Always you." She kissed his bland, android-like visage. "My little plaything."

HE AWOKE WITH a start. He had fallen asleep beside her. She might have killed him while he was vulnerable. But she hadn't.

A pounding at the thick wooden door, glazed a glossy blue. Stake sat up, heart thudding, then looked down at the woman beside him on the mattress. She lay on her back staring up at him. The way the light touched her black eyes at this angle, they glowed at him a laser red.

How long had he been asleep? And had she dozed off, too? Or been watching him all this time?

"Sir?" a voice called through the door. Private Henderson. Now, when Stake came in here, he posted only Henderson outside the door. He trusted him the most.

Corporal Jeremy Stake jumped to his feet and struggled into his blue-camouflaged uniform as swiftly as he could, but with his nerves singing it was an awkward enterprise. "Right there, Henderson," he said. He fastened his belt. There were no weapons holstered on it. He didn't bring them into the Earth Killer's room.

Still, she could have found another way to kill him while he slept. Had she spared him out of a sense of humanity, or was it only that she felt killing him would gain her nothing except her own death?

Hearing her move, he turned to see her pulling her own clothes toward her, more peasant attire than anything like a uniform: a sleeveless top that fastened down the front and pants that ended at the calf, in a darker shade of blue than her skin; her lovely, sky blue skin. Even as he rushed to get his boots on, he could barely take his eyes off her small, lithe body while she dressed. Her hips only subtly flared, but the thick mat of black hair below

her smooth belly belied her body's child-like
appearance. In leaning forward to step into her
pants, her long, long hair spilled down like ink to
hide her little breasts with their nipples the same
soft pink as her lips against that cool blue skin.

Finally Stake could go to the door and crack it
open. Henderson was a good man, didn't try to
peek in past him. "I'm okay," Stake told him.
"Just, uh, trying to get her to talk to me."

In a lowered voice, Henderson said, "Yes sir;
sorry, sir. But I thought you'd want to hear what
the other prisoner was telling Private Martin. She
just came and told me. It's about the Earth Killer."

As he left the room, Stake threw a glance back at
the woman named Thi Gonh. Now that she had
dressed again, she sat cross-legged on her mattress
on the floor. She gazed at him in return, her face
unreadable. Stake shut and locked the door
between them.

Private Martin was the only female in their unit,
and as they walked (another Colonial soldier had
come to guard Thi Gonh in Henderson's place),
Henderson suggested that this was the reason the
male prisoner had opened up to her.

They came to the room—one of those the clerics
had utilized as their quarters before the Earth soldiers captured their monastery—that was being
used as the young prisoner's cell. The guard posted at the door was Private Cortez, and he smiled as
Stake approached him.

"Hey," he said, "when can I have my turn, ah,
interrogating that little blue bitch?"

Stake stopped in front of the man. "Shut your
mouth, Cortez. You aren't to touch her."

"I see. Want her all to yourself, huh?"

"I said shut your blasting mouth. Now get the fuck out of my way."

"Yes... *sir*." Cortez stepped aside, and Stake unlocked the door to let himself and Henderson into the male Ha Jiin's tiny cell.

The male prisoner, who had not given his name, looked better off now that the medic had seen to his wound. He was as small and light in frame as the woman, with a short, bristling haircut. The light made his eyes flash red when it refracted off them, too. He lay on his thin mattress, the end of it doubled over to prop up his back.

"I hear you've been conversing with our Private Martin," Stake said to the young man, who had to be less than twenty. He wanted this information straight from the source. If the youth wouldn't talk as readily to him as he had to an attractive young Earth woman, then he'd get the story from her instead. "You said something to her about your partner, the Earth Killer?"

"Earth Killer." A grin spread open in his face; it seemed to flash back the light itself. "How could that traitor ever be known as Earth Killer again?"

His English was very good; this was the most Stake had heard him say. He stepped closer. "Why do you call her a traitor?"

"She let us be caught, with no fight. There are not many of you now. Maybe in here we could have beat you, or pushed you back."

Henderson couldn't stop himself from speaking up. "I seriously doubt that, partner."

"You did the right thing, surrendering," Stake told him. "Now maybe you'll make it out of this war alive. A smart choice doesn't make you a traitor."

"She is a traitor. Letting you take us—that is not her true crime." Now he turned his smile to Henderson. "You were one of the soldiers in the clearing. Reading your friends' letters. I remember your face."

Stake looked to Henderson. "What's he talking about?"

Henderson dropped his eyes. "It was a few hours before we came to the monastery, the day after Lindy and Lieutenant Babouris were killed by the sniper. Me and Privates LeDuc and Devereux were... well, we were all on the move, sir, but it was when the unit stopped to take a rest. The three of us crept aside into a tiny clearing. We had the personal belongings we'd taken off Lindy, and Privates Nguyen and Howland. We found some mail they'd printed out. We began to read the messages to each other, quietly. I don't know why. Maybe to pay tribute to them. LeDuc began it, by reading a letter Lindy's wife sent him. There were pictures in there of his children. And then I read a letter Howland's mother sent him, and there were even a few cookies in a little bag. I don't know if she shipped them to him or if he brought them with him. It looked like maybe he was just saving them, to have them. We each ate one of the cookies. And LeDuc was the first to start crying."

Stake glanced down at the Ha Jiin boy. His grin appeared wider.

"We all three of us were crying, very quietly so no one would hear us. Not the enemy. And not our friends."

"But we did hear you," the Ha Jiin broke in. "And we were watching you. And the woman had you in her sights all that time. Her finger on the trigger."

Stake turned to him, not daring to believe it. "She could have killed them?"

"More easily than she killed your two officers, and the two other men you were weeping for." He tipped his chin at Henderson. "But she waited. And waited. I looked at her. She let her gun down. I motioned to her—shoot them, *shoot* them. But she wouldn't. And when I tried to point my gun, she put her hand on my arm. She made me pull away with her. And I obeyed her."

"Why?"

"I had to obey her. She is higher in rank."

"No, I mean, why didn't she kill my men when she had the chance?"

"Why? Because she is a woman." He snorted. "She was strong when she was killing you from a distance, but she became soft when she was close enough to smell your tears."

Stake looked away then, as if he could see the Earth Killer through the walls that separated them. "She showed my men mercy, because they were defenseless just then. And because their loss touched her," he said. "That makes her human, not weak."

"Human, like you? She is fighting to keep our nation whole! She is fighting against demons that step into our world out of the air, from some hell we can not see! She kills your officers and soldiers, and then spares the men who weep over those same dead men? She is a traitor. And someday I will be back with my own people, whether it takes me a year or ten years. And I will report her to my superiors as the traitor she is!"

Stake lunged forward then, and stood over the boy, and pointed the sidearm he had ripped out of its holster. Pointed it down at the surprised hole where those bright teeth had been gleaming seconds earlier. "Who's soft now, huh? You'll be smelling your own tears in a minute. Probably your piss, too."

"Sir," Henderson said.

"Don't," the young man blubbered, shielding his face ineffectively with one hand.

Stake backed off slowly, and returned his jungle-blue pistol to its holster. "You owe that woman your ass, punk, whether you want to admit it or not." He turned to leave the room. "Come on, Henderson."

Returning to the Earth Killer's cell, Stake found its door standing wide open. The room was empty. For a moment, his eyes went wild, but one of his men close by told him that Privates Martin and Devereux had taken the woman to clean herself up. Stake himself had given his people orders to allow her this. He headed toward the single large room where the monks cared for themselves. There, he found the two Colonial soldiers posted outside the open door. He heard water splashing against a body inside, but didn't see her from this angle.

"I was talking to the male prisoner," Stake said to the unit's only female. "Good job using your womanly wiles, Martin."

Private Martin nodded. "I'll try to find out anything else significant. He hates our guts, but it looks like he wouldn't mind bedding down with an Earth woman if he had a chance."

"Speaking of womanly wiles, sir," Devereux spoke up, "some of us are getting concerned about you and this woman. The past couple of days you've been in there with her more than out here with us."

"Don't worry about what I do, private."

"I worry because you're our commanding officer now—corporal. And you're our commanding officer because that woman in there killed Babouris and Lindy. Is that so easy to forget, just because she's beautiful?"

"I haven't forgotten that. But did you know that woman spared your life a few days ago?"

"Martin told me. I don't believe it. Yes, we were reading letters in the clearing. Looking at pictures of Lindy's kids: a boy, five; a girl, two. Who'll never see their dad again, because that woman shot his face off. If you ask me, she didn't kill us just then because she thought it would draw too much fire, and her partner was already wounded. Not because she felt *sorry* for us."

"Believe what you want to believe."

"I will. And I believe you're fraternizing with the enemy. Or is that sodomizing the enemy?"

"You will show me respect, private!" Stake roared. He thought he could hear the Earth Killer tense her body motionless, just then, as she listened to them in the next room.

"When we get out of here, you may find yourself reported, corporal."

"If you do get out of here, you'll have that woman to thank for it."

"Yeah?" He smirked. "Like I say, it isn't just me who isn't too happy about how chummy you are with her. You know, you can't be with her every minute, as much as you might like that. And who knows; she might just try to escape. One of us might just have to shoot her in the back."

Stake stepped closer, until his face was inches from the other man's face. So close, that his features were starting to mold themselves into Devereux's angry reflection. "If someone makes that serious mistake, they might find themselves shot, too. In the front."

Martin put a hand on Devereux's shoulder. "You better do as the corporal says. No one has witnessed any improper behavior. We have to stick together, here. The Ha Jiin could move on this position at any time."

Stake's compack beeped just then. It was affixed to his belt, and he glanced down at it. "I'm going to take this call. See that woman safely back to her quarters when she's done, and get her some food." He then stalked off with Henderson in tow.

Stake detached the little computer and thumbed it on in front of his face. Another man's visage appeared on its little screen. That visage was covered in a camouflage of blue patches, ranging from pastel to indigo. But the camouflage was not makeup, Stake knew, nor was it even tattooing. It was the man's natural coloration, if natural were the right word. Stake understood straight away that he was looking at a clone. Many of the Colonial Forces infantrymen were copies cloned from belf masters—soldiers bio-engineered to be better fighters. Stronger, hardier, with enhanced hearing and vision, and in this case better equipped to blend into their surroundings. Since the Earth Colonies had only been involved in the so-called Blue War for three years at this point, the man's blue-based camouflage meant that this clone was probably only a year or two old. And yet, a moment later Stake realized that this being out-ranked him.

"Corporal Stake? I'm Sergeant Adams, of the 5th Advance Rangers. We're the men headed to rendezvous with you at the enemy temple."

"Yes, sir. Good to talk with you, sergeant," Stake said. In reality, though, he was always wary when dealing with clones. They tended to be grouped into their own units, and so there was often resentment or even hostility between them and the "birther" soldiers, as the clones had nick-named men like Stake. The birther men felt superior for not being a mass-produced product. The clones felt superior knowing that they were, in general, the better warriors. Stake tried not to fall into childish tribalism and counterproductive rivalry, as so many others did, but it was easy to get swept up in it when the derision was directed one's own way.

"Stake, we're in the Kae Ta Valley and things are a bit intense down here." In fact, Stake could hear a distant crackling of gunfire in the background. "I estimate we're going to be a few days behind in merging our unit with yours."

"Understood, sir. We'll continue to hold this position until you arrive, or until we receive new orders."

"Good man. Hey—we heard you caught the Earth Killer. Nice work, corporal."

"Yes, sir."

"Got to run. Places to go, people to kill. I'll get back to you ASAP."

"Thanks, sergeant." The man's patterned face vanished from his compack's screen, and he returned it to his belt.

A short while later, the soldiers ate some dinner and settled in, restlessly listening to the sounds of the darkening jungle as diurnal animals made way for nocturnal. Stake stole back toward the room in which Thi Gonh was kept. There, he found Devereux posted outside. The man looked agitated when he saw Stake coming toward him.

"Go get Martin to replace you," Stake told him harshly. "I don't want you guarding this woman anymore."

"Okay, sir," Devereux stammered, sounding strangely less cocky all of a sudden, "but why don't you go get Martin, and I'll wait here until…"

Beyond the thick door, Stake heard a muffled voice. A man's.

He pushed past Devereux, threw the glossy blue door open.

The Earth Killer lay on her belly on the mattress, her face squashed against it in profile. She was naked, and so was the man lying across her back. Private Cortez had his pistol in his fist, and he kept its muzzle pressed against the blue woman's skull. Hearing the door open, Cortez had raised his head. "Dung," he hissed. Thi Gonh opened her eyes.

The tip of Stake's boot caught the Earth soldier under the jaw. He then descended on Cortez with his fist. When he had rolled Cortez's moaning hulk off the small woman, Stake stomped him between the legs, and then on the face. He heard his nose break. Blood sparkled on his boot.

"Stop it!" Devereux shouted, trying to grab at Stake from behind.

Stake's pistol smashed across Devereux's jaw in an arc as he tore it out of its holster. He then aimed the weapon at the stunned soldier's face. Blood started to run into the palm Devereux clamped over his mouth. Cortez's faraway moans sounded like he was having some terrible nightmare.

"Anyone touches this woman again, I will kill them. I will... absolutely... kill them."

"She's using you!" Devereux sobbed. "She doesn't give a blast about you, or me, or any of us! She'd kill us all if she could!"

"Get out of here. And take your friend to the medic, before I decide to shoot his stinking jewels off."

Devereux dragged Cortez's nude body from the room, leaving a swath of blood. And Stake turned to look down at the prisoner. She had pulled her clothing to her, but held it balled up in front of her in clenched fists. For the first time, he saw her eyes were moist with tears that she was fighting to restrain. For the first time, she revealed to Stake that she knew some words of English, after all.

"T'ank you, Ga Noh," she said in her dark voice. "T'ank you, take care, take care of me."

Ga Noh. He remembered it now. Henderson had told Stake she'd referred to him this way, after seeing his face change the first time. Ga Noh was something like a chimera or a shapeshifter. A mystical kind of being; part human, part god. Maybe good, maybe evil.

"I'm sorry," he told her.

She held her hand out to him. He stared at it.

Using you, Devereux had said. Only using you.

Why had he found himself attracted to her, even before he'd learned that she had spared three of his men? Was it indeed just her beauty blinding him? Was the shapeshifting mutant so desperate for the attentions of a woman? *Any* woman? He felt a moment of contempt for her. Contempt for himself.

And then he took her hand.

PRIVATE INVESTIGATOR JEREMY Stake awoke to find that *Buddy Balloon* had been replaced by a late night talk show. A naked starlet sat giggling in the interviewee chair, luminous green tattoos twined around her overly large breasts like the vines of pumpkins. He turned his head to see that Yuki Fukuda's biology teacher, Janice Poole, had dozed off in her purple silk robe beside him. He stared at her profile for a few moments. Private Devereux had been dead for ten years now—killed the first day that Stake's unit and the cloned Rangers ventured out from the monastery together—but his words still echoed in Stake's mind. *Using you.*

He stole out of bed, gathered up his clothing. He was afraid that the sound of showering would rouse Janice, but this was not so much out of consideration for her. He just slipped into his things, buckled on his gun's holster, and stepped out into the chill of Punktown's night.

CHAPTER TEN
THE FRIEND

"I SAW AN elephant, Mom!" the little Choom boy said to his mother as she pulled him along the sidewalk, away from the mouth of the alley he was pointing into. It wasn't good to linger too close to alleys in Punktown, whether above or down here in the sector called Subtown, lest one be pulled inside that alley by a mugger or rapist, drug addict or addled homeless person.

The homeless person leaned forward out of the shadows a bit, watching the child point back at him. The boy's words meant nothing to him. He did not know he was being confused with an animal that the boy had an inaccurate understanding of, but which the homeless person did resemble in the most superficial of ways. For one thing, he had grown larger. He was taller now than most of the people he saw on the streets. This made them look at him more. That was why he preferred to venture out of the maze of alleys only when the lights in the concrete sky dimmed and artificial night fell over the twinned, shadow city of Subtown.

He turned away from the mouth of the alley, which teased him with its view of the lively bustle of traffic and people. People who, unlike him, seemed to know exactly where they were going. No, he turned the other way, deeper into the network of passageways behind and between the squat buildings that rose from the cavern's floor like stalagmites.

Behind an atypically wider structure called Fallon Waste Management Systems, the homeless person ducked beneath some thick pipes that ran out of the building's flank and curved to disappear into the floor of the back lot like gigantic tree roots that had nourished the building's growth. He passed through a gust of warm air blowing out of a huge fan behind a protective grille. There was something of a grotto back here that he hadn't chanced upon before. It looked very promising as a shelter, though the fan made the climate-controlled air warmer than he liked.

There were more pipes of varying thickness; a nest of them. Red valves locked inside clear plastic security boxes. Nevertheless, steam hissed out of leaks here and there. The homeless person had to get down on hands and knees to proceed deeper, and at last he came upon a little bower made from these pipes and a projection of the building that formed a corner. He discerned two eyes, brightly reflecting the light back at him, watching him approach. At first, when he noticed these eyes, the homeless person paused. But then he understood that this was one of those metal people he saw on occasion. He did not know words like automaton or robot, but he could comprehend that it was a creature not quite alive like himself. Usually they were moving. This one didn't move at all, and looked to be missing some of its parts. Though he knew these metal people were not alive, he also suspected that this one had in its way crawled into this hidden nest to die.

As the homeless person drew nearer to the robot, it spoke to him in a wary, shaky voice. "Who is that? What do you want?" it demanded.

The homeless person froze, confused. When another being poked its head out from behind the dead robot he realized that he had been mistaken, but he still did not know whether to withdraw, or wait for the hidden person to say more. Before he could do anything else, the person spoke again. More of her came into view, also. She was a woman, with matted yellowish-white hair, a wool hat pulled down over it. In one blue-veined fist she gripped a piece of pipe. Or maybe it was a piece of the robot she hid behind.

"This is my place. Can't you see that?" she rasped at him. Then, her nervous face twisted in an exaggerated expression of befuddlement. "What the hell are you? A mutant?"

He had heard that word used about him before, when people saw him on the street. The word didn't have the excited wonderment of the word "elephant" that the little boy had uttered.

The woman took in the homeless person's frayed, dirty poncho fashioned from a blue plastic tarp. "You're like me, huh?" she grumbled. "No place else to go?"

He didn't move. He was timid, because her voice was harsh and she still held that pipe, although she probably weighed as much as one of his stout limbs.

"I used to have a place, a nice place!" she blurted, as if accusing him for changing that situation. "I was born on Earth, not here, not down in this hole! I had a husband, and a good job—can you believe that? But we never had kids. Pollution got in my system. Oh, we couldn't afford to fix that, and we couldn't afford to adopt. Things went downhill when he lost his job, and then I did, too. Can you believe the way people are forced to live in this city? While those rich scum sit in their fancy restaurants looking down on the rest of us?"

The homeless person felt his insides gurgle with that unending, nameless hunger. Could the old woman hear it? He felt vaguely embarrassed at his own abject state, as if he were inferior even to her.

She took him in again with that crumpled squint. And as if she had indeed heard his guts churn, she said, "You're a big boy, aren't you? But you can't be eating well. Our type don't eat well, do we?" She lowered her makeshift weapon at last. "A big boy like you might keep the punks away from me. Do you know they steal my medicine? It's hard to get my medicine! I don't have a job like I once did, see! I have to sell scrap." She motioned toward the partially dissected robot. "Good thing I used to assemble electronics. I know what I'm doing, damn it! But these punks steal my medicine." She eyed the homeless person craftily. "A big boy like you, they wouldn't come close. Maybe we can help each other, huh?"

He said nothing. He was unable. But he thought he could make sense of her words, or at least her intentions, in some intuitive way. Using some latent ability.

"You can't understand a damn thing I'm saying, can you?" she grumbled. "Or can you? Come here. Come over here. I won't hurt you if you don't hurt me."

She gestured. He hesitated, still meek, a cowering giant. But at last, he crawled closer to her.

"I'm Dolly," she told him, still crouching behind the robot's carcass, still a little leery at the size and shape of him. "You got a name?"

A name. A name. *Did* he have a name?

"You look like a big fat baby," she mumbled. "I'll call you Baby. Or maybe Junior. Oh fuck it." She waved him on impatiently. "Come on. Come back here. There's a better spot behind here, if you can fit through. It's better, as long as those thieving punks stay out of it."

"Bastards like him are what put me out of my job," she said in an echoing voice, as she ducked through a conduit in back of Fallon Waste Management Systems. She had pushed aside a circular grille, secured now by only one screw at the top, to facilitate their entrance. She was referring to the robot they had left behind in the arbor of pipes. "So I don't mind stripping him down to pay for my medicine. Poetic justice, I say."

The homeless person still had to crawl on hands and knees, through a thin trickle of foul-smelling sludge. She glanced back at his movements.

"Just like a big baby. You probably wouldn't be any good protecting me if some punks did try to rob me, but the looks of you might scare them off." Dolly faced forwards again. "We're almost there."

The conduit intersected with a larger, downwards-angled passage, also circular but this time with inset lights spaced along its curved ceiling. The homeless person could walk on two legs, though stooped over double. This angled tunnel deposited them at last into a dark, dripping catacomb, a rat's maze of off-branching corridors. Water sluiced through run-off channels recessed into their floors, bundles of cables and pipelines both stiff and flexible snaking along their walls. The circulatory system and digestive tract of a megalopolis. Dolly put it more simply.

"Now we're in the guts of Punktown," she said triumphantly, like an explorer who had discovered an ancient, buried city. "But here's my little corner of it."

They stepped up onto a tiled platform above the miasmic stream, where a filthy blanket hung down from an overhead pipe. Behind this curtain was Dolly's corner of Punktown. There were some cardboard boxes of salvaged and stolen junk that comprised her earthly possessions. Tools she used to dismantle some of the machinery down here for scrap. Bits of the machines she disassembled. Some cartons of food. A mattress she now sat down upon. She gestured for the homeless person to sit on the bare platform beside her, and lean his broad back against the wall's white ceramic tiles.

Dolly lifted a red metal valve from amongst her plunder, and grinned like a carved and shriveled apple head doll. "Sometimes I guess I cause little power outages and plumbing problems for the folks up there, taking my scrap. Too bad for them! It's their own fault for not having better security under the city; they're lucky no terrorists have blown it all up or poisoned the water! One time a rat got into the electrical ducts of the factory me and my husband worked at. It got itself fried, and they lost power and had to send everyone home. From one little rat! So it serves 'em right. Build and build, fast and reckless. Knotting up more and more of these pipes until they can't tell one from another. People only care about today's profit, see, not keeping things safe for tomorrow. You think the government would regulate everything? Not when they've got businesses tucking nice crisp munits in their G-strings. Greedy bastards, all of 'em." She tossed the valve back into its carton. "One time some repairmen came down here with a maintenance robot to fix some problem I caused, and they threatened me. I chased those idiots right out of here, and I even got a hunk of their damn robot, too!"

Throughout this tirade, the homeless person had sat there with a respectful and uncomprehending awe, as if in the presence of a wrathful deity that could shut this whole city down and bring it to its knees if she wished.

"Well, it's about time for my medicine. Sorry, I can't share this, so don't ask, but I'll let you have some of that there." She indicated a sizable bag of stale potato chips with a resealed top.

The homeless person turned his head toward it. The smell made his innards do a slow-motion somersault, but he knew by now that it was fruitless to try to get those enticing morsels inside him. He turned his attention back to Dolly, and watched her as she administered her medicine.

From inside her soiled clothing the old woman had produced a syringe-like device. She held it up to one of the maintenance lights, squinting one eye at the transparent cartridge. A silvery glitter writhed within. "These are nanomites," she explained. "They'll crawl all inside me and make my pain go away for a while. You get lots of pain when you're my age, you know, and living the way I do." She lowered the syringe and pressed its tip against a fat blue vein in a stick-thin wrist. "They weren't meant exactly for this, but the man I buy them from reprograms them, see? To help people like me who got no damn health insurance for regular doctors."

Dolly sent a measured portion of the contents into her bloodstream. She let out a wheezy little sigh, then hid away again her syringe filled with sparkling, microscopic bio-machines. She rested her back against the wall, now, too.

"They'll go to work inside me," she said. "Like I used to go to the factory to make machines. Now it's the other way around, see?" She snorted a laugh, sounding dreamy already. "They'll crawl straight to my brain. Tickle me... tickle me... make the pain go awaaaay..."

Dolly shut her eyes in their pouches of wrinkles. The homeless person simply observed her. A calm came over her; he felt it vicariously, and experienced a welcome serenity. He was transported, briefly, from his daily anxiety. The hiding, the aimless exploration. The confusion that gnawed him hollow inside.

Soon, linked as he was with Dolly, he lapsed into his own sort of dreaming.

First, he remembered the boy who had called him an elephant, because of his grayish bulk and because of the restlessly coiling trunk-like appendages where creatures like Dolly had a face. Then, however, the boy metamorphosed into an older child: a girl child. But although she was a child, she was also his mother. Wasn't she? Because she cradled him to her chest. Yet how could such a small, delicate entity carry him in her arms? Then he remembered that he had been getting larger. Larger, every day. She had nourished him with her love. With her very life essence. Maybe that was what he needed to fill the chasm inside him.

He dreamed of her beautiful face, her avid eyes, her tender kisses on his plump little belly, white as opposed to the grayer hue of the rest of him. The little wings on his back stirring contentedly, as they did now, rubbing up and down against the tiled wall, making the blue plastic tarp that covered him rustle with their movement.

She cooed to him, his child mother. She cooed a name to him. And then he came awake, fully awake, with that name still resonating in his mind.

Now he knew what he was called.
Dai-oo-ika.

CHAPTER ELEVEN
ORGAN GRINDER

ADRIAN TABLEAU WAS short in stature but powerfully muscled, his graying hair neatly cut but undyed, his face as creased but hard as a clenched fist. Even with his custom-made five-piece suit and the marble-topped desk he sat behind, he still spoke with the tough accent of the streets that had shaped him. A former business partner named Grant Leery had said of Adrian Tableau that he hadn't worked his way up from the streets to his penthouse apartment from the inside, but rather had climbed up the outside like a giant ape scaling a skyscraper.

The face that presently filled Tableau's comp screen was softer, more intellectual in aspect. The man introduced himself to Tableau as Simon McMartinez of the Paxton Center for Missing and Exploited Children. While McMartinez talked, Tableau dropped his gaze to the toolbar at the lower edge of the screen. The Caller ID feature there told him that the call did indeed originate from the Center for Missing and Exploited Children, though the information also indicated that the particular device being used was a pay phone. That was a bit odd, but he supposed the man wasn't in his office at the moment.

After his introduction, McMartinez went on to say, "I understand, sir, that you filed a missing person report with the city police, regarding your daughter Krimson."

"Why, have you heard something?" Tableau said, impatient to get to the point.

"No, sir, I'm sorry, but I was hoping that we could lend you and the police some support with this case. We try to give them field investigative assistance in as many cases as our work load can handle."

"Well, I'd appreciate all the help I can get."

"Very good, sir. Might I come to your place of business right now and discuss this with you in person?"

"Yeah, yeah, sure. You know where I am? I can send my driver for you if it's easier."

"Ah, yes, actually—that would save me from using public transportation. Very good, sir. I'll wait in the lobby, then."

"Someone will be on their way." Tableau tapped a key, broke the connection, then tapped another key to contact his chief of security.

In moments, another face filled the screen. This face was covered in a camouflage of blue patches, ranging from pastel to indigo. But the camouflage was not makeup, nor was it even tattooing. It was the man's natural coloration, if natural were the right word. "Sir?" the man said.

"Jones, get down to the Center for Missing and Exploited Children." He recited the street address information that had been saved by his toolbar, as well. He then showed the man called Jones a picture of Simon McMartinez, a paused image from the call that his system had recorded automatically as it was programmed to do with all calls, until such time as he cleaned up its memory files of unnecessary data. "I want you to get this man and bring him here," he told Jones, as if his voice came from the frozen image of McMartinez. "He'll be waiting for you in the lobby."

"Very good, Mr. Tableau." Jones signed off, and his blue-camouflaged face vanished.

WHAT A GREAT idea to have Tableau's man come and pick him up, thought Jeremy Stake. He wished he had thought of it first.

Stake had anticipated that Tableau might check his Caller ID feature or trace the call. If Tableau doubted he was who he said he was, the meat magnate could later call the Center for Missing and Exploited Children and verify that a Simon McMartinez did indeed work there (though hopefully, he wouldn't be put through to the man himself). Or if Tableau cared to check any number of net sources, such as a phone directory, he might find an image of McMartinez's face, again to confirm his identity. It was for this sort of reason that Stake had decided to impersonate an actual person at an actual organization, rather than merely invent an undercover personality. But having Tableau's driver fetch him from the Center itself was just too perfect.

The only problem was that as Stake sat in the lobby waiting, a few people coming and going said hello to him, greeting him by name. One woman even looked at him quizzically and said, "Did you get a new hairstyle, Simon?" He smiled and pretended to be too busy talking on his wrist comp to answer her, and so she drifted along. But it made him anxious. What if McMartinez came down here right now from the building's third floor, on which the Center rented its offices?

Less than an hour ago, Stake had entered the Center and introduced himself as a private investigator hired by Adrian Tableau to find his missing daughter, Krimson. He had been introduced to Simon McMartinez, and had surreptitiously photo-captured the man on his wrist comp—several times, to be sure he got a clear, direct image. If he'd had more time, he might even have created a phony ID badge using one of these images, as he did when he impersonated forcers.

McMartinez said he hadn't seen Krimson's missing person file yet, but he called it up on his comp. He seemed genuinely concerned and apologized to Stake for not having been introduced to this case earlier; there were just too many kids going missing in a city of these proportions. But he promised to let Stake know right away if he came upon any information about the teenager.

Stake had then gone down to the lobby, locked himself in a stall in the men's room, and stared at the various images he had stolen of McMartinez's face, slowly transforming his features into those of the other man. As always when he needed to borrow an identity, Stake had been glad the man didn't have facial fair, wasn't obese or an octogenarian. Not that, in the latter two cases at least, his cells wouldn't have given their best effort. The planes of his face shifted, realigned themselves, as if the very bone of his skull were being molded, but as extreme as the process was it was without physical pain. When the metamorphosis was complete, he'd returned to the lobby to make his call.

And now, this simulacrum of Simon McMartinez looked up to see a man with a blue camouflaged face enter the office tower's lobby.

"Dung," Stake breathed.

It was not, of course, the first time he had seen a Blue War clone in the city of Punktown. But most of the clones who had survived the Blue War had been given jobs as miners on distant moon colonies, or made construction workers on orbital space stations, or made laborers in some other location that didn't intermix them greatly with a public too busy resenting clones as job competition to be grateful for their war service.

The clone veteran met Stake's eyes, as well, and immediately came walking toward him. But Stake had already guessed that this was Tableau's man. What else would a homunculus bred as a warrior be doing here in this silvery tower? And wearing an expensive black suit and a fashionable bowler hat, to boot?

"Mr. McMartinez?"

Stake pretended to end his imaginary wrist comp call, and stood up. "Yes? Are you Mr. Tableau's driver?"

"Yes, sir. I'm Mr. Jones, the security chief for Tableau Meats." He waved them back toward the lobby's revolving doors. "Will you come with me, please?"

They rode in Tableau's luxury helicar, which lifted above the congested street traffic and glided along invisible navigation tracks beamed through the canyons of steel and concrete. Its interior was heavy with Mr. Jones's high-priced cologne, which he seemed to overindulge in just to show that he could afford to do so on his salary. Or maybe the cologne and his fancy suit and bowler hat were his way of self-consciously compensating for his appearance—and origins. Stake couldn't help but lean toward the front seat and ask him, "So you were in the Blue War, huh?"

"Yes, sir. I was there for four years."

Me too, Stake wanted to tell him. "That must have been a rough ride."

"Yes it was. I lost my left foot in an engagement in the Kae Ta Valley."

"Really? Did you have it regenerated?"

"I don't believe that a cloned soldier would be deemed worthy of that level of attention, sir. No, I was given a prosthesis."

Ahh. Did Stake detect the slightest hint of resentment at the clone's station in life?

Then he frowned. The Kae Ta Valley? The cloned soldiers of the 5th Advance Rangers, led by Sergeant Adams, had been pinned down by heavy action in that location before rendezvousing with

Stake's unit, holed up in the captured monastery. But he told himself not to become paranoid. The Fifth couldn't possibly have been the only cloned unit to fight their way through the Kae Ta Valley. Anyway, even in the unlikely case that this man had been one of the Rangers (Stake didn't remember him, as they all looked alike anyway), his guise as McMartinez would prevent him from being recognized. Still, unsettled, Stake activated his wrist comp, called up McMartinez's image, and stared hard at it, lest his face begin to dissolve back to its default setting prematurely.

He needed to maintain his disguise. He had felt this was the best way to approach Tableau, and poke about the issue of his missing daughter. And maybe in poking at that, he might turn up Yuki Fukuda's stolen doll. He knew it was unlikely that Tableau would have answered questions put to him by a private dick hired by his business rival.

"I hope you can help Mr. Tableau find his daughter," Jones spoke up from the front seat. "He's very distraught over it."

"I'll do my best," Stake said. Without lying in that regard, at least.

IT WAS DIFFICULT for Stake to take in Tableau closely, at first, or even to hear his words. He was too stunned by the menagerie that formed the man's office, here at Tableau Meats.

The walls of the office were transparent, and behind this barrier were a dozen cells containing a variety of animals. These were natural specimens of the creatures his company produced in the form of headless/limbless battery animals. In one cell, a cow rested on its side in a bed of straw, its long-lashed eyes gazing back at Stake placidly. Two pigs in another cell. A cluster of chickens pecking at feed. A Kalian glebbi, a long-legged and long-necked reptile resembling a llama. Stake knew that the battery versions of these creatures, as produced in the manufacturing departments of this complex, would be bigger, plumper, without fur and scales and feathers to be removed. But what of that ape in one of the cells?

Stake had never heard about any race in Punktown that included such an advanced primate in their diet. This creature even looked bipedal, more of a hominid than an ape. But then he thought of the extradimensional race called the L'lewed, who bred a species of primate they had encountered on another world for sacrifice in a religious ritual. The L'lewed would have preferred to use more fully human beings for this purpose, but naturally that was frowned upon by the Earth Colonies. Could Tableau be producing the hominids here for the L'lewed's needs? Stake gestured at the creature, which was moving about its cell in an agitated way, back and forth, throwing them hostile looks and once baring its fangs in a cry they couldn't hear.

"Is this also a comestible animal, Mr. Tableau?"

Tableau turned to regard the creature, and laughed. "Oh, this guy is a one-of-a-kind, Mr. McMartinez. I once had a business partner named Grant Leery. We parted ways on, ah, bad terms. He liked to call me an ape in a suit, behind my back. So I had my lab people make this hairy fella from some of Grant's DNA that I got a hold of. But they tweaked it here and there, and we sort of regressed him a bit. I'm told my Grant is a fine specimen of *Australopithecus africanus*." He laughed again. "I had a hat made for him like an organ grinder's monkey, but he wouldn't keep it on."

"That's quite the unique revenge," Stake said, almost too stunned to feel disgusted.

Tableau faced his guest again, and looked like he regretted his candor. His mood became grimmer as he turned to the subject of his daughter. "I appreciate your help with Krimson. The forcers haven't done a damn thing, if you ask me. They suck enough tax money out of my ass to fund a half dozen precincts, but they can't turn up a single clue. And I've had my own security men dig around, asking questions, but... you know." He gestured at Jones as if to say, what can something that looks like that find out?

"I'll do everything within my power, Mr. Tableau."

"Here, come sit down. Coffee?"

"Um, sure."

Tableau motioned to Jones, who promptly left the room, bowler hat cradled in one arm. Looking back at Stake, the businessman's hard eyes suddenly narrowed. He tilted his chin toward Stake's hands, folded in his lap. "Wrist comp not working?"

"Sir?"

"You called me from a pay phone."

Stake glanced down at the device on his wrist. "Oh, right. No, no it isn't. It's glitched."

"Ah."

Stake, as McMartinez, asked Tableau to fill him in further on the circumstances of his daughter's disappearance. There had been no note left by her prior to her going missing and no message sent since, no calls to him from her, nothing; she simply hadn't returned home from school one day.

With an apologetic expression, Stake asked, "So do you think she might have run away with an older boyfriend, as the rumors have it?"

Once more Tableau's eyes narrowed, and his jaw thrust out more pugnaciously. "The problem with that theory is, I don't know this alleged person's name. She hinted to me that there was some older guy she liked—she wouldn't tell me *how* old—and I told her that any guy who tried to date her wouldn't be getting any older if he put a finger on her. She's sixteen! I don't care who her friends are fuc... seeing. I didn't want her getting taken advantage of by some horny punk. Well, after I told her how I felt, she wouldn't tell me a damn thing about him."

"But didn't she confide in any of her friends?"

"Either she didn't, or they've been covering for her. But I don't think they're covering for her now, because they know she could be in danger. And I've even offered some of her friends a reward if they put me on this boyfriend's trail, but they still can't tell me anything. So I don't know if there's a boyfriend involved in this or not. I don't know if I scared her away from dating him, or if she ended up protecting his identity even from her friends so I couldn't get to them."

"That's unfortunate," Stake mused aloud.

There was one bit of information he could provide Tableau, he knew, but he didn't dare. Not yet, anyway. That one of Krimson's friends claimed to have heard her voice on a Ouija phone. It looked like no one had shared that rumor with her father.

Instead, Stake casually introduced the matter that he had been hired to pursue. "Another funny rumor I've heard is that she envied a classmate of hers for having one of those kawaii-dolls that are so popular now. A very, very valuable one, belonging to a girl named Yuki Fukuda." He watched the businessman's eyes carefully after dropping this bomb. "Evidently this doll has been stolen. Is it possible she might have taken the doll and run off with it? To sell it, or…?"

Indeed, Tableau's eyes flashed with a predator's alertness. "Who are you talking to, to get a story like that?"

"Well," Stake stammered slightly, "I'm just starting out on this case, but I did put in a call to the Arbury School, and—"

"My daughter isn't a thief. And she hardly needs to sell stolen goods to make money, if you get my meaning." He waved his arms to encompass his office. "And for that matter, she has one of those dolls herself! I gave her the money for the stupid thing."

"Well, it's just that I heard she and Yuki aren't exactly the best of friends."

"Yeah, so? And that kid's father and I aren't the best of friends either, but my daughter wouldn't run away from home just because she stole a doll."

Stake glanced about the room at the animals behind the clear barrier. He was afraid to continue looking into Tableau's eyes; they were just too intense. He felt the knit of his face rustle on some nearly subliminal level. Maintaining his casual tone, he said, "Well, it's just that I'm told that doll was created at Fukuda Bioforms using some very controversial research."

"I don't know about that, and I don't care. I'm in the meat-making business, not the freak-making business like that arrogant son of a bitch."

Stake resisted the urge to bring up the hominid which presently crouched in its cell sifting through its fur for imaginary fleas. Though now Stake wouldn't put it past Tableau to breed fleas specifically for the purpose of tormenting that pitiful creature.

"As a product of that research," he said, "the doll could be very enlightening to another bio-engineer. Hence its extra value."

"Are you suggesting... you're not suggesting my daughter stole that doll to give to me, are you? So I could study Fukuda's techniques?"

"I'm just passing along the rumors that—"

"Well, she didn't!" Tableau snapped. "Even if she did steal it to give to me, where is she? Huh? Where is my daughter? This talk about that Fukuda kid's doll is not helping me out here, Mr. McMartinez. And you said you were going to help me find my daughter. I don't give a blast about John Fukuda's freaky research or his spoiled brat's toys."

"I understand, sir," Stake said, trying to calm the man.

Mr. Jones reentered the room then with a tray containing two coffees and a plate of croissants.

"About fucking time, Jones," Tableau grumbled to the clone, taking his own coffee.

"Yes, sir. Sorry," the war vet intoned.

Tableau addressed Stake again. "Okay, look, you keep in touch with me and I'll keep in touch with you. But you'll only be helping me if you stick to a realistic scenario."

"Mr. Tableau, I just feel it's in your daughter's best interest if we consider every possibility, no matter how far fetched it might seem at this point. As you say, Krimson is only sixteen. It's a volatile age. She might have done something impulsive and then, out of fear of the consequences, decided to run off. Either alone, or with her mystery man."

"I admit that mystery man angle is one we need to keep looking into."

"Well, that I'll do, sir."

Stake had finished about half his coffee when Tableau announced he had a business meeting coming up in fifteen minutes. Stake rose and the men shook hands again. The older man's grip was crushing. "Okay, then. Like I say, you keep in touch," Tableau said.

"Thanks for your help and hospitality."

Jones preceded Stake to the door and held it open for him. "I'll drive you back to your office now, sir."

"Jones, let Mr. Doe drive our guest back. I need you to be in that meeting with me."

"Very well, Mr. Tableau. Then I'll be right back."

The clone walked Stake down a carpeted hallway and into another office, its door labeled SECURITY. In this large room, Stake was disconcerted—if not surprised—to see two clones identical to Mr. Jones sitting at two of the desks.

"Mr. Doe—would you give our guest Mr. McMartinez, here, a ride back to his office at 969 Trade Avenue? The Center for Missing and Exploited Children?"

One of the two other clones stood up promptly, retrieving a bowler hat from where he'd set it down. "Certainly. Come with me please, sir."

Stake smiled over his shoulder at Jones as he was led out of the security office. "Thanks. Mr. Jones. See you again." He couldn't resist the playfulness of the words. As he accompanied the black-suited Doe to the heliport on the roof, it was as though his escort had never been changed.

THE NEXT MAN on Adrian Tableau's computer screen looked furtive because he was hiding in a toilet stall, and he was hiding in a toilet stall because he didn't want his coworkers to see him take this call on his wrist comp. And he didn't want that, because this man—Gordon Fester—worked for Fukuda Bioforms.

Jones stood by his boss's desk as Tableau spoke to this man, to whom he had approached and offered money shortly after Fukuda Bioforms had assimilated Alvine Products. "I had a terrible thought a little while ago, Fester, and I wanted to run it by you."

"Yeah?" the furtive face whispered. Tableau heard a toilet flush in another stall.

"You know my daughter Krimson is missing. Well, it's come to my attention that a rumor at her school has my daughter stealing a doll belonging to John Fukuda's daughter, one of those blasting kiwi things or whatever they are."

"Kawaii-dolls; yeah. His daughter Yuki's doll got stolen out of her locker, I guess. It's got to be worth a lot to him, because I hear he had a special team make it."

"Some kind of experimental research?"

"Right. The team was headed up by Pablo Fujiwara. Pablo was a designer at Alvine Products, who survived when the earthquake ripped through it."

"So Fukuda is hot to get this thing back."

"Yeah. I hear he hired a private investigator to look for it."

"Really? Do you know that person's name?"

"No."

"Find out. Because the terrible thought I have is this, Fester. If people think Krimson stole this doll, then that means John Fukuda might blame Krimson for it, too. And if Fukuda believes that, then maybe the son of a bitch has done something to my daughter."

On the computer screen, Gordon Fester widened his eyes and nodded in horror at the thought. "Wow. Yeah, I don't know."

"Well look into it! And get me the name of the detective he hired. If Fukuda has done something to Krimson—kidnapped her or... whatever—then he might have hired someone like that as muscle."

"I'll see what I can find out," Tableau's inside man promised, knowing that he'd be well compensated for his efforts.

Adrian Tableau disconnected, then looked up at Mr. Jones, who loomed above him like a statue. "If

Fukuda has hurt a hair on her head," he growled, "I'll skin that fuck alive. And I'll skin his daughter alive in front of him, before I do."

A peripheral movement caused Tableau to look up and see a blob of fresh feces splatted against the inner wall of the hominid's cell. It was glaring out at him defiantly.

"Jones," Tableau said, "you know how people crack open the skulls of living monkeys to eat their brains?"

"Yes, sir."

"Find me a chef who can do that."

CHAPTER TWELVE
GOING DOWN

WITH HER LONG hair gathered up in a loose pony-tail, Javier put a hand on the back of Mira's neck, but lightly, not so much guiding her head's movements as integrating himself with them. Meshed gears in a machine of pleasure. He leaned back slightly against the edge of the sink. His navel was at the level of her forehead. Both of them had removed their clothes, but neither had stepped into the shower. He stared down at her body. Her entire legs—plump and awkwardly bent—didn't even reach the level of his knees, but her torso was nearly of regular proportion and he admired the distended sphere of her bottom.

The pleasure was becoming too intense. He pulled back from her, reached down to that rounded bottom, took its cheeks in his hands and hoisted her up. Her legs hooked over his. With a gasp, looking in his face, she let him inside. He was afraid to hurt her, watched her eyes, but her mouth gaped open in something other than pain or protest. She put hands as small and dimpled as those of a toddler on his face, drew it to hers. Their tongues slithered over each other in a frenzy.

Javier turned them around and lowered Mira to the counter beside the sink. Bent over her. Her squat legs poked up, tiny feet resting on his hips. Again they stared into each other's eyes. Her face was beautiful; anyone would say it. His gaze drifted down her smooth chest, perfect skin pulled taut across it. Back to her eyes again. Her head was at a slight angle. He saw the purple veins almost lost in the black hair at her temples. Remembered her gift. Was she reading his mind just then? It unsettled him. If so, what was she seeing? Because he wasn't sure what was inside there, himself.

Then she panted, "Patryk."

"What?" Javier rasped, working toward his orgasm. He flinched. There was a loud knocking at the door of the bathroom, and Patryk's voice on the other side of it.

"Javier, you in there?"

"Yeah, hold on!" he yelled, angry. "I've gotta finish my shower!"

"Okay. Um, I just wanted to show you something."

"I'll be right there!" In a softer voice he hissed, "Can't leave my babies alone for a second!"

Mira smiled up at him, embarrassed. And flushed. And with something else shining in her large dark eyes that made Javier uncomfortable, weirdly sick in his guts. Something that made his heart beat faster with more than just exertion.

JAVIER SHOWERED QUICKLY so he'd reappear with wet hair, but from the looks that greeted him and Mira it didn't seem like the others were buying it. Satin, in his cybernetic pony, remarked, "Feeling all refreshed now, are we?" Javier ignored him, turning his attention to Patryk. Nhu pouted as Patryk extended the wrist comp that had been confiscated from her.

"I found blueprints for Steward Gardens on the net," he announced. "Filed with the Paxton Zoning Office."

"Good man," Javier told him. "What can we use?"

"There's a generator in the cellar, like she guessed." The tall youth nodded at Mira. "And a brainframe tied into all systems."

"An organic brain? A, what do you call it..."

"Encephalon," Mira said.

"Yeah," said Patryk.

"Nhu." Javier turned to her. "You're the techie. You think you could tap into that? Shut off these Blank People?"

"I could try," she sulked, "but—"

"I think there's something better than that idea," Patryk cut in. He tapped the device with a finger to draw Javier closer. The gang chief positioned his face directly above the little screen. Suddenly, the connection with his brain made, the image there filled the much larger screen of his mind. Patryk explained what he was seeing. "There's a maintenance chute down there. It connects up directly with the town system."

"Meaning?"

"It looks like we could get into the sewers. If we can do that, then we can pretty much go anywhere we want in the city."

Javier looked up at him, slipping his brain out of the wrist comp's enveloping sleeve. "Yeah?"

"It will be locked, I'm sure. The town doesn't want just anybody getting down into the sewers. But they do, anyway. So there's got to be a way in. If me or Nhu can't hack it, then maybe we can just force our way. Blast it if we have to."

Javier showed his sneer-like grin. "Man, I've gotta give you a raise."

"You've got to give me a salary first," Patryk replied.

Javier turned to address the others in the conjoined gangs. "Hey. Saddle it up. Looks like we're getting out of here, peoples."

AT THE REAR of Steward Gardens's B-Wing, behind the central area which on the ground level had served as a function room, the five remaining Tin Town Terata showed the seven remaining Folger Street Snarlers to the elevators that gave access to the two floors above. And to the basement level below.

They had taken all their essentials. Patryk had his backpack with their scant food and collected communication devices. And everyone had their weapons. As they neared the elevators, Satin—moving along in his insect-like manner—said to

Mott, "If you were smart you'd dissolve the body of your friend before you go. If the forcers find him here later, they'll come to Folger Street and question you."

"Blast you! I'm not melting my friend. Anyway, I don't have any plasma."

Satin held up his formidable Decimator .220 revolver. "I do. Green plasma, man, the best stuff. It won't leave anything. Eat his flesh, his bones, his clothes, his…"

Mott stopped and looked ready to go for his own gun. "I told you, freak, nobody's gonna melt my friend!"

"Hey." Javier looked back at them. "You two shut it and get over here."

"Anyway," the dreadlock-headed Choom grumbled, "our insignia is sprayed outside. If the forcers want to find us, they'll find us. Nothing we can do about that now. You got some bodies of your own back there in 5-B, don't forget."

"Yeah, but they don't have tattoos and gang gear like you punks do."

Javier contemplated the twin elevators. "I don't know. I'd hate to box myself in one of these and have it get stuck. If that brain down there is controlling the Blanks and the trash zapper, who's to say it won't purposely seal us inside a lift?"

"Didn't happen to us," slurred Nick, the mutant with the deflated-looking head.

"Well, you took a risk I don't wanna repeat. Come on."

Javier led them instead toward the stairwell and hoisted the metal door open. They began to descend, the metal steps clanging under their feet.

Struggling with them, Mira said, "I just hope we can get the basement door open. We haven't been able to before."

"I'll try my skeleton card," said Nhu, referring to the blank data card she had loaded with countless randomly generated key codes, using her home computer system.

Javier glanced at Mira as they tramped down the steps side by side. In a low voice, he asked her, "You okay?"

"Okay? In what way?"

"I don't know. You know. Just... okay?"

She smiled. "I guess."

"Sorry about the stairs. I'd carry you, but..."

"Oh please. I'm not a baby, you know."

"So I can't call you 'baby,' huh?"

Mira smiled at him again.

They reached the basement level hallway. Aside from the elevators, just a single metal door faced them, and upon it were stenciled the words: RESTRICTED AREA. Javier gestured Nhu forward. She produced her card and skimmed it through the reader. Nothing. She swiped it again. Tapped a couple of buttons in the keyboard.

"Dung," grumbled Tiny Meat, perched behind his larger brother's shoulder like some foulmouthed parrot, "this isn't going to work."

There was a beep, the red status button on the control strip turned green, the metal door slid open in its grooves, and two gray arms thrust out of the murk beyond in an attempt to seize Nhu by the head.

Another hand caught her by the arm and jerked her backwards, out of reach, with surprising force.

"Blast!" shouted Javier, firing his gun into the onrushing figure.

Nhu stumbled as she was whipped around, away from the open doorway. She spun in her savior's grip and looked into the skeletal face of Haanz, the spider-limbed Choom mutant. He had put himself between her and the door.

Javier's bullets had smashed back the first figure, but a second gray-skinned entity plunged out of the doorway and leapt at Satin. He lifted one of his robot-like prosthetic hands and caught the thing by the throat. He held it aloft, its limbs thrashing like those of a man at the end of a noose. Mott raised his gun and fired several shots through the dangling body before Satin could point his plasma-loaded revolver at it. The body went limp in his grasp.

A third creature leapt over the dead body of the first. Nick had a pistol, too, and he and Javier both hit the oncoming being—but its forward momentum caused it to crash into Javier nonetheless. The two of them went flying back to the floor. The gang chief struck his head against the opposite wall.

A fourth member of the Blank People tore out of the room, but now Big Meat and Tiny Meat both launched streams of acid into its face. The creature hit the ground, rolled, flipped up onto Javier, bubbling and steaming and kicking crazily, but Mira and Tabeth had Javier's unconscious body by the legs and they dragged him back toward the stairs.

"Hit the door! The door!" Nhu was screaming, cowering behind Haanz.

Five, six and seven fought to get through the door at the same time. A flurry of arms like biting hydra heads. Tiny Meat was knocked off his brother's shoulder to the floor. Big Meat was seized, and pulled into the cellar's gloom.

"Fuckers!" Mott roared, lunging forward with his gun but afraid to hit Big Meat as he disappeared screaming into the mass of bodies beyond—who knew how many. Then, abruptly, one of the Blank People broke out of the tangle and was jumping onto Mott like a lover, wrapping its legs around him, grabbing his head in its hands, and thrusting its thumbs into his eye sockets. The Choom wailed, went down onto his back, the thing still straddling him.

"Blast! Blast! Blast!" Satin bellowed, and he pointed the Decimator and fired. A gel cap loaded with corrosive plasma burst against the gray being's temple. Instantly, a luminous green fluid seemed to pour over the thing's faceless head, and run down the neck and upper chest like a burning lava. By the time the plasma flowed down the thing's arms and toward its belly, the head and neck were totally eaten away in its wake.

Still dissolving, the dead creature toppled sideways off Mott. But Mott did not sit up when relieved of its weight. Blood streamed out of his crushed eye sockets and trickled from his ears.

Nick was on the other side of the threshold, and made an attempt to stab at the keypad to close the door. He was grabbed by the wrist. Yanked off his feet. Pulled into the cellar. They heard his gun get off two shots before it was silenced.

Tiny Meat had righted himself, stunned, and turned toward the open doorway. "Big!" he screeched. "Big! You fucks! Fuck you, you fucking fucks!" And then he raced straight into the darkness, between the legs of the pressing bodies like a baby too small yet to even be walking. The others heard him continue his cursing, until the screamed curses degraded into just screams.

Barbie, also on the far side of the door, reached out to the keyboard next. She tapped some buttons, and the door began to close. Arms and half a gray body wedged themselves between the edge of the door and its frame, became pinned there. "Stand back!" Satin shouted, and fired several more gel caps. More hungry green fire spread across the reaching limbs and the upper body of the one that had almost made it through. Two arms dropped severed to the floor. In moments, there was nothing left of them but black smudges. The half a creature followed them with a thump, its own glowing green arms whipping uncontrollably. But these limbs shortened to stumps, and by then the thing wasn't moving anymore. It vanished too, again leaving only a kind of lingering shadow on the carpet.

The door slid into its groove. Barbie, of the five faces, tapped the key labeled, LOCK. They heard the control strip bleep as this was accomplished. The status light went from green to red.

The two gangs looked about them, dazed at their losses. Four of the Terata remained. Four of the Snarlers. And Mira bent over Javier, holding his face in her hands as she had done a mere hour before, when they had been alone in the bathroom together, and she spoke his name over and over.

CHAPTER THIRTEEN
SEANCES

JANICE POOLE WAS sitting behind her desk, and Jeremy Stake sitting on a corner of that desk, when someone rapped lightly on the biology classroom's door. It cracked open, and a girl of sixteen stuck her head into the room. "You wanted to see me, Miss Poole?"

"Come in, Caren," Janice told the girl. "I have someone here I want you to meet. His name is Mr. Stake, and he'd like to ask you some questions about your friend, Krimson Tableau."

The student had already ventured into the room but seemed to pause in a freeze frame at the mention of the missing girl. Caren Bistro was a fairly pretty girl, looking both proper and fetching in her school uniform, but she bore enough of a resemblance to her father Ron Bistro to unsettle Stake. Ron Bistro was the "Punktown Prince of Porn," the best-known male pornographic star in the city, and only recently Stake had watched a holovid of Bistro in a threesome with two androids, one patterned after the attractive wife of the current Prime Minister, and the other resembling the long-dead actress Brigitte Bardot. (*And Ron Created Woman,* he remembered the vid had been titled, and Bistro had portrayed a libidinous robotics designer.) Bistro made enough money to send his daughter to the Arbury School and to have bought her the kawaii-doll that presently poked up out of her backpack. Bup Be was its name; a Vietnamese expression for "doll." Bup Be had two black lines meant to represent its eyes, but no nose or mouth. Its long black hair was constantly stirring in a breeze without an apparent source; maybe it was being blown out of holes in the doll's own head, Stake speculated.

And her father made enough money to have bought Caren a nice, trendy Ouija phone.

Stake had at first thought to ask Yuki Fukuda to introduce him to this girl. After all, it was Yuki who had given him Caren's name. But he had feared that Caren would resent Yuki as much as Krimson had, and thus prove to be uncooperative. And so he'd approached Janice for assistance instead, figuring that her presence would intimidate Caren into being helpful.

"I already talked to the police about Krimson," Caren stammered, looking evasive. Too evasive for Stake's taste.

"I'm not the police," Stake told her, but he did not elaborate on just what he was, or who had hired him. "And did you tell the police about the messages from Krimson that you've been hearing on your Ouija phone?"

"Wh-what? Who told you that?" Caren said, glancing nervously from her biology teacher back to Stake. She looked like a deer poised to bolt. Bup Be turned its head ever so slightly, as if it were wary itself.

"Please sit down, Caren," Stake said, while he got off the edge of the desk and stood over her to be more physically assertive. She did as he requested, lowering herself into the nearest desk at hand. While he spoke, he tried not to look at the girl for too unbroken a stretch or with too much engrossment, lest he begin to bear a resemblance to Punktown's Prince of Porn himself, indirectly. "Caren, you know this matter is of the greatest importance; a matter of life and death. Krimson is your friend, and we need to do what we can to—"

"She's already dead," Caren interrupted him.

Stake stopped. Then asked, "So why do you say that?"

"Because of what you just said!" Caren whined. "Because I've heard her on my Ouija phone! Of course she's dead!" Tears began to cap her eyes.

"You recognize her voice?"

"She was my best friend! I know it's her!"

"And what kinds of things has she said to you?"

"Look, I really don't feel comfortable talking about this, okay? Krimson was scared of her father. She said he's a very scary guy. So if she was scared of him, then I'm scared of him, too. If this stuff gets back to him, he'll be mad at me for the things I know. The stuff Krimson didn't want him to know!"

"This won't get back to her father. I'm not working for her father. I promise not to involve your name in this, no matter what you tell me." Stake glanced at Janice. "You promise too, don't you, Miss Poole?"

"Of course! Caren," Janice said, leaning forward emphatically, "we only have Krimson's best interests at heart. If she is dead, then we have to establish that officially, don't we? Doesn't she deserve that? And if someone hurt her, doesn't she deserve to be avenged? The person who hurt her punished?"

Caren dabbed at her eyes. "Yes."

"So tell me, dear," Stake said, compassionate but firm. "What is it you've heard on your Ouija phone?"

"Oh God," Caren moaned, dropping her face into her hands. "The first time, I just heard her say my name. 'Caren. Caren.' Maybe that time I wasn't sure it was her, yet. But the next time I heard her, I definitely recognized her. She said something like, 'I'm in the void.'" Caren Bistro looked up, red-eyed. "They say creepy stuff like that. All of them."

"But did she say anything else that only Krimson might say?"

"Yes. The third time I heard her, she said, 'Caren. Tell Brat... love him. Caren. Tell Brat.'"

"And who is Brat? Is Brat her boyfriend? The older boyfriend she was rumored to be seeing?"

"Oh God," Caren groaned again, wagging her head, her hair falling about her face as if she might hide within it.

"Caren, please. Remember, your name will not come up, I swear it!"

"Yes," she sighed. "Brat was an older guy. Nineteen. She knew her father might hurt Brat if he found out about it. I'm the only one she trusted."

"And you've been a good friend, Caren. You kept your friend's secret like she asked. But if she's dead now, then there's no more reason to—"

"There *is* reason! I told you, her father will be furious if he knows I was protecting her like that! He already came to me and offered a reward if I knew anything! Do you know how tempted I was? But I don't trust him!"

"He won't find out about this. No one will. But please, Caren, what is this Brat's last name? Where might I find him?"

"I don't know where he went! I tried to phone him to ask him about Krimson, but his brother said he's disappeared, too!"

"Do you feel he could have been the one to hurt her?"

"Maybe. I only met him once, for a little bit. He seemed nice, but he was part of a gang, so I don't know."

"Part of a gang? Where'd she meet up with him?"

"Um, at the Canberra Mall."

"Do you know where he's from? The name of his gang?"

"Oh, um, she said Folger Street. The B Level, in Subtown. They're the Folger Street Somethings."

"Huh."

She sniffled forlornly. "You want to know what I think?"

"What's that?"

"I think her father found them together. Maybe in bed. And he went so crazy that he killed them both. So now he's trying to look like he's grieving, hounding the forcers to find her, while all the time he's the one who really did it!"

Stake and Janice exchanged grave looks. Could such a scenario be possible?

Regretting that she'd shared her theory, Caren frantically begged him, "Please, please, you can't tell anyone I said that!"

"I told you, my dear," Stake reassured her. "Not a soul. But I have to know the boy's last name. Brat...?"

"Brat Gentile. She called him Brat Genitalia." She gave a rumpled smile. "And he called her Smirk. It's Krimson spelled backwards. Partly."

Stake nodded. "Very good, Caren. You've been very, very helpful. And a very good friend to Krimson. But in a way it wasn't fair of Krimson to put such a burden on you. Don't you feel better now, for letting it all out to someone?"

"I guess," Caren Bistro whimpered. She reached behind her for a packet of tissues she kept in a zippered pouch of her backpack. In so doing, she dislodged Bup Be, which fell out of the backpack to the floor. It lay there in a yellow silk Vietnamese ao dai with white pants. As Stake watched, the doll lifted its stubby arms in the air, waiting for Caren to stoop down and retrieve it. Caren did so, and pressed the doll to her chest as if to nurse it. Without meeting Stake's eyes, she muttered, "There was one more thing Krimson said to me. Just two nights ago."

"Yes? And what was that?"

"It sounded like she said, 'Yuki's mom is crying.'"

"Yuki's mom?" Stake stepped closer to her. "Look, Caren, do you have your phone on you right now? Do you think you could try to—"

The girl's eyes went wide. "No! No more! No more!" And before Stake could attempt to calm her, Caren Bistro fled from the room, clutching the little Asian-looking doll as if rescuing an infant child from danger.

YUKI FUKUDA HAD changed into her "Hey Jelly!" pajamas, patterned with the popular big-eyed jellyfish image that had started the current jellyfish craze. She sat on her bed cross-legged watching her wall-sized VT, but her mind was on the man her father had hired to find Dai-oo-ika. Earlier that day he had asked her for Caren Bistro's name. Yuki wanted to call him now and ask him what mean little Caren had revealed, if anything, about having heard Krimson Tableau on her Ouija phone. But Yuki knew that her father would frown upon her contacting the detective on her own, and involving herself in the investigation unless Mr. Stake approached her for information directly.

Thoughts of Krimson Tableau speaking on Caren Bistro's Ouija phone put her in mind of her own Ouija phone.

Yuki unfolded her legs, got off the bed and padded barefoot across her sprawling bedroom's immaculate white carpet. She took the phone off her desk and then sat in the desk's chair, just swiveling back and forth and staring down at the toy-like little gadget in her lap. At last, swallow-ing, she activated it, depressed the button labeled SCAN, and slipped the phone through her glossy hair to press it to her ear.

Fizzing static: it was the constant background noise, no matter how much one fine-tuned and fil-tered with the controls. It could be diminished but not eradicated. Occasional crackles, brief louder spurts that sometimes made her flinch. Sometimes a voice emerged out of such a burst. A miserable wail. An angry inarticulate shout. But so far, noth-ing. Yuki let the scan feature run on. She would do her searching, and if they were willing, the essences that dwelt within that sea of static would come to meet her halfway.

She closed her eyes. She imagined herself in a bathysphere of sorts, a tiny one-person sub, lower-ing through the fathoms. Deeper, into an alien realm. With shadowy, amorphous forms like jelly-fish floating just beyond the sub's piercing lights. Deeper.

"Yuki."

Garbled. A mouth full of sizzling, hissing static. Distorted. Muffled.

But she knew it was her mother. She knew it in the little hairs that rose on her arms. She knew it in her cells.

"Mom," she whispered into the mouthpiece. "Mom, please talk to me."

"Yuki."

As always, the tears that could not be locked out slipped from beneath the closed doors of her lids. "Mom," her own voice quavered, "please tell me how you are. Please, please, Mom, I love you."

Then, more words, but chopped into fragments by the crackles. Words beaming from so far away, like a sun ray scattered and diffused through the ocean depths. It sounded to Yuki as if the distant voice had said, *"You are a... lone."* Alone?

"Mom? Hello? Mom?"

"Yuki."

This voice was not distant, unclear. Only too close, too loud, too firm. Her eyelids snapped open. Standing in her bedroom doorway was her father. His face immobile, though a demon's furious snarl seemed to be layered beneath its smooth mask.

"Daddy," she squeaked.

John Fukuda stepped into her room, tall and sharp-edged in the business suit he still wore. "I'm sorry I ever bought you that thing."

"Why, Daddy? What..."

"I heard you. I heard what you were trying to do. You're trying to contact your mother."

"But I did!" she protested. "Daddy, she's spoken to me before! I was afraid to tell you, but she has! I know it's her!"

"How can you know?" he snapped. "You were only a baby when she died!"

"You've shown me vids of her; your wedding vid!" she reminded him, her tears flowing copiously now, face half-crumpled like the tissue she gripped in her free hand. "But I just know. I know it's her! She wants to tell me something."

"Tell you what?"

"I don't know. I can only hear her a little."

He came nearer, held out his hand. "Give me that thing."

"Please, Daddy!"

"Give it to me!" he shouted.

With a sob, Yuki rose from her chair and hand-ed the device to her father. He pocketed it without a glance, and said, "I was foolish to have bought you this. I don't want you playing with your friends', either. If I learn of it, you'll be sorry. Do you understand me?"

"But why? Why don't you want me to—"

"Enough!" he bellowed. He had never yelled at her this way before, and she almost staggered back as if struck. He turned toward the door. "Go to bed now."

Yuki fell into her chair again as if her legs had gone out beneath her. And she buried her face in her hands, crying inarticulately like one of those sad creatures swimming in a vast ocean she could not glimpse, but which was essentially the air all around her.

EARLIER THAT AFTERNOON, after Caren Bistro had left, Janice Poole had come out from behind her desk and smiled at Stake lasciviously, as much as she dared to do within range of the camera that monitored her classroom. She whispered, "Want to come home with me after I finish up here?"

He gazed over her shoulder. Atop a counter that ran the length of the room were a number of tanks containing various animals, from fish to insects to rodents to a group of Kalian lizards much smaller than the edible glebbi, though these short-limbed specimens still had long, serpentine necks upon which perched smiling crocodilian heads. These creatures were piled atop each other in an unmoving orgy. At most, one of the periscope heads would turn lazily this way or that. At last, Stake said, "Umm, I'm not feeling that great tonight. I haven't been sleeping well."

"Ohh, really?" Janice stepped closer to him as if her proximity, the aura of her lust, might sway him. "Hey," she said. "Am I your girlfriend now or what?"

Now he looked directly at her, and smiled. "Am I your boyfriends?"

"Hm. Plural, huh?"

He grinned, felt a little guilty. "Sorry. Look, I really am tired. I'll call you tomorrow, all right?" And then he headed to her classroom's door. "Thanks for your help just now."

Janice folded her arms and raised an eyebrow at him. "Mm," was all she said as he left.

Now, he was back in his flat on noisy, colorful Forma Street. And now, alone, he almost regretted not going home with Janice after all. He remembered those lizards, taking mindless comfort in the contact of each other's bodies.

That, in turn, made him think of Thi Gonh.

Unanswered questions haunted him to this day, as if she had taken them to the grave with her. But he felt confident that she was still alive. This was because he had tried to find her, and had at least glimpsed her footprints before they vanished into obscurity. He had never returned to her world, her dimension, after the war—that was true. But he had called here and there. Sent messages. Sifted through the net. The first footprints had been clear enough, in fact.

When the 5th Advance Rangers had met up with his group and they had left the captured monastery, releasing the clerics detained during the occupation of it, the combined force of soldiers had taken the two Ha Jiin prisoners with them. It wasn't until the third day that an air cavalry vehicle had been able to rendezvous with the group, and carry the prisoners away for further, official interrogation. Sometimes prisoners were used in exchange for captured Colonial Forces soldiers. But Stake had feared that the Earth Killer would be too great a prize to trade. Too heinous a criminal to set free.

During those three days that they dragged the prisoners along with them, they had even engaged the enemy a few times (and it was in one of these brief firefights that Private Devereux, whose life Thi had spared in that clearing, was killed by another Ha Jiin's bullet). But it was from his fellow soldiers, many of them now camouflage-faced clones, that Stake felt the greatest threat. Not to himself, but to the blue-skinned woman. With Sergeant Adams now in command, he didn't have it within his power so much to protect her. Or be left alone with her. As it had turned out, however, the trek had been too dangerous and Adams too bent on his mission for any abuse to have been directed at the woman, besides the occasional hateful comment. Yet when the cavalry ship landed to spirit her off, Stake's anxiety had become even greater than before. Now, he would not be able to protect her at all. Now, in all likelihood, he would never see her again.

Standing in his dingy apartment, staring sight-lessly down into the bustle of the street, Stake remembered her eyes as she had entered into the craft and glanced back at him before the door slid shut behind her and the soldier escorting her. He remembered that there was nothing to remember about her eyes. Blank, dark, as mysterious as those of the lizards that had gazed back at him in Janice Poole's classroom. Black, flashing bright red, and then gone.

Upon returning from the field to the allied city of Di Noon, he had called this office and that officer, sent urgent and repeated messages. He urged any-one who would listen to show mercy to the Earth Killer, relating the story that her own companion had revealed to him—how she had herself taken mercy on three Earth soldiers vulnerable within her gun sights.

She had not been released to the Ha Jiin until after the war had ended, but it wasn't that much longer in any case. Still, as Stake continued to fol-low her situation, primarily through the news media and military reports, there had come yet another direction for his concern. After hearing the same testimony from her companion that had won her leniency with the Earth forces, her own government tried her for treason. But there was her record to take into consideration. Though she had spared three Earthmen in a moment of weak-ness, that did not return life to the many other soldiers she had not hesitated a moment in dis-patching. In the end, the Earth Killer had been awarded her freedom, dismissed from military service. And her people had given her a new moniker, half out of contempt, and half out of a kind of humor based on lingering respect.

She was called the Earth Lover.

The footprints of the Earth Lover had disappeared into the blue jungles of her planet after that. Trailed off into a private life somewhere, hidden from notoriety and shame. A woman turned patriot turned murderer turned pariah. Another live war casualty.

To this day, she remained as much a cipher to Stake as he was to himself. Was it her living ghost, or his own, that rattled its chains in the halls of sleep more disconcertingly? Or had he and she become one entity in a way, in an abstract form of his mimicry, his empathy? In trying to find her, he wondered, had he as much been trying to find himself?

She's using you, Private Devereux had told him. To keep from being executed by his men. Letting Stake make love to her, to prevent being raped again by the others.

In an alley below he saw two dogs of different breeds sniffing at a burst trash bag together. Like the lizards. That unthinking, instinctual need for companionship. He hoped that at least it had been this between them. Not just her using him. If not love, if not even affection, at least this. Was that too much for him to have asked of her in return?

As he had countless times before, he replayed her face on the screen of his mind, as she had appeared when he was atop her. She had seemed to have honestly lost herself in pleasure on two or three occasions. On one such occasion, her eyes had slitted almost entirely closed until only a sliver of white showed, as if she had gone into a trance. And she had cooed, in the softest tone he ever heard from her, "Ohh, ban ta like. Ban ta *like*."

Later, he had asked Private Henderson what "ban ta" meant. He had replied, "Ah, that would mean 'your lover.'" Then realization had shown in the other soldier's face. But he had said nothing. A good man, that Henderson.

And she had always called him Ga Noh. The chimera. The shapeshifter.

He recalled her eyes open, another time, as he crushed himself into her as though he might fuse their bodies, her left leg hooked in the corner of his elbow, her knee bent back to her ear and her foot bobbing, bobbing in the air with thrusts that were almost violent, almost rape. But those wide eyes were not hateful. Or afraid. Did memory distort them into something passionate?

He had buried his face, buried his soul, in the thick dark jungle between her legs. She had held his head there. Pushing him onward, urging him to lose himself further. And she had done the same for him, avidly lapping like a dog drinking water, her eyes on his all the while, watching for his pleasure and watching for his magic—until his shame at his gift and for how *he* was using *her* made him squeeze his eyelids shut.

He smelled her skin now. He smelled the hair of her head, her hair down there. Her hard slender calves were unshaven, hairy as a boy's. It excited him. A few hairs grew from the corona of her nipples. It enthralled him, all of it—every detail pretty or plain— because she was not a dream, not a fantasy; real flesh and blood, a creature of the earth and forest, hands not fossilized white like the aristocracy of her race but with dirt and blood under their fingernails.

Or was she? Was she so real, now? Hadn't she become a fantasy after all, like a porn movie android, like a seemingly three-dimensional actress in a holovid?

Why couldn't he forget her? He had tried. And sometimes, for months even, had succeeded. But some ghosts couldn't be exorcized.

Why had she returned again, as if reincarnated, at this time specifically? What was happening, or not happening, in his life to bring her back with such extra intensity?

The tease of Janice's attraction to him? The beautiful slanted eyes of Yuki? Or was it even John Fukuda, longing for his murdered wife? Aching for his dead twin brother, a missing half, the absence of which couldn't help but leave him shattered and incomplete? In empathizing with Fukuda too much, had Stake only reopened his own war wounds?

She *did* care for me, he chided himself. Hateful—afraid—of his doubts. He reminded himself of something else she had said. Something she had told him before being led into the air cavalry craft. Her tone dark and strong again, not her bedroom whisper.

"T'ank you, Ga Noh. T'ank you, take care, take care of me. Some time I take care you. I take care you, too."

Tears burned Stake's eyes like acid. Angrily, he swiped his wrist across his face. And then he pulled his window's shade.

* * *

WHEN JOHN FUKUDA entered his own bedroom, he heard a soft hissing sound and realized the Ouija phone was still activated inside his jacket pocket. He closed his door, slipped out the gadget, and stared down at it as if to melt it in the heat of his gaze.

Was that a tiny voice he heard? Small as the voice of an insect that had crawled inside the thing through a hole in its mouthpiece?

Slowly, as if afraid it might explode in his hand, explode against his skull, Fukuda lifted the device to his own ear. Held it an inch away from touching.

"James."

"My God," he whispered. He trembled more inside than outside. "Yuriko."

"James."

John Fukuda dropped the phone to the carpet. And then he stomped the heel of his shoe upon it.

CHAPTER FOURTEEN
THE OUTSIDER

DAI-OO-IKA LIFTED HIS eyeless head to watch Dolly appear out of the labyrinth of sewer tunnels, a plastic shopping bag in hand. She stepped over the streaming brook of a run-off channel and hoisted herself up onto the tiled platform that was their home, pulling the hanging blanket back into place behind her to offer some illusion of security. As she hunched down beside him and started opening her bag, the old woman paused to frown at her companion.

"Did you get bigger while I was gone, or what? I don't know how you keep looking bigger but you won't eat a damn thing I give you." She rustled through her bag. "Can't say I haven't tried. How about this?" She extracted a banana, all black and soft except for its end. She broke this off and extended it to him. The tentacles that were all he had for a face, ringed in black and silvery bands,

217

writhed and squirmed but did not reach out for the morsel. His hands remained on his knees. "No?" Dolly said. "Christ, are you fussy or don't you ever eat at all?" She crammed the good banana end into her mouth, then peeled the gelatinous rotting section and ate that, too.

Watching her, Dai-oo-ika thought of his child mother again. Nourishing him with her love. Embracing him to her chest. He missed her; a yawning canyon of inarticulate yearning. Yes, that was the hunger he always felt.

Dolly settled in beside him, sitting on her stained mattress. She produced her syringe filled with a metallic sand of microscopic nanomites, almost insects and almost machines. "Time for my medicine again, Junior," she told him. "You be a good boy and watch over me while I rest." She injected a measure of the nanomites into a vein in her wrist, then sighed and hid the syringe back inside her coat. She leaned her head against the tiled wall, closing her eyes. "Don't let those punks steal my stuff while I'm resting," she purred grumpily. "They try to... steal... my mediciii..."

Dai-oo-ika continued to watch her, as she had requested. He watched her eyeballs move back and forth beneath their thin lids as if tossing and turning under a ratty blanket in troubled sleep. He sensed that there was no rest for her species, even at rest. But then, he had his own disturbing dreams, didn't he? Not only of the past—of his lovely, angelic child mother, kissing his belly—but of a future time that would come, or at least was *intended* to come. He had been having one of these dreams just before Dolly had returned from foraging. Dai-oo-ika had envisioned a burning and mostly flattened city, stretching out black and twisted to all horizons. Below him, thousands of upturned faces and arms lifted in praise. The faces were a mix of human and nonhuman, but all were charred black, blistered by fire and deformed with radiation. Silvery pus ran out of heat-sealed eyes. Yet despite the pain these people must be feeling, they were singing to him, all in one voice of adoration. And he looked down upon them from a great height. For he was huge. Huger than an elephant. *Vast.*

He was their god.

Arms lifted, so many arms lifted as if to embrace him. It would take that many to embrace him. But when he had been small, it had taken only one pair. Having remembered those arms, he could not forget them again. How he longed to be enfolded in them just one more time.

Dai-oo-ika stirred, shifted his growing bulk. The blue tarp he had been wearing as a poncho made a crinkling sound as he removed it, but Dolly was too lost in her dreams to be bothered by the noise. He moved closer to her. And spread his thick arms, to embrace her. His friend. He loved her. She was all he had for a mother now.

Dolly gave a dreamy, muffled moan as her face was pressed against his white belly. He squeezed her tighter, until she not only indented his flesh, but began to slide into it. Where only moments earlier the flesh of his belly had been firm as the flank of a whale, now it was a yielding cloud of cells, a raw pudding of protoplasm that let Dolly's body break its surface, submerge beneath it.

Dai-oo-ika embraced Dolly until there was nothing left to embrace. And when he opened his arms again, she was gone.

He knelt there in their little corner of Punktown, surrounded by her cartons of junk, his arms spread empty. On one level, he felt nourished again at last. But on another level, the embrace had left him feeling only emptier still. His friend had fed him. And his friend had gone.

A confusion overwhelmed him. A sense of helplessness. He did not understand his world. He did not understand what he was, or what he should expect of himself. Had what he'd just done been against his nature, or a fulfilling of it?

Piercing through all this turmoil was one bright, burning ray. It shot out of him as if to burn this whole city to a crisp. Though he could not utter a sound, it was a howl to burst the eardrums—or mind—of every life form in the universe. It was something he had never felt before.

Guilt.

Along with the nanomites in Dolly's system he had absorbed her syringe as well, and the entire swarm now coursed through Dai-oo-ika, racing madly, exploring and mapping this terra incognita and adapting their programming to tickle and soothe a new kind of brain. But their thousands of minuscule claws only itched at it, scratched at it, irritated it instead. A maddening infestation of fleas in the hide of his mind. Gripped in a humming spasm, Dai-oo-ika spread open his wings, their struts like clawed fingers to rake an unknown enemy. Like the wings of a butterfly fresh from its cocoon, drying in the air. But at that moment, Dai-oo-ika wished he had never emerged from his chrysalis of forgetfulness.

Then, abruptly, he cocked his Medusa-faced head, as if a faraway sound had caught his attention. It was as though his silent howl of rage and loss had burned a tunnel through the ether, allowing this distant sound to come to him. It was like a ghostly but familiar voice. It possessed a quality of kinship.

He turned toward it, because he had nowhere else to go. He would follow the voice like a beacon. But rather than lead him up out of the sewers, it led him deeper into their maze instead.

"WANT ANYTHING FROM the caf?" Mirelle asked her coworker Suuti.

Mirelle was attractive, he supposed, for a woman of Earth ancestry, but he just couldn't get past those terribly small mouths of theirs. Still, the Choom found her company pleasant. They were cooped up together in this small monitoring office of Fallon Waste Management Systems for their entire shift, and so a harmonious atmosphere was paramount.

"Uhh, how about a mustard?" he said. Hot mustard was a traditional Choom drink that he had coaxed Mirelle into trying, and now she even bought the occasional cup herself. He began reaching for some change.

"No, no." She held up a hand. "It's my treat." Mirelle left the office, and Suuti leaned back in his chair, stretched and groaned. His bored gaze returned to the bank of status displays and security screens ranged above his terminal.

With Mirelle out of the room for twenty minutes or so (he figured she'd work a bathroom break in there), Suuti sat forward and changed one screen to play one of the porn vids he had secreted into the system. He was starting to select a Ron Bistro classic when a loud burst of static on another screen drew his attention.

A pixilated blizzard filled the monitor. Suuti frowned and lowered his gaze to the tool bar at the bottom of the image. One of the sewage conduits not so far from here: Section D-16. Suuti lifted his eyes again to see a vague dark form shifting behind the veil of static. Then, most of the crackling blizzard cleared, and Suuti saw the form more distinctly.

It had been moving slowly across the screen from left to right, but now the hulking figure stopped in mid-frame. A head like the body of a mollusk turned. It faced Suuti, and he knew that despite its absence of eyes, the head was seeing him, too.

MIRELLE REENTERED THE monitoring station with a cup of thick, steaming mustard in one hand and a tea for herself in the other. And she almost dropped both cups as she stood transfixed just one step inside the room, staring at Suuti. He was curled like a fetus in the far corner, hugging his knees, rocking and mumbling.

"Suuti, are you all right?"

His head lifted from behind his knees, his Choom grin huge. Suuti's eyes were swollen shut, pink and shiny, as if he had been badly beaten. Fat, silvery tears like mercury were beginning to leak out from their sealed lids.

"Outsider," he giggled, like a boy caught doing something naughty while Mirelle had been away. "Outsider."

CHAPTER FIFTEEN
UNBURDENING

"Corporal!" said Captain Rick Henderson, smiling out from Jeremy Stake's computer monitor. "This is a nice surprise."

"Nice to see you, sir," Stake told him, smiling back. "Thanks for the Christmas card. How are your wife and children?"

"Good, good, thanks. Hey you, don't call me 'sir,' okay? When we served together, you were the 'sir.'"

"Well, things have changed a lot since then. But if that's the way you want it, then don't call me 'corporal.' Fair?"

"Fair enough. How is the private eye thing going? Must be more fun than sitting embalmed behind this desk like me."

"Well, I have a bit of a private eye kind of favor to ask you, but it's not part of a job. Something personal." Stake repositioned himself in his seat edgily.

"Name it."

"The Earth Killer."

Henderson stared back at his former commanding officer for several beats. "The Earth Lover," he corrected him.

"Yeah. I've tried to find her over the years. On and off. Mostly from the Ha Jiin end of things, but their information systems leave a lot to be desired. I lost her trail some years ago."

"I don't have much to do with the Ha Jiin or the Jin Haa these days, Jeremy. But if you want me to, I'll certainly put out my feelers and see what I can find."

Stake hoped Henderson couldn't see the swallowing motion of his throat. "I'm just curious about how she made out after her trial and all. If she's okay now. You know?"

Henderson nodded. "Yeah. I know, Jeremy."

"I appreciate it. You ever need a free snoop job, I'm your man."

"I will keep that in mind. I've got a pain in the ass colonel over me who I'd love to see exposed as an S and M slave, or something."

Stake smiled again. "I've got another call to make, Rick. I'll talk to you again soon. Again, I appreciate this a lot."

"Seriously, I'll do all I can. You take care, Jeremy. Great to hear from you."

Stake signed off. Then, he made the second call he had alluded to. It was to the home of John Fukuda.

On Stake's monitor the owner of Fukuda Bioforms appeared weary, still wearing his business suit but with the collar unfastened. "Mr.

Stake," he said. "Hello. Do you have some news for me?"

"Some questions for you, Mr. Fukuda. Some things that may or may not have bearing on the theft. But I find them troubling."

"It's been a troubling night for me," Fukuda sighed. "I shouted at my daughter. I was very cruel to her. She's sleeping now, so I'll have to wait until the morning to apologize." Stake could tell then that he'd begun drinking.

"Well I'm sorry to call right now. I was hoping we could meet someplace, if you thought it wasn't too late."

Fukuda nodded distractedly. "Do you think you could come here to my home? I'll send the directions to your vehicle if you want to give me your program code."

"Thanks. Yeah, if you could do that it'd be great."

"NICE PLACE," STAKE said, looking around him as he followed his host across the veldt of living-room carpet. Fukuda had met him in the hallway outside his apartment after security had allowed the investigator through the foyer to the elevators.

"Would you fancy a blood orange martini again, Mr. Stake?" Fukuda asked.

"A coffee would be preferable, sir."

Fukuda turned and looked at Stake more closely. His eyes seemed to will themselves to sobriety. "Why don't we talk in the kitchen, then," he said.

Stake watched his client's back as he ordered them both a coffee from his state-of-the-art food dispensing system. "Sir, maybe I'm blurring the line between professional curiosity and personal curiosity, but I'd like to ask you a few questions about some things I've stumbled across in my investigation. Sort of by accident. Like I said, they may not have to do with this case at all, but I have to cover all angles. Every possibility. And…"

Fukuda faced him, handing the hired detective one of the coffees. "What is it you have to ask that requires such a lengthy set up?" He smiled as he said it.

Stake held his gaze and jumped right into it. "Your wife was murdered, I understand."

It was Fukuda who had to break their gaze. "Yes. That's true."

"And your twin brother. He's dead, too. The thing is, sir, I have to know if you have enemies. Either Tableau or someone else, who hates you a little more than I'd imagined." Stake pictured the hominid on display in Adrian Tableau's personal miniature zoo. "I've learned that Tableau can be a pretty vindictive guy."

"Adrian Tableau didn't murder my wife," Fukuda muttered, looking down into the steam rising off the black pool of his coffee. "Or my brother James, either."

"But you're saying James was murdered as well?"

"Are you familiar with the poet Robert W. Service, Mr. Stake?"

"As a matter of fact I am. He wrote war poems. He was a medic in Earth's First World War."

"Very good. And he has a poem called 'The Twins,' who are also named James and John.

Service's poems are very simple, plain, but I feel they have great impact. In this poem, one brother goes off to fight in the war, and while he's away the other brother steals his job. And then he steals his woman. The final verse reads:

> Time passed. John tried his grief to drown;
> To-day James owns one-half the town;
> His army contracts riches yield;
> And John? Well, *search the Potter's Field.*"

Stake watched Fukuda's face, waiting for more. Some elaboration. It didn't seem to be forthcoming. "Sir?"

"It was my brother James, Mr. Stake, who murdered my wife Yuriko."

"*What?* Why would he do that?"

"My brother and I were very close, which should come as no surprise. But there was always a competitiveness in our relationship, as well. I guess I was the more practical one, more disciplined. James was wilder, took more chances. Though one might say he had more imagination. When I started up Fukuda Bioforms, I offered him a position, but he didn't want to be subordinate to me. And I admit, I didn't want him as an equal partner. Not that I didn't want to share the glory, but I didn't trust his judgment. So James tried his hand at other enterprises. A string of unsuccessful enterprises. He worked for other companies in between these adventures, but he still wouldn't come to work for me. As the years went on, and he suffered failure after failure, I know he became more and more jealous of me. But his crowning failure was yet to come."

"And that was?" Stake asked, observing his client with almost scientific attention. As if he were a psychologist now instead of a private investigator.

"Steward Gardens," Fukuda went on. "An apartment complex just off Beaumonde Square. An expensive bit of property, as you can imagine, and James was proud as hell that he acquired the loan for it. He came to me and hired my services— at a greatly discounted price, of course; he consented, at least, to that—to produce the encephalon server that would be the brains of the complex. For this, I had to collaborate with an outfit that specializes in encephalon installation and programming, because my field of expertise lies more in the organic than the inorganic. That's why I outsource some of the work on the nanomites we produce, for instance. In any case, encephalons are not something we normally create at Fukuda Bioforms, for that reason, but James knew I had done it before. And the idea amused him that the tissues from which I would produce this semi-organic mind should come from his own brain."

"Huh," Stake grunted.

"Yes. A flamboyant touch. A Jamesian touch. As he liked to joke, he was 'really going to put himself into this place.' So, this I achieved. With the little outfit he hired, we produced and installed the computer brain. But that was actually James's secondary concern, in regard to my contribution to his dream project. What really intrigued James, what he hoped would give the place a uniqueness, a lure to fill all those apartments with ambitious young Beaumonde Street sharks, was his notion to provide a bio-engineered servant for each and every one of them. Seventy-two of them, in total. A simple sort of organic automaton, able to bring you a coffee. Change the sheets. Water a plant. Zap the trash. Not something to talk to, or trust to babysit your child. Or take to bed, in case you were wondering. Nothing with a mind that advanced. In fact, rather than develop a human-like brain for these life forms, I teamed with his encephalon crew to develop a computerized chip to serve as an inorganic brain. Actually, it wasn't even that. More of a remote receiver than a brain, because these servants would all share a single, communal mind: the encephalon we installed in the basement."

"I see." For a moment or two, Stake had envisioned the camouflaged clones he had fought alongside in the Blue War. And Mr. Jones, the war vet who worked for Adrian Tableau. But now he knew the golems Fukuda had designed for his brother had been nowhere near as human.

"And there was another attraction with these creatures. In theory, at least. Each was programmed to act as a security guard. A personal bodyguard for their owner, should they be attacked by a rapist or mugger outside their apartment. Because that was where each creature would be stored when they were not needed, in a little nook beside your apartment's outer door. I designed them to resemble statues, so that they would blend into the architecture of the building itself. An artistic flourish. But James's brainstorm again, naturally."

"But all this was a miscalculation? People weren't interested in having their own mindless slave to fetch their slippers?"

"James's miscalculation was in hiring that inept little team who worked with me on the encephalon, and on the servants' receiver chips. You get what you pay for, and they were cheap because they were young, cocky and inexperienced. There was glitch after glitch. James ended up suing them. Meanwhile, he was paying very sizable taxes on this property, owing money to its builders, and so on. I managed to stay out of the lawsuit for the most part, but James resented me for that. For not suing those idiots, myself. He accused me of 'sneaking out' of the whole mess. Turning my back on him. And now, four years later, with multiple lawsuits unresolved and liens by the town, the place is in legal limbo. A fly trapped in a web of red tape, even though the spider itself is dead."

"And so how did James die?"

John held up a finger, asking for patience. "James had one more reason to resent me. Envy me. My wife, Yuriko. A beautiful, beautiful woman. Sweet. Graceful." Fukuda drew in a long breath. "One afternoon, James came to my apartment while I was away. He tried to seduce my Yuriko. She resisted. And in a fit of anger, James killed her."

"My God." Stake wagged his head. "I'm so sorry."

"I came home while he was still there. In fact, I heard the shot and rushed in. I grappled with James. I got the gun out of his hands. And then I shot him. I'm the one who killed him. My own twin brother." The man had been avoiding Stake's eyes, but now he looked up at them at last.

"I don't think anyone would blame you for that."

"Well, the law thinks otherwise about such things. So I used my influence, my money, to cover up the situation. Yuriko was killed in a home invasion by an unknown party. James was killed in a hovercar wreck, his body badly burned, a week later." Fukuda smiled tremulously, held out his wrists in front of him. "Care to arrest me now, detective?"

"I'm not a forcer. And like I say, I can understand what you did. Finding your wife that way."

"My wife." Fukuda averted his gaze once more. "I tell you, I *worshipped* her. We had only been married two years. We had dreamed of having children."

"Dreamed? But, what about Yuki?"

"Do the math, Mr. Stake." He snorted a little laugh. "I never had a daughter. There was, and is, only Yuriko."

"What are you saying? That Yuki's... a clone?"

"Given my resources, how could I resist it? But despite how much I mourned her, despite my agony at not having her beside me, I couldn't bring myself to try to duplicate Yuriko exactly. How could the unique woman I loved ever truly be replaced? If one is to believe in the soul, then I felt Yuriko's soul had ceased to be. At least in this plane. The being I created from her—it was Yuriko, but it was also its own self. So in a kind of compromise, I reasoned that if something were to remain of Yuriko, it should be an offspring of sorts. The child she did not live long enough to give birth to. Though, of course, Yuki is more of a twin than a daughter. And more than a twin, too." Fukuda faced Stake with sudden sharpness, as if he'd been accused. "She is my tribute to Yuriko. But you aren't to think that I have ever acted in any indecent way toward her. I have never even been tempted. I've raised her as my daughter. That is the only way I see her, now."

"But she doesn't know any of this."

"No. I accelerated the clone to the age of twelve, four years ago. I thought it was a good age. A child old enough to be self-sufficient, and yet a charming companion for me. Old enough to resemble her mother. But still innocent. Anyway, I had a history built for her out of photographs and vids that are actually of Yuriko, expensively falsified records, and even by infusing her with memory-encoded long-chain molecules in a brain drip—a method for providing a clone with instant learning. Instant memories, real or imagined."

"I know," Stake said. It was how the cloned soldiers he had fought beside had been trained, enabling some—like Sergeant Adams of the 5th Advance Rangers—to outrank him though only several years old, physically.

Fukuda went on, "No, Mr. Stake, my dear child knows none of this. And she doesn't know that the woman she's been hearing on her Ouija phone, trying so urgently to speak with her, is actually herself."

"It isn't fair, you know. Not to tell her."

An angry spark was lighted in Fukuda's eyes, but a rising tide of tears extinguished it. "I will tell her,

one day. When she's old enough to fully understand. And forgive me."

"I'm sorry. That wasn't my place to say."

"Don't apologize, Mr. Stake. I'm the one who
should be apologizing to you, for keeping this
from you. But at the same time, for unburdening
myself to you. Forgive me. Please. *Forgive me.*"

Stake was shocked, then, when John Fukuda
took several unsteady steps toward him and
grasped one of his hands in both of his. He
squeezed it, staring into Stake's face, only a short
distance away.

And then Stake understood. By now, he figured
he must look nearly as much like Fukuda as his
brother James had. He knew that just then, it was
not he who Fukuda was begging forgiveness
from—but from the twin brother he had murdered
four years earlier.

"I forgive you," Stake croaked softly.

Still clutching his hand, John Fukuda burst into
sobs.

CHAPTER SIXTEEN
ALL OF THEM

JAVIER DIAS HAD awoken to a raging headache and tears and curses and missing friends.

Now on his feet again, he took in the faces of the survivors: Patryk, Nhu, Tabeth. And of the Tin Town Terata, there were Mira Cello, Satin, Haanz, and Barbie. Eight. But the question was, how many of the Blank People were on the other side of the basement door?

"Maybe all of them," Barbie said in the overlapping voices from two of the smaller of her five jumbled faces. "I mean, maybe there's a way they can get inside the cellar from outside. So that would mean all of them could come through that way."

"She's right," Nhu said, pacing madly up and down the dimly lit hallway with tears shining on her cheeks. "We can't risk opening that door again."

"But how would they be getting in there from outside?" Javier asked. "Patryk, you see anything?"

Patryk was examining the blueprints for Steward Gardens again on Nhu's wrist comp. "No. But I'm not sure of how well I understand everything in the blueprints."

"I don't think they have access from outside," Mira said to Barbie. "That dead homeless guy we found in here when we first broke in—do you remember where we found his body? In the hallway right above us." She pointed toward the door to the stairs. "He must have woken these things up somehow, by poking around down here. Maybe tampering with the brainframe to turn the utilities on. He managed to lock some of them in the basement, but others caught up with him and killed him, or else he just died from his wounds."

"Yes." Barbie nodded her amalgamated heads. "Yes, that makes sense."

"But even if there's only a limited number of them left in there," Tabeth said, "we don't know how many. And if we try to go back inside, we'll probably end up like our friends."

"We'll go in shooting like crazy," Satin growled. "All of us shooting in there at once."

"No!" Nhu cried, pacing, pacing. "I won't do it! You saw what happened! We have to go out one of the windows—it's the only way!"

"And you saw what happened to Clara," Tabeth reminded her. "Almost all the Blank People are still outside. That much is for certain."

"But it's only a short run to the street. Do you think they'd all take the risk of leaving the property like that? By the time they responded, we could be on Beaumonde Street already!"

"Maybe they won't stop there," Tabeth argued. "Maybe they don't care if they tear us apart right in front of the whole street. And we might not make it that far, anyway. These things move fast."

"Mira," Javier said, in a thoughtful voice. "You said you think you've been hearing the thoughts of the computer brain in here, a little." He motioned toward the door marked RESTRICTED AREA.

"Yeah. The encephalon. But I told you, I'm not powerful enough to tell it what to do."

"Could you at least try to concentrate on it, and see if you can find out how many Blank People might be left in there? If it's their server and they're linked into it, maybe you could count the connections?"

Mira nodded slowly. "I could try. I'm closer to the brain down here."

"Give it a shot."

"Don't even think about going in there again!" Nhu said. "Look, when we first came here and Patryk broke us in, did all the dozens and dozens of Blank People attack us outside then? No. Only when we stepped inside did it trigger their programming. When you Terata broke in, I bet it was the same. You approached the building, and they didn't wake up. But once you broke in, they did. They poured in, and you fought them back and locked them out. But think about it! They want to get in here and kill us because we're *inside!* If we're outside, they'll lose interest. Even Clara—think about it—Clara wasn't outside when they killed her. They pulled her out from inside."

"A good theory," Javier said, "but what about Brat? They killed him outside."

"Mira said the trash zapper did it."

"What's the difference? The brain is linked up to that, too."

Mira said, "Look, you can't predict these things—they're too erratic. Their programming is shot; it's like they're insane. Okay, maybe they didn't react to us at first, until they knew we'd broken inside. But now they have us targeted as criminals. If we go outside, they won't ignore us this time."

"Fine. Fine. Don't listen to me. Open that door again and die like the others did." Nhu stormed off down the hallway, threw open the door to the stairwell. They heard her clomping up its metal steps before the door swung shut again with a clang.

"Go after her," Javier told Tabeth. "Keep an eye on her."

"I'll go, too," said the cadaverous, quadrupedal Haanz, and he crawled off for the stairs like a daddy longlegs.

Mira approached the metal door that led into the basement, laid her small hands upon it. Then she rested her forehead against its cool surface as well, and closed her eyes. The others hushed as they watched her. Javier thought that the veins at her temples looked darker, maybe even thicker. He thought he even saw the flesh pulsing there subtly.

"Mm," she grunted distantly, as if dreaming.

* * *

"ARE YOU ON gold-dust right now?" Tabeth called, chasing after Nhu down the first floor hallway. "You are, aren't you?"

"It keeps me sharp, and I seem to be the only one around here whose brain is working right, if you ask me." She walked with brisk determination, turning into the lobby at its far entrance. At the lobby's back wall was a door into the maintenance area, which—like the basement—the Terata had not been able to access. At the front of the lobby were, of course, its double glass doors.

Tabeth saw that Nhu was heading straight for them, and reached out to snatch at her arm. "Stop it! Hey!" To Haanz she cried, "Go get Javier— quick!"

Nhu broke into a run, but called back, "Haanz, if you're smart you'll come with me! Come on!"

Haanz's expression had been one of desperate concern, but now the desperation took on another quality. A desperation not to be left behind by pretty Nhu. One of his long-fingered hands grabbed Tabeth by the ankle, and he caused her to fall forward onto her elbows. Then he was leaping past her, loping after the small Vietnamese woman.

Scrambling back to her feet, Tabeth began to draw her handgun. "Stop it!" she yelled. "You'll get us all killed!"

Nhu almost collided with the doors, stopped herself with her palms against them. There was a control strip alongside the frame, and she immediately jabbed at the big green button with the word OPEN stenciled on it in white. The security glass had been tinted an opaque black on the outside, but from inside she could see the fountain in front of the building. And beyond that, at the end of the wide walkway, distant hovercars gliding along the street. A short run. She could flag a vehicle down. She was attractive, someone would stop, and then she'd pull Haanz along after her.

At the touch of her finger, the double doors had begun to part open with a whisper, sliding along their tracks. Nhu was greeted with the smell of outside city air and the chill bite of autumn. And then, like a diver into a pool, she plunged through. She was aware of Haanz galloping through the opening doors in her wake.

Tabeth charged after them, pistol in her hand. But now she was less concerned with calling them back, and more intent on hitting the big red button labeled CLOSE.

Haanz heard Tabeth running behind him, running surprisingly fast, almost catching up. His head turned on its long, serpentine neck to see the gray figure sprinting after him. And launching itself into the air.

Nhu heard Haanz's cry, looked back, stumbled on a few more steps until she was at the scummed fountain. Haanz was howling now. The gray creature had him pinned to the walkway, one arm locked around his neck. Behind her, Nhu heard a hovercar beep its horn at another on the street.

"Dung," she hissed, ripping her pistol out of its holster. Even as she did so, she saw the Blank People popping out of their niches in both wings. On all three floors. One here, two there, three more on this side. Leaping down to the overgrown lawn.

She met Haanz's eyes, wide in his skull-like face, his Choom mouth opening huge to cry, "Nhu... *run!*"

"Fuck that," she said, and shot the being who had pinned Haanz through its faceless face. Its head jerked back, and its arms slipped from around the mutant. His head fell forward, his neck drooping limp. Broken. Haanz's eyes and his mouth did not close as his face thudded into the walk.

"Blast, blast, blast," Nhu sobbed, whirling to run toward the street again.

From inside, Tabeth saw her friend go down in the middle of a dozen gray bodies. Nhu got off a few shots. Two of the Blank People rolled away, dead. The rest hunched around her obscured form like vultures over a lion's kill.

Tabeth had not touched the button to shut the doors. Instead, she had entered a marksman's stance, extending her gun in both hands. She began picking off the Blank People around her fallen comrade. She didn't realize she was weeping and shouting obscenities at the same time. But when she saw the heads of the hunkered Blank People begin to turn her way, and more and more of them drop down from the balconies, icy terror overrode her concern for her fellow Snarler and she reached out to the red CLOSE button.

The man-like creature that stepped around the edge of the doorway to stand face-to-no-face with Tabeth was exactly like its many brothers, except for the number engraved into its forehead: 12-B. And the giant red penis spray-painted onto its front.

It seized her by the throat, and began walking her backwards. Tabeth fired her gun into its mid-section, the muzzle pressed right up against its gray flesh. The creature flinched with the detonations but kept walking her, and kept squeezing. Finally, though, it loosened its hold and slumped dead upon Tabeth as she herself fell onto her back, half unconscious from lack of oxygen.

The dead being with its mock phallus lying atop her like an incubus, Tabeth lifted her head to see the flood come crashing through the open front doors. A flood wave of gray, living flesh.

Then, before she could raise her gun again, the living wave descended upon her.

ABOVE—OUTSIDE—THE Snarlers and the Terata on the basement level heard the distant crackle of Nhu's and then Tabeth's gunfire. At once, Javier and Satin had their own guns out and were moving toward the stairs.

"Don't!" Mira screamed, jolting back from the metal basement door as if an electric shock had gone through her. Eyes bulging, she panted, "I was connected to the brain; I heard it. They've come through. The front doors are open. The Blank People are coming through."

"What about Nhu and Tabeth?" Javier asked.

"Dead. I felt their screams. Haanz, too. And now the Blank People are coming."

"All of them," Satin said, eyes hard and ready for a fight.

"All of them," she confirmed.

Even as she said it, they could hear the thunder of their footfalls upstairs. They heard the stairwell door fly open with a boom. The metal steps start to clang.

"Get into the elevator!" Patryk yelled, rushing to the nearest one and stabbing its OPEN button. The door slid aside without hesitation. He shoved Barbie inside, then Mira, and ducked in after them. Javier followed, and Satin last, whipping around to fire a few shots from his Decimator revolver as the first of the Blank People reached the basement level and flung open the stairwell's door. Splashed with hungry green plasma, several of them went down and impeded the others long enough for the elevator door to slide shut.

They heard hands without fingernails, hands without fingerprints, claw and bang at the closed security door as the elevator itself moved upward.

CHAPTER SEVENTEEN
THE VETERANS

"HEY, IT'S THE Man of a Thousand Faces," Lark slurred from the bar as Jeremy Stake entered the Legion of Veterans Post 69. "And all of them ugly."

But that was pretty much the extent of the Blue War vet's taunting, and when the Choom bartender Watt pulled a Zub draft for Stake, he explained, "He doesn't know that you helped him hit his head on the bar that time."

Stake smirked and took his drink to one of the tables. And it was as he sat down that his wrist comp alerted him to an incoming call. Stake checked its origin: Captain Richard Henderson. He took the call immediately, bending over the little device to let his mind become the computer's screen. There, he saw his old friend's face smiling at him, but with a somewhat leery look in his eyes.

"I found her, Jeremy."

Stake stared back at his friend a long few moments, but shook himself when he felt the sly crawl of his nebulous flesh. "That was fast."

"Things have opened up more on their world. And she's on the net now, where I guess she wasn't before. I contacted her myself, Jer. Her English has improved. I told her you'd be calling."

Stake nodded. "Thanks, Rick. I owe you."

"Well, she spared my life that day. I can't forget that. But are you sure you really want to do this? I mean, it's not my business, but just out of concern. You sure you want to go back like this?"

"There are some things I have to know."

"I understand. I think." Henderson craned his neck as if to peer over Stake's shoulder. "Looks like you're in a veterans' post. They all look the same. I should know—I got one as my hang-out, too."

"When you've been in a war," Stake said, "you live in the past as much as the present."

"I don't think it's just us vets," Henderson said. "I think all people do."

STAKE HAD TAKEN his hoverbike today, and he rode it back toward Forma Street, not wanting to call Thi Gonh from LOV 69. He was in his casual attire, not undercover, not on the job. A black sports coat over a white T-shirt, baggy khakis, beaten sneakers, and on his head a black porkpie hat. The silly little porkpie hat was, at least to his own eyes, an object of individuality. Something almost defiantly *him,* as if to compensate for the anonymity of his tenuous features. Something to paperweight his elusive self so it wouldn't blow away in the wind. He wore it even inside his apartment, sometimes. As he rode, he found himself reaching up to hold it down if the breeze gusted too much. Afraid to lose it.

However casually he was dressed, though, under his coat he still wore his favorite pistol in a shoulder holster. It was a Darwin .55, "the height of firearms evolution" as the ads proclaimed. On the job or not, this was still Punktown.

Coasting astride the bike, he again remembered being stationed in the city of Di Noon, with its streets flooded in bikes. And he remembered gaping up at Thi, riding astride him but leaning back with her smooth blue belly pumping fast, her own face composed with strength and control as she looked down at a more helpless likeness of herself, watching his transmuted face sadistically for the pleasure she was inflicting, and asking him, "Ga Noh *like?* Ga Noh *like?*"

Lizard atop lizard. It was the most primal of all impulses. The need of cells to lie alongside other cells. And he ached for her, even now. As if some vital part of him had been severed. Or never attached in the first place.

He arrived at his little tenement house at the end of the infamous street, jutting at its very corner like the prow of a ship pushing on through a glittering sea of vehicles. Rather than leave his hoverbike on the sidewalk, he got off to glide it into the lobby and store it under the stairs. He took the elevator to his top floor flat.

As he let himself into his apartment, Stake instantly took in how its air was heavy with a high-priced cologne, such as someone might overindulge in just to show that they could afford to do so on their salary.

A hand appeared from around the door to seize him by the lapel, almost dragging him off his feet. This person's other hand jammed the barrel of a snub-nosed Decimator revolver under Stake's jaw painfully. A second man closed and locked the door. Out of the corner of his eye, Stake saw that this man had a pump-action shotgun in his hands. He recognized it as his own, in fact. The man had found it in the corner between his computer desk and the wall.

Both men wore pricey and priggish black suits, bowler hats on their heads. And the flesh of their faces and hands was leopard-spotted in a camouflage of blue-on-blue.

The first man let go of Stake's jacket, instead slipped his hand inside it to relieve him of the Darwin .55. "Nice," he said, smiling and tucking it into his own waistband.

As Stake stood there between the two clones, a third one stepped into view from the bedroom. He was of course identical to the other two, but somehow Stake could tell that this one was Mr. Jones. The clone nodded courteously. "Mr. Stake."

"How did you get in here?" he demanded.

"That would be me," said the man with his shotgun. Was this one Mr. Doe, the clone who had driven him back to the Center for Missing and Exploited Children after his meeting with Adrian Tableau? "Skeleton card," he explained.

"So what do you want?"

"You're a Blue War vet," observed Jones, strolling about the room now, and pointing to a case containing several medals that Stake had mounted on one of its walls. They were largely barren otherwise, and he particularly refrained from hanging photos or paintings of people, lest he begin to look like them. In his private lair, he wanted only to be himself. Whoever that was. To that end, there was only that one photograph of himself, should he need to stare at it upon his arrival home.

"Why do you ask?" Stake joked drily. As if, from the clones' appearance, it wasn't apparent.

"Very funny," said the one with the shotgun.

Stake smiled, feeling a bit smug. These men didn't remember him from his visit to Tableau's company; he was sure of it. But then, that returned him to his question. "I asked you what you're doing breaking into my apartment?"

"We work for Adrian Tableau, Mr. Stake," Jones explained. "He's the owner of Tableau Meats."

"I see. And?"

"And, *you* apparently work for John Fukuda. Owner of Fukuda Bioforms. A business competitor of Mr. Tableau's."

"How do you know that?"

"We have our sources," purred the one with the revolver barrel prodding his throat. Its blade sight was scraping his skin.

"It's come to our attention," Jones went on, still pacing, "that Mr. Fukuda suspects Mr. Tableau's daughter Krimson of stealing his daughter's expensive kawaii-doll. And its value seems to be increased by the fact that the doll was created using unconventional research that Mr. Fukuda obtained after he took over the former Alvine Products. It's possible Fukuda even suspects Mr. Tableau of coveting that research, and hence encouraging his daughter to steal the doll for him."

Stake's mind was racing. He could see that this information had come through his own lips, in the guise of caseworker Simon McMartinez. But still, how had they learned of him—Jeremy Stake, the private investigator hired by Fukuda? They had their "sources," the one with the Decimator had said. Who would that be? He doubted Janice would have betrayed him. Had Caren Bistro overcome her fear of Tableau? But then, she hadn't known that Stake worked for Fukuda. Was the source someone who worked under Fukuda, then? Stake could envision Tableau paying for the eyes and ears of such a person.

"What's your point?" he asked Jones.

"Our concern is that Krimson Tableau has been missing now for about two weeks. Our employer is worried that John Fukuda, suspecting Krimson of this crime, may be responsible for her disappearance."

"What? No... no. Fukuda hasn't done anything to her."

"And you wouldn't do anything to her, on Mr. Fukuda's behalf? Kidnap her, perhaps? Or something even worse?"

"Don't be crazy! Yes, okay, Fukuda hired me to find that doll. And yes, he thinks Krimson might have something to do with it, because Krimson hates Yuki Fukuda the way her father hates John Fukuda. But Fukuda did not kidnap Krimson Tableau. And I would never do something like that for any client, or for any money."

Would they go so far as to torture him? Though strictly forbidden, torture had not been unknown in the interrogation of Ha Jiin prisoners, by soldiers cloned or otherwise. Might they even intend to kill him? Stake gauged his chances of surprising the three clones. Brushing that revolver away from his neck with his left arm. Grabbing his Darwin out of the man's waistband and bringing it up to take out the shotgun man. Then back to blast the first man. Then wheeling and plugging Jones before he could jerk out whatever iron he carried. Maybe. Maybe he could pull it off. But Stake dreaded the scenario. As strong and fast and skillful as he was, these men were designed to be even stronger, faster, more skillful. *Three* of them. And one of him, with guns only inches away.

"And we're just to take your word on that?" said the shotgun man. "Put our trust in your professional ethics?"

"Hey, bring me down to the nearest forcer precinct. I'll submit to a truth scan in a minute. Yes, Mr. Fukuda would like to know if Krimson took the doll. So yes, I've tried to find her myself. In that regard, I'm actually helping Tableau, aren't I? The more people looking for his daughter, for whatever reason, the better."

"You're more and more the saint by the minute," said shotgun man.

"If Fukuda took Krimson, then why doesn't Yuki have her doll back?"

"Because Krimson never took it," Jones said, stopping opposite Stake a few paces away. As if he might strike him. Whip out his gun to execute him. "He may have her in custody to use in bargaining for the doll if he can establish that Mr. Tableau possesses it. Or even, realizing his error in kidnapping her, Fukuda might have murdered Krimson Tableau and disposed of her to hide the fact that he captured her."

"That's all nonsense. Paranoid nonsense your boss is feeding you. You guys should know better."

"It's your blasting boss who's the paranoid one, *corporal*," said the Decimator man. He had studied Stake's medals, too, obviously.

"Hey, mate, we all fought on the same side once."

"Yeah? Not anymore."

"Oh my God," Jones said in barely a whisper, taking a step nearer to Stake. "Your face is changing. You're starting to look like us."

Dung, Stake thought. Not in color, he knew from spending time with their sort in the past, but definitely in form.

Decimator man leaned around in front of Stake for a look. "Not us," he corrected. "You. He's a chameleon."

"Why are you copying me?" Jones asked harshly.

"I can't help it," Stake snapped.

"So you're like us, huh? A belf?"

"No. I was born, not grown. I'm a mutant."

"I see. Better to be a mutant than a clone, I guess."

"Your words, not mine."

The Decimator's muzzle ground itself against his jawbone more painfully. The front sight broke his skin and he felt a bead of blood run down his neck. "Wanker," the man snarled.

Mr. Jones looked Stake up and down. "Don't be so smug, my friend. You might still be a belf and not know it. Your designers could have given you a false history. A brain drip of memory-encoded long-chain molecules, the way they trained us."

"Why would they go through the trouble of making me think I was a birther?"

"Maybe it had to do with the work they programmed you for in the war. I mean, why would they have used you, if not to exploit your ability? Were you a spy? A deep penetration scout?"

"Stop fucking with me. You're not going to convince me I'm a factory product like you bastards."

The shotgun's stock smashed him in the ribs, and Stake went down on the floor, feeling as if he'd been hit with a load of its pellets. The Decimator now pointed at the top of his porkpie hat. But Jones hadn't deemed to pull his own gun. Calmly, he said, "Maybe you're a pet that madman Fukuda cooked up in one of his labs. And it's him who put a bogus history in your head. Digest that for a while, Mr. Stake."

"Blast you," he wheezed.

"In the meantime, I suggest you think about the wisdom of withholding information that might lead us to the whereabouts of Krimson Tableau, dead or alive. If you come forward to help us, we'll be lenient, even if you had something to do with it. After all, you're just a tool. But if we have to come back here again, we may be in a less civil mood next time."

"I'm going to continue looking for that doll," Stake said evenly. "And if I find Krimson Tableau along the way—dead or alive—I promise to let you know. But I will assure you again, I had nothing to do with her disappearance."

"And you can assure us that Fukuda had nothing to do with it, either?"

Actually, Stake couldn't assure them of that. The man was still too much of a mystery to him. Too full of surprises.

"Not as far as I know," was the best he could say, rising to his feet again slowly so as not to alarm them. He winced, a hand to his side.

Shotgun man took the Darwin .55 out of his comrade's waistband and walked into the bedroom. He apparently left the shotgun and pistol in there to return them to Stake, because he came back without them. Meanwhile, Jones had moved toward the door.

"Remember what I said, Mr. Stake. Don't be foolish, now."

"I won't if you won't."

The last one out was Decimator man, and he gave a mocking military salute before Stake closed the door in his blue-mottled face.

A FALSE HISTORY. If he were just a "pet" created by John Fukuda himself, as part of some game, some play—the scope and purpose of which he couldn't fully imagine—would his maker go through the trouble of faking these medals framed on the wall? The pictures of his parents that he kept, but locked away? The same way Fukuda had manufactured a history for Yuki, his wife-turned-daughter? No, it was too illogical in his own case. At least the idea that he himself was a military clone, designed for his chameleon abilities, made more sense.

But it wasn't true! *It wasn't!* He knew who he was. He had had parents. A past. All these memories were real. He knew them as intimately as he knew this very second.

He turned to look across the room at his computer.

Rick Henderson had given him the number by which to contact her, via net connection. On her other world. In her other dimension, almost as far away as their one week together.

Stake sat down in front of his computer. And at last, began the call he had fantasized about making for a decade gone by.

It rang and rang on her end. He let it go on for five minutes. What time was it, there? And if someone finally answered, might it be a boyfriend? A husband? A daughter or son?

He was about to disconnect, filled with that thought, when her face appeared on the screen. He flinched, felt nausea lurch into his guts.

Her hair was parted on the side, drawn back behind her head but he could tell it was still as long as ever. Where the light gave it a sheen, it went from black to metallic red. Her blue face, like that of some beautiful apparition, had maybe lost a layer of youthful softness. But he had never seen her eyes, or her little smile, so soft. Or heard her voice, when she spoke, sound so gentle.

"Ga Noh."

"Hi," he said, trying to make his own smile look casual. "Hi, Thi Gonh. It's good to see you again. My friend told you I'd be contacting you, then?"

"Yes. Your friend. Hen-da-son."

Stake nodded. "Good. Thanks for talking to me. How are you?"

"Thi is good," she said. "How are you, Ga Noh? You married now? Children?"

"Me? No. No time, I guess. Busy working."

"Work what?"

"I'm a detective." He saw her features pinch together in confusion. "I'm like a policeman, but for money."

"Ah." But it looked like she only partly got it.

"What are you doing now, for work?"

"I have good money. Farm. Big farm." It seemed to Stake that she watched him more closely, watched for his reaction, when she added, "My husa-bund and me."

"Ah." He nodded again. *Husband*. "You got married."

"Yes. Six years married."

"Congratulations. Wow. Ah... any children?"

"Oh, no." She shifted slightly, uncomfortably, as if embarrassed at a failing. "Thi body no good."

"*No*, don't say that. Your body... you..."

His words trailed off. He wanted to vomit. He wanted to cry. He wondered if it were too late to go out after Jones and the other two clones— and shoot them. Shoot their blue-patterned faces off.

Now Thi narrowed her eyes as she scrutinized him even more intently. Why? Was he beginning to change? To mirror her face, as he had done the first time she had told him her name? Mirror her face, as he had done when their bodies were knotted behind the closed blue door of her cell?

"Ga Noh, what happen?" She pointed at the screen.

"Huh?" He touched the blood trickling down his neck, and understood. "Oh. I, ah, cut myself shaving." He made shaving motions and grinned stupidly. Broken-heartedly.

"Ga Noh," Thi said. "You okay? Okay?"

"I'm okay."

"Why you call me? You need Thi take care you? Help Ga Noh?"

"Help? Oh no. No. I just… I just lost track of you so long ago, and I've always wondered how you were. After the trial and all. I'm just happy you made out all right. I'm relieved."

"Someone hurt you, huh?"

"Hurt me? No. No, I'm okay."

"Someone hurt Ga Noh." Her face had become harder, grim.

"Don't worry about me. It's just my job. It's crazy sometimes." He cleared his voice. "Hey, look, I have to go. But I was talking to Rick—Henderson—and I just thought I'd check in with you and say hi. Now that we aren't at war with each other anymore, huh?"

Her eyes still probed him. Sniper's keen eyes. "Thi worry you. Very worry."

"No. No, really. Look, I have to go. Maybe I'll call again sometime."

"Call from where? Where you now?"

"Punktown, on Oasis. I was born here."

She glanced behind her before she continued. "I am afraid husa-bund angry Thi, talk to Ga Noh."

"Yes, yes, I understand."

"But you need Thi, you *call*. Okay?"

"Sure. Same here. You need anything, call me. Just store my number, all right?"

"Mm."

"Okay, then. Well... nice to see you. Goodbye, Thi, okay? Goodbye."

Sadness in her face. It truly looked like sadness. *Ask her!* part of him shouted. But what did it matter now what, if anything, she had felt back then? What that had been all about. A husband now. Another life entirely, as if a different woman had been reincarnated inside the same body.

"Goodbye, Ga Noh," she said.

He pressed a key, banished her face. Then let his head droop. And laughed. Wagged his head, and laughed.

"Fool," he muttered. "Stupid, stupid fool." Ten years, for these five minutes. And now it was all over, wasn't it? This was his closure. Finally over, with a whimper. With a chuckle.

Stake lifted his head to make another call. To let John Fukuda know about the visit from Tableau's cloned thugs. And to let Fukuda know that his own life might be in danger.

Back to the case, to take his mind off the call he had just made. The emptiness that it had filled only with pointed, painful heaviness, like the obsolete detritus of their war. Razor wire and spent cartridges, blood-crusted knives and mud-caked guns. Back to the case, because it was all he had.

CHAPTER EIGHTEEN
CONJOINED

As HE PASSED through a wide section of tunnel, Dai-oo-ika noticed that two youths in shabby clothing were watching him, crouched as they were on a catwalk above him, but when he turned his head their way they ducked back into a narrow opening. He was tempted to go up the ladder there after them, in order to take more nourishment, but he did not want to be distracted from the unseen beacon—the silent vibration, almost like a voice— that drew him on and on through the entrails of Punktown. It promised him understanding of his condition, of himself, at its source. Or at least, it was his desire that it would be so.

Some stretches of tunnel were utterly without light. It didn't inconvenience him one bit. His senses had become heightened; the thick tendrils of his face touched—like Braille—the particles of light from which images were constructed. They caressed the currents of sound like a hand dipped in a flowing stream, and the airborne spores of scent adhered to them and dissolved into their silver/black-banded flesh.

On he burrowed. On. Like an archeologist in subterranean ruins, hoping to excavate and piece together the fragments of his memory. There had to be more than just his name, the face of his child mother, snatches of dream. There had to be.

He reached the limits of underground Subtown, but came to a ladder, which he climbed up, up, to a higher level of the netherworld. At one point he crawled on all fours on a web-like metal grille and watched a subway train speed by below him, washing him in a flow of warm and stinking air. Now, just below the crust of the city, he continued following the beckoning call. A voice almost as familiar as his mother's.

He came to a sealed circular grate, but it was not the first that had blocked his path and he pushed it out of its frame with a tortured screech of metal. Dai-oo-ika entered a polished white tunnel, glossy as the inside of a leviathan's intestine. He crawled along this for a short distance, warm air like the wake of that subway train blowing hard against him. But he was a fish diligently swimming upstream against the current. At the end of this air vent he encountered a fan spinning inside a cage. He bent his thick fingers between the bars and tore the cage out of the mouth of the tunnel. The fan came with it in a burst of sparks, the blades whirring to a gradual stop. He bent this obstacle to one side, the fan blades merely the petals of a giant flower for the crushing.

Dai-oo-ika found himself in a long passage that vanished into darkness in either direction, despite the maintenance lighting. The tunnel was crammed with pipes that sheathed power cables and plumbing that conveyed water both fresh and fouled—many of these conduits labeled with tags or even by color. Spaced along the tunnel were rungs set into the tiled walls, these leading up to hatches stenciled with words he could not fathom. But he did not need to read them. He went unerringly to one set of rungs, and hoisted his bulk up them. The metal hatch was locked, but he yanked it clear of its socket with one hand and let it crash below him.

The access chute was narrow, and he had to squeeze his heavy body through it like the boneless mass it truly was, just as an octopus can ooze its body through the barest crack. But he was able to stand erect again once he had entered the basement of the apartment complex called Steward Gardens.

There were a number of interconnected rooms. Dai-oo-ika could stand in them with only a little stooping. Here were the support systems of the structure above him. Its softly humming generator. Cabinets sparkling with indicator lights. Monitor stations with screens that showed colorful scrolling data, or fizzing static, or were black and dead. Dominating one room was a huge tank containing the generic soup of fermented bacteria that the apartments' food fabricators could mold like clay into a variety of programmed meals—could have, had the soup not gone bad. Dai-oo-ika sensed the seething microscopic life within, but it did not interest him. It was not a sustenance that would have nourished him, even if it were still viable.

But he took all this in only briefly. The source of the voice in his head was here, so loud now. As he moved toward it, however, several stealthy figures crept out of the gloom.

Dai-oo-ika felt the vaguest sense of kinship with these four figures. Their origins were at least in part the same as his own. Like him, they had no eyes but still appeared to see him as they approached in a widening semicircle. Their skin was gray, as his was predominately. All that distinguished one from the other of them was the number marked on their foreheads.

But they apparently felt no kinship with him. They clearly saw him only as another intruder.

The first of the creatures to bolt and leap upon him tried to dig its fingers into his flesh. This angered Dai-oo-ika, and he plucked the clinging creature off him with one hand, flung it across the room. Another rushed him, but he batted it away and it thudded hard against a wall. He caught the third and fourth in his arms—and pulled them tight in a squeezing embrace. Pressed them against his swollen white belly. Until, much as they squirmed in his arms, they began to sink into his flesh as if it were a pool of milk.

One of the two he had repelled tried to rise, but he moved toward it with one of its brothers' legs still protruding from his belly for a moment before it slipped out of sight. He picked up this stunned creature and embraced it, too. As soon as it had submerged, he turned his attention to the last of the four. It was flopping in a seizure on the floor.

It didn't put up a fight, only convulsed in his hands as he fed it headfirst into his mid-section.

Nourishment. He savored it. He felt stronger still. And now he focused his attention on the voice again. Followed it to the very core of this building which, in a sense, the owner of the voice made a sentient thing—though sentient in a damaged way. Steward Gardens was like one immense living entity that didn't quite know what it was, either.

The encephalon was a mass of grayish, convoluting tissue thatflattened into a vertical transparent frame, about four feet tall by two feet wide by six inches thick. Wires snaked out of the massive brain, floating subtly in the greenish amniotic solution that kept it alive. There were more computer stations in this room, but the brainframe itself was the very soul of the building.

Dai-oo-ika approached the glass cabinet slowly, its fungal green glow upon him. What was its relation to him? Brother? It felt more like… father. Creator. A god's god. He reached out his right hand and placed it flat against the surface. The brain's thoughts poured into his palm, flowed up his arm and into his flesh toward his own nexus of thought. He jolted a little at the strength of their connection, and the glass around his hand shattered. The nourishing solution began to leak out and patter on his feet. But Dai-oo-ika did not pay heed. He pressed his hand inside the cabinet, and now laid it upon the knotted brain tissue itself. The voice running into his arm turned to a bellow.

A stigmata-like hole opened in his palm of its own volition. The coiled brain matter started to unravel, to be sucked into the hungry mouth in his hand. It diminished in its frame as more and more fluid splashed free.

Like a dead parent's belongings packed away in an attic steamer trunk, Dai-oo-ika had compacted the inorganic material he could squeeze no sustenance from, but which he had not yet bothered himself with ejecting as waste product, into a cavity inside himself. This tight bundle included Dolly's clothing and crushed shoes. But he had not quite figured out what to do with her nanomites, being in that gray area between organic and inorganic, so as much as they had made his mind itch with their busy work he had tolerated them, accepted them as part of his evolving condition.

Now, they seemed to sniff the encephalon, and it aroused them in its abundance. The microscopic machine-animals raced through Dai-oo-ika's system, through his arm and into the brain tissues even as he drew them into himself. Then they began racing back and forth between the two entities, as if to help facilitate his absorption of the huge organ, a nest of eager worker ants. He had subconsciously altered their programming, or was it they who had gnawed away the membranes clouding his own programming? In any case, the nanomites worked at a frenzied pace to marry the two bodies together at the cellular level, a corps of wartime surgeons, incising and cauterizing, transplanting and mending with their tiny mandibles, tiny tool limbs.

The wires plugged into the brain were sucked into Dai-oo-ika's hand, as well. As with the other inorganic material he had drawn in, these were not dissolved and digested. Even when the last of the encephalon was gone, and only a little fluid pooled at the bottom of the frame, the wires still streamed out of his palm.

He slumped down heavily to the floor as if in a swoon, sitting in the puddle of amniotic solution like a drunken Buddha. His arm was still draped inside the frame but he was unmindful of the fangs of glass that pinned his wrist there. The other ends of the wires ran into relays that communicated with the little room's various computer stations. And now, all the monitors that had been showing colorful data or fizzing static or dead blackness flickered and revealed the same image. It was grainy, streaked with scratches and blips like damaged celluloid, but beneath this clutter Dai-oo-ika could see a burning and mostly flattened city, stretching out black and twisted to all horizons. Below were thousands of upturned faces and arms lifted in praise. The faces were a mix of human and nonhuman, but all were charred black, blistered by fire and deformed with radiation. Silvery pus ran out of heat-sealed eyes. Yet despite the pain these people must be feeling, they were singing to him, all in one voice of adoration. And he looked down upon them from a great height. For he was huge. He was their god.

Dai-oo-ika understood the cosmic web of Fate then. He understood that he and this brother/father had needed to become united (was it *reunited?*) in order to both realize their potential. In order to fulfill their destinies.

CHAPTER NINETEEN
INTERVIEWS

ON HIS VEHICLE'S sound system Stake played a jazz piece called "Yesterdays" from Twentieth Century trumpet player Clifford Brown. It was melancholy, and melancholy music from any era or planet, for that matter, was all right by him. He was piloting the hovercar down a wide, multilane ramp into Punktown's subterranean sector.

Caren Bistro had told him that Brat Gentile belonged to a gang down here in Subtown. The B Level of Folger Street. "The Folger Street Somethings," she had said.

Above him now, a solid sky with clouds of steam hissing out of the crisscrossed network of pipes up there. Stake slowed the car as the ramp fed into a grid of streets and the early morning traffic along this one congealed to an ooze. Among the work-bound pedestrians walking along the sidewalk he spotted several that glowed a luminous blue. Each

269

of them turned its head to smile directly at him. One of the translucent blue figures stood at the curb with her thumb sticking out as if to hitchhike, her long hair blowing dreamily. It was then that a whispery voice spoke to him inside his vehicle.

"Open your world to Séance Friends—for the strongest, clearest Ouija channels in Paxton." He had left the holographic hitchhiker behind him a moment ago, but now she stepped up to the curb ahead of him again, her eyes seeming to look into his. The voice went on, "Make a special friend who can tell you about the long past, or even about your own future."

"Bastards," Stake said. It was legal for such advertisements to intrude into one's sound system, justified as "ambient sound," like hearing someone else's radio blast from another car. The ad didn't replace his music, but overlapped it, and that was invasive enough. It continued with a testimonial: the voice of a young girl.

"My spirit guide told me I'll die before I'm twenty, so your next ghost friend could be me!" She giggled.

Stake shut his sound system off altogether.

Further along, he made his way through a neighborhood of gray-skinned, blue-turbaned Kalians. Tenements and shops had hung black banners outside, and there was a group of protestors that shouted at the passing vehicles. Several helmeted and armored riot forcers made sure they didn't overflow into the street itself to block traffic. Stake glanced out at their furious, black-eyed faces. "What's their problem now?" he muttered.

He remembered what Janice had told him about the Kalian deity called Ugghiutu. "Sort of the

Kalian God and Satan in one body." One of the so-called "Outsiders," exiled from this dimension but waiting to return to power. He thought of the former owners of Alvine Products, their lunatic plan to design and grow a horde of giant monsters to reclaim the universe.

Despite the strict religious beliefs of most Kalians, Stake had never encountered a neighborhood that didn't have its street gang, and he soon noted a cluster of Kalian boys who wore blue satin jackets to match their turbans, which they wore facing backwards. But these were not the gang kids he was searching for. He continued on, until he arrived at last on Folger Street.

Stake cruised along the entire length of the extensive street. When he finally reached what appeared to be its end, he turned around and came back from the other direction.

He didn't spot a single gang kid. That is to say, he saw no apparent gang outfits, and what was the point of being in a gang if you didn't flaunt it, announce it in some way, brazen and proud?

Stake didn't know the full name of the gang Gentile belonged to, but he thought he knew gang graffiti when he saw it. On the face of one tenement building, in between two windows, someone had sprayed a very large, stylized dog's head baring its fangs, in red paint that glowed like neon. Though they didn't exhibit any obvious gang peacockery, there were three tough-looking kids sitting on the tenement's front steps, apparently in no hurry to be off to school.

Stake found a parking spot along the curb a little ways up, and then backtracked to the tenement building on foot. With animal-keen instincts, the kids noticed his approach right away. He hadn't been able to think of any guise he might have called up, seated in his car and browsing through the faces on his wrist comp, in order to gain their confidence. Couldn't think of an actor's role he might adopt. And so he figured he'd just jump right into it without pretense.

"Hey," he said in greeting as he came to the steps. The preteens looked a little too young to be in a full-blown street gang; maybe a tadpole gang. But you never knew. The adolescent gang called the Martians—after the god of war—was one of the deadliest in Punktown. "Do you guys know a kid named Brat Gentile? I'm a friend of a friend and nobody seems to know where's he got off to."

"Oh, please, officer," said one of the three, a Choom girl with her spiky hair dyed a metallic silver, her long mouth in a smirk. As young as she was, she'd had her eyelids surgically altered so as to look exotically slanted.

"No, no, I'm not a forcer. I'm a friend of Brat's girlfriend, Krimson. Krimson's gone missing, too."

"I don't know who the hell you're yakking about."

"Brat's in a gang from around here, the Folger Street Something-or-others."

"Snarlers," said one of the two boys seated beside the girl. "The Folger Street Snarlers."

"Snarlers. So do you know Brat?" he asked the boy.

"I'm sure I'd know his face if I saw him. But I haven't seen him or any of the Snarlers in a while."

"What do you mean?"

The second boy spoke up. "It isn't just your friend of a friend that's missing, Mr. Forcer. Nobody's seen any of the Folger Street Snarlers for *days.*"

"MR. GENTILE?"

Stake almost said Genitalia, because it had been running through his mind that Caren Bistro had said that was Krimson Tableau's playful nickname for Brat. Caren had also said, in Janice's classroom, that Brat had a brother whom she had contacted while trying to find out what had happened to her friend. Stake had been grateful to find his phone number listed on the net.

"Who is this?" asked the face on the hovercar's console screen. Theo Gentile appeared to be in his mid-twenties, and wary didn't begin to address the look in his eyes.

"My name is Jeremy Stake, sir. I'm a hired detective. I'm looking for a girl named Krimson Tableau, and I understand that your brother—"

"I don't know anyone by that name!" Gentile snapped.

"I'm told he calls her Smirk. She's your brother's girlfriend."

"I don't know where she is. I don't even know where my brother is! Who hired you?" Stake began to stammer a reply, but Gentile cut him off. "I just got back from Miniosis. You go tell your boss—I don't know anything!"

Theo Gentile disconnected. With a sigh, Stake started up the vehicle and pulled out into traffic. In his earlier cruising he had already established where the local police precinct house was located.

"IT WASN'T MY turn to babysit the Folger Street Snarlers today," growled the beefy forcer behind the counter, not even bothering to look up at Stake. "Why don't you go earn your dirty money, gumshoe, instead of asking us to do your work for you?"

"Gumshoe?" Stake murmured to himself with a disgusted smile.

But a woman at a desk behind the burly officer looked up and said to him, "Eric mentioned something about the Snarlers not being around." Then to Stake: "Want to talk to Detective Moudry, sir? He's had a lot of dealings with the gangs around here."

"Yeah," said the first forcer. "He even took a bullet in the neck from one of the Snarlers. He had to kill the blasting punk."

Stake ignored him, said to the woman, "Yes, please, if it isn't too much trouble."

She got the plainclothesman on the phone, and a minute later he stepped out from some inner office and gestured for the woman to buzz Stake through the security door. Stake followed him back toward his office.

"Yeah," Moudry said, glancing at Stake with a cop's appraising eye. "It's funny. I'm hearing the Snarlers haven't been seen, and a couple of their family and friends are starting to get edgy."

"What do you think about that?"

"I don't think they've all been killed in some big street war; that'd be hard to keep from being noticed. I just been figuring that they're lying low for some reason. Maybe they're keeping their heads down because some other gang is gunning for them. They had a bad scuffle with a Tikkihotto gang called the Morlocks last year."

"It just seems funny to me, because I'm looking for the girlfriend of one of them and she's missing, too. A girl by the name of Krimson Tableau, nick-named Smirk by her boyfriend."

"Don't know her," Moudry said, opening his door for Stake, "but wherever they're hiding, I guess she must be hiding, too." They both seated themselves. "What's her boyfriend's name?"

"Brat Gentile."

"Gentile," Moudry echoed, doing a search through his computer files. "Hm. I don't have an arrest record for him, but I do have his name here on a list I made of the current gang members." Then a light seemed to come on in some dusty back storage room of the detective's mind. "Ohh, Gentile. Yeah, yeah. I know his brother, Theo. Theo was in the Snarlers himself for years. These kids come and go, so it's hard for me to keep up with all of them. But we got a history, the Snarlers and me."

"The man up front said you got shot in a scrap with them one time."

Moudry waved it away like it was all just part of the game. "That was nine years ago. Javier Dias wasn't even the leader back then."

"He's the current leader?"

"Yeah. Not a total scumbag, as far as these things go. But I had him in not too long ago on suspicion of a warehouse fire. These punks get thrown a bone sometimes for torching places in insurance scams." He punched some keys. "This is him." He swiveled his monitor for Stake to see. An interrogation room vid played on its screen.

The camera showed Moudry standing, sipping a coffee, while a young man sat behind a table with a water bottle in front of him. The camera zoomed in close on Javier Dias: wiry, tightly wound, with a pompadour of curly black hair, and wearing a white leather jacket. When he spoke, he talked out of one side of his mouth and through gritted teeth in an effect that seemed as much like partial paralysis as it did toughness.

"You're wasting your time bringing me in here about this dung, Moudry," Dias said to the detective with familiarity. "Why you got to be harassing me all the time? You still hurting from that slug in your neck? That wasn't me, remember?"

"I remember. And I remember putting a slug of my own through Banshee's skull for it."

"Yeah, yeah, all in the past, right?"

"Exactly. I'm talking about now. I'm talking about the fire in the old Magog Industries warehouse."

Moudry stopped the vid and started to say something, but Stake asked, "Would it be okay if I saw a little more of that?"

The plainclothesman shrugged, and continued playing back the recording.

Earlier, while pretending to adjust his shirt collar, Stake had covertly captured some still shots of Detective Moudry on his wrist comp, thinking that his face—familiar to the Folger Street Snarlers and perhaps their kin—might come in handy. But now, he started taking a new series of shots, from the screen in front of him.

BRAT GENTILE DIDN'T have an address of his own listed in any current directory, but when going on the net for his brother's phone number Stake had found that Theo Gentile and his wife lived on Folger Street themselves.

On the front steps of Gentile's tenement building, Stake depressed the key for his apartment number until a familiar face appeared on the monitor screen, warier than ever. "What?" it barked.

On his own monitor screen right now, Theo Gentile would be seeing the attractive face of a young man with high cheekbones, who talked out of one side of his mouth and through gritted teeth in an effect that seemed as much like partial paralysis as it did toughness. "Hey man, let me in, quick. It's Javier."

But both the picture and sound would be shot with distorting static. It was not a malfunction, much as Stake hoped that would appear to be the case. He owned a cheap multipurpose scanning device that he had brought with him from his car's glove compartment. He was holding this instrument just below the security system's lens. He had used it numerous times before so he knew its field, as presently adjusted, would disrupt the image with snow and distort the audio as well. Gentile would be able to see his transfigured face—but not too clearly. In addition, he wore a ski hat over his hair and stood close to the lens so it wouldn't be noticed that he did not possess the trademark white leather jacket of the Folger Street Snarlers.

"Wh… Javier?"

"Javier Dias, you stupid fuck!"

Gentile's wariness didn't seem to be assuaged much. "Javier, man, what's the blast? Where's my brother?"

"That's what I want to tell you. Hurry up before somebody sees me out here. There's this creepy guy going around who says he's a private detective, asking about me."

"Yeah, yeah, that wanker called me, too!"

An indicator light went from red to green and with a click the door came unlocked.

Gentile had opened the door to apartment 12 on the second floor and Stake had stepped inside before the young man could take in that, in addition to being without his leather jacket, this Javier was several inches taller than he should be. Stake saw the pistol in Gentile's other hand and went for it immediately, seizing his wrist and spinning him around in a move he'd learned in combat training, then slamming Gentile's front against the closed door. Gentile cried out, tried to pull the trigger in an attempt to at least shoot Stake in the leg, but Stake bent his wrist back almost to the point of breaking and the pistol clattered to the floor. Stake drew his own weapon, the Darwin .55 that Mr. Jones and his men had considerately returned to him before leaving his apartment, and let Gentile feel its touch behind his ear.

"Wanker, huh?" Stake said.

"Javier, please, man, please," Gentile blurted.

"Calm down," Stake told him, no longer imitating Javier Dias's voice as he recalled it from the police vid. "I'm not here to hurt you. I only want to ask some questions, then I'll leave."

"You're not Javier."

"And you're not your brother, but you'll do. Where's your wife?"

"At work!"

"Good. I'm going to let you go, and you're going to sit. You sit nice and I won't have to be impolite anymore. Got it?"

Stake kicked the dropped pistol away, then stepped back to retrieve it and to let go of Theo Gentile. He turned around, furious and frightened and confused. He repeated, "You aren't Javier."

"I'm that private detective who called you earlier. If you'd talked to me then I wouldn't have to be visiting you now."

"I'll call the forcers on you, dung-licker!"

"Go ahead, I just came from there. Talked to an old friend of yours named Moudry. Anyway, it's in your best interest to cooperate, Gentile. We both want the same thing: to find your brother Brat."

"And what do you want him for?"

Stake motioned with his gun. "Come on, sit down."

Gentile hesitated. "How is it you look like my friend Javier now?"

"A little genetic trickery of mine. If it starts to slip, don't get spooked."

In the next room, Gentile complied and lowered himself into a chair. "You work for Adrian Tableau," he said, "don't you?"

"Hands on the armrests," Stake ordered, afraid another weapon might be tucked in the cushions. "No, I don't, but I am looking for his daughter, Krimson. So you admit now that you know she's involved with your brother."

"I don't know anything about that girl; I only met her a couple times."

"Why are you so scared, Mr. Genitalia? Who are you hiding from?"

"Hey, like I told you on the phone, my wife and I just came home from visiting with her family in Miniosis. I get back here and my brother is gone. Not only that, but his whole gang is gone. I don't know if another gang did something to them, or if it has to do with that girl's father, or what. So I been watching my ass until I found out more. I didn't want my wife to return to work but she thinks I'm overreacting. I don't think she's taking this seriously enough!"

"So Brat told you Krimson's father is a dangerous man."

"Yeah. He said her dad would highly disapprove of him going with her. You *sure* you don't work for him?"

"No," Stake assured him, "I wasn't hired by him. I was hired by the father of a schoolmate of Krimson's. I believe Krimson stole this girl's kawaii-doll, and I'm trying to get it back."

"What? That's all you're really looking for?"

"Yes. It's an expensive doll. To tell you the truth, I don't care about Tableau's daughter, except that I feel she's the one who stole this doll."

"Yeah, she took it," Gentile said, not looking ready to believe that the bio-engineered toy was Stake's only concern.

Just like that—confirmed at last. "Did she tell you that herself, or was it your brother?"

"Brat told me. He called me when I was in Miniosis, because he was upset. She ran out on him or something and he said it was strange."

"Ran out on him? Tell me what he said. About the doll... everything."

"Then I have to show you his room to explain. Can I get up?"

"Okay. Slowly."

Gentile rose from the chair, rubbing his twisted wrist with a bitter look of accusation thrown Stake's way. Stake followed him with his gun held loosely, but ready, as the former gang member led him into a little hallway off the living room. He opened one of the hall's doors, and the two men entered Brat Gentile's bedroom.

The walls were lost in a dizzying kaleidoscope of graffiti, like dozens of Jackson Pollock paintings superimposed over each other, some in neon colors that glowed in the dark. Stake nearly winced. There were fake painted windows and bogus open doors that looked out on surreal savannahs or ocean depths, populated by fanciful animals. Here and there posters of music stars or favorite movies added another layer to the chaos, including a poster of a Kalian glebbi grazing on a plain. Stake remembered the live specimen he had seen in Adrian Tableau's little menagerie.

"My brother loves animals," Gentile said, watching Stake.

"And he loves Krimson Tableau, too, huh?"

"Let's get it clear: it was her idea to take that doll. Brat had nothing to do with that. He told me so, and he had no reason to lie to me about it."

"But did he say if her father put her up to it?"

"Why would he do that?"

"The father of the doll's owner is a business rival of Tableau's."

"Huh. I don't know anything about that. What I got from it is that Smirk just did it because she hates that girl. Brat said her father got Smirk a kawaii-doll of her own, but it wasn't a very exclusive model so she didn't like it—she wanted this other kid's. I take it she's pretty spoiled, this Smirk. Rich girl, you know? Brat said she's a handful."

"Did you see the doll yourself?"

"No, I was away by then. But when he called, Brat told me she had it with her when she came to see him the last time. That would be two weeks ago." Gentile shook his head. "I really don't know what the big deal is with those stupid dolls. I guess it makes 'em think they look sexy, like little girls." He snorted. "Well, I suppose it does. I got to admit this Smirk is a hot little monster. I can see why Brat would put up with her dung. But I knew she'd be trouble, sooner or later."

"What did he say happened the last time he saw her?"

"Okay, well, he said she came over here after school. Matter of fact she'd just taken the doll, and showed it off to him all proud and nasty about it. He said it was a weird thing, with like an octopus face and little devil wings. It moved, too. Like a baby on drugs, is how he said it. He said it was kind of alive."

"But Brat told you she ran out on him?" Stake was running his keen eyes over the paint-slathered walls, the ratty furniture, the dirty clothes draped and heaped where Brat had left them before disappearing, himself. There was even a greasy pizza box still on a little coffee table, a number of empty bottles of Zub beer ranked beside it, as if Gentile had been afraid to tamper with a crime scene. Stake presumed that the rich girl had taken a perverse satisfaction in slumming with her less than affluent paramour.

"I'm getting to that. Like I said, Smirk came here after school to show him the doll, and then they went to bed for a while. Y'know? After that Brat dozed off. When he woke up, his girl was gone. He told me he thought it was funny that she didn't wake him up to say goodbye, but at first he figured she just didn't want to bother him. Then, he saw this."

Gentile moved to a cabinet filled with a clutter of music and movie chips in their jewel boxes, magazines, other odds and ends. He shoved aside the stack of jewel boxes and dug out an object that he'd stashed behind them. He turned and offered the object to Stake. It was a young girl's pocketbook.

"She wasn't here, but this was hanging on the back of his computer chair. And her clothes were folded on the chair, too. Even left her shoes. I got all that stuff hidden away, too. Anyway, when he saw her clothes and all he knew something wasn't right. So he got worried, and ended up calling me. He sure couldn't call her father. Smirk told Brat herself that her father is one mean bastard.

Connections with the Neptune Teeb family and everything." Gentile squirmed a little. "Maybe I shouldn't have said that."

"I've met the man. Wouldn't surprise me if he had friends in the syndy."

Stake had taken the pocketbook from Gentile and sat on the edge of the bed to open it on his knees. Makeup, a package of tissues, a little palm comp (Krimson didn't care for the wrist comp variety, he supposed). And a black hand phone, with cute-eyed sheeted ghosts all over it: a Ouija phone.

Gentile went on, "I blocked the palm comp from being traced, in case her father figured on trying to home in on its whereabouts." That could be done, even if the device were currently inactive. "I have her backpack, too, with some school dung in it. Books and such. There was room enough inside that maybe she brought a change of clothes with her. But even so, why leave her school uniform with Brat?"

"But the doll..."

"He said she didn't have her own kawaii-doll when she came over. But yeah, that's the only thing she took with her when she left, apparently—the kawaii-doll she stole from that other girl."

"So last time Brat saw her, they were both in bed."

"Right. They were lying around naked, you know. Lovey-dovey, pillow talk. She picked up the doll and hugged it, all giggly, he said, trying to be cute. Brat couldn't stand the touch of it, himself. Anyway, somewhere in there he fell asleep."

Stake got up from the edge of the bed and turned to survey it again. The sheets were still in disarray, as they must have appeared to Brat on the day he had awakened from a deep, post-coital and maybe post-alcoholic slumber to find his young girlfriend no longer beside him.

Observing the hired detective, Gentile said, "Christ-o-mighty, man, now you're starting to look like me a little bit. Or what it would look like if Javier and me had a love child." He snorted again. "You doing that on purpose?"

"No," Stake said. "Mind of its own."

Gentile's gaze shifted to sweep the room as Stake's had, but with more melancholy. "I wish I'd come back from the in-laws' place as soon as he called, but how was I to know what would happen? I figured the little she-beast was just playing games with the poor kid. He didn't call me again, and when I came home he was gone. I thought he must be with his crew, but when he didn't show up I went out looking for the Snarlers and I couldn't find any of them, either. That's when I got the chills, man, deep chills."

"I have to say," Stake agreed, flipping up the pillows to peek under them, "it's very disturbing. I can see Tableau coming after your brother, but I don't know what to make of the whole gang going missing."

"I'm trying not to think so negative," Gentile said. "Maybe the Snarlers have gone underground with Brat to protect him from Tableau. Maybe they're all okay."

"That does sound like a strong possibility," Stake reassured him. But as for Krimson, he thought the odds were less in her favor. Seeing her Ouija phone had reminded him of Caren Bistro hearing the missing girl on hers.

He got down on hands and knees next and looked under Brat's bed. A sock, a porn magazine, dust bunnies. On the far side of the bed, though, he noticed something more interesting. He rose, walked to the foot of the bed and started pulling it away from the wall. Gentile came over to help him. "What?" he said.

Stake pointed down to a square hole in the wall at floor level. A grille partially covered it. Only partially, because the grille had been pulled out of its frame at one corner and bent upwards. "That an air duct?"

"Yeah. And before you ask... no, I didn't know it looked like that. But there's no way Smirk could have fit through there, if that's what you're thinking."

Stake stared at the air vent. "That's not exactly what I was thinking," he said.

CHAPTER TWENTY
RUNNING TO STAND STILL

FLOOR THREE. THEN, the button for the basement again, before the door could open. Sometimes when they briefly stopped before ascending or descending yet again, they heard fists pounding on the outer security door. Thank God the things didn't think to try the elevator keyboards on each floor. Thank God the elevator's mechanism had not given out and trapped them somewhere between floors. Javier had visions of the Blank People shimmying up the cable from below. Or worse, dropping down the shaft from above onto the top of their carriage, and prying open the hatch above their heads.

The elevator had to keep moving and moving, like a shark that will die if it stops passing water through its gills.

Javier looked at Patryk, who leaned his tall body in the corner, playing around on Nhu's wrist comp.

He felt a fondness and a bittersweet pride. The last of the Folger Street Snarlers besides himself. Quietly strong, loyal and calm, with an unquestioning faith in his leader. But Javier felt no less fondness for the others, despite the flaws that might have led to their deaths. How could he have outlived them? He was twenty-five. Some of the others had been teenagers. He had passed through more fires in his life on the streets than they had, but had still come out the other side where they had not.

So far.

He took in the last of the Tin Town Terata. Barbie had fallen asleep, hunkered down near Patryk's feet with her arms around her knees. Her two cognizant faces had closed their eyes, but the largest of the five faces flicked its eyes back and forth madly as if in a panic. REMs, Javier realized. For the sake of room inside the cramped elevator, Satin had folded up and collapsed the limbs of his mechanical body as best he could. He glowered at something only he could see, but occasionally roused from his distanced fury to glance around at his remaining comrades as Javier was doing.

And Mira. She had fallen asleep, too, curled on her side like a child at his feet. He wanted to kneel down close to her and touch her hair, her face, her shoulder, but was too self-conscious in the presence of the others. Why was he so attracted to her? Had this circumstance drawn the two of them together only because they needed each other? He had heard that the nearness of death brought out the instinct to fuck, to procreate, to continue the species. Could that impulse have found a more tender manifestation in the both of them? If he had

met Mira on the street would he have done anything except maybe crack a joke behind her back
to Mott or Hollis? He had had beautiful women of
all races. Whole women. Mutants were to be
scoffed at, shunned, or at best pitied. Maybe she
had used her gift, he kidded himself. Got inside his
brain and twisted it like a balloon animal into the
shape of love.

Whatever the case, whatever the cause, that was
what he felt when he lowered his eyes to her again.
He felt love.

The elevator had reached the basement level.
Javier was quick to poke the button for Floor
Three. They began to rise up smoothly through the
body of Steward Gardens again.

Javier noticed Satin's eyes were on him. They
had an angry look, but then they always did. He
realized the mutant had been waiting to say something to him. Maybe waiting for quite a while.

"You like our little girl, huh?" he grumbled.

Ha, Javier thought. Maybe Satin had a touch of
a gift, himself. "Yeah," he said. "I like her."

"Yeah, well, she likes you, too." Satin turned his
eyes away. "Can't blame her. She needs a man with
those extra touches—like arms and legs. Real arms
and legs. Not much someone like me could do for
her."

Javier understood a lot then; not that he hadn't
suspected it before. "Hey. I seen you fight those
Blank People. If it wasn't for you, you most of all,
none of you Terata would be alive right now. Mira
wouldn't be here right now." The gang leader
chuckled. "I know I wouldn't want to go up
against you, man."

Satin returned his gaze to Javier. And smiled.

"Uhh," Mira said.

Javier flicked his eyes back to her, saw that she was shivering violently. Her strong features were clenched in an expression like pain. No longer caring what the others thought, he crouched down beside her and gripped her shoulder, leaning his face in close to hers. "Mira! Mira, wake up!"

"Javier," she murmured, as if talking in her sleep. But he could tell it wasn't quite that. "Something in the basement. Somebody. Something."

"What is it? What do you see?"

The purple veins at her temples stood out engorged and throbbing. Their branches were spread wider than he remembered them, touching the ends of her eyebrows and the tops of her cheekbones like cracks in the porcelain head of a doll. "Javier, there's something in the basement now." She spoke clearly but her eyes were still crunched shut. Awake but not. "It's swallowed the brain. The encephalon. Merged with it. It's sitting down there, getting bigger. Stronger."

"What is it? What are you talking about?"

"Dai-oo-ika." Then she gave a shudder, and seemed to change her mind. "Outsider. Dai-oo-ika. Outsider. The Spawn of Ugghiutu. Outsiders... the *Outsiders*..."

"Okay, that's enough—wake up." He shook her. "Wake up."

She didn't open her eyes, but her features relaxed somewhat and her trembling became more subdued. Javier stroked her hair and looked up at Satin, who said, "We got to get out of here. We can't keep riding up and down in this thing forever. We have to make a run for it."

"We'll die, like Nhu," Patryk said.

"What else can we do?" Satin growled. "There's nothing else left. The question is, do we go out the front door or through the basement?"

"The building is too full of them now," Javier said. "We'd never even get to the front door alive. But we don't know about the basement. Unless the Blanks are getting in from outside, there might only be a few left in there."

"Nhu took her key card with her, didn't she?"

"We don't need it anymore," Patryk said. "She overrode the basement lock-out and now we have access to general door functions."

"Well, what about that thing Mira is talking about? What's that mean?"

"I don't know," Javier said. "But of the two choices, I guess we're going to have to make a run for it that way."

"There's another idea," Patryk said. "Nhu's idea."

"What was that?" asked Satin.

"Call the forcers in here. They're the lesser of two evils. Let them fight the Blank People. We might even be able to escape more easily while they distract each other."

Javier held Patryk's gaze for several long seconds, and then said, "Let's do it."

"Okay. Her wrist comp is acting funny—I can't get on the net—but there's some hand phones in my backpack." He slung it off his shoulder and fished around inside. He produced one of the little devices and passed it to Javier.

Javier took it, recognized it as Tabeth's. He activated it, punched the emergency number for the police, and held the phone to his ear. Hissing, crackling static. He made some tuning adjustments, but to no avail. He tried to call other numbers programmed into Tabeth's address book. He couldn't get through on those, either. "Let me see another one," he said.

Patryk traded him Hollis's hand phone. Again Javier tapped out the number for the forcers and pressed the device to his ear.

A sizzling, fizzing aural clutter, rising and falling in waves. Then, through it, teases of multiple voices, surfacing briefly then submerging again, elusive fish in an ocean of static. But Javier heard one voice that he recognized. It was almost comical, because it was a high-pitched voice cursing with hysterical vehemence.

"Fuck! Fuck you! Fuuuck!"

"Tiny Meat," he whispered.

The voice faded away. Patryk was watching him. "Some kind of interference. It shouldn't disrupt the net *and* the phones."

Javier put away Hollis's phone, now essentially become a Ouija phone. He looked down at Mira again, slumbering peacefully now. "It's that thing in the basement doing it," he said. "Whatever it is Mira was talking about." He knelt down to gently wake her up. "But we got no choice. We're going out that way."

CHAPTER TWENTY-ONE
VISITORS

JOHN FUKUDA WAS dropped off at his apartment complex by one of his company's security people, but when he entered the foyer he was a little surprised to see the building's own security team was not represented. Still, he didn't think too much of the empty security desk until he buzzed for the elevator and two men appeared around a corner in the hallway, taking their place to either side of him as if merely waiting for the lift themselves. An innocuous enough scenario, but Fukuda was not put at ease by the fact that these men—however nattily attired in black suits and bowler hats—both had a blue camouflage pattern across their faces and hands. Not after the call he had received from Jeremy Stake yesterday, about being visited by three men of this same description.

Fukuda slipped his hands into the pockets of his suit jacket and smiled casually at the man on his right. "New in the building?" he asked.

"Oh, I don't think a fancy place like this would rent to a couple of mere belfs, do you?"

"I shouldn't think they'd discriminate. It's against the law. As long as one has enough money." Fukuda turned to the other man. "Visiting someone, then?"

The elevator door opened to reveal a young woman inside the cabin, her face entirely covered in a pixel tattoo that currently played a film loop of dolphins gliding along underwater. Even so, she gave the two camouflaged-faced men a suspicious, disapproving look as she emerged.

"Iris—hi," Fukuda all but blurted. "Nice to see you."

The woman paused and looked at Fukuda a little strangely. "Hi, Mr., um…"

"Fukuda."

"Yeah, hi. Ah, how's your daughter?"

"Good. Good, thanks."

"That's good." The dolphins were replaced by another film loop of teeming, glassy jellyfish. "Well—have a good night."

"You, too."

Fukuda's neighbor walked off in the direction of the complex's front doors. Watching after her, the man on his left said, "You asked if we were visiting someone. The answer is yes." He took hold of Fukuda's elbow. "We're here to visit you."

Fukuda began to jerk his arm free of the clone's strong grip, but the other stepped close to him and Fukuda felt the muzzle of a gun poke into his ribs. "Get inside," said Mr. Jones.

The three of them entered the elevator cabin and its door whispered shut. Fukuda said, "There's a camera in here, you know."

Mr. Doe grinned. "There are a good number of Blue War clones in Punktown, Mr. Fukuda. And every one of us looks exactly the same."

"Push the key for your floor," Jones commanded.

"Push it yourself."

"We don't know the precise floor or number. So would you kindly accommodate us?"

"Why don't you tell me what you want?"

"In the privacy of your apartment."

Fukuda made no move to touch the keyboard. "I am not bringing you inside my apartment."

"Afraid your lovely daughter might be home from school? Don't worry, she isn't. She had her driver bring her and some friends to the Canberra Mall."

Fukuda's jaw tightened. "You sons of bitches are watching my daughter?"

"It's not *your* daughter we're interested in, Mr. Fukuda."

"Yes, so I gathered. You work for Adrian Tableau."

"Will you push that button so we can talk about this in a more comfortable location?"

"There's nothing to talk about. I don't know anything about Tableau's daughter. She has nothing to do with me."

"No? But you seem to be of the opinion that she stole your daughter's special little toy."

"I am examining all possibilities about that matter."

"Including the possibility that Mr. Tableau's child took it? His *missing* child?"

Fukuda looked from one mottled face to its indistinguishable duplicate. "What did you do to the guard in the lobby?"

"He's alive. Just resting. Our other friend is watching over him."

"Go back and tell your boss that his criminal tactics won't work on me."

On the other side of the door, someone punched the elevator's call button. Doe quickly tapped the button for the second floor, and the cabin began rising. "You'd best take us to your apartment, Mr. Fukuda, or things may become ugly."

"Really? I thought you already were ugly."

Jones drew back his arm and struck Fukuda on the ear with the pistol's butt. Fukuda yelped and fell back against the rear of the cabin, clutching his ear with one hand and raising his other arm to ward off a second blow. "All right! All right!" he cried.

The clone holstered the handgun and nodded politely. "Thank you, Mr. Fukuda."

JEREMY STAKE WAS pinned under Janice Poole when his phone rang through his wrist comp. He strained to reach it on her bedside table. For a moment, playfully, she took hold of his arm in both hands to stop him, but when he looked up at her hotly she let go of him right away. He almost dropped the device, fumbling it into his hands.

But it was not her. Not Thi Gonh. The screen showed only darkness. There was sound, however:

"You asked if we were visiting someone. The answer is yes. We're here to visit you."

"Get inside."

"There's a camera in here, you know."

Stake could see that the call was coming from John Fukuda's hand phone. He didn't know that the darkness of the screen was the darkness inside Fukuda's suit jacket pocket, or that Fukuda had covered up the beeps of the buttons as he punched in Stake's number by talking loudly to his neighbor Iris. But Stake could at least figure out that his employer had called him so that he might overhear this conversation.

"What..." Janice started to say, but he gave her another fiery look, this time with a finger to his lips. He activated the MUTE key so he and Janice wouldn't be heard on the other end. The voices continued:

"Push the key for your floor."

"Push it yourself."

"We don't know the precise floor or number. So would you kindly accommodate us?"

Stake scrambled out from beneath Janice, almost toppling her off the bed. "Tableau's men are at Fukuda's apartment."

"Maybe you should call the forcers."

"He didn't phone the forcers. He phoned me."

Stake began to dress hurriedly. As he did so, he only hoped that since his employer was being clever, he would also have the foresight to leave his apartment door unlocked.

It was fortunate that Janice's apartment was much closer to Fukuda's than was his own. By the time he reached Fukuda's place on his hoverbike, better able to negotiate the tight evening traffic than his hovercar, Stake figured he would have lost his physical resemblance to Yuki's biology teacher—who watched him from the bed as he gathered up his holstered Darwin .55.

"WHAT IS THAT?" John Fukuda asked warily. He had been placed in a chair in the center of his living room's sea of expensive carpeting, his hands cuffed behind his back. "Truth serum?"

Mr. Jones had removed his bowler hat, exposing his hairless head, which looked like a blue planet of many continents as seen from space. He was making an adjustment to a syringe-like instrument. In a pleasant, conversational tone, he said, "Recently I read an article about truth serums and truth scans. It said more and more corporate types are having firewall chips implanted in their brains to block the effects of such serums, I suppose in case an ambitious coworker wants to loosen their tongue by spiking their coffee. Mainly, though, the chips are to prevent scans from reading their minds. Apparently they're afraid that business rivals engaging in espionage might try to access their thoughts through phone calls or other remote means, or even by putting telepathic mutants on their payrolls."

"That's all very interesting, but I don't have a chip like that."

"No? Well, would you tell me if you did? So you see, I don't trust truth serums and truth scans." He held the syringe up to the light, squinting one eye at the transparent cartridge. A silvery glitter writhed within. "What I trust is pain."

"What are you talking about?"

"These are nanomites. You ought to recognize them, huh? You produce similar creatures yourself. I used this type with a lot of success in the Blue War, on Ha Jiin prisoners. Oh, it was against the code. The nanomites were for emergency surgical procedures in the field. But their programming is adaptable." He held the instrument ready, and then moved toward his prisoner.

Fukuda stiffened. He had to force himself not to get up and bolt. Lounging back on a love seat nearby was Doe, aiming a handgun in his direction. Fukuda knew it was a type that fired beams instead of solid projectiles. He said, "Look, I told you the truth! I swear it on my daughter's life! I don't know what happened to Krimson Tableau!" Jones pressed the syringe's tip against the side of his neck. "Please, don't!"

There was no pain. Was it his imagination, though, or did he feel the rustle of thousands of microscopic clawed feet as the machine-like insects scurried into his system?

Jones pocketed the syringe, and in its place produced a little remote control device. He held it up for Fukuda to see. "It's simple, really—like a toy. One button will make the nanomites go to work on your nerves to bring about excruciating pain. And this button, here, will make them repair the damage they cause. They're very good at doing either." He smiled. "We're just waiting now, giving them a little time to spread around and make themselves at home."

From the love seat, Doe snickered.

"Please, listen, you know I'm a wealthy man. I can pay you men a great deal of money to stop this."

"We have a sense of loyalty, Mr. Fukuda, do you know that?" Jones's amicable demeanor began to crumble away. His eyes shone, and he spoke through clenched teeth. "It might seem hard for you to believe that factory-produced mannequins like us could have such principles. You might even believe that we're merely following our robotic programming, by substituting a corporate commander for a military one. But I'll tell you something—most vet clones like us are breaking their backs right now in asteroid mines, or constructing space stations, or some other slave labor work. Mr. Tableau gave the three of us a job we could be proud of. A job that lets us walk the street with birthers like you!"

"I didn't make you men, did I? I don't manufacture human clones!"

"What I'm saying is, you can't buy our loyalty. It's about more than the blasting money." Jones was so animated now that as he spoke he sprayed spittle in Fukuda's face. Had his skin tone been natural, he might have been flushed deep red. But he calmed himself enough to glance at a clock on one wall. Regaining his composure, he found his smile again. "I think that's enough time."

Mr. Jones pointed the remote at Fukuda, who yelled, "Don't, don't, don't!"

He started to shoot up from the chair but the pain slammed him back down hard. It was difficult to tell exactly where it was coming from—seemingly everywhere at once, like electricity crackling along every nerve. Fire up and down his arms and legs. Fire in his neck, making the cords stand out, fire across his back, in his fingertips and in the sensitive nerves at the head of his penis. He screamed. Tears bubbled up in his eyes.

Jones thumbed another button. The nanomites went to work fast to repair the gnawed nerves, but to Fukuda the process was agonizingly slow. He slumped in his chair nearly unconscious, drooling onto his shirtfront. He felt like he must be bleeding from every pore, though there wasn't a mark on him. It would have been hard to prove a military prisoner had been tortured, should someone investigate. Fukuda was a man possessed, but the tormenting demon inside him had receded. For the moment.

"They're like us," Jones went on. "Like soldiers. We were programmed with martial arts training, to break and tear another person to pieces. But we were also trained in ways to heal the body with just our hands. Set a broken bone. Get kicked-in balls to come down into the scrotum again. Stuff an eye back in a socket, if it was still attached."

"I don't know," Fukuda mumbled, still drooling. "I don't know where she is."

"I'd be afraid to admit it, too, if I'd killed her."

"I didn't kill her, you fu—"

Jones pressed the first button again. The nanomites became piranha again. Fukuda began to scream again. Once more he shook in his chair like a man being executed through electrocution.

There was no gunshot, really, just a *poof*, because the Darwin .55 was a pricey gun with a lot of features, one of which was an optional silent mode. Thus, it was as though Doe's wrist simply exploded on its own through some extreme medical anomaly. The ray blaster dropped to the floor with his severed hand still wrapped around the grip. He howled in surprise as much as agony.

Jones whirled around and saw Jeremy Stake there in the doorway behind him, holding his pistol in both hands to steady its aim. "Reverse it!" he snarled.

The clone pressed the button to turn the nanomites from demons back to angels, from soldiers to healers. Fukuda slouched down limp in his seat with a deep groan.

"Okay, now drop that thing!" Jones let the device fall to the carpet. "Hands on your head!" Jones complied, lacing his fingers atop his skull. As when he had ranted to Fukuda, his eyes shone and his teeth were clenched.

"You're a fool getting in this deep, Stake. You should walk away from all this now."

"You fuck! You fuck!" Doe was wailing, clutching his arm to compress its veins. He started rising to his feet.

Stake shifted his eyes to him. "Sit down!"

With the stump of his wrist squirting blood in rhythmic pulsations, the clone reached his remaining hand into his jacket for some backup weapon. *Poof.* This time, the .55 projectile went through the vet's throat and shattered something glass across the room. This time, the clone obeyed Stake's command. He dropped back onto the love seat, a wave of vividly red blood washing down his bright white shirtfront.

"I *told* him to sit down," Stake muttered.

"You fuck," Jones hissed, the same words as Doe and in the same voice. Yet, he had the better sense to remain motionless.

Stake moved further into the room. He circled around Mr. Jones until he came to Fukuda's chair, and reached down to the manacles binding his wrists. "What's the release code?" he snapped. Jones gave the numbers, and Stake punched them in with his free hand while keeping the Darwin trained on the security chief.

"You'll die for killing my man."

"Soldiers die, Mr. Jones. Like one of you told me, we're not on the same side anymore."

His hands now free, Fukuda rose from the chair shakily. He scooped up the dropped remote, afraid Jones would stomp on the pain button.

Stake went on, "If Fukuda did do something to Krimson Tableau, he'd have just told you. So you found out what you needed to know. Go back to your boss and tell him that."

"You're going to let him go?" Fukuda panted.

"As opposed to?"

In a whisper, Fukuda said, "We should take care of him, like that one!" He motioned toward Doe's corpse with its surprised-looking open eyes and flowing throat wound.

"I came to protect you. I'm not an assassin."

"Such a good soldier," Jones mocked.

"You and me both, huh?"

"Whatever. Let him go," Fukuda said. But he went to Jones and dug inside his pocket, fished out the syringe device. He saw that only a portion of its contents had been injected into him. Without hesitation he then jammed the tip of the instrument into Jones's side and injected him through his shirt. The entire remaining dose.

Jones spun and elbowed Fukuda in the face. He fell back onto the carpet, but the remote was in one hand and he pointed it like a gun. Depressed one of its buttons.

The clone instantly dropped to his knees, his mouth wide in a cry that wouldn't come. His eyes quivered in their sockets, as if they might burst from some pressure behind them. Then he pitched onto his face, unconscious but still giving spasmodic jolts.

"Enough." Stake took the remote from his employer and thumbed the button to order the nanomites to make their repairs. He pocketed the device. "You're lucky this is directional, or you would have just put yourself on the floor with him."

"I guess I didn't think of that." Fukuda placed a hand on Stake's shoulder, wagging his head. "Thank God you got here."

"Well now we've got to get him and his friend out of here. Where's the third one?"

"Apparently he took out the security man in the lobby, and has him restrained somewhere. Probably in the security office."

"What a mess," Stake seethed, his eyes roving over the scene. "What a blasting mess."

"Yes, and we have to get rid of them before Yuki comes home."

"How well can you trust your security people?"

"Very well, I think."

"We could go to the forcers with this, but I think we should dump Doe's body and drop off Jones near Tableau's company. If it comes back to us later on, a memory scan would show it was justifiable and it was just a clone, anyway. So why don't you call some of your men over here in a car. And you'd better have one of them stay with you in your place at all times now, until this is over and squared away."

"All right. Uh, what about number three, downstairs?"

"We'll have Jones talk to him and send him away, when he wakes from his nap." Stake knelt down and used Jones's own manacles to cuff his wrists behind his back. He then patted him down and took two pistols and a switchblade knife off him. "Jeesh," he said to himself. "Fucking Clone Ranger." He rose to face Fukuda again.

"I can't say you didn't warn me that Tableau might make a move, but I guess I still couldn't believe he'd go this far."

"Look, Mr. Fukuda, I told you I talked to the brother of Krimson's boyfriend. I told you the boyfriend didn't know where she went off to. But I didn't tell you all of it, maybe because it sounds crazy." Stake then went on to relate the circumstances of Krimson Tableau's disappearance from the Gentile brothers' Subtown apartment. All the personal belongings, clothing included, she had left behind. Finally, he described the ventilation grille that had been bent open behind the bed where Krimson had been resting with her lover.

Fukuda furrowed his brow. "I don't see where you're going with this."

"Now we know for certain that Krimson made off with the doll initially, yes. But later, I'm thinking the doll made off with *her*, in a way."

"*What?*"

"I think the doll escaped through that air duct on its own, after it did something to Krimson while she slept right there beside Brat Gentile."

"Did something? Did what—*eat* her?"

"Who knows? How does that thing feed, anyway? Like an amoeba?"

"What are you talking about? It gets what little nourishment it needs through photosynthesis. That doll could hardly consume a human being, then climb down from the bed, tear open an air vent, crawl away God knows where. None of that. The best it can do is wriggle and squirm a little! You met Yuki's friend Maria, remember? And you saw her kawaii-doll, Stellar. I created that doll, too. Dai-oo-ika is no more advanced a life form than that! A slug would be more active—and sentient."

"But Dai-oo-ika wasn't made in the same way Stellar was, isn't that right? You used a different approach for him, didn't you? Something sort of radical?"

Fukuda became wary. "What do you mean?"

"Hey, look over there, Mr. Fukuda!" Stake barked. "There's a dead man soaking his twelve pints into your nice expensive love seat! I did that, and now I can expect Adrian Tableau to make my life interesting. I guess you didn't think I needed to know about it before, and I guess I didn't think so either, but now I need you to tell me everything! Dai-oo-ika... you created him with information you inherited when you bought up Alvine Products, didn't you?"

Fukuda touched his lower lip, split by Jones's elbow, and studied the blood on his fingertips.

"Even if I get Dai-oo-ika back, I don't dare return him to Yuki as a harmless toy. If I'd known from the start the danger I might have placed her in..."

"So it's true, then. And it wasn't just about your poor sad daughter, or even about a costly kawaii-doll. You can't let Tableau or anyone else get their hands on your special research."

Fukuda lifted his head and smiled at the detective with something like defiance. "If I can believe what you're saying, then maybe he even did something to Tableau's daughter out of anger. Knowing she'd taken him from Yuki." He almost sounded proud of the creature for that. His surprising prodigy.

"I can't believe you'd be so irresponsible as to use that fanatical cult's data to make a *toy* for your child."

"It was an experiment! But I didn't expect anything extreme to happen. The designer I put in charge of the project didn't anticipate any danger, either."

"I thought you were supposed to be the practical brother, and it was James who had the crazy schemes."

"James wasn't crazy!" Fukuda said. "Just more creative than me. More daring."

"Well, being daring and being reckless are two different things. Your best bet, if we can even hope to catch Dai-oo-ika now in this whole blasting city, is to just destroy him."

"Let's not get ahead of ourselves. First, as before, we find him. Whether he walked away on his own or not."

"I'd like to talk to your designer. Just on the small chance that he might come up with something useful in tracking the thing down."

"His name is Pablo Fujiwara. He used to work for Alvine Products, in fact."

"Lovely."

STAKE AND TWO of the security crew from Fukuda Bioforms rode down in the elevator with Mr. Jones. Knowing the martial training Jones had been instilled with from his conception, Stake kept the manacles on him and his Darwin .55 leveled at his back. Shortly after Jones had awakened, Stake had instructed him to call the third Blue War clone and tell him to go fetch their vehicle and wait outside. And to be sure not to try anything stupid when their party arrived in the lobby. Stake had also inquired about the apartment complex's guard. Jones had related that the man was drugged unconscious, but basically unharmed, in the security office. Fukuda had then said he would offer the security man some financial persuasion for not forwarding this whole matter to the law.

"What are you going to do about Mr. Doe?" Jones asked now, as they descended.

"I took your two guns. One of them has plasma bullets, I see. So I'm going to melt him."

"You'd be wise to melt yourself, too, because that's the only way you're going to be able to escape me, Corporal Stake."

"Just doing my job, Mr. Jones. Like you."

"My job will be done when your skull is cracking between my palms. I should have killed you at your flat, but I guess I got all soft because you were a vet. We're all permitted the occasional lapse in judgment, right?"

"I suppose."

"And your lapse of judgment is letting me live, now."

"Yeah? Time will tell."

The elevator reached the ground floor, and Fukuda's three men watched the clone cross to the front doors, looking as dignified as he could in his pricey suit and bowler hat, despite his wrists being cuffed behind his back and the incongruous coloration of his flesh. At the doors, he turned to give Stake a nod that was not polite, not friendly. It was an assurance. *We will conclude this business another day.*

Stake nodded back at him.

CHAPTER TWENTY-TWO
THE CONVERTED

THE TRASH ZAPPER behind Steward Gardens gave the appearance of sinking into the drifts of autumn leaves that were ever accumulating as winter inched nearer like a glacier. The dead pig-hens heaped on the ground nearby were utterly buried now, as if under piles of another species of dead creature. No new pig-hens came to roost on the heliport atop the building's roof. By now they had learned that it was not safe for them; dangerous things might appear, fast and predatory. The huffing, snorting sounds their little tapir snouts made were no longer heard. Just distant traffic surging and beeping, and the leaves rustling whenever a gust of breeze stirred them. But presently there came a noise to break that calm. It was a metallic squealing sound: loud, rasping, screeching. The two retracted mechanical arms of the zapper had unfolded and were stretching upwards toward the overcast sun. Straining, their talons spread wide, as if to tear a hole in the sky and reveal another dimension lurking beyond its fabric. As if to tear the veil off the face of a god.

In the basement of Steward Gardens, the huge tank in which fermented the bacteria-based generic soup that supplied the building's food fabricators began to rumble and shudder. From every fabricator in every apartment came loud liquid belches, and then a sudsy and foul black muck was disgorged, running across marble counter tops to plop onto the kitchenettes' floors. The rotting substance was like the many advancing pseudopods of one vast, amorphous organism.

As Mira Cello had told Javier Dias, on the third floor of A-Wing there was a little movie theater. For four years it had been languishing in darkness, but at last its wall-sized vidtank flickered to life. At first, the holographic screen only contained static, like a raging sandstorm trapped inside an aquarium. Then, fragmentary images started to take shape from the storm. These images coalesced into a burning and mostly flattened city, stretching out black and twisted to all horizons. Below were thousands of upturned faces and arms lifted in praise. The faces were a mix of human and non-human, but all were charred black, blistered by fire and deformed with radiation. Silvery pus ran out of heat-sealed eyes. Yet despite the pain these people must be feeling, they were singing, all in one voice of adoration.

The door to the theater opened, letting in a bit more light. A dark figure walked down to the front row, and stiffly took a seat. Following closely came a second figure, which seated itself beside the first. Another figure. Another. The next row began to be filled.

Soon, every seat in the theater was filled with an identical gray figure that gazed upon the screen raptly, in spite of its lack of eyes.

DAI-OO-IKA HAD GROWN impatient with the irritating busywork of the nanomites; it was redundant for the most part, anyway. So he commanded them all to file through his swelling body to that special cabinet where he stored inorganic trash, and crawl back inside Dolly's syringe. However, they couldn't find their way into the device again, so he had them gather in one of her compacted shoes instead. There he ordered them to die, which they obediently did.

But the wires in his body he liked. The wires linked him with the building's systems, so that it became an extension of his body like a protective exoskeleton. The wires even linked him with the net. He tested the net's waters with curiosity, sent his thoughts out like spiders along the invisible strands of its web. He watched a man and woman in a naked tangle on their bed, gazing at them through the cyclopean eye of their computer screen. Through another such window he saw a woman seated at her computer but sobbing into her hands; she, too, didn't notice him staring at her. Sad, desperate, frail little creatures, these. Though the woman's tears made him feel a pang for his mournful child mother.

There was one man seated at his keyboard who did look directly into Dai-oo-ika's face on the screen. The man screamed, fell back from his chair, staggered to the door. But there he stopped. And when he turned slowly around again, he was smiling and his burned-shut eyes oozed mercury tears.

There would be more time later for such exploration, experimentation. Maybe he would even be able to extend his consciousness along multiple—countless—strands of the web simultaneously, instead of only one at a time. Like a god who can hear the prayers of millions at once.

For now, he had his current flock of new followers to finish converting. Before he converted them in another way, in his own unholy communion.

THE FIVE OF them had their guns in their hands. Satin checked the six plasma capsules in the cylinder of his cannon-like Decimator .220. Even Mira held Brat's gun, which Javier had given her. Javier had succeeded in awakening her, but knelt down low beside her with an arm around her waist, as if to comfort a child roused from troubling dreams.

"You okay there, baby?" he whispered.

"Aside from a killer headache. I think I need a foot rub."

"Ha. Next time we're alone," he told her. "And nice guy that I am, I'll rub everything else, too."

"I bet you didn't do *that* to your mom."

Javier returned his eyes to the floor indicator, his demeanor becoming serious once more as the elevator descended for a final time toward the basement. "Be ready to move," he told the others. "Ready, now."

The cabin touched down. This time, they did not jab the keypad again to send it back toward the upper levels. This time, they waited for the door to automatically slide open.

They had already noted that there were no hands slapping or pounding against the outer security door, but when it slid open they were too surprised—and too wary—to feel real relief that there were no Blank People outside the door waiting for them.

Javier emerged first, whipping his gun this way and that, followed by Satin. Up and down the hallway, there were none of the bio-engineered entities to be seen. Patryk moved quickly to the door to the basement proper, but Mira put a hand on his arm before he could hit the button to open it. She looked to Javier and whispered, "It knows we're out here."

"But what is it, Mira? The Blanks?"

"No. Something else."

"The brainframe?"

"I... yes. But something more. I don't know." She shook her head. "I don't know."

"You called it 'Outsider' before, when you were in your trance."

She scrunched up her face. "I don't remember."

"We have to *go*," Barbie cut in, looking around wildly with her multiple sets of eyes. "Before they come back."

Javier held Mira's nervous gaze, but he nodded to Patryk. "Do it."

There was a beep, the red status button on the control strip turned green, and the metal door slid open in its grooves, but this time no gray arms shot out at them to drag them inside. There was only silence beyond, and an odd, unpleasant smell, almost rotten but almost like burning plastic.

Again, Javier led the way, followed by Mira and Barbie, with Satin and Patryk bringing up the rear. Patryk closed and locked the door after them.

"Where did they all go?" Satin hissed to Patryk.

They crept through a room with metal workbenches along the walls, maintenance tools hanging from racks above them. Machinery hummed softly, and the brightness of overhead emergency lights only made the shadowy areas seem darker by contrast. Across the room gaped a doorway like the entrance to a cavern. Was there a kind of deep, liquid burbling coming from in there? Maybe the tank that supplied the raw material to the apartments' food fabricators, because that foul rotting smell was becoming stronger.

Mira took Javier by the arm to stop him. "We should go back. Go out the front door."

"But aren't all the Blanks still up there?"

She seemed to stare off into the ether itself. "Yes... yes. I can sense them clearly, because they're all in one place. But they aren't moving."

"Because they're waiting up there to ambush us," Satin said. "Come on, come on, we can't risk it!"

"We're close now," Patryk told them. "The maintenance chute is in the room just beyond this one. We get through that, and we hit the town sewer system."

"Mira," Barbie said, "that big brain in there is messing up your thoughts. It's glitched. Just try to shut it out!"

Mira glanced at the black maw of the doorway, and back to Javier. She tried on a tremulous smile. "Okay. Okay. Let's just do this."

Javier touched her hair, then turned toward the doorway.

There was only a single emergency light that had not extinguished in the largish room beyond, but even that one was flickering. The only steady light came from banks of monitors, these showing a tempest of static through which a city skyline struggled to appear. The pale, bluish glow of these screens shone weakly on a glistening dark hulk that appeared to dominate the center of the room. The stench emanated from it, and Barbie cupped a hand over one of her faces' nose and mouth but the others had to suffer. "What is that, there?" her dual voices whispered in different tones.

Another rumbling gurgle. Then the slithering rustle of movement, as if an immense anaconda had just shifted its coils across each other. Javier thrust out an arm to bar the others.

"It's something alive," he hissed.

Patryk had been wearing the goggles his father had once used in his work, pushed up on his head, and as soon as they'd entered the grotto of a room he had slipped them down over his eyes and adjusted them for night vision. As he brought up the rear, only he could clearly see the mountain of flesh that sat at the center of the room.

"Jesus *Christ*," he said.

Only he saw the faceless head turn slightly at the sound of his voice. The sprawling, swollen creature withdrew part of its consciousness from the teaching of its acolytes. From its plucking at the strands of the net. It focused on these tiny intruders. Without eyes, with its mass of silver and black tentacles swarming, it looked directly at Patryk specifically.

He screamed.

Javier swung his gun up and fired blindly, into the heart of the silhouette. "Run! Run! Run!" he shouted. "Go around it! Behind it! Go, go, go!"

Satin caught Patryk under one prosthetic arm and dragged him along, extending the other arm to launch a plasma capsule from his revolver. He missed what he took to be the thing's head, the corrosive green plasma spreading over some equipment behind the creature. Sparks sputtered into the air and a row of monitors went out. Abruptly, the vague cityscape vanished from every screen, replaced by static alone. What the green incandescence of the plasma might have illuminated somewhat, the black smoke from melting gear only further obscured. Satin kept moving, afraid to fire again lest he hit Javier or Mira in the darkness and the pandemonium. The leader of the Folger Street Snarlers was holding off in front of the vague creature and blasting shot after shot to cover their escape.

Javier pushed Mira to run after Barbie and Satin. "Hurry, baby! *Go!*"

His gun clicked empty at last.

At the rear wall, behind the mountain of flesh, Barbie found the maintenance chute already unblocked for them. Enough light from the utilities tunnel beyond shone through to make the way clear. Just before she scampered through on hands and knees, wheezing from exertion and fear, she glanced over her shoulder and saw the back of the behemoth in the pallid radiance from the open hatchway. She saw two projections that might have been ribbed fins like the dorsal fin of a sail-fish. Or wings. If the latter, they were far too small and fragile to ever lift such a dinosaur in flight. But they frightened her. They made her think that what she was seeing was a demon.

Mira started to scurry around the perimeter of the dark thing, Javier moving behind her. The snaking appendages observed them both, but it was the small being's mind that commanded the demon's attention. As if with numerous serpents' tongues, it could almost lick the thoughts that crackled from her mind into the air.

Satin pushed Patryk into the access chute. He was babbling, sobbing, clawing at his goggles to get them off his head as if he feared their rubber frames would melt into his skin. Poised on the rungs set into the wall of the utilities tunnel, Barbie took hold of the boy and helped pull him through. Satin couldn't see past the shoulder of his pony when he tried to turn his head, but he shouted out for Mira and Javier blindly.

Two of the striped tendrils lashed out, extended like thrown spears. They wrapped themselves around Mira's head.

"No!" Javier almost fell over her, caught hold of one of the muscular shafts and tried to tear it off her. He had dropped his empty gun.

The tendrils started to contract, then, jerking Mira off her feet, raising her into the air. Her legs kicked and she clawed at the coils across her face as they tightened.

She had let go of Brat's pistol. It struck the side of Javier's foot, and he hunched down, felt for it frantically. "No, no, no!" he bellowed, as he looked up and saw Mira being drawn close to the mound of flesh. He scooped the gun into his hand, and pointed it up at the indistinct hump that was the thing's head.

But he might hit Mira.

But that might be for the best.

"Come on!" Satin roared, unable to see what was happening on the other side. He was tempted to put a plasma bullet into the creature's back now that he could see its gray flesh more clearly in the light from the utilities tunnel, but the plasma was dangerous as wildfire, and his friends should be coming around its flank, coming any moment. He started folding his cybernetic body into the access chute. The limbs could make it but his torso, broader and inflexible, became wedged.

Javier hesitated, torn, and in that moment the creature brought Mira against its chest. She was engulfed into the heart of shadow. At first, that was what Javier believed. But then he knew it was more than that. Terribly more than that.

He rose, thrust the pistol, and cried, "You *fucker!*"

The arms came for him next. One slapped over his wrist, looped around it, squeezed. He let go of the pistol's grip but the trigger guard hooked his index finger. Another limb looped around his throat. He was lifted. He hovered in mid-air. Floated closer to the engorged mass.

He was brought almost level to the face, and an instinct made him close his eyes so that he could not make it out. Snakes... Medusa... he would turn to stone. As soon as he shut his eyes, he heard a voice in his head. It was distant, watery, like a voice over a Ouija phone.

"Javier," the voice said.

He opened his eyes.

Only inches away from the creature's chest. But now the arms began to lower him. To loosen from his neck and wrist. He was dropped and fell onto his hands and knees, gasping for breath.

"Javier," the voice said again, growing fainter. *"I can't hold it."*

"Mira," he croaked.

"Run!" she blurted, surprisingly loud.

Javier was up and running, then, skidding around the side of the creature. Behind it he saw the lighted access passage, and pushed off to one side was Satin's abandoned pony like the shed husk of a gigantic spider. Barbie had reached in to help unbuckle him and pull his odd little larva of a body through. She cradled him in her arms now.

Javier dived into the chute, shot through it, almost fell to the floor of the utilities tunnel beyond. He looked up to see Patryk seated against the wall. His eyes were red as if a caustic chemical had been sprayed into them, but when they turned his way Javier knew that his friend could still see.

"Where's Mira?" Satin said.

"Dead," Javier told him. He still had Brat's gun in his fist, and he squeezed it as if he might crush it. Crush it like black coal into a glittering diamond, a crystal from which red laser beams burned, shooting out between his clenched fingers.

"Fuck! Fucking hell!" Satin groaned. He looked up at the access chute. "What are we going to do now?"

"We're going to go." Javier took Patryk by the arm and helped him to his feet. "We're going to go home." But his eyes returned to the blackness at the end of the access chute he had just plunged through. And his hand still squeezed his gun's grip. Crushing it. Crushing.

CHAPTER TWENTY-THREE
DEADSTOCK

"This is a prime example of Black Angus cattle," John Fukuda said, pointing to the specimen in question. "A thick neck and straight back, a wide brisket and round rump, a thick rib eye, and perfect intramuscular fat."

"And no troublesome head or legs," Stake added.

"Unnecessary parts. But if you like to dine on heads and legs, maybe I'll grow a special breed just for you," Fukuda joked. "Do you want me to throw in tails, too?"

Stake took a step closer to examine the animal, if it could still be thought of in that way. It occupied one of many narrow pens lining both walls of a long central hall, each creature in this section identical. Several hoses were inserted into the blunt stump of the thing's neck, and one hose emerged from its back end. It rested upon its belly and the flipper-like vestigial limbs that were all it had for legs. It did not stir or shift its body in any way, and its sides did not even rise and fall in the act of breathing. Stake wondered if he would even hear a heartbeat if he were to put his ear against it.

"We use better, more up-to-date processes than what Alvine Products was using," Fukuda boasted, as they continued on down the high-ceilinged hallway. "And we're always experimenting with new ones."

Stake stopped short when he heard a loud burbling sound from one of the headless cattle. He turned to see a young woman in a white uniform making adjustments to a support system on a small rolling cart. On its bottom shelf was the pump that circulated the animal's fluids. The worker looked up and smiled apologetically at Stake for distracting him. To him, it had sounded like the creature had just been decapitated and blood had been gurgling out of its neck. However, the great living carcass appeared undisturbed in its blissful, dreamless state of oblivion. Stake commented to Fukuda, "You should breed office workers like this. Corporations would love you."

"What do you think I have working in my administrative department?" Fukuda took Stake by the elbow. "Kidding." They continued on. "By the way, last month I had an entrepreneur of sorts approach me with the request that I design a headless, limbless breed of human female for a brothel he was hoping to establish at an asteroid mining outpost. His staff, as such, would need a minimum of care. And no pay, of course. 'The perfect woman,' he joked to me. 'No head to complain with, no legs to run away.'"

"What a fuckbag," Stake murmured.

"Huh? The clones, or him?"

Stake gave Fukuda a look. "Him. So what did you tell him?"

"I declined."

"Out of a sense of outrage, or because you thought it might make you look bad?"

"Outrage?" They had come to the end of the hallway, and a transverse corridor offered them a choice of directions. Fukuda gestured to the right. "Would you like to see our pork pigs? They come from a fine heritage, a very old breed—extinct in its natural state, actually—called Gloucestershire Old Spots. Very moist meat, with a fine texture. Or are you in the mood for chicken?"

"If I see much more, I might become a vegetarian."

"I didn't take you for being squeamish. And you seemed to enjoy that steak I treated you to in the Bioforms cafeteria."

"I'm just anxious to talk to your man, Fujiwara."

"Of course. I'll cut the tour short, then." He indicated they should go to the left. "This way."

As they walked down this narrower connective hallway, Stake asked, "So Fujiwara works here, instead of at your main building?"

"He keeps a lab here and another at Bioforms, as he has projects going at both facilities. He's one of my best researchers and designers. He has imagination. That was why the owners of Alvine were so keen on hiring him."

"He was never charged for what their cult was trying to do?"

"What they were trying to do is open to speculation, since it never happened. One could say the creatures they were secretly breeding were an army of monsters for some apocalypse they saw coming. Or one could argue they were an experimental brand of meat product. Anyway, the owners are all dead now. Pablo was just one of their team, doing as he was instructed. He was questioned, but not prosecuted in any way."

"But did he reveal all of his research to the authorities?"

Fukuda smiled over at Stake. "Of course not. People have to pay for such knowledge. And pay others not to ask too much about it."

They arrived at the Research and Development department; specifically, lab suite RD-3. A recognition scanner appraised Fukuda and buzzed him in. Trailing him into the brightly lit series of large, interconnected rooms, Stake wondered idly if the scanner were good enough to have seen through his mimicry had he presently been imitating his employer.

The two men passed work counters covered in computer systems, arcane equipment, printed documents, petri dishes, and the scattered remnants of take-out food and coffee. A holographic model of living cells had them hovering and crawling in the air above one counter, each individual cell as big as a tea saucer.

They found Pablo Fujiwara alone in the farthest room. Stake didn't know where to look first—at the man or his specimens. Both were equally eye-grabbing. Fujiwara was a slight man with close-cropped hair but a great, curling and waxed Salvador Dali mustache. He was wearing a *Buddy*

Balloon T-shirt, featuring that VT show's star, the 150-pound sphere that was Buddy Vrolik. Beneath his image were the words: SOMEBODY KILL ME. It was Buddy's catchphrase, and he said it at times of duress (as when his family members were having one of their frequent arguments) and at times of overwhelming pleasure (as when a visiting comely female dropped something in front of him and bent over to pick it up). Fujiwara's pants were of a peach-colored leather. Stake realized they were like Janice's bed sheets: living human skin cells. He saw a small support pack clipped to the waistband, to keep the cells alive. A matching leather jacket was draped over the back of a chair.

When they'd come in, Fujiwara was sprinkling something that looked like fish food into a tank filled with a greenish solution, in which writhed a mass of large, fat and lazy eels. They had gill slits but no fins nor even eyes, nothing more than a soft little beak-like mouth, which opened blindly to catch the raining feed. Fujiwara smiled at the approaching men. "My new pets," he explained. "Do you like boneless chicken?"

"Those are chickens?" Stake said.

Fujiwara was as enthusiastic as an artist at a gallery showing. "A step backwards in deadstock evolution, maybe, but it's all about building the better mousetrap. Or better mouse. I know there are those markets that wouldn't purchase this breed or even its meat, because they have brains and the animal lovers will be barking, but these cuties would actually be easier to set up and harvest than the plugged-in battery chickens. So we'll still find our buyers."

Stake tapped on the glass as he watched them, then motioned toward a much larger eel-like creature that rested in a long tank dominating a counter against one wall. The tank was so narrow that the thing had no room to move, lying at the bottom like a pinkish log. Stake was reminded of a jumbo-sized shawarma in a Middle Eastern restaurant, ready to be shaved for a sandwich. The living cylinder had a mouth and gill slits but again, no other features. "And what's that? The king of the boneless chickens?"

"Boneless pork," Fujiwara said proudly. "I call it my five-foot-long hotdog."

"Yummy," Stake commented.

"Pablo, this is the investigator I told you about," Fukuda cut in. "Jeremy Stake."

Fujiwara shook his hand, and his expression became a bit more serious, maybe even a little wary. "Hi. You want to know about Dai-oo-ika."

"Him, and Alvine Products. What were you doing for them?"

Fujiwara picked up a take-out coffee and sipped it, avoiding Stake's eyes in the process. "I was doing my job. Following orders. Designing and developing."

"Monsters?"

He snorted. "What a word—monsters."

"Well, what were those things they had you making?"

Fujiwara hesitated, still not looking at him. "A kind of life form unfamiliar to us in this dimension." Then, he admitted, "A kind of army."

"To bring about some kind of apocalypse?"

"I didn't see the whole picture, you know—I wasn't part of their cult. I was just one blind man, with his hands on one part of the elephant. But yeah, they seemed to think some big cosmic event was nearing, or else they were going to set it off, and the army was a part of that."

"But how much havoc could this army create in a colony like this, no matter how big and dangerous the creatures became? If I wanted to bring about a local Armageddon, I think I'd make microscopic creatures instead. A plague."

Fujiwara met his eyes at last, and looked very grave as he said, "They would have gotten *very* big, my friend. And I didn't understand everything about them, but if they'd been allowed to develop fully and mature, it seemed like they were going to have some powerful attributes. Gifts. A range of psi abilities."

"You say another dimension. So you didn't design these life forms from scratch."

"I was given a very unusual DNA sample, and some very unusual information on a chip. They called this chip the Genomicon. I was told the DNA was from an extradimensional life form, but not from any dimension the Earth Colonies have had interaction with, to my knowledge. I don't know if the Kalians bought it on the sly from a Theta researcher, or what. And they sure as hell weren't about to tell me that much. Anyway, the DNA was degraded—prehistoric, actually—and I had to sort of extrapolate. Patch it back together."

"Is Dai-oo-ika the same kind of life form you were growing for the Kalians?"

"Oh no, but related. Another extrapolation. I consulted the Genomicon in making him, too. No, the creatures for the Kalians weren't as anthropomorphic, though they had some similarities, of course. The Spawn, as they called them, had gills like sharks and just two forelegs, and they were a dark purple color, though like Dai-oo-ika they were eyeless, with only sensory organs like tentacles for a face—a little bit like the eyes of Tikkihottos, I suppose, but I think these were also the creatures' psi organs."

Stake turned toward Fukuda with deliberate slowness. "Again, nice pet for your sweet young daughter. You should have made a plague, too, and put it in a locket for her."

Before Fukuda could say anything, Fujiwara continued, while beginning to nervously twist one end of his mustache around and around his finger. "Look, Mr. Stake, you've got to be discreet with this information, okay? The cultists that didn't die in the earthquake got themselves assassinated by a rival group called the Children of the Elders, who want to make sure this apocalypse never happens. I don't want these Children coming after me, too, thinking I'm part of the Ugghiutu cult."

"Mum's the word. I just want to find this doll, this Dai-oo-ika, for your boss here. Did he tell you my suspicions? That Dai-oo-ika might have harmed the girl who stole him, and ventured off on his own power?"

Fujiwara began pacing, twisting and twisting his mustache. "I thought I'd inhibited his growth. And limited his intelligence."

"He's a precocious child."

The bio-designer made a little groaning sound. "How do you think he harmed her?"

"One of the monsters at Alvine Products consumed a rescue worker like an amoeba would. Could Dai-oo-ika do that?"

"Dai-oo-ika has light harvesting complexes, for photosynthesis."

"I'm asking you, do you think he could do what that Alvine monster did?"

"How should I know? I didn't even know *they* could do that, let alone Dai-oo-ika!"

"Scientists," Stake said.

"The best thing you can do, in my opinion?" Fujiwara looked up at Fukuda while he paced. "When you find our friend Dai-oo-ika, you should destroy him. If you're still able."

Stake and Fukuda looked at each other grimly. Fujiwara himself had just echoed Stake's earlier sentiment. Would that be enough to make Fukuda listen?

Stake returned his gaze to the bio-designer. "Maybe you ought to destroy that Genomicon, too."

Fukuda spoke up. "It's in my possession now," he said. "And I'll... consider it."

CHAPTER TWENTY-FOUR
PLEASANT CONVERSATIONS

WHAT HAD EARNED Ron Bistro his status as the "Punktown Prince of Porn" was no doubt his very ordinariness, which made it easier for the men who watched his vids to identify with him. It made them less intimidated by the proceedings, made them feel they too might frolic with the likes of a Simone Pattycakes or the belly-dancing twins, Ufuk and Ulku Istanbul. Well, at least through Ron Bistro his fans could do so vicariously. He had come into fame when, on the set of a picture he was shooting back when he was a mere camera operator, the scripted action had developed into an all-out orgy and Ron had been dragged by one actress out from behind the camera. His inept enthusiasm had endeared him to his future audience. Now, ten years later, he was less inept in front of the camera, though time had made him all the more ordinary looking.

Today wasn't the first day he had personally dropped off his daughter Caren at the Arbury School, nor the first time he had applied his charms to his daughter's schoolmate, Yuki Fukuda. But Yuki had not watched any of his vids and didn't find him any more charming than the fathers of her other schoolmates (in fact, there were quite a few who she found much more worthy of a crush), and as for his wealth—well, again, every Arbury girl's father had a wallet that bulged more in the back than anything Bistro had up front. So Yuki merely smiled and nodded politely as Caren's dad tried to make small talk with her, in front of the school before the first bell had sounded.

"So are you in any of Caren's classes?" he asked her, beaming. He had obviously forgotten that he'd asked her this on earlier occasions. She figured he was confusing her with other Asian students with whom he had flirted.

"Yes, a couple," she answered. She glanced toward the parking lot. She still saw the vehicle that had brought her to school waiting there in the student drop-off zone, a Fukuda Bioforms security man by the name of Nelson Soto behind the console, keeping an eye on her until she was safely inside. Soto was a quiet, serious young man who Yuki found very worthy of a crush, though he didn't seem receptive to the idea, himself. She couldn't make out his expression from here, but she picked up the distant vibe that he wasn't pleased with this older man's nearness to her.

Caren had distanced herself from her father, standing in a knot of friends, each with a kawaii-doll poking up inquisitively from their backpack and with a Ouija phone pressed to their ear. Bistro gestured toward them with one hand, the other resting against Yuki's back to direct her attention. "Do you play with those creepy things, too, Yoshi?" he asked her.

Yuki watched Caren's squinting face as she strained to listen to whatever it was she was hearing.

"I used to," Yuki said distractedly, still staring at Caren, "but my father took it away from me. He said it was morbid."

"Aw, he's got to loosen up, huh?" Bistro rubbed his hand up and down her blazer-covered back as if to console her. "It's just a little bit of fun, right? No harm in that."

Yuki heard a car door slam, glanced around to see Nelson Soto leaning against their vehicle with his arms folded, wearing dark glasses and a frown. She couldn't help but smile a little at this, as if his concern for her were of a personal rather than professional nature, but she turned back to Bistro and said, "Let's go over and see what they're doing." She knew Caren hated her, having been friends with Krimson Tableau, but she counted on the girl behaving herself in the presence of her father.

Bistro started to protest, preferring their more personal conversation, but kept up with Yuki as she moved toward the little cadre of teenagers. "Hi, Caren," she said brightly. "I've been chatting with your dad. Pick up anything interesting today?" She pointed to the tiny phone.

Caren's eyes were molten when they shifted her way, and she was ready to growl something nasty for having been disturbed—and by this girl, no less—when she saw her father ambling along behind Yuki with that big goofy grin he wore when approaching an actress on camera. So with strained politeness she said, "Shh. I'm trying to hear her, okay?"

"It's Krimson, isn't it?" Yuki said.

Eyes on Yuki but with her ear focused elsewhere, Caren only nodded.

"If it's for me," Bistro quipped, "tell 'em I'm out!"

The bell sounded. Like programmed animals, the girls milling around outside the school turned and filed toward the entrance, under the similarly watchful eye of the school's security man, inside his weapons-scanning booth. Caren's little group began to break up, but Yuki didn't want to let it go. She knew her father's hired man Jeremy Stake had questioned Caren about Krimson, but because of their enmity she had not been able to ask the girl about it—and of course her father was not very forthcoming with details of the investigation into Dai-oo-ika's theft.

"We were all talking to her," said another girl over her shoulder, more openly helpful, as she started for the entrance. "We all heard her at the same time. Pretty clear, too."

"Well she's gone now," Caren said with a hint of resentment in her tone, lowering the device.

"She must've heard the bell, too," said her father, trying to be noticed.

Yuki said, "Caren, what does she tell you?"

Caren Bistro hesitated to repeat what she'd heard, because of how spooky it was listening to her friend through this instrument, the same one they had once taken turns listening to with giggles of delicious fear. Recently Caren had sworn never again to listen to this or any other Ouija phone, but the first time her phone had rung to let her know a channel was open—that voices were being received—she had found herself drawn back to it.

As much as she disliked Yuki, Caren could not bring herself to tell her what she had told Stake: that Krimson had once said, "Yuki's mom is crying." But she did finally admit, "The other day she said something about your doll, Dai-oo-ika. But I couldn't make that out too well. And she said something funny just now that makes me wonder if she's really dead, after all. Though I guess that's just wishful thinking. You don't hear live people on Ouija phones."

"What did she say?"

"She said, 'I'm at Steward Gardens. Steward Gardens.' Wherever *that* is."

NELSON SOTO SAT with the engine of his hoverlimo running without sound or vibration, waiting in the drop-off/pick-up zone of the Arbury School lot for the dismissal bell to sound. He could still smell Yuki's too-fruity girlish perfume, from when he'd brought her to school hours earlier. Whenever he escorted her, he couldn't help himself from stealing peeks of her in his rearview monitor. That adorable face, those adorable legs emerging from the tartan skirt, but he would never dare act upon his desires—even though she seemed flirtatious toward him. He respected his boss, and Yuki herself, too much for that. He took a professional approach to his work.

In his rearview monitor he now caught sight of a black-garbed figure approaching his limo from behind. He immediately recognized the uniform as that of a Paxton law enforcer. The forcer wasn't going to hassle him about waiting here, was he? Surely he didn't take him for a pedophile stalking pretty teenage girls. Again, not that he didn't allow himself to peek.

Yes, the forcer was coming to talk to him. He rapped with the back of his gloved hand on the driver's side window, which Soto lowered with a tolerant sigh. He looked up at the man. The forcer wore a beetle-like black helmet with its visor down. A voice over a microphone said, "Can you state your business here, sir?"

"Look, I'm just waiting here for the daughter..."

The little gun that came up in the forcer's other hand was not a standard police issue. It was small, silent, fired a bright blue ray beam straight into Nelson Soto's forehead. It cauterized its own path as soon as it burrowed it, minimizing the spilling of blood, but when he slumped back in his seat Soto was just as dead as if Mr. Jones had emptied a shotgun into his skull.

Jones reached in, deactivated the door lock, and ducked inside the car, shoving Soto over to the passenger's side. He shut the door and adjusted every window's tint so they would appear fully opaque from the outside. And then, as Soto had been doing, he sat waiting for the bell.

When Janice Poole looked through the lobby windows and saw Caren Bistro's famous father talking to a tall, long-legged black student, she decided to go outside and chat with him a bit herself. She had watched a good number of his vids, one of them with Jeremy Stake, who had not been cooperative about mimicking the star. Ron Bistro had flirted with Janice before—though, to her irritation, he seemed to much prefer these kids—and if her sullen and distant Jeremy kept evading her as he had been doing, she might just have to give in to Bistro's Everyman charms.

Janice left the building in a stream of departing, chattering schoolgirls, buffeted by them a little. The traffic of teenage bodies grew momentarily congested, and she sighed, trying to remain patient. She craned her neck to see if Bistro were still there. He was, but her eyes flicked to take in another adult figure. A forcer in black uniform and helmet had stepped up to Yuki Fukuda and taken her gently by the arm, guiding her toward the same hoverlimo Janice saw waiting for her every day. From Yuki's body language and expression, even at this remove, Janice could tell the child was confused. The forcer opened a back door for Yuki, then pressed inside after her. When the vehicle started forward, Janice assumed that the usual driver (who was rather cute, if unfriendly) was up front behind the controls.

But Janice could have sworn she'd heard the start of a cry from within the car, just before the forcer pulled the door closed behind him. A cry of surprise or alarm, from Yuki.

* * *

AGAINST THE WALL between the doors of the two shipping/receiving docks, three loader robots were stored in a row, their chipped yellow paint indicating that they'd seen a lot of use before this place had been abandoned. Yuki had thought all three of them were dead, but when her kidnapper moved across the room, she saw the automaton in the center turn its head a little to follow him with its eyes. Its eyes, its whole aspect, seemed to express a great melancholy. The middle robot had the coils of a thick black cable looped around its neck, and a plastic loading pallet leaned up against it. To Yuki, it looked forlorn at being hidden away here. Trapped here. Like herself.

She sat in an old office chair, a small girl made smaller by the great, empty and echoing space that surrounded her. It was as though she drifted far out to sea, clinging to a scrap of wreckage to remain afloat. She was not bound, but she might as well have been. The two men in forcer uniforms had their guns in hand at all times, though they had both removed their helmets—to reveal bald heads and identical faces entirely covered in blue camouflage. One man called the other Mr. Jones. Jones called him Mr. Smithee.

The men who had killed her father's driver, poor handsome Nelson, had taken the stolen limo into a warehouse or factory district that she didn't recognize. Was it the terrible slum called Warehouse Way? But the drive from her school hadn't seemed long enough for it to be that. It didn't matter. Wherever it was, she didn't want to be there. Wherever it was, she knew she was in grave danger.

But despite their threatening appearance and the presence of their guns, the men had not been violent toward her. They had not abused her sexually, or even verbally, beyond giving her terse commands. It was very apparent that they were just doing a job. And waiting for someone else to show up.

It wasn't long before he did.

A man entered the spacious, largely vacant shipping department from its opposite end, and walked toward Yuki and her two captors. His expensive shoes clicked against the floor and he wore a five-piece business suit personally tailored to his short, powerful body. The man's graying hair was neatly cut, his face as creased but hard as a clenched fist. When he planted himself before Yuki, he stared down into her face with an intensity that bored straight through her. His husky voice revealed the tough accent of someone raised on the streets.

"Do you know who I am?"

Yuki had been crying, on and off, since she had first seen Nelson Soto's dead body slumped down in the passenger's seat of her father's hoverlimo. Tears ran afresh from her red and swollen eyes, and she whimpered, "Nooo."

"I'm the father of your classmate, Krimson Tableau. Do you know *her?*"

Yuki had been too panicked, too disoriented, to formulate any clear theories about what was happening to her, but now things made a terrible sense. "Yes," she answered, sniffling.

"I think your father knows her, too, little girl. And I think he knows what happened to her. Your father believes my daughter did something to some fucking toy of yours, doesn't he?"

"No," she whined. "No, I don't know, *please.*"

"Look, I don't want to have to hurt you. But I'm not getting anywhere with your father, and now he's not getting you back until he gives me some answers. Dead or alive, he had better let me know where my daughter is. Or I'm afraid he's going to start feeling the feelings I'm feeling. Don't you think that's fair enough?"

"Please... I think I know where Krimson is."

If Adrian Tableau's face could grow any more intense, it did. "You do? Where is she?"

"Her friends heard her on their Ouija phones today."

"What? Those goddamn things?"

"She told them she's at a place called... called Steward Gardens."

"And where the hell is that?"

"It's not too far from Quidd's Market," Yuki went on hopefully.

"Beaumonde Square?" one of the camouflaged men spoke up.

"Yes. One time my dad took me to Quidd's Market and he drove me down the street to see Steward Gardens."

"Why?" Tableau demanded.

"Because he said my Uncle James owned that place, but it never opened up because of problems."

Adrian Tableau looked around slowly at his two waiting security men. "Leave her car here. We'll take mine."

Mr. Smithee came over and took Yuki by the arm, to help her up from her chair and to escort her while walking. As the four people crossed the room toward its exit, the middle of the three forgotten robots turned its head to watch them, looking all the more morose at having lost its temporary company so soon.

CHAPTER TWENTY-FIVE
REVELATIONS

His MEETING WITH Pablo Fujiwara fresh in his mind, for an hour now Jeremy Stake had been searching out and reading archived news stories on the net regarding the cult that had formerly owned Alvine Products, and used its resources to create a bizarre army.

Nearly all of the human-like Kalian race worshiped the demon/god Ugghiutu, but this particular schismatic group had not been content with merely paying him tribute, had instead been intent on awakening him from some sort of spell he was under. Reanimating him from his living death. Or was that merely metaphorical? Maybe this crop of life forms was just meant to represent Ugghiutu, supposedly reborn in new flesh as a colony of animals, though perhaps possessing a communal mind. At least, that was what one of the more adventurous articles suggested. Most of the major news outlets seemed to have treated the idea of an army of monsters as the ludicrous plot of an overzealous group of crackpots, dismissing any real threat—despite several rescue workers having been killed by a few of the awakened creatures before they, too, were consumed in the fire raging through Alvine as a result of the earthquake that had all but gutted the complex.

Still, some of these more audacious journalists not only took the threat more seriously, but drew connections to other cults and ominous events, here on Oasis and on other worlds as well. They cited the existence of a Tikkihotto cult, a Choom cult, even Earth-based cults with similar beliefs centered around a race of god-like "Outsiders" that awaited their rebirth and return to power. Nineteen years ago there had been a major incident right here in Punktown, when three vast, insectoid creatures had attempted entry into this plane of existence, the extradimensional entities apparently summoned by a sect of beetle-like Coleopteroids (or Bedbugs, as the race was nicknamed). The government had become involved, even killing one of the titanic—though still immature—creatures. They had been called Gatherers by the Bedbug cultists, but these journalists linked them to the Outsiders that the Ugghiutu followers spoke of.

Accompanying one of the articles was a painting taken from an ancient Kalian text that portrayed great Ugghiutu in one of the guises he could manifest. The illustration was captioned "The Black Cathedral." Apparently Ugghiutu would form his amorphous black flesh into the semblance of a temple that would appear in remote places, and lure the unwary inside as unwilling sacrifices. This temple, consisting of himself in tribute to himself, exhibited a looming dome in the center (a head? Stake wondered), minarets made of entwined tentacles, and two flat-roofed wings of several floors that framed the central rotunda.

Such folklore-like elements aside, Stake was open-minded about what he read. After all, the woman he loved was an extradimensional being herself. And look at the great power she had wielded over him. Conquering, and laying to waste, *his* world.

Stake went to a net bookstore called Shocklines to order two books relevant to these matters; *Monstrocity,* a non-fiction account of the Alvine Products controversy, supposedly written by a man who had opposed the Ugghiutu cult, and *Everybody Scream!*, which dealt with the night the three Gatherers had attempted to cross into this dimension to wreak havoc. But while Stake was looking up the books, a call for him came over his comp and he switched the screen to vidphone mode. When he saw the call came from Janice Poole, he let it through.

She didn't look like her usual flirtatious, smiling self. She looked surprisingly grim. "Jer," she said, "I think I saw Yuki Fukuda abducted in front of the Arbury School a little while ago."

"What?" he hissed. "You *think?*"

"It was her car, but a forcer was making her get inside, and then he got in after her. I thought I heard her cry out. I don't know where her regular driver went to."

"Maybe he was in on it. Got paid off. Did you tell the police?"

"No. In case it really is the police, for whatever reason."

"I doubt that. It has to be that blasting Tableau. Did you call Fukuda?"

Janice seemed to squirm inside her skin for a moment. "I called him first. He didn't want me to tell you, but I couldn't hold it in anymore."

"Shit, Janice! How long ago did you see this?"

"I'm sorry, Jer. It was about forty minutes ago. Maybe longer."

"Dung!" he shouted. Then he fought to control himself. "Okay, look, I'm going to call Fukuda myself. You'd better let me know quick if you hear anything new!"

"I will, I promise. I'm sorry. And you keep in touch with me, too, okay?"

He cut the connection, muttering curses, and punched up John Fukuda's number.

Fukuda answered promptly, and right away Stake noticed two things. That Fukuda was inside a moving vehicle, and that his face looked even more grim than Janice's had been. "Detective," he said.

"Mr. Fukuda, I just got a call from Janice Poole. She told me Yuki's been taken."

"Yes," Fukuda said in a voice that was oddly flat and composed, though perhaps only out of numbness. Out of a crushing kind of fatalism. "I received a call from the person responsible, telling me that he had her and instructing me not to contact anyone about it. And a few minutes ago he called again to tell me where to meet with him. I'm on my way there now."

"You're doing what? Don't be crazy; it's a trap."

"I'll hear what he has to say. And then he can hear what I have to say. I'll do whatever I can to satisfy him. If killing me satisfies him, so be it, as long as he lets Yuki go free."

Stake snatched up his black sports coat, shoved his arms into it, and clapped his porkpie hat on his head. He transferred Fukuda's call to his wrist comp and continued their conversation that way as he tore out of his apartment.

Realizing from the image that Stake was on the move, Fukuda said, "Where are you going?"

"I'm going where you're going, so tell me where it is."

"I can't do that."

"You have to, damn it!" He didn't want to wait for the tenement house's elevator, so his feet were a flurry down the stairs.

"If the person in question sees you with me, he may do Yuki some harm."

"He may still do her harm—you and her both! Do you think he'll let you two live to implicate him in this, after he's done questioning you?"

Fukuda glanced from the road ahead of him to the vidscreen on his console, locking eyes with Stake. After a hesitation, he spoke weakly, letting Fate continue to buoy him on its currents, wherever it might wish to carry him. "Steward Gardens. He's taking her to Steward Gardens."

"That place your brother built. In Beaumonde Square."

"Yes."

"So why there?"

"I don't know. I suppose because it's abandoned, private. I don't know how he found out about it. He must have researched me."

Stake had reached the lobby, and dragged his hoverbike out from under the steps where he was permitted to store it. He walked it to the front door and out into the failing light of dusk in Punktown. The late autumn air had a sting to it. Stake straddled the machine, and then it was whisking him along, insinuating and inserting itself into the slots and narrow passages between the hovercars and various other types of vehicles clotting the streets. Throughout this, he maintained his exchange with Fukuda, shouting to be heard over the roaring and beeping of the traffic.

"Why don't you stop somewhere and I'll meet up with you before you go on? Better yet, why don't you just back off, and let me handle this?"

"I told him I'd be there, and I'll be there. Yuriko died because of me once already. I didn't bring her back just to get her killed all over again."

"I see. So you're going to commit suicide, essentially, to atone for your sins."

"You don't know the half of my sins, Detective Stake. Though now might be as good a time as any to confess them."

"I thought you already had."

"I'm afraid I've been less than honest with you about things. Told you a distortion of the facts. You see, I'm not John Fukuda." Again he linked his gaze with Stake's through their vidscreens. "I'm James Fukuda."

An aqua-colored hovercar had slowed to a stop directly in front of Stake's bike due to a snarl-up in

the traffic. He nearly collided with it, his ass jolting up from the seat as he braked. But it was his
brain that felt thrown forward with the momentum. He returned his attention to his wrist comp,
squeezing the bike's handles as if to cause them
pain, the muscles in his jaw squeezing as well.
Fukuda was waiting, giving him space to react. He
reacted. "You're James Fukuda. The dead brother.
So was it you all along I've been dealing with, or
have the both of you been taking turns fucking
with me?"

"There is only me," Fukuda told him. "It's my
brother John who's the dead one."

The traffic had begun moving again, but like
chunks of ice in a nearly frozen river. Stake spat a
profanity. He glanced up at a helicar that flew
directly above him along a strand of the invisible
navigation web strung between the skyscrapers, a
taxi with the identifying number 23 boldly black
against its yellow-painted belly, making it look like
a giant bee. He wished he was up there, inside that
craft, not down here locked in this crawling glacier. Fukuda had gotten a head start, and he had
been closer to Beaumonde Square than Stake had
been from their points of departure. Regardless of
the small bike's maneuverability, he feared he'd
never overtake Fukuda on the way to Steward
Gardens.

"Why did you lie to me before?" Stake shouted.

On Stake's little screen, Fukuda's eyes were
turned away—presumably while he watched the
traffic ahead of him—as he replied, "The story I
told you before is that the brother named James
was in love with Yuriko, the wife of the brother

named John. That part was true. But what wasn't true, was that Yuriko resisted James's advances, and in a fit of anger James killed her. I then said that John came home to find his wife dead, and the brothers struggled. In despair at finding his wife murdered, John grabbed the gun away from James and shot him with it."

"I remember."

"The fact is, Yuriko loved James, as he loved her. As *I* loved her. My brother John... well, I told you he was the successful one. Practical, dedicated to his business, unwaveringly strong. But he was also cold, Mr. Stake. He was so obsessed with his company that he became distant from his wife, even distant from me. Yuriko was very sensitive, very gentle and affectionate; she needed to be *loved*. She was not a bad woman. If anything, I was a bad brother."

"So you started an affair with her."

"One day, as I suppose was inevitable, John discovered the truth. Caught us together at his apartment. Not in bed at that moment, but he understood. In his rage, he took out a gun and shot and killed Yuriko. Then he turned on me. I got the gun away from him. And because he had killed the woman I loved, I killed him, too." Fukuda let out a long, ragged sigh. "Almost the same story I told you. But with some critical differences."

"Let me spare you telling me the rest. John was the successful one. You were the dreamer, the loser; you were saddled with Steward Gardens, your biggest failure yet. So you assumed your twin's identity, and took over his business."

"I was the more imaginative brother, yes. But I was also the envious brother. I coveted my brother's wife, and I coveted his success. In my greed, I stole them both, didn't I? At the cost of their lives. So I tried to bring them back, in my way. I resurrected Yuriko through Yuki. And I resurrected John through me."

"Do you think getting yourself killed now will redeem you?"

In a choked voice, James Fukuda said, "I only want my daughter back."

"Pull over and let me catch up with you, damn it!"

"Why do you care what happens to me, Mr. Stake?"

"Because you're paying me to," he snapped.

"I don't think so. I think it's your nature to care."

"Whatever you say."

Once more the traffic became bogged down, and in frustration Stake glanced again at the freer movement of the helicars overhead. That cab, numbered 23, had paused above him as well, even though the traffic was more open up there. Irritated vehicles beeped at it, or switched to other navigation beams to veer angrily around it. What was it waiting for?

Me, he realized. *Dung.* Tableau had obviously put a tail on him. Eventually they'd see that he was headed for Beaumonde Square, for Steward Gardens, and then they'd be ready for him. Well, so be it. He'd deal with that problem once he arrived there.

"I'll be there soon," Fukuda said from Stake's wrist comp, his voice growing increasingly shaky. "I'd better sign off."

"Fukuda, I'm telling you—"

"You should turn around and go home, Mr. Stake. This is my affair now."

"It always was. Look, if you won't let me help you, fine—but let me help Yuki."

For a moment Fukuda didn't reply. Then he said, "We must follow our own destinies, detective. If that is your choice, then that is your destiny. For me... well, it's time to accept my destiny, instead of hijacking my brother's. Now I really have to go. I just can't bear to look at your face any longer."

And with that, James Fukuda broke their connection.

Stake didn't have to switch his little computer's screen to mirror mode to know whose face he had begun to assume.

CHAPTER TWENTY-SIX
CONVERGENCE

THEY HAD LEFT the hoverlimo—with Nelson Soto still slumped down in the passenger's seat—behind at the warehouse, and taken Adrian Tableau's luxury helicar. So it was that Mr. Jones brought this craft down into the parking lot on the roof of Steward Gardens' A-Wing.

They disembarked from the vehicle, the chill wind up here making a streaming pennant of Yuki's long hair. Evening was falling, the sky deepening to blue, a background against which the kaleidoscope of city lights began to dazzle. Squinting against the wind, Tableau walked close to the edge of the roof and for a moment watched the traffic on distant Beaumonde Street as the first wave of office workers made their way home, leaving their more ambitious brethren to sit at their desks for a few hours longer. Tableau still resented their kind, despite his now greater success, just as much as when he had mugged them as a teenager. Because of his background, he trusted his security team of retired Blue War clones more than he did any of the office drones under his employ.

Mr. Smithee had gone to the door that gave access to the building's interior, prepared to use a skeleton key card to override the lock. But he turned to the others to announce, "It's already open."

Tableau looked down at the overgrown gardens that set the apartment building back from the street, the dead vines entwined through the metal trellises, the scum-filmed fountain in the center of the front walk. "Blasting haunted house," he murmured to himself, before joining Jones and Smithee, who flanked the sniffling teenage girl. He had a gun of his own under his expensive jacket, and he drew it from its holster before they passed through the rooftop doorway.

The little party descended to the third and top floor of A-Wing, emerging in a murky corridor behind the large room central to this level. Jones stepped forward to lead the way, his ray blaster held ready. Not the first time in his life he had taken point. They passed the elevators, turned a corner and found themselves looking down another dimly lit hallway, with numbered doorways on their right—the first of these being 36-A. On their left: two more widely spaced doors giving access to the room that comprised this floor's center. Tableau himself took Yuki by the arm now, and whispered harshly, "If you've walked me into a trap, you're going to be one sorry little girl."

"I didn't," Yuki sobbed. "Krimson told Caren this is where she is."

Smithee flicked his eyes about warily. The sounds of street traffic had been left behind them, entirely blocked out. A silence like deafness, incongruous to this city. Had he not known differently, the veteran might have believed he was deep beneath the earth, as when he had stalked through the tunnels in which the Ha Jiin had long stored their deceased. The same tunnels in which, during the Blue War, their living soldiers had hidden, popping up from concealed hatches in the jungle floor to attack like the reanimated and vengeful dead.

Jones was keeping his eye on the numbered apartment doors, but it was the nearer of the two doors on his left that opened, just a few feet ahead of him. He whirled, bringing up his pistol, as a figure walked stiffly out into the hallway.

The entity had the form of a man, but unfinished, with the barest suggestion of a nose and eye sockets—no true features other than the number 32-B etched into its forehead. It was gray-fleshed and without clothes. And it turned as if it had no awareness of Jones and his pointing gun whatsoever, shambling off in the direction of the elevators and stairwell.

"What the blast was that?" Tableau hissed after the thing had trudged past him. He felt Yuki crushing herself against his side, as if he might protect her. "I thought it was a ghost!" he said.

"A belf," Smithee whispered, recognizing the bio-engineered life form as something remotely like himself and Jones, though on another branch of the plastic evolutionary tree.

Jones moved closer to the open door and began to peek inside, immediately jerked back as another figure lurched out of the darkened room beyond. It brushed against his arm but again seemed unaware of or uninterested in his presence, following its brother down the hallway, identical except for the number 21-A that Jones had glimpsed on its forehead.

He ducked into the doorway once more, and this time could see that the room served as a miniature theater. On its screen, however, there was only a fizzing and crackling sea of static, which once or twice flashed an image that didn't quite solidify. Accompanying these flashes was a burst of sound that suggested a multitude of voices moaning or chanting all at once, but the static drowned them out again.

There were a few heads silhouetted against the screen. One of these last remaining audience members stood, turned awkwardly, and started walking toward the doorway. Jones stepped back to let the faceless being pass, and stagger off down the hallway in the same direction the other two had gone, disappearing around the corner as they had. For the third time they heard the metal stairwell door squeal open and bang shut.

"Let's see where they're going," Jones said, leading the party back the way they had come.

"If those things have done something to my daughter..." Tableau began, but he didn't complete the unthinkable thought.

The four of them descended to the ground floor, but there was one level lower than that. The basement. Mr. Jones hesitated, looking down into the stairwell. Had the three mannequin-like beings gone down there?

"I think we'd better stay up here," he said guardedly, straining his hearing toward the gloom below. The basement level emergency lighting was stuttering, nearly dead. "Fukuda will be coming to the front entrance."

"But if those things are down there, they might have my daughter," Tableau said, pressing close beside him. He held Yuki behind him by her wrist.

"When Fukuda gets here, maybe he can tell us where she is, specifically."

"He doesn't know!" Yuki spoke up.

Tableau looked back at her with his teeth clenched together. "What do you know about what he knows?"

"Daddy."

Tableau whipped his head around to peer down the stairwell again. "Krimson?" he blurted.

Jones looked at his employer, surprised.

"Krimson!" Tableau shouted. He started forward, but Jones blocked his way with his arm.

"Sir, what is it?"

"What is it? Didn't you hear her call to me?"

"Your daughter?"

"Yes—down there!"

"No, sir, I didn't."

"Krimson!" he shouted again. "Are you down there?"

"Daddy."

A person, little more than a shadow, shuffled just barely into view at the bottom of the stairs. The person was shortish in stature, and had a feminine outline; she looked, in fact, like she wasn't wearing any clothes. She lifted her arms up toward them. Toward Adrian Tableau.

"Daddy."

This time even Jones heard the barest whisper of a teenage girl's voice in his head. Behind him, Yuki mewled; she'd felt the word scuttle across her brain like a centipede, as well.

Tableau lurched against Jones's arm, but he grabbed onto his employer and held him back more forcefully. "Don't, sir."

"Let me go, you fuck!" Tableau raged. "That's her! It's Krimson!"

"It isn't," Jones said. "It isn't her."

The figure below them took several steps closer to the foot of the stairs, still extending its arms in a beseeching gesture. It had stepped into the faltering light. For a moment, the light almost kicked in at full force. It briefly reflected on smooth, gray flesh, and glistened on a long cord that trailed behind the figure, from the base of its spine like an immense tail that ran off into the darkness. The tail was striped in black and silver bands and slithered with a sideways motion of its own, as if it were the body of a giant snake. Or an immense tentacle, tethering the female figure to something unseen.

"Oh God," Tableau moaned, when he saw the apparition had no eyes, no mouth.

"What is that thing?" Smithee said, craning his neck to see over their shoulders. "What the hell is down there?"

With shocking speed, the figure lunged onto the steps, began running up them. Tableau was strong, but Jones was stronger; he flung the man aside to tumble across the floor. He then slammed the door shut, and Smithee threw himself at the metal surface just as Jones did. The two clones pressed their shoulders against it with all their weight.

Crouching beside Tableau, too terrified to attempt flight, Yuki screamed when she heard the thing on the other side of the door hurl itself against the metal. It banged a fist, or maybe even its head, against it repeatedly.

Lying on his back, Tableau let out a strangled scream of his own and clutched his head, which was filled to bursting with the word, *"Daddy... Daddy... Daddy... Daddy... Daddy..."*

"Open the door," Smithee barked at Jones. "We've got to shoot it!"

"No, no, don't!" Tableau cried out.

"It isn't her!"

"It *is*. It's part of her, part of her, inside something else," Tableau sobbed. Blood started to trickle from his nostrils. He thought the seams of his skull were spreading apart.

Then suddenly there was no more pounding. No more wailing in a familiar voice inside their heads. The presence had withdrawn. But for the moment the two security men kept themselves pressed to the door, not trusting the silence.

"Krimson," Tableau groaned, still lying on the floor despite the voice having left his skull. "Krimson." The teasing manifestation of his daughter, meant to convince him that she was still alive, now only confirmed to him in some mysterious and terrible way that Adrian Tableau's daughter was dead. *Dead.*

"That's something of Fukuda's down there," Jones said. "It has to be."

Tableau finally dragged himself back to his feet. "He can tell us what it is when he gets here," he panted. "Right before I shoot his blasting eyes out."

"No," Yuki Fukuda bawled. "No... *nooo*..."

EVEN AS HE called Krimson Tableau's flesh ghost back to him, Dai-oo-ika couldn't be sure if he had sent her out, or if her own absorbed essence were responsible. In his present state of flux, he was still something of an alien to himself. Whatever the case, he had modified one of the Blank People he had assimilated so as to render the girl's form. But now that form came walking back to him, dragging behind its umbilicus—which was actually one of the tendrils that composed Dai-oo-ika's face, much attenuated.

The female figure crawled up the hillock of his great belly, then embraced him as her new father. And began to sink away into the primordial ooze of flesh from which she had come, in a kind of reverse birth. He broke off the end of his tentacle from her spine, and the appendage contracted to the same length as the rest.

Another figure entered the room. One of the last remaining Blank People. This creature, too, approached its master so as to add its flesh to his own. Its contact as it crawled upon him was an irritating distraction, however, and he almost swatted his supplicant off him like an ant. He was being bombarded with too many confusing feelings, sensations. He had previously sensed the creature above him named Adrian Tableau, the one that his extended essence had just ventured forth to meet. And now he sensed another familiar presence up there. Not familiar to some ill-digested splinter of another creature's mind, embedded in his own. No, this presence was familiar to *him*. But it was an echo from another, earlier life or incarnation. This echo was as distant and muffled as the voice of a child's mother as heard from beyond the womb, a voice remembered by a mere fetus of the god-like being he was close to becoming.

Still, the voice Dai-oo-ika had heard inside the muffling womb of his head haunted him deeply.

"*No,*" that familiar voice had bawled. "*No... nooo...*"

As THE FOUR of them made their way toward the smaller lobby structure that connected Steward Gardens' two wings, they passed the last few mannequin beings walking in the opposite direction. On impulse, as the last creature approached him, Adrian Tableau lifted his handgun and fired three rounds in rapid succession into its rubbery gray head. The two clones were startled and Yuki yelped. The thing dropped at their feet and flopped in a dying convulsion.

Tableau glared at his companions. "All right—come on!" With his pistol he motioned for them to continue onwards. "Fuck Fukuda's toys."

CHAPTER TWENTY-SEVEN
REUNIONS

JAMES FUKUDA PARKED his hovercar to the right of the building. His was the only vehicle in this lot, which curved around to the apartment complex's rear—though he had seen one lone helicab perched atop the roof, as he had approached Steward Gardens along Beaumonde Street.

It had been quite a while since he had entered these grounds, and their neglected state depressed him. Some small animal scurried ahead of him through a tangled underbrush that had once been a neat row of hedges, geometrically perfect in shape. He recalled the plans for these gardens as designed on computer, and as they had appeared when finished, back when Steward Gardens had had a future. In a way, it had never even had a past. It was a stillborn thing. Something that made him feel sadness, embarrassment, even loathing. Could Tableau really appreciate the humiliation of forcing him to come here and face this place again? Face who he truly was, and why he had locked that person away for the past four years, just as the doors of this place had been locked up?

But they were not locked, he saw. The front doors were wide open, as was every window of both wings, gaping blackly like rows of eye sockets in a titanic skull. But stranger still was that every one of the bio-engineered "stewards" was missing from its nook between the apartments' outer doors. When had that happened? Could thrill-seeking youths be responsible for spiriting away so many of them?

The side path he had taken from the parking lot joined the main walkway to the front doors. When he came to the fountain he paused to glance back at the street, the traffic flowing past, cars containing people bent on their own destinations, troubled with their own problems. He did not know that when a gang girl named Nhu and a mutant named Haanz had recently died in this yard, none of the people speeding by who had happened to look over and glimpse their strange deaths had bothered to call the forcers, even with communication devices right before them on their consoles or around their wrists. This was Punktown, after all.

Still watching the distant movement of the street, Fukuda felt that this was the last time he would ever see the world outside this building again. All along he hadn't realized the true destiny for this place, but now he understood. He had built Steward Gardens like pharaohs had once built pyramids for themselves. As a tomb.

He smiled bitterly when he recalled his brother John's mockery, comparing James with his army of quasi-alive statues to the Chinese Emperor Qinshihuang, who had filled his tomb with an army of 8,000 terracotta warriors. No wonder the encephalon had never worked right, no wonder this place had been cursed, when John had agreed to help him but had done so without faith, without enthusiasm, without the support he should have shown for his twin brother.

James shook his head. Shook away the anger. Hadn't he left it in the past yet? Hadn't he accepted that the anger should only be at himself? Couldn't he learn that lesson at last, before he went inside to meet his punishment?

Before he could will himself to go inside, however, someone came outside to meet him. Perhaps the person had been watching him from within, and grown impatient.

Though he was dressed in a forcer's uniform, and though the Blue War clones with their blue-mottled faces all looked the same, Fukuda knew from past experience that this was Adrian Tableau's top security man, Mr. Jones. The one who had tortured him, and the one he had tortured in turn.

Jones had a gun in one hand, and beckoned Fukuda with the other. "Mr. Fukuda," he said calmly, "would you please come this way? We've been expecting you."

ONCE HE HIT Beaumonde Street, it hadn't been hard to find. There was a name on the large plaque outside the structure, its letters deeply recessed into a slate-gray background, like an epitaph carved on a tomb: STEWARD GARDENS.

Jeremy Stake noted that there was one vehicle parked in a lot to the right of the building, and a helicar on its roof. It didn't surprise him that Fukuda had reached this place before he could, but he swore under his breath anyway. His hoverbike had been delayed by the snags in traffic, but he prayed that Fukuda's larger vehicle had been delayed even worse, shortening the time between their arrivals.

Stake overshot the building and continued on to an office block next door. He left his bike in its lot, thinning out as evening set in, and jogged back toward the apartment complex on foot. He entered its unruly grounds as warily as if he were creeping through a jungle of blue vegetation, bent low and darting from cover to cover. He moved in on the left flank, not wanting to come straight at the front doors. Every window stood open. That was odd, but it would grant him a stealthier entrance.

As he got closer to the building, he glanced up at the darkening sky several times, expecting to see a helicab with the number 23 on its belly floating above him, but he had lost sight of it when he had entered Beaumonde Street. So, had he only imagined that it was following him? Paranoia, perhaps, but he couldn't blame himself for that.

The Darwin .55 was out of its holster and nosing ahead like an anxious bloodhound.

When he reached the building itself, Stake squatted below the window of one of the apartments, poked his head up gingerly to peek into the unlit room beyond. Judging the room to be empty, he hauled himself over the sill. He was inside.

The door leading out of the apartment and into the hallway was open. When Stake stepped into the murky corridor, he saw that every one of the inner doors for the apartments had come open, like the windows. Open like the eyelids of a corpse. He detected a distant shouting that the hollowed-out husk of the building caused to echo.

He ran lightly in that direction.

"LET ME GO to my daughter!" Fukuda exclaimed, as Jones held him back. Tears had filled his eyes at the sight of her, sitting in one of the front lobby's chairs, again unbound but with one of Mr. Smithee's hands resting heavily on her shoulder. "If you've hurt her in any way..." he began.

Smithee grinned. "You'll do what?"

"Daddy," Yuki was sobbing, holding out one hand to him. *"Daddy."*

"Did you check him for weapons?" asked Adrian Tableau.

Jones nodded. "Nothing. Not even the syringe he injected me with last time." Jones showed an unsettling smile to the man whose arm he gripped.

"You injected me with it first, you fucking belf!" Fukuda snapped back at him. He saw a look come into Jones's eyes like that of a leopard before it springs onto its prey, but he shifted his anger to his business rival. "I'll tell you what I told your toy soldiers the last time, Tableau. I had nothing to do with your daughter's disappearance! I hired a man to look for Yuki's kawaii-doll, as I'm sure these thugs have told you. And I admit my investigator did track your daughter down to an apartment in Subtown, on Folger Street. The apartment of her boyfriend, named Brat Gentile. He was the last person to see her, not me. They slept together, his brother told my man, and when he woke up your daughter had disappeared."

Adrian Tableau came close to Fukuda, his lower jaw thrust forward. "I've heard this boyfriend dung before. If my daughter had a boyfriend I'd have found him by now. And even if she did, who's to say you didn't snatch her as soon as she left this alleged Subtown apartment? Or are you suggesting this boyfriend did something to her?"

"You ask *him* about it! He's gone missing now, too, so he's the one you need to be looking into."

"Oh, I'll look into it, all right. But right now I'm looking into you."

"I'll talk to you all you want, but you have to let Yuki go. She's a *child*! She's *innocent*!"

"A child, like my Krimson?" Tableau suddenly bellowed, spittle flying in the other man's face. "An innocent, like my daughter? Oh, we can't let anything bad happen to *your* daughter, can we?" Tableau looked past Fukuda toward Smithee, gave a barely perceptible nod. Fukuda turned his head to see Smithee drop down into a crouch beside the weeping teenager. He removed the shiny black shoe from her right foot, as gently as a shoe salesman. He then pinched the edge of her navy blue knee sock, and began rolling it down, exposing her hard youthful calf.

"Stop it! Stop it, you fuck!" Fukuda roared, trying to throw himself at the man, but Jones pulled him back and now took hold of his other arm as well, wrenching them both behind him.

"Don't," Yuki cried, but she only watched helplessly as Mr. Smithee pulled the balled-up sock off her foot.

"Mm," Smithee said, running one finger along her wrinkly sole as if to tickle her. "Cute." Next he wiggled each toe, starting with the biggest. "This little piggy went to market. This little piggy went home." When he came to the last and tiniest toe, he didn't let go, held it by its plump end. From his holster he drew his pistol, which he pointed at the base of the toe, the muzzle brushing cold against her skin.

"No, no, no, no!" Fukuda screamed.

"Oh, it won't bleed much," Smithee assured him. "The beam will cauterize the wound. But her foot won't be so pretty afterwards, I'm afraid. Especially if the next little piggy goes to market. And the next. And the next."

"Please," Yuki begged, "why don't you try to talk to Krimson on a Ouija phone? Why don't you just ask *her* what happened?"

"Yes, yes, do that!" Fukuda blubbered. He wished he hadn't stomped Yuki's phone to pieces after all. Wished he had it in his jacket pocket right now.

"I'm not here to play with blasting toys!"

"I know you don't want to try that approach, because then it means she's dead. But if she is dead then you'll want to know why, and you could hear that from her own lips!"

"Her own lips? Her own ectoplasm, you mean? Listen to you, Fukuda. And here I thought you were a man of science."

"I was skeptical about them before, too, but—"

"Enough about the damn séance phones or whatever the blast they call them!" Tableau began to pace. They all waited, watching him. When he faced Fukuda again, he said, "Krimson *is* dead; I have no doubt about that now. I saw her ghost a little while ago, in fact, right here in this building. It was some kind of belf thing with no face. But it was her. Her spirit was inside it—I *felt* it. Now I think it's time for you to explain *that* to me."

"Explain? I don't know what you're talking about!"

"Your brother owned this place, correct? That's what your kid told us."

"Yes, but..." Fukuda broke off, and then he opened his mouth and nodded. "Oh, wait. What you saw, it wasn't your daughter. I designed a whole crew of belfs for these apartments. They were to be servants and bodyguards. Some of them must still be around. They look like the thing you described. Gray, with no real face. That's what you saw, not your daughter."

"Yeah, yeah, we saw those things. This one was different. And I heard my daughter's voice up here!" He tapped his temple with his fingers.

"You're distraught. You imagined it. You have to calm down and think rationally, Tableau! What you're doing here is not only dangerous to me and my daughter; it's dangerous to *you!* Look, you haven't hurt either of us yet. I swear to you, I won't tell a soul that you took us here. Why don't you go to the forcers and tell *them* your suspicions about me? Let them handle this, as you should have from the start. They can give me truth scans, memory scans, I'll consent to anything. They'll prove to you that I'm innocent! And if I'm not innocent, then they'll punish me, won't they? I'll go with you willingly—right now!"

"Forcers," Tableau snorted. "I did a little time as a kid. I've had my share of forcers. And I know too well that truth scan or no truth scan, if you put a little padding in a forcer's wallet he'll tell me your grandma built a time machine and assassinated what's-his-face, James F. Kennedy."

Mr. Jones spun around, eyes hardened. He had released one of Fukuda's arms in order to pull his beam gun out of its holster. The others all looked at him and saw that he was facing the open front doors. Upon entering the lobby they had tried to close them, but the keyboard hadn't responded. The building's power system was apparently out of joint.

"What?" Tableau asked.

"I thought I heard something out there," Jones said in a low, ominous voice. He kept Fukuda close to him, in case he needed him as a hostage. Or a shield.

Tableau glared at Fukuda again. "You did come alone, didn't you? Because I'd hate to have to tell my man Mr. Smithee, there, to slice off your little girl's nose instead of her toes."

"I came alone, I did, I swear."

Because the clone called Smithee held a gun against Yuki's flesh, Jeremy Stake had intended to shoot him first. But it was Adrian Tableau whose eyes abruptly turned in his direction. Adrian Tableau who spotted Stake at the far end of the gloomy lobby, by the entrance to the rear hallway of A-Wing.

"The fuck you did!" Tableau snarled, swinging his gun around to point across the room.

Stake's gun was already pointed.

Tableau was a veteran of the streets. But Stake had also, in his way, been a soldier of the streets before becoming a soldier in another dimension. Their guns seemed to fire simultaneously, though the hired detective actually got his shots off first.

Two of the Darwin's solid .55 slugs struck Tableau in the head; one through his left eye and out the back of his skull, the other crushing his nose and deflecting downward to emerge through his lower jaw. Virtually faceless, he still managed to squeeze off one last wild shot into the ceiling as he crumpled to the lobby floor.

Smithee had maintained his crouch beside Yuki, and in fact she sat between him and the gunman. He hunkered down even more, but lifted his pistol from her foot and began firing across the room.

Stake had started to duck back around the corner of the hallway entrance, but the clone had had his military training before he was even out of his nutrient bath. One of the ray bolts hit the detective in the lower left abdomen and went straight through his body like the solid shaft of a spear. Stake fell before he could make it to the entrance, going down hard on his back. He growled at the searing pain, but had still managed to hold onto his pistol.

Smithee had tracked Stake's falling body with his gun, but before he could fire more ray bolts a bare foot stomped him hard in the temple. In his squatting position, the blow actually sent him off balance and knocked him onto his side—dazed despite the genetically engineered thickness of his skull.

"Back off, Stake!" Jones yelled across the lobby, jabbing his own handgun's barrel into James Fukuda's ear.

Mr. Smithee lifted his head, quickly regaining his senses, and his eyes blazed up at Yuki Fukuda. "Bitch!" he hissed, moving his gun to aim at her again. But not at her foot this time.

At her face, glistening with tears.

"Please," Yuki sobbed, "don't!"

DAI-OO-IKA HAD BEEN flexing new muscles, reaching out with all the new flesh he had nourished himself on. Not the many pairs of gray arms; those were no more. He was reaching out with all of his body at once. He had found he could make his entire substance soft or firm at will. He could flow almost like a fluid, boneless, and then go solid as stone. He extended himself in all directions simultaneously, until no one room of the building's basement contained him. He now filled every room, like a flood of concrete that had been pumped in and then hardened. But he was not something to fit a mold, to be contained. This was just an eggshell. Soon he would reach out *beyond* its fragile barriers, shatter and emerge from it. A temporary coffin beneath the earth, from which he would *arise*, reborn, as his worshipers had predicted.

And yet, as if to distract him from that great destiny, as if to hold him back, there was that echo growing more and more familiar with each reverberation. He could not hate it, however much it impeded him. In fact, it inspired a perplexing emotion in him. A confusing yearning, as he heard the voice inside his mind say, *"Please... why don't you try to talk to Krimson on a Ouija phone? Why don't you just ask her what happened?"*

And he flinched—a quivering vibration that radiated throughout all his sprawling flesh like the ripples from a stone flung into a lake—when that same voice sobbed, *"Please... don't!"*

Suddenly, he not only heard the voice (mother, mother, mother's voice) but saw the speaker as well; through gauze or a fog, but he saw her. The sweet face that had once leaned over him, planted kisses on his chubby belly. *His* god. The god's god. And he saw other creatures, somewhat like her but different. He saw one of these creatures pointing an instrument at the mother-goddess. A hurting instrument, like that creature had fired into his belly in the city below the city, when he hadn't yet understood his hunger.

Mother.

Dai-oo-ika flexed his muscles again. Began to soften, so as to reach out further this time.

"YOU'RE UNEMPLOYED NOW, Jones!" Stake shouted, as he struggled to get his legs under him. He only fell onto his back again, and a wave of grainy black static passed over his vision. His next comment, little more than a gurgle between his clenched teeth, barely carried across the lobby. "This is over!"

"I don't happen to like being unemployed, Corporal Stake," Jones called back, and he increased the pressure of the gun barrel inserted in James Fukuda's ear. He threw a quick look at Smithee, who still had his handgun trained on Yuki's beautiful face. "Maybe you'd like to become unemployed, too, huh? I think that's only fa—"

The first beam, a blue so intense it left a brief afterimage on Stake's eyes, entered the rear of Mr. Jones's skull and emerged from his forehead, like a ray blazing from some mystical third eye.

The second blue beam went in one of Mr. Smithee's ears and came out the other, as if he were merely an insubstantial, holographic image in its path.

"Christ," Stake hissed, his eyes going from Jones to Smithee and back to Jones again, in time to see the security chief's own eyes roll up white and his body go slack, falling away from Fukuda like a marionette with its strings cut.

The gun flipped over in Smithee's hand, the trigger guard still looped around his finger, and swayed there a moment before it slid off and clunked to the floor. Black wisps curled out of both ears, and his nostrils besides. Then he crumpled and lay curled at Yuki's half-unshod feet.

Stake rolled onto his side in another effort to regain his footing, for an unthinking and instinctual moment desperate to reach the cover of the hallway again—expecting a third sapphire ray beam to come streaking his way next. And this person, whoever it was, was an even better shot than Smithee. This time he wouldn't get it in the side, but straight through the melon. Someone outside those open front doors; a damn good shot...

...a trained sniper...

Stake snapped his eyes at those open doors. His mind clicked into focus.

...an Earth Killer.

Despite his agony, and inspired by his intuition, Stake managed to get onto hands and knees, and from there shakily to his feet. One hand now pressed against the hole burned through him and the other lugged the Darwin, which felt much heavier than it was. His eyes were on the front doors as he began trudging toward James and Yuki Fukuda, but he saw no one outside in the darkness of falling night.

That cab, he thought. Number 23.

The sound that Jones's keen ears had heard out there.

"Thi," Stake whispered, staggering, trying to maintain consciousness.

Yuki rose from her chair as if invisible ropes that had bound her there now dropped away, severed. She stepped around Smithee's fetus-curled shape as James Fukuda rushed to her, and he seized her in a painfully tight embrace. Kissed the top of her head again and again.

"Daddy," she wept against his chest.

"Baby," he chanted, as if more to himself than to her. His own falling tears slid away into the midnight river of her silken hair. "Baby. My baby."

Stake saw them and held off from approaching any further, letting them have their moment. Despite being doubles, impostors, shadows of their true selves, their emotion was as real as anything he had seen or ever was likely to see. He envied them for it.

At last, Fukuda loosened his arms from around her, and smiled wearily over at Stake. He began to say something, but a look of concern came over him when he saw Stake weaving there unsteadily, his hand clamped to his side, his complexion almost gray. Fukuda's concern for the man was mixed with another disturbing emotion. He saw the barest reflection of his own features still clinging to the private investigator's countenance, as a result of their conversation over their vidphones.

"You're hurt," he said, taking a step toward him.

Fukuda's eyes were on Stake—on his brother's fading, possessing spirit—and Stake's eyes had turned again toward the open front doors, the camouflaging darkness of night. Was she watching him still? Watching over him?

Neither saw the silver/black-striped appendage until it had lashed out of the gloom and slapped itself around Yuki's waist. Her cry, however, quickly regained their attention.

None of them could understand what it was, at first; not the two men who saw it nor even the girl in its embrace. A gigantic python, coiled around her, was the first thought that came to Stake in his delirium. The great tentacle ran almost the full length of the lobby, from where it had emerged: the same hallway from which he himself had entered the lobby just a little bit earlier.

Then he recognized the silver and black bands on the appendage, though he had never seen the kawaii-doll itself before, only in pictures he'd been shown. Stake understood, and was in awe. A god is owed awe.

The tentacle pulled Yuki backwards. It did not crush her delicate body. It did not lift her off her feet. But it was immensely strong, and insistent. She had to dance backwards to keep from being dragged on her heels. In starting toward Stake, Fukuda had let go of her, but he managed to leap forward and grasp one of her outflung arms. Father and daughter wailed to each other. For a few seconds, they were able to hold on to the other's hand.

An amorphous form began squeezing itself into the far end of the lobby, bulging through the narrow hallway entrance. A shapeless, gray and glossy mass. More and more ballooning out of the doorway. Fluid but weighty. The python-like extremity was rooted in it.

Yuki and her father only held on to the ends of each other's fingers, now. And then, their hands were torn away from each other. Fukuda howled, falling onto the floor with the momentum.

Stake leveled his gun past Yuki, at the mounding tissue that was oozing into the far end of the room. Steadying his aim with both hands, he fired shot after shot into it. Even in his lightheaded state, the thing was hard to miss, and every projectile found its mark. But were there even any organs to hit? Nerves to feel pain? The tumor-like flesh barely rippled. It leaked just the thinnest trickles of clear, viscous fluid before the holes closed up, disappeared.

Fukuda scrambled to his feet. Stake lowered the Darwin and rushed at his employer, as swiftly as his pain and dazedness would allow.

The serpentine arm retracted or shortened. It was withdrawing into that billowing storm cloud of raw flesh. Yuki was pulled back... back... arms reaching, mouth and eyes wide.

Stake collided with Fukuda, threw his arms around him, before he could charge at the creature. "Let me go!" Yuki's father protested.

Yuki was pulled back... back... until all of the arm but the coil around her waist had vanished into the gray flesh. Then, her body impacted against it, as if she had fallen onto the mass from high above, fallen into a pool. She broke the surface. A slow-motion sinking away into that pool's thick gray waters.

"Yuki!" her father called.

Her face with its wide beseeching eyes was swallowed. Just her slim arms now, her splayed fingers. Then they, too, submerged.

"We have to get out," Stake said in Fukuda's ear. "We have to get out of here."

"We have to save Yuki!"

"She's gone. It has her. And it will get us next."

He would come back here later, maybe with Pablo Fujiwara in tow, or at least armed with whatever advice Fujiwara could give him. Or perhaps he'd even have to involve the authorities. The police or the Colonial Forces, of which he had once been a member. But for now, particularly in his current condition, there was nothing he could do but get his client safely out of this place.

Stake wrestled Fukuda toward the door. The Darwin fell from his hand in the struggle but he ignored it. The black static had lowered in a curtain over his vision again. He felt his arms around Fukuda weakening, slipping away.

Strong arms lifted Stake up again. Fukuda? Fukuda, coming to his senses and realizing that they had to get out. Fukuda dragging him backwards toward the open front doors.

Before he passed out, Jeremy Stake let his head fall back and stared at an upside-down face with blue skin and black eyes that flashed a laser red.

CHAPTER TWENTY-EIGHT
DAY OF THE DEAD

THE FOLGER STREET Snarlers' regular contact was
not there when they met the new arms dealer, but
he had forewarned Javier Dias to expect a KeeZee.
Thus, Javier knew to be looking up high before the
motel room's door even opened to admit them.
The KeeZee was almost seven feet tall, but that
was only part of his ominous aura. The being's
jagged-jawed head looked like a monkey wrench
with a thin, grayish-black skin vacuum-formed to
it. His long hair had been woven into thin braids
decorated with glass beads, which reminded Javier
of his dead friend Mott. The alien's three tiny
black eyes gleamed down at Javier lidlessly. The
body under the black jumpsuit was a solid mass of
muscle.

Javier had never heard one of them speak before.
The jaws barely moved, but the muscles and tendons in the thing's throat seemed to knot and twist

with a tortured effort. Even then, what reached Javier's ears was a translation as filtered through a device pinned to the breast of the alien's jumpsuit.

"If you already have weapons on you, you'd better hand them over first," the towering being told them. "I've got a scanner rigged just inside, so it will know if you're hiding even a penknife."

"I thought Rabal told you we were trustworthy," Javier said, referring to their regular dealer, a Kalian. But he obliged by slipping out and passing to the KeeZee the gun that had belonged to Brat.

"I don't even trust Rabal," the KeeZee told him. "That's how I stay out of prison. And how I stay alive."

Next into the room came Patryk, wearing dark glasses to protect his still red and sensitive eyes. He handed over a pistol as well. Then Barbie, of the five faces, entered the rented room. She relinquished her own handgun, followed by a boot knife nicely balanced for throwing. Lastly, in stalked Satin in his new cybernetic pony, though it was actually far from new. It was bulkier and more awkward than his previous sleek black model, its yellow enamel paint chipped and blistered, but at least it moved his pupa-like body from here to there. Scowling suspiciously, he directed one of his mechanical limbs to turn over a stubby little pistol-like submachine gun.

"Your iron could be better," the KeeZee remarked, locking the weapons inside a suitcase resting atop a bed too short to accommodate his looming frame. "Interested in upgrading?"

"Maybe next time," Javier told him. "Our finances are limited. Right now we want to concentrate on the stuff that Rabal said you could get for us."

"As you wish."

The KeeZee knelt down to drag two larger suitcases out from under the bed. The mattress creaked from their weight when he set them down. He flipped both lids open, and took a step back to let the others see around him.

"Huh," said Satin.

"Whew," two of Barbie's faces said. Her largest face just gurgled and dribbled some saliva.

"That should be enough for what Rabal talked about," the KeeZee said.

"Anything we should know about this?" asked Javier.

"Yeah," the KeeZee's fabricated voice grunted. "Be careful."

Money changed hands. Satin's powerful cybernetic arms hoisted both pieces of luggage, as if he were a bellboy employed by this seedy establishment. Confiscated weapons were returned. Seeing his guests out, the KeeZee asked Javier, "So what are you folks, a street gang or something?" His tone, even translated, sounded a bit derisory—but people of his vocation made their living off street gangs. Javier suspected the derision had to do with the two mutants. Javier wasn't happy about that. Nor was he happy about the being's lack of discretion in asking him such a personal question, but he answered anyway.

"Yep," he said. "We're the Folger Street Terata."

* * *

IT WAS WELL into night, but better than that, it was raining hard besides. Even the most ambitious worker at the office block next door had gone home hours earlier. Except for Quidd's Market and some notable theaters and restaurants in Beaumonde Square proper, this was not an area that seethed with nightlife. During the working week, the moneyed took themselves straight to the safety of their upscale apartments—such as, had it ever opened, Steward Gardens would have provided.

Safe from the stabbing cold of a pounding, late autumn rain. Safe from the criminals, the addicts, the gang members that might venture as far afield as Beaumonde Square if boredom or curiosity or restlessness compelled them, hoping to score one extra-fat wallet to pay for a larger than usual measure of seaweed or purple vortex, buttons or beans, kaleidoscopes or red shockers.

Javier Dias had tried all those substances and more in his twenty-five years. But tonight, his blood was pure. His mind was clear. It was not the first time he had been focused on avenging fallen comrades; he'd been doing that for over ten years. Yet, tonight it felt different. He felt much, much older now. By decades. By centuries. It was both a bad and a good thing, in ways he was only beginning to understand.

Javier had bought the hovercar they rode in from his cousin, Santos, at a great discount. In addition, this week Santos had given Javier a job doing such odds and ends as polishing the outsides of the pre-owned vehicles, and sometimes cleaning the blood of their former owners (often gang members, drug dealers, pimps, and low-level gangsters) from the interiors. Santos promised to take his younger cousin under his wing, to have him selling the used and repossessed cars himself within the year.

As had been a popular style for a number of years, most of Santos's vehicles sported elaborate artwork on their hoods and sometimes on their flanks and bonnets as well. The reproduction of a mural by Diego Rivera or a painting by Frida Kahlo, or a whimsically disturbing engraving such as *El fin del Mundo* by Jose Posada. A lot of Day of the Dead motifs, rich with skulls and skeletons in sombreros, and a lot of blood-soaked crime scene photos from ancient tabloids such as *Alarma!* Years ago, when visiting Santos at his lot—his fat cousin's face ever hidden under a brightly colored wrestler's mask, different every year—Javier had fantasized about owning a vehicle with this latter type of embellishment: the glassy-eyed or shotgunned face of a murder victim filling the whole canvas of the car's hood. Now, strangely, he found these vehicles distasteful. Now, he only wanted something cheap but reliable.

So the five of them rode in a battered hovercar with vividly purple Day of the Dead figures cavorting all over its lime-green body. It was not exactly nondescript, particularly for the Beaumonde Square area, but again—it was night, and raining in torrents of near biblical proportions, as if the sky had been rent open to reveal a strange sea hiding behind it: the inverted sea of another dimension.

There was the sound of a gun's slide in the car, as a first round was fed into the chamber. Javier knew it was Brat Gentile's gun, which he had given to his brother, Theo. Theo had heard about the reappearance of the last of the Folger Street Snarlers. Theo had sought them out. And when Javier had told him his story (the real Javier this time), Theo had asked to come along tonight. With the gang again, just like old times.

"Steady there, man," Javier advised him.

Theo grunted. The fear that had filled him lately had been eclipsed by his bloodlust. He stared out his window as Javier pulled into the lot to the right of Steward Gardens.

Earlier that evening, before the rain, there had been a vehicle parked here. They did not know that. They didn't know that a woman with blue skin had forced the vehicle's owner to help her carry another man, who was unconscious, to this vehicle, and then drive the three of them to a hospital. The vehicle's owner had resisted at first, because someone he loved had disappeared inside the building, but the blue woman had persisted, and the man had given in, knowing that there was nothing to be done. Javier and his friends were not aware of any of this. And because of the dark and the downpour, they had not spotted the helicar abandoned in the lot atop the building, either.

All Javier knew was that he had to come here tonight... *tonight*. Oh, he had planned on coming back. But there was something about tonight. Something that had alerted him, something that drew him. An intuition? An instinct? It was probably the dream he had had the night before. As he cruised the hovercar around to the rear of the building, where it would be best shielded from the street, fragments of the dream floated to his consciousness like the debris from a ship sunken in lightless depths. The fragments began to coalesce. The sunken ship of his dream arising, as if a film played in reverse.

In the dream, he had been walking through the streets of a city. But the city could not be Punktown. Couldn't be. Because a city with the feral spirit of Punktown, the pulsing life, the humming vitality— however polluted and diseased—surely could not be reduced to this carbonized ruin. This snuffed-out, three-dimensional shadow.

What buildings remained standing to either side of him (the rest crumpled to mountains of twisted rubble) were mere skeletons of girders. Hollow shells. Blackened husks. Vehicles still clotted the streets, but depending on their material were fused together or melted into barely recognizable shapes like puddles of candle wax. The sky was black with clouds of soot, and scattered fires still burned across the city's jagged horizon, making the bellies of the clouds glow red.

If this was, in fact, Punktown, where were its people? The millions upon millions of Earth colonists, most of them by now having been born here, and where were the native Chooms? And the many other races that had settled here, in lesser numbers? The gray-skinned Kalians, the tendril-eyed Tikkihottos, the beetle-like Coleopteroids, the sightless Waiai, the scaled Torgessi and so many, many others? He saw no mutants. No clones. Not even their skeletons. No trace of any of them, at all. Unless... unless this black, glittering ash that covered the cracked pavement. Unless this obsidian sand that crunched under his soles.

Gusts of wind swept the dust up into his face occasionally, but he wore protective goggles over his eyes. Patryk's, maybe. But it wasn't the dust that caused him to wear them. It was something else. Something he was afraid to look upon with his naked eyes. As much as he dreaded this *something*, however, it was what he had come here to find.

Finally, signs of life. Voices carrying on the wind, like the ash. Muted, at first, muffled. But as he got closer and closer, they didn't really become that much clearer, only louder. He could not make out what the owners of those many garbled voices were saying. Whatever it was, they were saying it all at once, their droning voices lifted in a monotonous chant.

Javier turned the corner of a street, and found himself looking down a particularly wide boulevard. It was filled with people from one charred shore to the other, thousands of people perhaps, yet all of them had their backs to him. It was just as well. From the looks of their ragged clothing and their burnt scalps, it was better that he could not see their faces. They looked like an army of the dead. Not only were their voices raised to the sky, but their arms as well. They seemed to have invited this annihilation, and praised it still.

He didn't study them too long, however. He merely noted them peripherally, because there was something else that commanded his attention, froze him in his tracks as if he had been turned to stone by the sight of it. It was the *something* he had come here to find.

It loomed at the far end of the street, filling the end of it and then some. It was as tall as some of the intact buildings that flanked the broad avenue. Impossibly vast, impossibly alive.

This creature, this entity, would have soared even taller had it not been crouched on its hind legs, its arms resting on its knees as if it sat upon a throne. Its color was primarily gray, though its swollen belly lightened to a translucent milky white. Its hands and feet looked like the fleshless digits of a skeleton, but were webbed as if it might be an aquatic being, and this impression was furthered by its two great wings, which—large as they were—could not possibly support its bulk in flight. These appendages were tightly ribbed, resembling the dorsal fin of a sailfish, and thus might have been more fin than wing. In addition, the thing's head evoked incalculable ocean depths, devoid of all light. Without eyes, without ears or any other features except a cluster of squirming tentacles where a face should have been, each tentacle ringed with silver and black stripes, each tentacle thick as a tree trunk. The "ocean" this creature was meant for, however, might have been the ether of another dimension. Or a black gulf that yawned between dimensions.

There was also something about the entity that suggested the mechanical, blended with the organic. Portions of the thing's skeleton seemed to be external, like the cage of ribs above the swell of its belly, and the complex bones of its limbs, but these structures appeared machined rather than grown.

There was a network of pipes snaking between the bones, wires like veins running in and out of the glossy skin, the neck thick with bundles of cables that communicated between head and body. Steam issued from crater-like ports in the elbow and knee joints. Heat that made the air about the entity ripple was vented from grilles—or were those gills?—in its mountainous form. And beneath the skin of the being's domed head bulged the knotted convolutions of a brain (*encephalon*, Javier thought numbly) with no skull to contain or limit its growth, its emanations.

Was this the entity's intended form? Its *true* appearance? For some reason, rather, it bespoke to Javier a kind of *confusion* of the flesh. A barely checked chaos. As though, in laboring to achieve its ultimate manifestation, the creature had consciously or unconsciously emulated features of its environment. The building it had gestated inside. And the city that surrounded that building.

Too mesmerized to feel terror or anything much but awe, Javier watched as several smaller forms came scuttling out of vents or gaps in the titan's body, scurried across its surface, then burrowed back inside. From this distance he couldn't tell if they were gray, human-like figures crawling on all fours, or huge insects like microscopic nanomites mutated into a much larger state. Or some combination of both.

Yet now his attention was diverted from the creature, back to the crowd of chanters gathered to pay it homage. He realized they had lowered their arms, and that they had all begun to turn in unison. Every one of them, turning to face *him*.

They had no eyes; those had been fused shut. But they grinned. And as if in a single rumbling voice, the congregation chanted one phrase much clearer than what they had uttered before.

"Kill me," they all said at once. *"Kill me."* Each time, louder. *"KILL ME."* Until the sound became so thunderous, it didn't seem to come from their mouths anymore. It seemed like a booming thought transmitted from the very brain of the colossus, instead.

"JAVIER? HEY."

With a supreme effort, he tore his eyes away from the creature, turned his head to see Patryk standing there—no, sitting there—beside him. Sitting beside him in the front seat of the lime-green hovercar. Javier didn't even remember bringing it to a stop in the parking lot, and lowering it to the pavement. The rain flowed down the windshield in sheets. Because it was dark, Patryk could bear to go without his shades, and his eyes peered at Javier with concern.

"Are you okay?"

Javier nodded slowly. After a few moments in which to calm the racing of his heart, he grunted, "Let's go."

The two of them, with Theo also lending a hand, unloaded Satin's mechanical pony. Once on the ground, Satin was able to unfold its limbs and raise himself to a walking position. The pony's yellow paint shone dully in the murk, but the other four had dressed entirely in black, Javier and Patryk even wearing black ski hats pulled down to their eyebrows.

Javier opened the trunk. In it lay the two suit-cases. Rather than lift them out, he merely unlocked and raised their lids to give access to their contents.

Before coming here they had already broken the green clay into pieces, rolling them into soft worms. They had molded other chunks into spheres between their palms, like snowballs. Like grenades.

The explosive compound was a "smart material." The primitive mind incorporated into its very substance was receptive to signals transmitted from a little device Javier carried in his pants pocket. The material could be programmed in any number of ways. Different chunks could be deto-nated individually, like grenades if thrown. Or, all of the material could be made to detonate at once.

Satin was too clumsy for stealthy work, and so he would remain with the hovercar to notify the others by hand phone should a forcer patrol car come nosing around. Also, he and his submachine gun were ready to cover the retreat of the others, should they come running with Blank People—or that whatever-it-was they had encountered in the basement—in pursuit.

The other four wore pouches with shoulder straps, and into these they loaded the balls and worms of green clay. Then, they exchanged grim looks, and scattered into the wet darkness.

Barbie and Theo approached the right side, or B-Wing, of the structure together, each of the opinion they were watching over the other. They squeezed between two hedges, then Theo helped Barbie pull her awkward bulk over the low wall of the ground floor walkway, which corresponded with the two balconies above it. On the other side, they immediately hunkered down and reached into their pouches for the first worms of clay. Wheezing, Barbie pressed hers against the base of one of the black metal doors to the apartments. The dark windows spaced across the building made her nervous. Might a number of Blank People leap out at her at any moment? As she rose to move on a little bit, and plant another piece of explosive putty—Theo doing the same in the opposite direction—she eyed the nearest window more closely. The brows of several of her faces knotted in confusion. Had the window been barricaded? There was something pressed flush against the open frame. She took a step closer, and even started to reach out to touch the barricade but quickly withdrew her hand.

It was a slate-gray material, glossy as plastic, that blocked the window's opening. A wall of living flesh.

Patryk had stolen around to the far side of the building: A-Wing. He, too, began flattening worms of clay against the base of Steward Gardens. He, too, looked up and realized that every open window was blocked by gray flesh. He shuddered, but kept up with his task. This was the thing that had nearly blinded him. The thing they had come here to kill.

Javier had moved to the front of Steward Gardens. He had just positioned a worm of clay against the foundation of the building when his hand phone beeped. He brought it close to his face. "Yeah?" he hissed.

It was Barbie, whispering in blended voices. "Guys, the thing's gotten *huge*. It's pushed up against all the windows. It's ready to bust out of this place."

Javier studied the windows across the front of the building, noted the way the city's distant lights glistened on the wet dark skin that filled them. "I see it. Looks like we can forget about going inside to plant the rest of the stuff. Just keep moving around the perimeter. Boys, you got that? Do not attempt to go inside."

A pause, and then Patryk joined in the conversation. "Got it."

"If you say so," Theo added.

Javier pocketed the hand phone and scurried to the next position. The numbered black doors had made him nervous, before. He had expected one or more of them to fly open and reveal—what?—standing there. But now he knew there was only more of that gray flesh bulging behind them.

He came to the edge of B-Wing's front, and looked over at the smaller section of the complex that connected the two wings and contained the lobby.

He saw the front doors. He saw they stood open. And he saw there was no glossy gray flesh filling the space. The threshold was black, empty. It gave access to the building's interior.

Javier had risen unconsciously from his crouch. He began walking toward the front doors, oblivious to the rain that smashed and soaked him. From his pouch, he extracted a round ball, which he held ready in his right fist. From his pants pocket, his left hand withdrew the remote device. His thumb poised itself over the key that he had programmed for the arming of individual grenades. He pointed the device at the ball in his fist to link them. And kept approaching those gaping front doors.

Once, he had confessed to Mira that as a Folger Street Snarler he had torched cars and abandoned warehouses for a cut of the insurance money. He had always made certain there was no one inside those warehouses, not even a single squatter. So he had done this sort of thing before. But not with this level of equipment, and not with the intent to kill. His heart hammered. He could not calm it this time.

Just paces from the open front doors now, but still he could not see inside. Javier slipped away the remote to trade it for the hand phone. "People," he said into it. "Where are you at?"

"Almost done," Patryk reported.

"Me, too," said Barbie.

"I still got some left," said Theo.

"Just leave the bags with what you have left against the building, and get back to the car," Javier told them. "I'll meet you in a minute."

"Where are you now?" Barbie asked.

"Just go," he commanded.

He switched back the phone for the remote, and then Javier walked the rest of the way to the front doors.

He stood at the very threshold, expecting some trick, some booby-trap to be triggered. This close and he still couldn't see anything at all within the building. He might as well have been looking into the vastness of outer space. Stupid; he had not thought to bring flashlights for them, maybe too afraid that their beams would be seen by cars moving along Beaumonde Street. And just as he thought this, a light came on in the lobby before him. A single, distant and weak emergency light had stuttered into life. Startled, Javier very nearly pressed the button on the remote that would give the grenade a three-second delay for throwing. He took one step inside.

Another step, and he realized that the light was buried like a fly inside amber. The light shone through a translucent wall of flesh; he couldn't yet tell how thick. The flesh formed a tunnel through the lobby, seemed to have vaguely ribbed sides and a curved or arched ceiling. Javier grew warier still, fearing that this living chute would abruptly contract, squeeze down to crush and eject him. Or swallow and digest him. But he took another creeping step.

On his fourth step, he saw a figure detach itself from the gloom ahead of him. A figure that became a silhouette against the weak, imprisoned light. Javier halted his advance as their two bodies regarded each other.

"Javier," said the figure, so small that it might have been a child. But he knew better than that. He recognized her outline, her proportions, even though her head seemed strangely smooth and hairless.

"Mira!" Javier said. The grenade of his heart had been armed. He almost lunged forward right then and there, to grab her up in his arms and run with her out of this place. He almost burst into tears. She was *alive!* That monster in the cellar had captured but not killed her, and now she had found her way out! She had been waiting for him, waiting for him to return and take her away from here.

"Javier," she said again, and this time even though he recognized her voice, he realized he was not hearing it with his ears. It was bypassing his ears to go directly to his brain. But she could do that, right? She had her gifts, didn't she? "Don't come any closer," the voice in his mind continued. "I don't want you to see me."

"Mira... I got to get you out of here!"

"I can't leave, Javier."

She took a few stiff, waddling steps toward him to lessen the space between them just a little. He saw that she held something in one hand. She was dragging a length of rope or cable. He grasped that it was secured to her. She was bound. Still a prisoner.

No, not bound. It tethered her, yes, but now Javier understood the rest. He understood because he saw Mira's silhouetted flesh glisten around the edges as it moved against the pallid light. The light glistened on the silver and black striped cord, too, though he still couldn't tell if it were attached to her front, like an umbilicus, or her back. For a moment, because it was uneven and distorted by the ribbed walls of the flesh chamber, a little of the light had slid around the side of her face. It was dark in here, yes, so it might only have been an illusion that she had no face. Might have been, but he doubted it.

"You son of a bitch," Javier said, shaking his head slowly from side to side. His tightening fingers made indentations in the clay he held. It began to mimic the lines in his palm, like imitation flesh patterning itself intimately after his own. "You son of a bitch..."

The familiar outline came to a stop. "It's me, Javier. He took me. He's taken others, too. He swallowed his own mother."

"You're one of those things!" Javier shouted. "Like the Blank People!"

"You want to destroy me. Good. You have to destroy me, Javier. You have to set us free. Even *he* wants to die now."

"Who are you talking about?"

"The Outsider. He swallowed his mother. He swallowed her fear and it hurts him. He's confused. He's... lost. He wants it all to end, Javier."

"This is a trick."

"You must do what you came to do. I didn't come to stop you. I only came to say goodbye."

It was Mira. It was a trick, yes. A forgery. But it was still Mira at the same time. He knew it. He just didn't want to believe it. And yet, he was also desperate to believe it.

"I'm sorry I didn't save you," he croaked. Tears had started from his eyes.

"You can save me now. Please hurry. Part of him wants to die. Part of him wants to stop hurting. But part of him wants to destroy. Destroy everything. And that part is growing. Soon, that's all of him that will be left."

The outline extended both its short arms, like a child asking for a hug. A lover asking for a parting embrace. But Javier knew, without her voice in his mind even having to tell him, what she really wanted him to do.

He closed the distance between them. As he came, he thumbed the pouch's strap off his shoulder. He got just close enough to pass the pouch of explosives into her waiting hands. He did not want to brush her imitation flesh. He did not want to see her face any more clearly. He backed off quickly once she had folded the pouch against her chest.

"Thank you, Javier. You have to go now. Please hurry."

"I'm sorry, Mira," he said, backing off further for the doorway behind him. The night and the rain.

"Don't be sorry. It will be okay now."

He paused at the very threshold again. "Love you." He'd never said it before. To a girlfriend, to his mother, to any of the Snarlers.

The one buried light flickered out. The voice flickered out in his head, but he heard in a trailing, ghostly whisper, "I love you, too."

THE OTHERS HAD just managed to get Satin inside the car when Javier arrived and let himself into the driver's seat. Patryk, Barbie, and Theo piled in, and the hovercar lifted from the wet pavement.

"Where were you?" Barbie asked.

"Inside. I left my bag in there. We got to get out of here, fast."

She saw the remote gripped in his right hand as he started the vehicle moving with his left.

The remote had an impressive range, its signal not scattered or impeded by the rain or intervening structures. The lime-green car had left the parking lot of Steward Gardens. It had returned to

Beaumonde Street and sailed further down that affluent boulevard until they'd lost sight of the building in their wake. Only then, when he could no longer see it, did Javier push the key on the remote. He didn't point it behind him; he didn't have to. He didn't even turn his head to look.

But the others looked back, astonished by their handiwork.

Over the tops of the office blocks arose a miniature mushroom cloud, growing fast as if nourished by the rain, like a towering tree with a storm-churned head of leaves. Even with the hovercar making no contact with the street itself, they felt the vibration of the blast ripple through it, rattle them in their seats.

The column subsided quickly, its ominous head dissipating, but before it did it billowed and seethed against the black sky, like a gray mass of formless flesh.

EPILOGUE
LIMBO

IT MADE JEREMY Stake angry to find a message from Thi Gonh on his wrist comp, once he was conscious enough to realize that he lay in a hospital bed. Once he had remembered her face, hovering over him, inside the lobby of Steward Gardens.

It made him angrier still that it was not even a recorded message with her face, her voice, addressing him from the wrist comp's screen. Instead, it was a written message. And to further his disappointment, the English was just too good, indicating that she had used a Ha Jiin-to-English translation program to compose it. To him, it did not sound like her at all.

"Ga Noh,

I am back home now. Before I left the doctor told me you would be well.

I hope you understand why I could not stay. I had to lie to my husband about where I was going.

I told him it was business on Oasis about our farm. I don't know if he believes me.

I hope you understand why I watched you for several days but never let you see me. I have already dishonored my husband with my deception. But I was concerned when I saw your face on the phone screen. I followed you a while and you seemed okay. I was going to leave but I am glad I remained a little longer. I was pleased that I could help you fight your enemies.

If you need me again please you must be honest next time and tell me."

"Okay. I need you," Stake whispered as he read the words. He read on, gazing directly down at the device so that its screen filled the front of his mind itself. The words would leave their afterimage there, etched into his brain like a stinging tattoo.

"Once you took care of me. I was happy to repay that debt..."

"Debt," Stake echoed bitterly.

"...and I would repay it again a thousand times. Be well Ga Noh.

Your Ban Ta,

T."

For a few moments he had to digest the Ha Jiin words "ban ta," which she had not translated to English. But Stake knew perfectly well what they meant. Henderson had told him, long ago. He just wanted to be sure he was reading them right, be sure that they would not change when he looked back at them. So he read them again and again.

"Ban ta," Henderson had told him, meant, "your lover."

Stake closed the message and lay back heavily on his pillow. Then he reached out and beeped for a nurse.

"Yes?" a dry voice asked from a speaker. He didn't know if it were a human or a robot. Not that it made much difference, he'd found from previous hospital stays. A tough business at times, being a soldier. And a hired investigator.

"When can I get out of here?" he asked. And in a low murmur, he added for his own benefit, "I need a drink."

But he found he wasn't angry anymore.

BASS-HEAVY MUSIC thudded from a jukebox, a sports program played on one giant VT screen and a muted soap opera (watched avidly by several drunken gray-haired men) on another. Neons glowed fuzzily through cigarette smoke, and a genie-like holographic woman belly-danced inside a large plastic bottle advertising Knickerson beer. Stake seated himself on one of the stools at the bar.

Without having to be asked, Watt pulled a tap with his insect-like prosthetic arm to fill a glass with Zub beer and placed it in front of him. "You doing okay, man?" the Choom asked him gravely.

"Never been better. I think I'll take a shot today, Watt."

"Hey, Stake," slurred a hulk down at the end of the bar. Still no one had told Lark that Stake was responsible for his own recent trip to the emergency room. He momentarily diverted his attention from the alcohol-dazed woman on the stool beside him. Stake had to admit she was attractive for a mutant, except for having one bulbous eye four times the size of the other. Defiantly, she called further attention to their mismatched state by wearing too much makeup around them. Lark went on, "What the hell did you come home in one piece for if you're going to get yourself all shot up now?"

"It's something to kill the time."

"Well, I hear that. Time's all we got left to kill these days, huh? But next time you run into some trouble on the job, you call your buddies down here at LOV 69, will ya? We'll cover your ass. Right, Watt?"

"I'd be more afraid of taking a stray bullet from you than from someone else," Watt told him.

"Aw, blast you, ya fuckin' wanker."

Lark turned back to the woman weaving precariously on her perch, her larger eye looking especially glassy and bloodshot, and Watt pulled a Clemens Light for another veteran.

Stake was halfway into his own beer when his wrist comp alerted him to a call. His heart quickened, but it was not her, of course. From the little screen, Janice Poole smiled up at him. He did not engage the screen so that it filled his mind, this time. "Hey," he said.

"Where are you, mister? I hear you left the hospital this afternoon."

"I'm having a beer at my Veterans Post."

"Sounds exciting. How do you feel? I came to see you yesterday but you were out of it."

"I feel fine. A little stiff."

"Stiff can be good. I've missed you."

"Sorry. Things have been busy lately."

"Yeah." Even with her image this small he could see the skeptical expression on her face. "Well, Yuki's father called me a few minutes ago. He's the one who told me you'd been discharged. I think he was checking to see if you were with me. He probably needs to talk to someone."

"I'm sure he does. He's called me a couple times but I didn't answer. I guess I'm not ready to talk to him yet."

"Well, he told me a little of what happened." Janice shook her head. "She was so dear. It's too terrible, Jer. Too terrible."

"I wish I could have saved her."

"Fukuda told me you did what you could. He said you were very brave."

"That's generous of him."

"That place where Tableau had Yuki... did you see on the news it blew up? Good thing you have an alibi, being in the hospital, but I guess the authorities have already questioned Fukuda about it."

"I've got some questions about that myself."

"Well, he told me he has no idea how it happened, and he said he'll submit to a truth scan to prove he had no hand in that. I hope not, because a couple of people in surrounding buildings were killed in all the damage."

"That's awful. But it could have been worse. Much worse." Stake did not elaborate further. Did not mention Dai-oo-ika. His personal theory, because traces of explosive material had been mentioned on the news, was that Thi Gonh had used more of her military expertise. In that regard, he was glad she was off Oasis and back in her own dimension. If he himself were truth scanned as part of the investigation—which he deemed likely—he hoped her name never came into it.

"Have the forcers spoken to you yet about Tableau?"

"They saw me in the hospital right before I left. They know me and all the respectable private dicks in town; they know I'm not some mad dog. They give us a bunch of dung but in secret they love us, because we tackle a lot of headaches that they don't have to deal with except in the aftermath. But I'm sure I'll still be seeing some mess before it all gets filed away."

"I've heard Tableau had syndy connections. Not afraid of that?"

"Nah. He wasn't in bed with them to the extent that they'd come after me, I'm sure."

"Well, I hope you're right." Janice shifted to a brighter tone in an attempt to restore their spirits. "So, my dear, are you interested in my own brand of nursing? I can be quite the nursemaid. It's better for you than that beer you're sipping. And maybe you can put on your Dr. Lambshead mask for me, hmm?" *Lambshead, MD* was a popular VT show, popular largely because of the sexy young actor who played the titular skilled physician, treating (and romancing) a multitude of sentient races on a far-flung space station.

"Maybe another time. Like you said, Fukuda needs to talk, so I guess I should return his call."

"I get the message, Jer."

"Janice…"

"You know, there's nothing wrong with being attracted to someone because of their personal attributes. Because they're funny, or they're gentle, or good in bed, or you like red hair or green eyes..."

Or blue skin, Stake thought. He cut in, "But Dr. Lambshead's attributes are what you'd be seeing, Janice. What are my attributes? Am I *me* to you, or just a channel remote?"

"Oh for God's sake, Jer. You know I care about you. But if I do find your gift exciting, so what? What's the alternative for you... a woman who finds it freaky and disturbing? Does it really hurt you that I became attracted to you because of that?"

Ga Noh, the Earth Killer had called him. Wasn't it much the same? Hadn't she become attracted to him because of his gift, as well? But, Stake thought, it had also been different. For Janice, he was a malleable toy. To the Ha Jiin woman, he had been, as Henderson told him, "A chimera or a shapeshifter. A mystical kind of being; part human, part god."

"Janice... I'll call you. I will. But right now... right now I just need some *me* time."

She sighed. "Whatever you say. Call me if you get lonely. We all get lonely, Jer. I know I do." And with that, she vanished from the wrist comp's tiny screen.

Stake gave a sigh of his own. Time for that shot. He tossed it back in one throat-searing swallow.

BEFORE HE STARTED another beer, and forgot who it was he meant to call, Stake finally contacted

Fukuda. The man picked up immediately. His miniature face showed a wan smile. "Well, hello. Welcome back from the dead."

An odd thing to say, Stake thought. Or at least, uncomfortable, given the circumstances. "Janice Poole said you were trying to reach me."

"I just wanted to know how you were, mostly."

"Care to join me for a few beers? I'm at the Legion of Veterans Post 69, on Diode Avenue."

"I'm on my way, then."

"Better hurry. I have a head start."

"I won't be long."

"Great. See you then, Mr. Fukuda."

The anemic smile faltered a bit. "You can call me James." Then he signed off.

WHEN JAMES FUKUDA entered LOV 69, he found that Stake had moved from the bar to one of the tables for more privacy, and that he was drinking a coffee instead of beer. "Have you quit before I could start?" he joked.

"I'm just waiting for you so I can start again," the detective told him.

"Then I'll get this round." Fukuda went to see Watt about two fresh drafts.

When they sat across from each other, they formed a silent and uncomfortable diptych. Stake expected Fukuda to ask him about the Ha Jiin woman who had come out of nowhere to get them safely from Steward Gardens. Fukuda, Stake was sure, expected and dreaded the subject of Yuki. But that part was inevitable, wasn't it? So he thought he might as well broach it first.

"Mr. Fukuda... James... I'm so sorry about Yuki. I've been wondering if it wasn't my fault. If I hadn't come in there guns blazing like a cowboy..."

"No. No, Jeremy, please. At that point there was no other way. They were about to torture her, weren't they? At least she had a chance at being rescued, that she never would have had if Janice hadn't told you she'd been kidnapped. But maybe it would have been better that way. You wouldn't have been so seriously injured. And I would have perished alongside Yuki, as I deserved."

"Don't say that. You gave her a brief life filled with love. You don't deserve to die for that. The men who deserved to die are dead."

Stake said that, but even he had to admit that—his methods aside—Tableau had only wanted to find the daughter he loved. And his security men had only wanted to do a good job for the man who had given them a life after the war for which they had been manufactured. Still, Stake had no room for remorse. After all, every enemy he had ever killed had been a child at one time. At some point, all life was innocent.

Fukuda said, "Maybe it was wrong giving her that life. It was a selfish thing, done to alleviate my guilt. I brought a human being into existence just for a way to redeem myself. But at the time, I told myself it was for Yuriko. That was why I made her my daughter, not my lover. I didn't want to lust for her again. My lust for her was what killed her the first time. But it didn't matter, in the end, did it? I still got her killed anyway. It may not sound scientific for the owner of Fukuda Bioforms to say, but it makes me think that she was not fated to be reborn. That I was trying to cheat her destiny."

"Who can say? I don't know if I believe in destiny. But once I didn't believe in ghosts, either."

"The owner of Fukuda Bioforms." Fukuda echoed his own words with a tinge of bitterness, staring off at one of the large VT screens as it played a commercial that managed to seem loud even with the sound muted. "There is no redemption for me. I think I can come to peace with that, in a way. That's *my* destiny."

Stake tried not to look at Fukuda's face for too long. On top of everything else the man was feeling, he didn't need to see his brother resurrected in front of him once more. So staring through his beer glass, the seething bubbles like cells on a microscope's slide, Stake said, "You know, any time people purposely conceive children, they really do it for their own pleasure. Not to further the human race or anything noble like that. Well, excepting our biological programming to further the race, misguided as those instincts may be. But anyway, like I say, that impulse is no less selfish than what you did in creating Yuki. Right?"

Fukuda heaved a sigh and tried on a smile again, returning his gaze to Stake. "Have you ever wanted children, Jeremy?"

"Yeah. Little blue-skinned children," he joked.

Fukuda narrowed his eyes with speculation. "Hm."

Stake realized he'd said too much. He did not want to discuss the mysterious Ha Jiin woman, or the reason for the destruction of Steward Gardens, the fate of Dai-oo-ika, or whether Fukuda would now be sure to order Pablo Fujiwara to destroy all the remaining research from Alvine Products. At that moment, he just wanted to go empty his bladder to make room for the beers to come, so he said as much to Fukuda as he rose from the table. "Be right back," he told him. "And the next round's on me."

"I'll be here," Fukuda replied.

The detective had been gone for a few moments, during which time Fukuda's eyes had wandered back to the muted VT's splashy brightness in the gloom of the bar, when a beeping sound came from inside his jacket. He flinched. For a second, he hesitated in reaching into his pocket, but a couple of other patrons glanced boozily his way. Throwing a look toward the direction in which Stake had disappeared, Fukuda nervously produced a little hand phone. It was a new, state-of-the-art model called the *Planchette,* with the orange outlines of Day of the Dead skeletons cavorting across its black surface.

The beeping continued, announcing that a channel had opened. Contact had been established.

Slowly, as if afraid it might explode in his hand, explode against his skull, Fukuda lifted the device to his ear. Held it an inch away from touching.

"*Daddy,*" a voice said, tiny and remote.

There was much crackling, hissing static. She was saying more, but he could not make out the words, the message she wanted to relate.

"What is it, my love?" he said into the mouthpiece. Tears quivered in his eyes, and his own voice cracked as he pleaded, "Please speak louder. I can't hear you. *I can't hear you.*"